THE FOURTH CART
I

STEPHEN R P BAILEY

The Fourth Cart I

Copyright © 2012 Stephen R P Bailey

All rights reserved.

ISBN-13: 978-1514303504

ISBN-10: 1514303507

www.stephenrpbailey.com

All characters in this novel are fictitious and any resemblance to real persons, living or dead, is purely coincidental.

The front cover image is provided courtesy of www.freeimages.com in accordance with their terms and conditions.

Novels by the same author:
The Fourth Cart I
The Fourth Cart II
The Fourth Cart III

Forward

Amidst the chaos of the Tibetan Uprising in March 1959, monks loyal to their God-King fought to keep treasured artefacts from the clutches of invading Chinese soldiers. Four horse-drawn carts full of gold and precious jewels left Lhasa in the wake of the fleeing Dalai Lama. Three carts were captured by pursuing soldiers. The fourth cart escaped, but appeared to vanish off the face of the earth.

In the early 1970s, the tale of the Fourth Cart was much circulated amongst the farang hanging around the bars of Patpong, Bangkok's red light district. One bar-fly even claimed to be the sole surviving witness to the fate of the legendary cart and would show listeners an enormous ruby which he insisted was part of the treasures still lying buried in Tibet.

For Nick Price, a brash young English lad on the lam, the allure of buried treasure was too strong to resist. With a wife and two kids to feed, as well as his inflated ego, he saw the Fourth Cart treasures as his financial salvation. So he came up with a plan to retrieve the treasures and cajoled his mates to join his mission. Unfortunately, it was a hasty, ill-conceived plan with devastatingly tragic consequences that would haunt him for the rest of his life.

Consequently, it came as no surprise to Nick when, twenty years later, it appeared someone from his past was out for revenge.

Chapter One

Midnight, Saturday 27th April 1991

Nick Price tried to convince himself that the creaking noises were normal, nothing more than the old manor house settling down for the night. He knew it was caused by the dissipation of heat stored up during the day in the building's fabric. As the night brought coolness, eerie sounds would be given off by expanded wooden floors and central heating pipes contracting back to normal. There was nothing else to it he tried to convince himself, no matter how spooky it sounded. It would happen every night. Yet tonight he could swear there was something more.

He stood looking down from the first floor galleried landing at the great inner hall below. Pale moonlight filtered through from the glass panelled roof above, casting ghostly silhouettes as it fell. He drew in a deep breath, placed a firm hand on the gallery rail and eased forward a few quiet steps, his stomach knotted.

He removed a solitary key from his trouser pocket. It was large and heavy, so typically characteristic of Victorian mansion doors. And tonight it was cold to the touch. Unnaturally cold, he thought. He felt for the keyhole, set within an ornate brass doorplate, realizing his hand shook as he inserted the key.

The door opened without noise or resistance. Three seconds later he was inside. Leaning back against the safety of the closed door, he could hear his heart pounding. He wiped away a bead of sweat from his forehead and waited for the darkened objects in the room to come into sharper focus.

He knew precisely where he wanted to go. He ignored the light switches, wary of attracting unwanted attention from anyone who may be asleep in adjacent rooms. Under the bed, he knew, lay a tatty old leather suitcase. And between where he stood and the bed was a clear path, free of any furnishings. Six strides later, he knelt, groped under the bed's valance, pulled out the suitcase and placed it on top of the empty bed.

The clasps flicked open at the lightest of touches, the opened suitcase revealing a jumbled collection of clothes, hairbrushes, make-up and photographs. He rummaged at the bottom until his hands found the object of his desire, a small leather pouch.

Moving towards the window, he opened the pouch, withdrew a magnificent ruby the size of a small plum, and held it at eye level in the moonlight. He stared at it for what seemed an eternity, lost to its hypnotic powers.

Images of Buddhist artefacts, of gold and jewels sparkling in a lamp lit cave, came flooding through from a dark, tormented part of his memory. The venture into Tibet was supposed to have been The Big One, the thing that would make him the happiest man in the world. How could he have been so deluded? How could he have let his lust for money blind him so? How could he have let it take Maliwan's soul?

As a cloud of despair rose from within, the hairs on the back of his neck bristled. The atmosphere in the room changed. Someone was closing in on him from behind; a hunter nearing its prey. And then he felt a presence. Stronger and closer. Much closer. His head turned and, out of the corner of his eye, a body materialized out of the shadows. It was Maliwan, back from the dead, gliding across the room towards him, her unworldly body floating above the floor. He watched in disbelief as her hand reached out, pointing in his direction. Accusing him. His mouth dropped open as a primal scream rose from deep within his chest.

And then a lamplight came on. Less than two feet away was the face he had fallen in love with on a beach many years ago. Its mouth opened as if to curse him.

'Daddy, what on earth are you doing in here?' The voice was blunt. 'It's past midnight. Why are you creeping around like a burglar?'

But Nick hadn't heard. His legs buckled and he slumped to the floor, crying. 'Jesus, Nit,' he replied to his daughter. 'You scared the living daylights out of me.'

Nittaya squatted down beside her sobbing father, hugging him as he sat cradling his head. She picked up the ruby that had fallen to the floor, turned her head towards the suitcase lying on the bed and said, 'Daddy, this really isn't healthy, going through Mum's old things.'

Nick sobbed a few moments longer before responding, 'I know, Nit, it's just that today's the anniversary. She's been gone from me eighteen years now.'

Nittaya gave vent to a deep sigh. 'Oh, Daddy, I'm so sorry. I forgot.' She nestled closer to her father. 'But don't you think she'd want you to move on?'

Nick wiped at the tears cascading down his cheeks. 'How can I move on, Nit? I was never able to say goodbye to her.'

Nittaya gently squeezed her father's hand.

'I'd have given anything to have been able to hold her and say sorry.'

Nittaya turned to face her father direct and said kindly, but firmly, 'Daddy, you can't keep blaming yourself for her death. It's eating you up.'

'I know that, but you don't understand ...'

'What I do understand,' Nittaya interrupted, 'is how much you loved each other. And she'd be really proud at what you've achieved since your days in Bangkok. You've built up a really good business, you donate huge amounts to charity, and you're loved by me every bit as much by Mum.'

Nick took a moment to compose himself before saying, 'I really don't know how I'd manage without you, Nit.'

Nittaya got to her feet and offered a hand to help her father up. 'You probably couldn't,' she replied with a smile. 'Which reminds me, we've got the launch on Monday. And it's me who's got to spend all tomorrow going over last minute plans for the party. So come on, bedtime. I need all the sleep I can get.'

Chapter Two

With his world-weary face tilted down, Nick Price studied the scale model of a proposed shopping-cum-residential complex, a mere stone's throw away from Brighton's beachfront. For years the site had been a derelict eyesore; a once proud amusement arcade, no longer in fashion with the town's holidaymakers. He said nothing for a whole minute, his lean, craggy features showing no emotion as his eyes took in the design. His audience of architects, bankers and engineers, gathered in the plush function room of the Thistle Hotel, showed signs of unease.

It was Nittaya who broke the silence. 'Come on Daddy, say something for goodness sake.' No one else would have dared interrupt her father's thoughts.

'Well, I'm not too sure about this roof terrace, it's a bit ...' Nick stopped short as he caught a glance of rebuke from his beloved daughter. Instead, he allowed his face to crack into an ear-to-ear smile. 'It's wonderful, Nit. Truly wonderful. You and Somsuk have worked really hard on this haven't you?'

'Todd helped us, Daddy. You shouldn't forget him.'

Nick turned and winked at his old mate, Todd. He knew where the credit really lay. And he also knew he didn't have to praise his old friend in public. Their relationship went far deeper than that. 'Yeah, I know that. It's just that I'm so proud of you. Your first major business venture. I just wish your mother could have been here to see it.'

Nittaya put her arm round her father's waist. 'I know, Daddy. I do too.'

Nick brushed aside a stray hair from Nittaya's face before saying in a commanding voice, 'Now then, folks. There's just one small but vital matter to clear up. Are you sure you can build this out for under fifty million?'

'Forty-seven million, almost to the penny,' a quantity surveyor replied. 'We've secured fixed price quotes for the build plus all incidentals. Interest and bank fees on top, of course, but that shouldn't be more than another five million.'

'And you've got a buyer at sixty?'

'The Bank of Kyoto,' Todd responded. 'They've already signed a memorandum of understanding. They'll sign contracts as soon as we can confirm that finance is in place for the construction.'

'So what are you waiting for?' Nick retorted.

Todd winked at Nittaya before replying, 'We just need you to give your final blessing, Nick.'

'And a big fat cheque too, no doubt?' Nick grimaced, but inside, deep down inside, his heart warmed. He'd done the mental arithmetic in a split second; two million pounds each for Todd and himself, same for his two kids. A sweet deal, indeed, for little risk and no real effort.

'It would certainly help, Mr Price.' The response came from a man in a business suit a few feet away. 'As you're the senior partner in this project, we really do need to have your equity stake deposited with our bank to get the ball rolling.'

Nittaya looked with expectation at her father. His heart melted at the sight of her pleading eyes. 'Well, I suppose it's too late to pull out now,' he jested. He handed over a brown envelope to the banker and sighed as though dispensing a cheque for five million pounds was a daily chore. 'Let's break out the champagne and open the doors, the press are going to be here any second.'

A mixture of cheers and sighs of relief filled the room. Corks popped, glasses were filled and trays of nibbles were handed around as a large crowd of pompous looking civic dignitaries wandered into the room at the appointed hour.

Never one to enjoy the pomp associated with these occasions, Nick withdrew to one side with Nittaya in tow. Todd would do the honours, pumping hands, making small talk, massaging egos. Todd always did, he was a natural at public relations. It was Todd's forte, and his reward was for his ego to be massaged as he basked in the spotlight.

It was, therefore, with a heavy heart that Nick watched Todd steer in his direction a large bearded man wearing the chain of office of the Leader of Brighton Borough Council.

'Martin,' Todd said as he drew closer, 'let me introduce you to my old friend, Nick Price.'

The Council Leader grabbed Nick's hand and shook it for far longer than was socially appropriate. Nick could almost read the councillor's thoughts; no doubt the man would dine out on the experience for months to come. He knew he was a local talking point; poor boy made good, generous benefactor, white knight to local charities, or an evil conniving property developer with half the council in his pocket. The press was divided, as were the people of Brighton.

'Now then, Martin,' Todd cut in, 'you must come and have your photograph taken standing next to the model of our town's new state-of-the-art shopping complex.'

'Of course, Todd, but we really should wait for my special guest.'

A frown formed on Nick's forehead. 'Special guest?' he asked. He threw a look of bewilderment in Todd's direction.

'Geoffrey Rees Smith, of course,' the councillor replied in a cordial manner. 'Our very own esteemed Member of Parliament. We couldn't leave him out, now, could we Mr Price?'

'What?' Nick retorted. He could feel his cheeks burning.

'Martin,' Todd exploded, 'I don't believe this! You didn't tell me you were going to invite him. I thought I made it clear that guests had to be approved in advance.'

'Come now, Todd,' the councillor replied wagging a finger in Todd's face. 'We're talking about a great coup here for both of us. Geoffrey was appointed Home Secretary in last month's cabinet reshuffle. For goodness sake, we can't possibly miss out on this opportunity. Think of the publicity we'll both get.'

Nick threw Todd a doubtful look and was just about to say something impolite when the door burst open to the sound of raucous laughing. He moaned as he watched the tall, broad, imposing frame of the Home Secretary stride into the room, his demeanour as ostentatious as was possible.

'Bollocks!' Nick muttered, attracting a recriminating look from his daughter.

'Bollocks, indeed,' Todd responded under his breath.

A feeling of foreboding settled on Nick as he watched the arrogant politician proclaim his arrival by greeting everyone in a loud voice. He felt the blood drain from his face as a pain surged through his chest. He grabbed hold of his daughter's arm moments before he felt his legs wobble.

Nittaya looked at her father in horror. 'Daddy? Are you all right, Daddy?'

'Sorry, Nit, I'm just having one of my funny turns.' He watched in dismay as the councillor moved in on the politician, mouth wide open in an ingratiating smile, followed close at heels by Todd.

'Geoffrey, thank you so much for coming,' the councillor said with a flamboyant waving of his arms. 'So good of you to find time, you must be so busy these days.'

'I am indeed, Martin,' Rees Smith boomed in response, as if determined to let the whole room know of his importance. 'Still, anything I can do to promote the town's image, you know me, I'm always pleased to help.'

The false smile refused to shift from the councillor's face. 'Let me introduce you to the project's founders.'

'By all means,' Rees Smith responded with one of his own insincere smiles.

The councillor turned to face Todd who seemed to be taking an unusual interest in something on the ground. 'This is Todd Conners. He's a long-time associate of mine on the council.'

'How do you do,' the Home Secretary said. But as Todd raised his eyes to make contact, Rees Smith's smile turned sour, his extended hand fell limp to his side.

Todd folded his arms across his chest and responded with a curt greeting. 'Hello, Geoff.'

'And over there,' the councillor continued unaware of the apparent drama, 'is Nick Price, the senior partner in this venture. Todd, perhaps you would be kind enough to make the introductions?'

Rees Smith's eyes turned in Nick's direction.

Even from thirty feet away in a crowded room, Nittaya had missed nothing. She prodded her father. 'I think you're wanted, Daddy. The Council Leader's trying to get your attention.'

If looks could kill, Nick would have been a happy man as he stared daggers at the politician.

'Come on, Daddy,' Nittaya said with glee. 'This should generate some good press coverage.' She linked arms with her father and set off across the room.

Nick got dragged against his will. He stopped a few feet short of the Home Secretary and fought back the bile rising in his stomach.

Todd coughed, breaking the atmosphere. 'Geoff, may I present Nittaya.'

The Home Secretary's attention diverted from Nick's piercing eyes. His face dropped as he took in Nittaya's beauty and radiance. 'My God,' he muttered, 'but you're . . .'

Todd coughed again, much louder. 'Geoff, Nittaya is Nick's daughter.'

'I, um,' Rees Smith spluttered as he threw a sideways glance in Nick's direction. 'Sorry, Nittaya, it's just that you remind me so much of your mother.'

Nittaya looked astounded. 'You knew my mother?'

Rees Smith frowned. 'A lifetime ago. You were just a baby if I remember correctly.'

Nittaya turned and looked inquisitively at her father, but received no reaction. She met Todd's eyes, and received an affirming nod. 'So you already know my father then? And Todd too, presumably? How? I'm sorry, I don't understand. How did my mother know a Home Secretary?'

'I wasn't Home Secretary back then. Not even a politician. I'd just graduated, had some time free. I went travelling around the world, seeking adventure. I stayed in Bangkok for a while and went to your father's bar a few times.'

Nittaya looked with scorn at both Todd and her father. 'Nobody mentioned this to me.'

'No,' Rees Smith responded quietly. 'I'm sure there was no reason to. You know the old saying, about ships passing in the night.'

Nick had been standing frozen rigid to the spot, a far-away look in his eye. Beads of sweat had broken out on his forehead. He could find no words to say.

Nittaya squeezed her father's hand as though urging him to snap out of his reverie. Smiling at the Home Secretary, she said sweetly, 'It's been very kind of you to attend today, sir. Can I persuade you to have an official photograph taken standing next to the model of our new complex over there?'

'Yes, of course,' Rees Smith replied with a genuine smile. 'I'd be delighted.'

Nick was dragged further across the room. As he was shuffled into position next to the Home Secretary, a flashlight temporarily blinded him. He cursed inwardly. Eighteen years had been a long time. Too long.

Chapter Three

It had been a beautiful sunny Saturday afternoon in early May, warm enough for Detective Chief Inspector Jack Magee to walk over the hills above Lewes in shirt sleeves. He and Jenny had taken their two kids, Carolyn and Jason, up to Black Cap for fresh air and exercise, to let them play in the woods and to stand on the concrete trig point pretending to spy pirate ships sailing on the distant sea. Magee was a true Lewesian; born, schooled, living and working in the county town.

Whenever he could, Magee would jog or walk over the Downs. Especially around the old racecourse, from where one could see a white painted house nestling prominently on top of the hill to the south. His parents had bought the former two-up two-down miller's cottage forty years ago when he'd been a toddler and had, as a labour of love, worked hard on it for twelve years to create a perfect haven. With its large rustic garden, swimming pool set amongst the ruins of the old mill and being surrounded by fields, the property had been an idyllic childhood playground. It had broken his young teenage heart the day his parents sold and moved out.

The peaceful day lasted until Magee had got comfortably settled on the sofa and halfway through a comedy on television. At ten minutes before nine the telephone rang. He gave his wife a pleading look and said, 'Would you mind, Jenny? It's probably your mother.'

'Unlikely,' she replied. 'I've already spoken to her today, she doesn't need anything.' Jennifer Magee nevertheless got up from her end of the sofa and walked out into the hallway, muttering over her shoulders, 'And at this time of night it's almost bound to be for you.'

Magee closed his eyes and prayed otherwise. He knew she was likely to be right, but there was always hope. Seconds later came the words he so desperately wanted not to hear.

'It's for you, Jack!'

The call made Magee's heart sink. He removed Carolyn from his lap, walked out into the hallway and dodged a playful slap from his wife. He smiled at her as he took the phone. 'Yes?'

'Is that DCI Magee?' an impersonal voice asked. 'Sorry to disturb you, sir.'

There was a certain way those words were spoken that unnerved Magee. Every time it was the same; a sort of cross between genuine sympathy and perverse delight at knowing someone's night had been ruined. 'Yes,' he snapped. 'What is it?'

'There's been a murder, sir. Over in Hove.'

'Hove? Christ man, I'm in Lewes. Isn't there someone else that can deal with it? There must be someone on duty who lives nearer?' It was a desperate plea, one he knew would be ignored.

'Sorry, sir. Superintendent Vaughan gave instructions for you to go. It's a high profile case.'

'Oh, for Christ sake!' He cupped the phone and swore in more colourful language. He knew precisely what high profile meant to his boss; a potential embarrassment to the upper echelons of the Force, so don't mess it up unless you have an urge to rejoin traffic control. 'What's the problem with it?'

'The victim is a local dignitary, sir. Well, was, rather, I should say. Mr Todd Conners. He's on the council.'

'On the council? You mean he's a councillor?' Magee was astonished. The victim's social status came as a surprise to him. It was at a level far below his interpretation of the word dignitary. He'd expected a Bishop at least.

'And several members of the press are there already. Waiting outside the house, I understand.'

'Oh great!' Magee caught sight of his reflection in the hall mirror. Mr Grumpy Face, Carolyn had named it. It wasn't attractive. It made him look ten years older. He tried a smile, but failed to make any improvement. 'How did that happen then? With the press, I mean.'

'We don't know, sir.'

Magee could guess though. It wouldn't be the first time the press had beaten the police to a crime scene. Chances were they'd been tipped off by a busybody neighbour. 'All right, give me the address,' he mumbled, as he sought to find the pen and scribble pad which usually lay by the phone. Twenty seconds later he finished the conversation by saying, 'I'm on my way.'

Magee bade goodnight to Carolyn as she staggered drowsily up the stairs, promising to be back soon. The lie hurt deep. He kissed his wife goodnight, pretending not to hear her low sigh.

Within fifteen minutes of leaving his house in Highdown Road on the Neville Estate, Magee turned his car off the A27 Lewes to Brighton by-pass into Dyke Road Avenue and proceeded into Tongdean Avenue. Turning into a side road, the house he sought soon became apparent; an enormous colonial style mansion, outside of which stood a morbid group of onlookers hungry for details. He ditched his car on the kerb and moved towards the drama. Holding his warrant card up in front, he fought his way through the congested sea of people. Not that any identification was necessary, for even to a novice officer his crusty expression marked him out as the officer in charge.

'Damn!' Magee cursed, as a camera flash dazzled him. He ducked under a strip of crime scene tape, strode up the driveway and disappeared behind the front door, relishing the relative peaceful respite from the noise outside.

'Right then, who was first on the scene?' Magee barked at a group of uniformed officers standing in the hallway.

'I was, sir.'

Magee took a notebook out of his jacket pocket. 'Name?'

'PC Fuller, Sir.'

'And where's the body?'

'Upstairs, sir. First bedroom on the left.'

'Fine. Lead the way, please, Fuller.' Magee took a white protective suit proffered in his direction, struggled to squeeze into it, almost split a pair of slip-on shoe covers as he forced his feet in, then mounted the stairs at a brisk pace. On entering the bedroom, he found a lone boyish looking photographer busy taking shots of a bloodied body of a man on the floor. He waited a full minute before taking an exaggerated look at his watch.

The action wasn't lost on the cameraman. 'Just one more shot from the front, please, if you don't mind. Then I'll be gone.'

Magee tutted, thinking that a fashion photographer would have taken fewer shots of the latest cat walk sensation, Kate Moss.

'Okay. Finished. He's all yours, Sergeant.'

Magee bared his teeth. 'Detective Chief Inspector to you, sonny.'

'Really? Sorry about that.'

Magee glared with contempt at the departing photographer, then knelt down for a closer examination of the dead man sprawled on the floor. The fact that a knife was sticking out of the man's chest was not unusual in his line of work. What was unusual, though, was its appearance. The hilt appeared to be an ivory carving of a Buddha. Six inches long, he reckoned. Not your everyday common household weapon. Close up, the Buddha's eyes seemed to stare back at him, hypnotically. He blinked hard to shake off its spell.

As a commotion erupted outside the room, Magee looked up and caught sight of a dishevelled young woman noisily entering the room adjusting the fit of her protective suit. She squatted alongside the corpse.

'Evening, sir,' DS Melissa Kelly responded in answer to Magee's scowl.

'And a good evening to you, Melissa. Glad you could make it out on a Saturday night.' It then dawned upon Magee why his boss had dropped the case his way. It would provide a great opportunity, no doubt, for the man's niece to chalk up a murder case on her CV. And it had been made plain a few months ago, in no uncertain words, that it was his job to ensure Melissa learnt the art of detecting well.

'Has the police doctor examined the body yet?' Magee barked at no one in particular.

'Yes, sir,' came a prompt answer. 'Do you want to speak to him?'

'Please,' Magee mumbled. 'In a minute.'

'I'll let him know then, sir.'

'Thank you,' Magee replied to a disappearing back. He turned his attention to his sergeant. 'So, come on then, Melissa. You're here to learn. What do you see?'

'Caucasian aged about forty, I'd say, slightly more perhaps. Well built, though running to fat. Throat slit, probably by the same weapon presently protruding from his chest.'

'And?'

'There doesn't seem to be much else to say, sir. It's pretty obvious how he died.'

'True, but then the cause of death will be established at the post mortem. You need to be able to work out the how, why and when. Look around you. What do you see?'

'Well nothing, sir. It's just a bedroom.'

'And?' But there was nothing more forthcoming from his sergeant. He sighed wearily as he stood up. 'Okay, okay. Stick to the basics. Write some notes, talk me through what you're jotting down.'

Melissa wrote fast as she reeled off the mundane things she observed, while Magee moved around the room. What struck him instantly was the tidiness of the room. The furniture looked to be in place, no ornaments broken, nothing seemed unusual or out of place. Even the victim looked neat, except for the blood. The clothes were in almost perfect condition; there was no ripped shirt or jacket as he might have expected if there'd been a fight. In fact, there was no sign of a struggle having occurred, and the only blood in the room was either on the body or on the carpet immediately surrounding the body.

The only odd thing was the vomit he found on the floor of the en suite bathroom, though he guessed its presence was the result of someone finding the body. Wife he suspected, though it could just have easily been one of the fresh faced officers downstairs. He would create merry hell if his crime scene had been messed up by a novice. He walked around the room a couple of times before nodding his head in satisfaction.

There was only one conclusion Magee could make. Todd Connors had died where he was attacked. The man had been standing near his bed when the murderer walked up to him and slit his throat. It was the only explanation of the jet of blood in front of the body. Then the assailant stabbed the victim in the chest. At no stage did the victim try to fight back, he must have just stood there and taken the punishment.

Magee realized Melissa was still running a commentary. He listened for a few seconds and then turned and caught her eye. 'But what are your general observations, Melissa? Try to get a feel for what happened. Try to picture the sequence of events. Who was where? How did the action go? What evidence is there to back up your thoughts? That's what's important.' He then spent a couple of minutes with her replaying the action that he thought had occurred.

'Now do you see? It's vital to work out the action of the crime. Remember that, please, if you never learn anything else from me. Next time go for the general picture, it's so important. Without working that out, you're sunk. You won't know what evidence to look for. And if you do find anything unusual, don't ignore it if it doesn't fit the picture you've built up.'

'Yes, sir,' Melissa replied as her head bobbed up and down.

'And most important of all, remember that catchphrase you were taught in training; see beyond the victim, see the killer.'

Melissa nodded for the umpteenth time. Magee could see in her eyes she was beginning to understand where he was coming from, but would she have got there by herself without his help?

'What about a religious aspect to the case, sir?'

'Religious? What makes you say that?'

'The carved handle on the dagger. I've never heard of Buddhism being associated with a murder case before. I thought religious murders usually concerned deep, often distorted, Christian beliefs.'

Magee half-smiled in response to his sergeant's attempt at credibility. 'Do you know anything about Buddhism?'

'A little. Well, I probably know as much about Buddhism as I do about Christianity.'

'Which would cover the back of a postage stamp, I suppose?'

'No, sir,' Melissa replied sharply, then softened her manner and added, 'Well, two stamps perhaps.'

Magee smiled despite himself. 'Okay, Miss Expert, try this one for size; does Buddhism encompass the concept of sin like Christianity does?'

He watched Melissa's facial expressions as she thought about that one. It took her some time to conjure up an answer and, when she did venture to speak, she looked as if she wished she hadn't opened her mouth in the first place.

'They have moral codes governing social behaviour, sir, if that's what you mean, sir. Thou shalt not commit murder, theft and such like. The teachings of The Lord Buddha describe them in detail, if I remember correctly.'

The crunched up eyebrows on Melissa's face hinted at something different. 'You've studied Buddhism, have you?'

'Well, sir, I've visited several temples in Thailand. I've even read the tourist catalogues. Well, you have to do something in between, erm, well,' Melissa hesitated, as if trying to find the right words, 'well, in between meals on holiday shall we say. Mind you, I've never seen a Buddha carved on a dagger before. Buddhism is supposed to be a peace loving religion. I wouldn't have thought it would be allowed. It seems curious in itself. It doesn't seem to fit in with Buddhist beliefs.'

Magee nodded his encouragement. 'But what about Buddhist ceremonies though?'

'With a dagger? Buddhists don't sacrifice animals, sir. Nor do they hack off, erm, I mean circumcise, that is, the boys. Or girls, for that matter.'

Magee frowned. Clearly Melissa's trips to the Far East had been wasted.

'Anyway, it's a nice knife,' Melissa continued. 'Easy to trace I should imagine.'

Magee winced. 'I doubt whether the poor bastard on the floor would concur with your description. Unusual perhaps, but "nice" is hardly an appropriate adjective is it?'

Melissa seemed to reflect on the matter for a few seconds. Looking somewhat chastised, she replied, 'No, sir, I suppose not.'

'Come on. There's nothing more for us in here. Let's go back downstairs.'

PC Fuller was waiting for the two of them on the landing outside the bedroom. Magee turned to him and asked, 'What time did you arrive?'

'Just before eight-thirty, sir. We were here within minutes of Mrs Conners' call to the station.'

'And when did the press get here?'

'Within ten minutes of my arrival, I suppose, sir.'

Magee frowned. 'Ten minutes, huh? Are you sure?'

'Quite sure, sir.'

Magee pondered on the length of time it may take a news reporter to hear of a murder and get to the location. 'Looks like our killer may have sought attention,' he muttered on the way downstairs.

'You think he phoned the press?' Melissa piped up. 'Earlier? But that means this was planned.'

Magee smiled, pleased she'd caught on to his reasoning. 'Indeed. Keep it to yourself though.'

'Sir?' PC Fuller called down to Magee as they made their way downstairs. 'There's something else you need to know.'

'Yes?'

'She had a gun, sir. Mrs Conners, that is.'

'A gun? What type?'

'A revolver, sir. She was holding it when we arrived. It's been taken away already. No shots fired.'

Magee nodded his thanks. At the foot of the stairs, PC Fuller introduced the police doctor. 'Thank you for waiting, sir. I'm Detective Chief Inspector Magee, this is Detective Sergeant Kelly.'

'Jenkins,' replied the middle aged doctor by way of introduction. 'How may I help you?'

'I just want to know the story. From your angle, that is.'

'Straight forward, I should think. An extremely sharp knife has cut the victim's throat. I imagine the post mortem will determine it to be the same one that's still up there. It must have been done with considerable force, the wounds are very deep. The assailant must have been standing right in front of the victim when the throat was slashed.' Dr Jenkins gave a wry smile and added, 'And he's right handed of course.'

'He, you say? Not a she?'

Dr Jenkins let out an impatient sigh. 'All right then, he or she. Sorry, I'd been led to believe that sexual equality has yet to reach the Sussex Constabulary. Person unknown, of male or female gender. Is that the correct parlance these days?'

'I only want clarity, sir, because of the wife. Is she strong enough to inflict those wounds?'

Dr Jenkins appeared to consider the matter for a while before replying, 'Yes. Yes, indeed. Mrs Conners could have been strong enough. Given the right conditions, that is. Yet I doubt it very much, Chief Inspector.'

Magee's eyebrows raised a fraction. 'And why is that, sir?'

'Not enough time. I've been here since about eight forty-five. Death occurred between eight and eight-fifteen, nearer the latter time in my opinion. The body was still very warm and fresh when I arrived, the blood was only just beginning to congeal. Mrs Conners must have come across the body within minutes of death, if not seconds. If she'd done it herself then she would have been covered in blood. Yet there's not a splash on her and I don't think she would have had time to shower and change before I was called out.'

'I see.' Magee mentally struck off one potential suspect from his list. 'Could you demonstrate the attack to the victim's throat, please?'

'Of course. Right hand holds the knife down here by the left leg, whips it up at a slight angle from left to right. A bit like a tennis backhand swing.'

The doctor's action confirmed Magee's suspicions. Todd Conners must have just stood his ground while it happened, which meant that he must have known, perhaps even trusted, whoever had done it. Surely, he reflected, no one in their right mind would let an intruder walk up to them that close, wielding a knife, without some attempt at self-defence.

'Okay. Thank you, Doctor, sorry for holding you up.' Magee bade goodnight and watched the doctor's back disappearing out the front door before contemplating his next move. 'Who's next, Fuller?'

'Well, Mrs Conners is in the sitting room, and there's a suspicious character we picked up outside earlier on. He's in the kitchen.'

'Oh? And just what was this suspicious character doing outside?'

'Watching the house next door, sir. Well, so he says anyway.'

'Hmm. Okay, we'll get to him later. We'll see Mrs Conners first.'

Magee followed PC Fuller into the sitting room to find a woman in a crumpled heap, sobbing, on a sofa. 'Mrs Conners? I'm Detective Chief Inspector Magee. This is my sergeant, Melissa Kelly. I'd like to ask you a few questions now, while the events are still fresh in your mind. How do you feel about that?'

Susan Conners nodded her head, snuffled and said, 'That's okay.'

'I gather from PC Fuller that there appears to be no sign of a break-in, nothing to indicate that the house has been burgled. Do you agree with that comment, Mrs Conners?'

'Yes. Though I haven't checked thoroughly.' She rubbed at her eyes and reached for a glass of what looked like brandy.

'Did you hear anything? Any screams? Anything unusual?'

'Nothing, Chief Inspector. Sorry. I was in my own bedroom doing my hair and make-up. I had the television on quite loud. Deliberately so, actually.'

A sudden tensing of Susan Conners shoulders wasn't lost on Magee. 'Deliberately so, Mrs Conners? Why was that?'

'So I couldn't hear my shit of a husband shouting at me to get a move on.'

The outburst had been venomous. Magee frowned; perhaps he'd been too quick to take in Dr Jenkins' comments. 'Did your husband normally shout at you?'

'Only when we were going out for the evening. I used to play stupid games with him. I would never be ready on time. It infuriated him and he would shout at me.' She paused a moment. 'Sorry, that must seem childish to you.'

'Tonight was no different?'

'No. No different at all. Maybe if I had been ready on time, then this wouldn't have happened.'

'Yes, well, we shouldn't speculate on that, should we? You might have got involved yourself. Forget it. Where were you going tonight, by the way?'

Susan Conners shrugged her shoulders. 'Just a Masonic do. Nothing really special.'

'Your husband was a Freemason?'

'He was a property developer, Chief Inspector. The Masonic fraternity is good for business contacts. Everything my husband did was for business. Making money was his life.'

Magee tried to put on a smile. 'Not a family man, then?'

'No, Chief Inspector. Not Todd. He had the kids packed off to boarding school as soon as they could walk, and they don't like coming back much. Can't say I blame them.'

'What mood was he in tonight? Worried? Happy?'

Susan Conners let out a deep sigh. 'Foul as usual.'

'Why was that?'

'He always insisted on me going out with him in the evenings so he wouldn't lose face in front of his friends. But he always resented having to take me along. And I resented him resenting me. Such evenings were always doomed from the start.'

'Did you ever fight? Did he ever strike you, for instance?'

Susan Conners looked up and caught Magee's eye. 'Are you suggesting I killed my husband?'

Magee fell silent for a few seconds, waiting for Susan Conners to take another shot of her drink. When she looked calmer, he continued, 'So, he never hit you, then?'

'No, he never hit me. Todd was an aggressive man, but never violent. He worked out all his frustration in the office. He got through a succession of young secretaries, if you catch my drift.

That's no secret, by the way, I'm sure you'll pick up on the gossip soon enough.'

'In time, Mrs Conners. All in good time. So your husband wasn't a physical man then?'

'Physical? No, that's just what our problem was. Todd hasn't been physical with me for nearly ten years.' She dabbed her eyes with a tissue.

'Can you think of any reason why your husband would be murdered?'

'None specifically. Though I'm sure you could find a few ex-tenants with a motive. He wasn't a pleasant man, at times, Chief Inspector. As I said, he made his living from property development. Sometimes that involved evicting little old ladies from their crummy damp flats. Occasionally it would get dirty. Todd never flinched from throwing squatters out on the street, or taking the roof off a house to flood the sitting tenants out. Do you get the picture?'

Magee got the picture all right. And losing your home was certainly a strong enough motive to commit murder. 'I understand that you were holding a revolver when PC Fuller arrived. Where did you get it?'

'It was Todd's.'

'Do you know how to use it?'

'Not really. It just gave me a sense of security while I waited for the police to turn up.'

'Where was it kept?'

'In Todd's bedside cabinet.'

'How long had he possessed it?'

'I'm not sure. Years, I suppose. He's certainly had it ever since we were married.'

'What was the reason he had it?'

'I have no idea, Chief Inspector. Maybe he suspected this day would come. I really couldn't say. We never discussed it.'

Magee contemplated the pathetic figure of the sad, dishevelled woman in front of him. If a gun had been around the house, then surely it would have been a preferred weapon if she had planned to kill her husband. It would have been far safer than to engage in a knife attack.

'Just one last question, Mrs Conners. The knife that was used, does it belong to you?'

'No, Chief Inspector. It does not.'

'You've never seen it before?'

'Never. It's hideous, with that ugly carving on it. I wouldn't have a thing like that in my house.'

Yet she'd have a gun in the house, Magee reflected. 'Thank you, Mrs Conners. I won't disturb you any more tonight. I may have other questions later, if you don't mind. We'll have to go through your husband's personal effects, business affairs and so on. That will no doubt lead to a certain degree of intrusion. Do you want anyone to stay with you here tonight, or do you wish to stay with relatives? I'm afraid we'll be working all night, the spotlights and noise may disturb you.' Privately, he was thinking she would be out like a light after the amount of brandy she appeared to have downed in the last few minutes.

'Thank you, Chief Inspector. But the house is all yours. I've telephoned a friend, he'll be coming to collect me in a minute.'

Magee was just about to excuse himself when he heard shouting coming from the front hall, and the front door slamming. He went out to investigate, only to find a constable on the floor with blood seeping from his nose. A few seconds later the front door reopened and two constables led in a rugged, handsome young blond man straining against handcuffs.

Magee asked, 'What on earth's going on?'

'This bastard just laid Johnson out, sir. We got him before he managed to get far.'

'What was he doing in here?'

'I mentioned him to you before, sir. Earlier this evening, he was sitting outside in his car watching the house next door. I asked him to come inside and give a statement. Johnson had been sitting with him in the kitchen waiting for you, sir. A few moments ago he decided to do a runner.'

Magee gave the struggling man a quizzical look. 'That wasn't very nice, sir,'

The man ceased struggling. 'I've been framed. You bastards! You're going to pin this on me, aren't you?'

Feigning innocence, Magee asked, 'Are we, sir? Why would we do that?' But there was no answer forthcoming. He studied the man's face for a few seconds before demanding, 'What's your name?'

Again, there was no reply from the blond man.

'His name's Mansell, sir,' interjected PC Johnson. 'Paul Mansell, according to his driving license. Age twenty five, this month. A Kemp Town address.'

'Well, Mr Paul Mansell. We'll talk later. Tomorrow morning, I suggest. A night in the cells should loosen your tongue.'

'Are you going to charge me with murder?'

'Not yet,' replied Magee. He then turned to the constable with the bloody nose. 'Book him for assaulting an officer, resisting arrest, withholding evidence, anything you like, Johnson. Nothing too serious, though, just enough to keep him locked up until we've all had a good night's sleep.'

Magee left Paul Mansell to face the wrath of Johnson and his colleagues then spent a while searching the house, confirming his theories about the case. There were no obvious signs of a break-in and no ransacking had taken place. He hoped the Scene Of Crime Officers would come up with something meaningful. For the time being, though, he decided he might as well go home and rest. There seemed nothing more to be gained from searching the house; no reason not to leave the case in the capable hands of his sergeant.

Magee was about to leave the house when the front door opened and a neatly dressed man in a black suit stepped inside. As their eyes met, Magee's jaw dropped in shock. 'Nick Price,' he hissed. 'What the hell are you doing here?'

Nick Price's upper lip turned into a snarl. 'Well, well, if it isn't PC Plod himself.'

'Get out of here, Price, this is a crime scene!'

Nick Price squared his shoulders and spat back, 'Fuck you, Magee! I've been invited.'

'By whom?'

'Susan.'

'Susan Conners? You know Susan?'

'I certainly do. She phoned me an hour ago, asked me to come over to sort this mess out. And I can see why.'

'Meaning what?'

'What do you think, you twat.'

Although Magee was taller and larger than Nick Price, the smaller man held his ground firm. In fact, Nick Price looked as though he was steeling himself for the first punch.

A slurred voice came from nearby, 'Nick? Is that you, Nick?'

Nick Price backed off, a look of hatred welling within his eyes. He jabbed a finger in Magee's direction. 'One day, old son, as promised, I'll get even with you.'

Magee sighed heavily as Nick Price disappeared into the sitting room.

A voice from behind said, 'Wow! What was that all about, sir?'

Magee turned abruptly to find Melissa looking concerned. 'Hmm? Oh, nothing.'

'Wasn't that Nick Price? The property developer?'

'Yes it was.'

'You know him, sir?'

'We've met before a few times. It's never been a pleasant experience.'

'He looked as though he was going to take a swipe at you, sir.'

'Yes. I thought so too.'

'Why would he want to do that?'

'Nothing, Melissa. It's ancient history.'

'But Nick Price is a respectable businessman, he's well known for his charitable works. Why would he want to pick a fight with a policeman?'

Magee shrugged off the comment. 'Just shows you can't believe everything you read in the newspapers. There's a dark side to that man.'

'That sounds ominous.'

'No doubt. Anyway, if you don't mind, I'm going home now. You can wind up here. Get SOCO to finish up, get the statements together and we'll go through it all tomorrow.'

'Tomorrow? On a Sunday?'

'We'll interview that Paul Mansell character in the morning.'

Melissa's shoulders sagged. 'Right. Goodnight then, sir.'

Magee left the house, pleased to distance himself from Nick Price. He stepped out into a blinding bright arc lamplight that was illuminating the property, only to be faced with an army of reporters. Even a television crew had arrived, hovering like vultures.

PC Fuller, standing nearby, looked almost apologetic as he said, 'They're waiting for a statement, I'm afraid, sir.'

Magee grimaced then walked down the driveway to do battle with the press. He put his arms behind his back, drew in a deep breath and said, 'Good evening, gentlemen.'

But before Magee could speak further, he was bombarded by a barrage of inane questions shouted in unison by a pack of speculative journalists. 'Gentlemen, please, if I may speak?' He waited a few seconds for a gap in the melee. 'I can confirm that a death has occurred here tonight. I cannot comment on whether it was a domestic matter or not. A man is helping us with our enquiries. However, we are unable to comment on his possible involvement. That's all for now, gentlemen. If you will allow me through, please? Thank you.'

Magee pushed his way through the journalistic scrum, wondering what sort of warped minds reporters must possess to ask the sort of sacrilegious questions now being shouted in vain at his disappearing back

Chapter Four

Nick Price eased Susan Conners' limp body down onto a guestroom bed, maneuvered her head onto a pillow, slipped her shoes off and pulled a bedspread up to her neck. He wasn't going to undress her, or even loosen her clothes. He wasn't in the mood, and he certainly didn't want the situation misinterpreted when she woke in the morning. Mind you, he reflected, the way she'd been knocking back the brandies, he doubted she would have any thoughts in the morning other than for her hangover.

He turned the light off, closed the door, crept along the galleried landing and unlocked the door to his sanctuary. He sat down on a tatty bamboo chair, Maliwan's favourite. Given to her by her grandmother on their wedding day and shipped back to England along with everything else from their room above Lucy's Tiger Den.

After a few moments collecting his thoughts, he found Maliwan's voice coming to him.

You're not smiling tonight.

'Sorry,' responded Nick. 'It's been a difficult night.'

Tell me about it.

'Do you remember Todd?'

Tell me about him.

'Todd Conners. He was a regular in the bar, for a couple of years. I got on quite well with him. So did Ronnie.'

Was he the one that was always making eyes at me?

'That's him.' Nick smiled. Maliwan would come over all girlish when a customer flirted with her. It was one of the many things he had loved her for.

I thought you didn't like him looking at me?

'I didn't,' replied Nick with all seriousness. 'But he was a good worker, I needed him.'

So? What about him?

'He died tonight.'

I'm sorry.

Nick was silent a full minute before choosing his next words. 'Mal? It's started hasn't it?'

Started? I don't understand.

'You know what I mean, Mal. Todd's death was no accident.'

Was he murdered?

'He certainly was. A vicious attack with a knife. A knife that just happened to have an effigy of a Buddha carved into the handle. Makes you think, that, doesn't it?'

Of what?

'You know. What we did in Tibet.'

Maliwan's voice fell silent.

'Susan said there'd been no fight. She said it had been as if Death had just come up silently and taken him away.'

He let his head sink into his hands, and tried to obliterate a fleeting memory of his tortured past. 'He's coming for us, isn't he?'

Chapter Five

DCI Magee sat in an interview room busying himself with the contents of a file that had been faxed from a police station in Arnos Grove during the night. He was not in a good mood. Being stuck in a dingy office with no window, on a bright sunny morning, was not his preferred choice of weekend activity. 'This report is particularly damning,' he murmured to Melissa. 'It says Mansell was a bit of a tearaway when he was a young lad.'

Melissa took the report and began reading the front page in silence. After the first paragraph, she gave a response. 'That doesn't make him a murderer though does it, sir?'

'No, it doesn't. But it seems he met up with Nick Price at an early stage.'

Melissa looked up. 'You think the two are involved somehow? I didn't think SOCO had come up with anything yet?'

'They haven't. No yet anyway, as far as I know.' Magee sat back and shrugged. 'And as our good Dr Jenkins said last night, the killer would probably have been covered in blood. Mansell wasn't. However, he was there and may have had the opportunity to clean himself up afterwards.'

'But you think Nick Price was involved, nevertheless?'

'Anything's possible, Melissa. The only thing we've got to go on at the moment is that Susan Conners knows Nick Price and he, in turn, knows Paul Mansell. All three were there last night, and we've no evidence to suggest anyone else was. So, maybe there's something going on between the three of them.'

'Like what?'

The Fourth Cart I

'I really don't know, Melissa. Not yet anyway. A few obvious motives spring to mind. Insurance, for instance. Then there's love. That frequently leads to recriminations when broken hearts are involved. Hopefully, something may come to light when we start to dig into Todd Conners' affairs.'

'And in the meantime?'

'In the meantime, Melissa, we'll just have to bait Mansell, push him a bit. There's certainly enough ammunition in this file to get him hot under the collar. With luck, he'll snap under pressure.'

'It says here he got let off with a warning for . . .' Melissa put the file down as the door opened and Paul Mansell was led in, restrained by handcuffs.

Magee gestured towards the chair on the other side of the table. 'Sit down, Mansell.' He turned to the escorting officer and said, 'Take the cuffs off him, please.'

'Sure that's wise, sir?'

'Quite sure, thanks.'

Paul Mansell sat down and faced his two inquisitors with a look of trepidation in his eyes. 'Are you going to charge me with murder, Chief Inspector?'

'We'll come to that matter in a minute, Mansell. First, I thought we'd just have a quiet chat. You see, I have your file here, from Arnos Grove. I'm sure you know what's in it.' Magee flicked briefly through the large pile of papers and gave Mansell a wry smile.

'Christ, that's ancient stuff. I was young then. A very different person to who I am now.'

Magee cast his eyes down to the dossier and read out, 'Petty theft, vandalism, expulsion from school for violence, social service reports. Quite a hard case, weren't you? And still are, judging by last night's little drama.'

Paul Mansell bowed his head. 'You've got me wrong, Chief Inspector. I'm not a "hard case", as you put it. Not any more. Not that I ever was before. I was just a mixed up kid. The reports must say that, surely? That part of my life is all in the past. I've been clean for nearly nine years now.'

'Nine years, eh? Let me guess,' Magee paused for effect as his upper lip curled, 'your conversion to the path of righteousness occurred as a result of meeting Nick Price?'

'Yes. Yes it was actually. And there's nothing funny about it. I met Nick when I was sixteen years old. He straightened me out. That's the god's honest truth.'

'Really? Forgive me, Mansell, but I find that hard to swallow.' Magee gave Mansell a stern look. 'You see, I know the real Nick Price. He was giving me trouble a long, long time ago.'

'Nick is not a villain, he's a decent guy. Yeah, of course he had a hard time in his youth. So what, who hasn't? But he's not like that now, he's a family man. It's people like you who continue to blight his name. It's out of order.'

Magee gave a snort of derision. 'You think so? I hope you won't be calling Price as a character witness, it won't make you any friends around here.'

'And why would I need a character witness? You haven't charged me with anything yet.'

'No, I haven't, have I? So, let's keep this conversation civil. Okay?'

'Right.'

'Good. Now then, to other matters. Last night, for instance. What were you doing outside that house in Tongdean Avenue? Be very precise about it, please.'

'As I told one of your officers last night, I was working on a case. I do security consultancy and investigative work. I have a legitimate practice. I've been doing it for a couple of years now. And yes, before you ask, I do a fair amount of work for Nick. These last few days, however, I was working for a client named Cracknell. I was keeping his wife under surveillance, at the house next door.'

Magee sneered. 'What for? What was your brief?'

'I was supposed to be on the look-out for strange young men. I guess Cracknell suspected his wife of having an affair. Maybe he wanted grounds for a divorce. That's not my concern. I just gather the evidence for the client.'

'You were employed direct by this Mr Cracknell?'

'Yes, I just said that.'

'Did you ever meet him?'

'No.' Paul Mansell squirmed in his seat before adding, 'He telephoned me and sent some cash in advance.'

The body language had not gone unnoticed by Magee. 'How were you to contact him should anything arise?'

The Fourth Cart I

'I wasn't to. He said he would phone back after a week. I didn't care. It was his money after all.'

'So you were tailing Mrs Cracknell constantly during the last few days then?'

'No. Specific times only. Two to five o'clock in the afternoon and seven to eleven in the evening.'

Magee reflected momentarily on the significance of the times. 'Why was that?'

'Haven't a fucking clue,' Paul Mansell spluttered. 'Sorry. Look, I don't know. That's the god honest truth. Cracknell was in charge. Guess he knew when she was at it.'

'So you have no written confirmation of your client's wishes?'

'No, none. As I said, it was all done by phone.'

'This is all rubbish, Mansell. You know the Conners don't you?'

'Who are the Conners?'

The reply seemed to have been delivered in a genuinely innocent tone, but Magee was having none of it. He gave a weak smiled as he said, 'Nice try, Mansell. Mr Conners, the man who was murdered last night.'

'I don't know a Mr Conners. Honest!'

'Really?'

'I swear I don't!'

'Nick Price seems to know the Conners. As, I believe, you do.'

Paul Mansell looked confused. 'What?'

'Oh, come on, Mansell. Todd and Susan Conners.'

A faint sign of recognition surfaced on Paul Mansell's face.

'Come on, Mansell,' Magee persisted, 'Don't say you don't know them. She called Nick Price last night to come over to her place, after her husband was found dead.'

'Nick was there last night?'

'As if you don't know!'

'Todd?'

'Yes, Todd Conners.'

Paul Mansell looked sideways to the door, as if he was going to bolt.

'Tell me, Mansell, were you and Nick Price in this together?'

'Sorry?'

'I reckon Todd Conners and Nick Price were in business together. Did Nick Price order a hit?'

'A hit? I don't understand?'

'For goodness sake, Mansell! You said yourself you're in the "security business". We all know what that means.'

'If it's the Todd I'm thinking about, he's an old mate of Nick's. They go back a long way. Why the hell would Nick want to order a hit on a friend?'

'I really don't know. That's why I'm asking you.'

'He wouldn't have done it.'

'Really? Convince me. Tell me what you were actually doing there last night.'

'I've told you the truth already, Chief Inspector! Why the hell would I lie? If I was involved in a hit, as you put it, why would I sit around all evening waiting for you lot to turn up? I'd just piss off as soon as the job was done, wouldn't I?'

'I have no idea, Mansell. That's what I want to know myself. Maybe you're just some sick sod playing games with us. Arsonists tend to hang around their fires to see the effect. Maybe you're inclined the same way.' He tapped the file in front of him meaningfully, and added, 'Maybe you wanted to draw attention to yourself, like you did when you were younger.'

'Sorry to disappoint you, Chief Inspector,' Paul Mansell hissed. 'I enjoy my life now. I have no wish to draw police attention and I certainly have no desire to serve a life stretch. I was scared shitless last time I was in a cell. It made me think about what I was doing with my life. I vowed then to pack it in and be a good boy.'

'Yes, talking about that, just how did you get off that last charge? That was pretty serious wasn't it? Caught in the act, according to these records.'

'I was just lucky, I guess. Perhaps your colleagues heeded my plea for forgiveness. I don't know, I never really thought about it. At the time, I was just glad that particular nightmare was over with.'

'That was when you first met Nick Price, you say?'

'Yes. That's correct. Nick came to visit me whilst I was in the cells. I hadn't a clue who he was. I'd never seen him before. He just marched into the station with a lawyer and cleared the matter up.'

'Just like that?' Magee was incredulous. 'How wonderful to have friends in high places. I notice that the owner of the store you trashed didn't press charges. That must have taken a fair bit of persuasion. Compensation? Or threats perhaps?'

'I have no idea,' Paul Mansell replied with an uncaring shrug.

'And you just received a caution! Deary me! That must have cost Price a lot of money. Come on now, Mansell, there's more to this than you're letting on. Price must have paid a fortune in bribes, or sold his soul to the devil, to get you off with a caution. Why did he do it? I don't believe you were a stranger to him. Nick Price is no knight in shining armour, he doesn't go around helping strangers in trouble. It couldn't possibly have been the first time he'd met you.'

'Chief Inspector, I swear I'm not lying! I don't know anything about Nick bribing people to get me off that charge and I don't know how, or why, he did it. All I do know is that I've been very grateful to Nick ever since. He's a good friend; he treats me like his kid-brother. He lets me get away with murder...'

'Really?' Magee raised an eyebrow in Melissa's direction.

Paul Mansell gave a sigh of despair. 'It's just a saying, for god's sake. Look, Nick just lets me do things other employees wouldn't be allowed to get away with. He treats me like close family. I meant nothing more by it. Okay?'

'Okay. Have it your way. So, you're grateful to Nick Price, you owe him one maybe. Do anything for him, would you? Do his dirty work for him perhaps? Like taking care of Todd Conners?'

'Nick doesn't murder his business associates. Nor his enemies either. He's not like that.'

'If I find out about a business deal between Nick Price and Todd Conners that went wrong, you're in trouble. You know that don't you, Mansell?'

'Okay. Fine, anything you say. But I stand by what I said.'

'Fine!' Magee closed the dossier with a finality and pushed it aside. 'So then, back to last night. What time did you arrive in Tongdean Avenue?'

'Seven o'clock exactly. As instructed.'

'And you sat watching the Cracknell's house from your car until the police arrived?'

'Yes. I'm glad the message has finally got through to you.' Paul Mansell relaxed into a slouching position for a moment whilst Magee sat in silence. Suddenly he jerked forward and his eyes screwed up into a frown. He then threw his head back and laughed.

'What's the matter, Mansell?'

'The murder was committed between eight and eight twenty, am I right?'

'You tell me, Mansell. You were there, not me.'

'My instructions. My non-written, non-provable instructions, as you'll no doubt remind me, were to leave my car at precisely eight o'clock and walk south down Tongdean Avenue and into the cul-de-sac that runs along the back of Cracknell's rear garden. From there, I was to observe the bedroom. There's a clear view from that cul-de-sac, though I had my binoculars with me. And I was to return at precisely eight twenty.'

'Add Peeping Tom to murder shall we?' interjected Melissa with a chuckle. Both men glared at her.

'Thank you, Melissa,' Magee said through gritted teeth before returning his gaze to Paul Mansell. 'Did you observe Mrs Cracknell? Throughout the time you were snooping around the back, that is?'

'Yes I did. The curtains were open, despite it getting dark. God knows why. She was wandering around, getting her kids ready for bed, brushing her daughter's hair, that sort of thing. I could make out a television glaring in the corner of one of the rooms. She was there the whole time until I left at eight twenty. I remember thinking it a waste of time as I wandered back to my car.'

Magee felt stumped. If Mansell was indeed telling the truth, then it was likely he'd just established an alibi. He met Mansell's stare, nodded his head and said, 'Melissa, get your pen ready, please. Now Mansell, I want you to describe every one of Mrs Cracknell's movements during those twenty minutes. You don't need me to tell that you your freedom may depend on this, do you?'

'No, you don't. Okay, here goes.' Paul Mansell closed his eyes and reeled off detail after detail, much of it seemingly petty and insignificant.

Melissa wrote rapidly, while Magee sat in silent contemplation and studied Mansell's face. He had watched guilty men lie smoothly before, even those that had given long detailed accounts of events that had never occurred. Here though, he knew that he was watching an innocent man fighting for his life. Yet something still troubled him. Something just didn't fit. Mansell was in it up to his neck; his gut instinct told him that, beyond question.

'Coffee anyone?' Magee asked as he rose to leave the room. He needed some fresh air.

The Fourth Cart I

'Yes please, sir,' Melissa replied, still writing.

Paul Mansell nodded his appreciation.

Magee left the room, feeling dejected. Five minutes later he re-entered the interview room with three cups of coffee and an assortment of sachets of sugar and dried cream.

'Thank you,' Paul Mansell said politely. 'I think that's it. I can't recall anything else.'

Damn those eyes, Magee thought. There was no guilt in them, not even a hint of nervousness. He sighed at the loss of another potential lead.

'Okay, Melissa. Let's wind this up.' Magee stood to leave the room, turned to catch Paul Mansell's eyes and said, 'This had better check out, or I promise we'll be meeting again.'

Chapter Six

It was barely nine-thirty in the morning when DCI Magee caught himself staring out his office window at Black Cap in the distance. It had become a ritual, his way of easing tension, coping with stress, the familiarity with the hills enabling him to imagine the views and the pleasure of filling his lungs with fresh air. It was one of the few benefits of working in the Sussex Police Headquarters building in Malling; the views were good, if you liked hills.

After a few moments of bliss, he sat down and continued the task of wading through a variety of reports that had landed on his desk since the murder occurred two days beforehand. Most were exceedingly boring, many were full of technical jargon. As he reached for the dictionary for the twentieth time, he wondered if his colleagues deliberately chose obscure words to make him feel inadequate.

Overall, he was disappointed with what he read. The reports revealed nothing he didn't know or suspect already. The only new information to emerge was that Mr Cracknell emphatically denied having engaged Paul Mansell to spy on his wife. It was an unfortunate inconsistency, but the truth couldn't be proved either way. What he needed was a new angle.

He rose, stretched his legs around the office for a few seconds, pulled back his office door and called out, 'Melissa? Come in here a second will you please?'

'Sure,' came the reply.

The Fourth Cart I

Magee sat back down as Melissa entered the room. He pointed to the array of files on his desk and said, 'You've read all this lot, haven't you? What's your take on it?'

'Can't say, sir. Not enough to go on at the moment, I reckon.'

'No clues, no motives and no witnesses. Except for Paul Mansell of course, but do we trust him? And what of his connection with Nick Price?'

'Coincidence?'

'I don't believe in coincidence.'

'Maybe just a red herring, then?'

'I don't like that idea either.'

'So?'

Magee swiveled his chair round and took a peek at the distant hills before replying, 'I'm convinced Todd Conners knew his assailant. I'm sure that the two of them had been standing talking and that the attack came as a total surprise to Conners.'

'What about the location? Odd place to choose for a talk isn't it, by the side of his bed? Unless it was with a lover, of course.'

Magee agreed. 'Mrs Conners certainly implied that her husband had many affairs. But she also said they would have been undertaken in his office. And don't forget he was going out for the evening. It seems unlikely that he would have a lover there, in his bedroom, at that particular time. Remember she said he'd only just shouted at her to get a move on.'

'So you reckon the assailant just walks into the house at eight o'clock and up to Conners' bedroom without being detected. Then, after no more than, say, a couple of minutes conversation, kills him and walks out, unnoticed, and without leaving a trace?'

'Yes,' Magee responded. 'I suppose so.'

'Paul Mansell, then. He was the only one that could have done it.'

Magee grimaced; he had already been down that line of reasoning. 'No, Melissa. I've decided to give Mansell the benefit of the doubt for now. His account matches the statements of the Cracknell family far too well. He couldn't possibly have known some of the things described in his testimony if he'd been inside the Conners' house instead.'

'Yes. There is that, but . . .'

'But, Melissa, I want to keep an open mind. I still need to establish the significance of the Buddha effigy on the dagger, if it has any that is.'

'Do you want me to check with . . .' but Melissa was interrupted by the ringing of Magee's telephone.

Magee lifted the receiver, only to hear a voice say, 'I've got the Home Secretary on the line for you, sir.'

Magee recognized the voice as being that of DC Deborah Collins, but was otherwise dumbfounded. 'I beg your pardon, Debs?'

'I said, sir, that I have Mr Geoffrey Rees Smith, the Home Secretary, on the line for you, personally.'

'That's what I thought you said.' Magee took a moment to compose himself. 'Well, you'd better put him through then, I suppose.' He covered the mouthpiece and said, 'Sorry, Melissa, this sounds important. It's the Home Secretary apparently.'

Whilst Melissa withdrew from the room, Magee sat upright and took a deep breath. 'Good morning, sir. This is Detective Chief Inspector Jack Magee, how may I help you?'

'Good morning, Chief Inspector.' The Home Secretary's voice was saccharine, causing Magee to take an instant dislike to the man. 'A local news item caught my attention last night, concerning the murder of a Brighton councillor. I understand he was murdered in his own home, in his bedroom of all places, and I gather that you are leading the investigation. Is that right?'

Magee scratched the back of his head in puzzlement. 'That is quite correct, sir.'

'May I ask how the investigation is going?'

'Slowly, sir. It's far too early to comment on it yet. I'm still collating reports.'

'No indication of the murderer's identity then?'

'None at all, sir. It was a very professional job.'

'Professional? You mean it was a hit man?'

'Not necessarily, sir, although it could have been. I really meant that it was well planned and well carried out. The murderer seems to have left no trace, no fingerprints, nothing that could help us to identify him.'

'What about that man you apprehended at the scene? The one that ran out of the house and was tackled to the ground. I saw that escapade on television.'

Magee's head sunk, briefly, despairing of the direction the conversation seemed to be heading. 'I let him go, sir.'

'For god's sake, why?'

Magee bit his lip and waited for a surge of irritation to pass before venturing to answer, 'Because I believe him to be innocent, sir.'

'Then why did you arrest him in the first place?'

'Suspicion, sir. He'd been surveying a neighbour's house during the evening. But it turned out he was just a private investigator on a case.'

'And he didn't see anything?'

'That's right, sir. He saw nothing of the murder or murderer; he was round the back of the victim's house at the precise time of the incident.'

'What was that man's name, Chief Inspector?'

'Mansell, sir, Paul Mansell.' The telephone fell silent. For a moment, he thought the line had been severed. 'Sir? Are you still there, sir?'

'Yes, sorry,' Rees Smith mumbled, 'my secretary interrupted me. How old is this Paul Mansell?'

'About twenty five, I believe.'

'So this Paul Mansell character is now roaming free?'

'Yes, sir.' Magee was seething. The Home Secretary's tone was bordering on ridicule.

'Well, I hope for your sake he's innocent!'

Magee jerked the phone away from his head as the outburst left his ears ringing. He waited a few seconds before replying, 'I certainly believe he is, sir.'

There was another long pause. Magee remained quiet, assuming the Home Secretary was collecting his thoughts.

'I apologize for being tetchy, Chief Inspector, the burdens of this office can make me snappy at times.'

'I'm sure they can, sir.'

'Look, Chief Inspector, the reason I called was to inform you that I'm taking a special interest in this case. It's just the sort of thing that the public are very worried about, they want to know that they are safe in their own houses. This sort of affair makes them very concerned indeed. It's very disturbing for little old ladies in particular. At the last election we pledged to increase resources to combat crimes just like this. Unfortunately, resources mean cash and that means a larger share of the tax burden. To justify the increased cost we need to show better results. I'm using this murder as a test case for our electors' attitudes. I want to see positive steps taken and a quick solution found to this case. I shall be taking confidential opinion polls to find out the public's attitude as the case progresses. Therefore, I would like to be kept informed of all matters relevant to the case. I want copies of all reports and interviews to be sent direct to me please, marked "Urgent and Confidential". I'll make sure the copies sent to me will be destroyed later. Don't get my intentions wrong, Chief Inspector, I have no wish to interfere with your case and I will not censure any interviews you wish to conduct with the press. Do you understand my request?'

Magee responded sharply, 'Yes, sir.' He understood his situation perfectly. His head had just been placed on a chopping block. The public was his jury, the Home Secretary his executioner.

'Thank you, Chief Inspector. I want to be able to assure the public that we have things under control. I know it sounds patronizing, but we can't have our voters, I mean the British public, worrying about sleeping safely in their beds, now, can we?'

'No, sir, we can't have that, can we.' Magee's hands were shaking, he felt he could scream.

'Well, as I said, Chief Inspector, keep me informed. Hope you succeed quickly. Goodbye for now.'

Magee replied, 'Goodbye, sir,' through gritted teeth, only just managing not to snarl. He slammed the receiver down and swore, 'Shit!'

Most of the staff in the open plan office turned in the direction of Magee's room. It wasn't often that they heard someone lose their cool quite so loudly.

'What the bloody hell does he think he's playing at! Bloody politicians! That's all I sodding well need.' Without rising from his chair he yelled out, 'Debs!'

Seconds later, DC Collins poked her head around Magee's office door and said, 'You shouted for me, sir?'

'A copy of all this crap for His Highness the Home Bloody Secretary, please!'

DC Collins stood resolute by the door.

The Fourth Cart I

Magee looked into her burning eyes and regretted raising his voice. He sighed and looked at her sheepishly. 'I'm sorry, Debs, I didn't mean to shout at you. That bloody man just got to me rather badly, that's all.'

'So we all gather, sir,' replied DC Collins. A mere flicker of a smile appeared on her lips. She gathered up the pile of reports whilst Magee sat quietly trying to regain his composure. As she was leaving the office, Melissa stepped in, a newspaper in hand.

'I take it that conversation didn't go well, sir.'

'You noticed.'

'I think the whole building did.'

Magee rubbed his chin. 'Rees Smith wants to be kept informed of the case. He wants copies of all the reports.'

'Isn't that unusual, sir?'

Magee crossed his arms and replied, "I'm not sure. I suppose it's within his domain, being Home Secretary. He gave me some political claptrap about it being a test case for voters' satisfaction with the Government's latest crackdown on crime.'

'But you don't believe him?'

'I don't know. I've no reason to doubt him. Although it does seem rather odd. I suppose I should check it out with Superintendent Vaughan.' He caught DS Kelley's eye and asked, 'Why are you smirking?'

Melissa stepped closer to Magee's desk and placed the newspaper down. 'Last Friday's Sussex Express, sir. Didn't you read it?'

Magee shook his head. 'Can't say I did. My thoughts were elsewhere over the weekend, I didn't get an opportunity to read it. Why? Have I missed something?'

'In light of that phone call, well, maybe.'

Magee pulled the paper closer. Towards the bottom of the front page ran the caption "Local entrepreneur unveils city redevelopment project". He skimmed through the story and turned to the inside front page for the continuation. To his astonishment, there lay a picture of Nick Price standing behind a scale model of his latest project. And standing alongside Nick Price was Geoffrey Rees Smith. Magee's jaw dropped. 'What the hell is going on here?'

Chapter Seven

Magee spent the remainder of the morning puzzling over Rees Smith's intervention. He didn't believe in coincidence, not when it came to crime, but neither could he think of any good reason for there to be a connection. By early afternoon, he reasoned he had to question Nick Price, no matter how much he'd prefer otherwise. The Rees Smith conundrum would have to be placed on the back-burner.

As Melissa drove up Lewes High Street, north past the Neville Estate and onwards towards the villages of Offham and Cooksbridge, Magee sat in the passenger seat in quiet contemplation of what the consequences of his visit may be. Twenty three years ago, fresh out of Hendon, he'd been eager to prove himself. Too eager perhaps, since it had led to a fight in the street with Nick Price. It was a fight that Nick Price appeared not to have forgotten. His eyes glazed over as he stared vacantly out the car's window, his mind lost to the past.

At Cooksbridge, the level crossing barriers were down, and a queue of cars stretched back over a hundred yards. As they waited for the London train to come through, Melissa broke the silence by asking, 'So, what's the real Nick Price like then, sir? Is he just like he's portrayed in the newspapers? Mean and nasty?'

Magee would have preferred not to answer. 'I couldn't say I really know him. We first met when we were teenagers. Nick Price was a foul mouthed, uncouth yob and I had a bit of a ding-dong with him.'

'Sounds intriguing. Are you going to tell me more?'

'No, sorry. I'm not.' Magee sunk back into the car seat.

As the train passed, and the barriers lifted, Melissa said, 'I can't picture you as a teenager, sir.'

Magee snorted. 'Cheeky pig! I'm not old. I'm only forty-one. And I'm still fit for my age. You know I go for a run up on the hills most weekends. It's just that you're twenty years younger than me, Melissa. It's a big age gap, that's all.'

'I know that, sir. It's just that you've been in the Force since before I was born, haven't you? It makes you seem old, a different generation. Like my uncle, he's always harping on about his long service.'

'You're comparing me to Superintendent Vaughan? Thanks a bunch. He must be well into his fifties.'

'I didn't mean it that way, sir. It's just that I feel I'm only just starting out in life.'

Magee screwed his eyes shut and thought about how time flies. 'Is that supposed to make me feel better?'

'No, sorry. Anyway, you were stationed in London when you met Nick Price?'

'Limehouse, in the East End. Nick Price considered it to be his territory. He thought he owned the place. His manor as he referred to it. It was a very different world back then.'

'This was back in the sixties?'

'Yes. Summer of sixty-nine, if I remember correctly. I was just nineteen. Price was the same age.'

'I like that. Summer of sixty-nine. It sounds like a line from a song. Are you nostalgic for those days, sir?'

Magee shook his head sagely. 'Some pretty dreadful things used to happen back then.'

'Such as?'

Magee shrugged. 'You must have watched police dramas on television that are set in those days. The storylines might be dramatized, but some of the things portrayed are pretty true to life.'

'You had some bad experiences?'

'Guess so. I was no different to the others.'

'Corruption? Gangland killings? Backhanders to the police?'

Magee caught Melissa's enquiring stare. 'I think we should change the subject. And keep your eyes on the road please.'

'I won't tell anyone. Promise'

Magee snorted. 'I don't doubt that, Melissa. It's just that I don't appreciate slurs on my character.'

'We're supposed to be a team, aren't we?'

'That may be so, but it doesn't entitle you to delve into my private life.'

'I thought we were talking about work.'

'Sometimes work crosses the boundary into one's private life.'

'Now you've got me intrigued. Come on, sir, spill the beans.'

Magee shook his head. 'Sorry, Melissa. On a more fortuitous day perhaps. Anyway, we're nearly there now. You can see Price's house through the trees over there to the right.'

Melissa glanced quickly to where Magee pointed but returned to her conversation. 'But there's bad blood between you and Nick Price?'

Magee nodded. 'You saw his reaction to me at the Conners house the other day. That's why I'm a bit apprehensive about meeting him now, in his own home. Without armed back-up, that is.'

'But you're going in, aren't you?'

'No choice, Melissa. Not now, not with our precious Home Secretary's interference. That sort of pressure makes the top brass react irrationally. Our dear Superintendent Vaughan wants me to explore every possible angle; "Don't leave a stone unturned" is how he put it.'

'And Nick Price is a stone that needs turning over?'

Magee shrugged. 'Who knows? He's got some dark secrets in his past; I know that for a fact. I'm going to give him a shake, see what falls out. Turn right here at the Rainbow Inn, his estate's just a hundred yards further along. Next right. This is it; Price's Folly. It used to have a quite acceptable name for a country house. Conyboro Hall. Then it became Conyboro School. He bought the place about three years ago and renamed it after himself of course, pretentious git that he is.'

But Melissa wasn't listening. As she drove up the tree-lined drive, she looked in awe at the estate with its coach house and stables to the left, formal lawns to the right, fields and woods in the distance.

'Wow! This is beautiful,' said Melissa.

'It certainly is. You can't see it from here, but there's a swimming pool just round the corner from those lawns, and there's a lake down the bottom of the fields.'

'You've been here before, sir?'

'Many times, yes. When it was a school. Every summer there'd be a fete here, to raise money for new equipment for the kids. Those lawns would be decked out in stalls and refreshment tents, people were allowed indoors if it rained.'

'I had no idea it was here.'

'There's no reason to. The summer fetes stopped once Nick Price bought the place. It's strictly private property nowadays and I get the impression he's not too keen on advertising its presence.'

The drive swept around to the left then opened up into a large parking area in front of an imposing Victorian red brick manor with wings on each side. Magee's stomach knotted as he got out of the car and advanced towards the double-width front door. To his dismay, two security men, each restraining a Doberman on a chain leash, came out to greet him.

'This is private property,' the larger of the two guards grunted. 'No visitors allowed.'

Magee held up his warrant card. 'I don't doubt it. Just tell Mr Price that we're here to see him.'

'You don't have an appointment,' the other guard growled, in unison with his dog.

'It's just a social call. Nothing official.' Magee waved his warrant card in the direction of a CCTV camera perched to the side of the entrance.

'Mr Price doesn't socialize with pigs!' It was the first guard talking in a grunt again.

'Now, now. That's not very friendly. I was led to believe that Mr Price was a decent upright citizen with nothing to hide. So Paul Mansell says anyway.' Magee directed himself to the camera, 'Paul could be in trouble, Mr Price. Maybe you can help him. I gather you're fond of him. He's a potential suspect in a murder case.'

The two guards seemed about to hurl more abuse at Magee when an electronic bleep behind them caught their attention. They turned to see a green light flashing on an intercom unit, and promptly walked off with the dogs without a further word.

'Guess we let ourselves in.' Melissa said as the guards disappeared through an open archway in a nearby hedge. As she put her hand on the door handle she said, 'I think I'm in the wrong game, sir. I could do with a house like this; my one bedroom flat in King Henry's Road is far too cramped.'

'It would cost too much, Melissa, and I don't just mean in terms of money.' He had meant it to be an astute remark, but it came out sounding paternal.

Melissa shrugged her indifference.

'You're obviously still at an impressionable age, Melissa. You'll grow out of it by the time you're lumbered with a mortgage and the responsibility of children.'

'Lumbered is the word, sir. You won't catch me in that situation.'

'Huh! You wait and see. Life has a nasty habit of trapping you just when you least expect it, or want it, for that matter.'

'I can wait. There's far too much to enjoy in life. Marriage is at the bottom of my list of things to do. Who needs a man anyway? Life finishes with marriage.'

Magee was surprised at the reaction. 'You think so? That's a bit cynical isn't it, for one so young?'

'I call it realistic. I know what I want to do in life and it certainly doesn't involve being chained to a desk or mortgage company.'

'You're living in a dream world.'

Melissa sighed. 'I wish I could.'

'It doesn't exist, you'd better get used to it.'

'Beg to differ, sir, but it does.'

'You think so? Where exactly?'

'Well, countries like Thailand. They offer warmth, clear blue skies, magnificent scenery, unbelievably clear tropical waters and a freedom to do whatever you want.'

'Really?' Magee shook his head in disbelief. 'I'm not convinced. You'll have to tell me more about it sometime. Come on, enough malingering, push the door open.'

As they stepped into an entrance hall, a maid dressed in a black uniform appeared and held open the door to reveal a large inner hall with a galleried landing running around the first floor level.

'Wow!' Melissa craned her neck to take in the splendour of the mansion. 'I could just see myself living here. I wonder how much the rent would be.'

'Dream on,' Magee whispered in response.

'This way, please. Mr Price will join you in a minute,' the maid said, holding open another door and ushering them into the forty-foot long lounge. Last time Magee had been in the room, it had been scruffy and had had enough chairs and sofas to cater for forty children. Now, it was rather tidier, and decorated in a style more appropriate for a country house home. As Melissa appeared fixated taking in the delights of Victorian plastering, Magee wandered across the room to the bay window, through which there was a panoramic view of the Ouse Valley down to Lewes and his beloved hills in the background.

Moments later the door opened and Nick Price entered wearing a mean expression on his face, and said, 'So then, we meet for the second time in a week. You looking for a re-match?'

Magee stood firm, but squirmed as Nick Price moved closer, staring threateningly into his eyes.

'I don't want any trouble, Mr Price.' Magee was already regretting coming without the support of ten men armed to the teeth and wielding pickaxe handles.

Nick Price stopped dead in his tracks just inches away from Magee. 'Constable Jack Magee,' he muttered. 'You know something, I swore to myself I'd kill you one day. Very slowly and very painfully.'

'I'm a Detective Chief Inspector now.'

'Well bully for you, Magee. You're still the same asshole who laid into me when I was on the ground!'

Magee felt his face burning. 'I can only apologize for that incident.'

'Incident?' Nick's fists tightened into a ball. 'You call that an incident? I nearly died because of you, you fuckhead!'

Magee leant back slightly as Nick Price, face reddened, menacingly moved an inch further forward.

'Daddy!' A sharp voice came from a doorway to the side of the room. 'What's happening? Who are these people?'

Nick Price bit his lip and whispered, 'We'll sort this out later, Magee.'

Magee breathed a sigh of relief as Nick Price backed away from the confrontation.

Nick smiled in his daughter's direction and said, 'Nit! Didn't know you were in the library. Allow me to introduce you to Detective Chief Inspector Jack Magee. Magee, this is my daughter, Nittaya.'

Nittaya shook Magee's hand and beamed a radiant smile. 'Pleased to meet you,' she said.

'Likewise,' Magee responded. 'And this is Detective Sergeant Melissa Kelly.'

Nittaya shook Melissa's hand, turned to Magee and asked politely, 'Have you been offered coffee?'

'Umm, no, we hadn't got that far.'

'Annie,' Nittaya called to the maid who was waiting in attendance by the door. 'Would you bring us some coffee please?'

'Sure, Miss Nittaya.'

'There you are, Daddy, that's how you should behave. Now, let's all sit down like adults.' They followed her instructions. Nittaya sat on a sofa next to her father, and linked arms.

Nick Price smiled as he looked at his visitors. 'Nittaya is my pride and joy, Magee. Along with her brother, Somsuk, of course. They're both following in my footsteps, in the property development business. Doing really well, so far, too. She's got far more of a brain than me, haven't you, Nit?'

'And far more social grace,' Nittaya added. 'Why were you being so aggressive just then?'

'It's nothing, Nit. I just got riled about some unfinished business with Magee.'

'From the bad old days?'

'Yeah, from the bad old days.' Nick cringed, as though he knew a reprimand was coming his way.

'Apologize,' Nittaya said.

'What?'

'I said, Daddy, apologize to the nice police officer for your aggressive behaviour.'

'But . . . but . . .'

Nittaya stared her father straight in the eyes and said, 'No "buts", Daddy. Go on, apologize.'

Nick Price turned to Magee in apparent desperation. Magee, for his part, was dumbfounded. Never had he expected to see Nick Price tamed by a woman; no matter that she was his daughter. No matter that she was the most beautiful woman he'd ever seen.

'You too, Chief Inspector. You must have done something to upset my father, so it's only fair that you apologize as well.'

'Nittaya,' Magee responded in a courteous fashion. 'The apology is due solely from me, not from your father. This unfinished business your father refers to, it's entirely my fault it's been brought into your house.'

Nittaya nodded her satisfaction then turned to her father. 'Well?'

Nick bent his head like a scolded kid and muttered, 'Sorry, Magee.'

'There we are then,' Nittaya said with a smile. 'Shall we start the conversation again?'

'Have you got kids, Magee?'

'Yes. Two.'

'And can they wrap you around their finger like this one?'

Magee smiled in response. 'It's been known.'

'She's everything to me,' Nick said as he caressed his daughter's head. 'Her mother had the same effect on me.'

Magee frowned. 'Had?'

'We were together for less than three years before I lost her. That was eighteen years ago, still seems just like yesterday.'

Magee could see a far away look forming in Nick Price's eyes. 'I'm sorry,' he said. 'Truly, sorry. I didn't come here to intrude.'

'No. No, I'm sure you didn't,' Nick replied as the maid came back in to the room with a tray of coffee. 'You said something about Paul being in trouble?'

Magee cleared his throat. 'The other night, as you know, Todd Conners was murdered. We picked up Paul Mansell in the neighbourhood. He admits he was sitting outside, in his car, watching a neighbour's house for half the evening. He says that he was working on a case.'

'So?'

'You knew Conners. You've done business with him I assume?'

'Yes, indeed. He's just helped Somsuk and Nittaya put together a project in Brighton. So what?'

Magee decided to go straight for the jugular. 'I understand that Paul Mansell has worked for you on and off over the years. I'm working on the theory that you and Conners fell out over some business matter and that you sent Mansell over to teach him a lesson.'

Nick Price remained impassive. 'Todd's an old mate, Magee. I don't murder friends. Nor anyone else for that matter.'

Magee continued unperturbed. 'I believe Conners was murdered by Mansell on your instructions. Mansell is now playing a silly game with me, pretending he was there on some domestic divorce investigation.'

'Murdered?' Nittaya gasped. 'Paul, a murderer? On Daddy's instructions? That's absurd, Chief Inspector.'

Nick Price said nothing, and sat expressionless.

'I shall be tracing Todd Conners' business affairs thoroughly,' Magee continued. 'And if I find something that went wrong, and that you were involved, then both you and Mansell may well be charged with murder.'

Nick Price had sat in silence, his face set in stone. Once Magee had finished his accusations, he broke into a smile. 'Very good, Magee! You almost had me going there for a minute. Problem is, it's nothing but tosh, isn't it? My deals don't go wrong. Especially not with Todd, he stood to clear a couple of million on our recent deal. I had no gripe with him, or him with me. And any money he made out of me over the years, whether up front fees or backhanders from suppliers, was well earned. He was straight with me, Magee, he didn't hide any side deals he had going, we'd share them anyway, people just expected him to want them. So then, you said that this was an unofficial visit, right? There's no arrest warrant or search warrant I take it?'

Magee shook his head in reply.

'Good. So what the fuck do you really want?'

'Daddy!' Nittaya yelped.

'Sorry, Nit.'

Magee was surprised at the reaction, for not only had Nick Price taken the accusations calmly, he'd dismissed them as the idle threats they were. 'Why did you take a liking to Paul Mansell when he was a lad?'

'Paul was very disturbed when he came to work with me,' Nick replied. 'Guess I saw a piece of me in him. I felt sorry for him.'

'It must have cost you an arm and a leg to get him off the charges hanging over him. That last bit of trouble he got into was pretty severe. How did you wangle it?'

Nick Price laughed before he replied. 'You don't seriously expect me to answer that do you, Magee?'

Magee allowed a smile. 'It was worth a try. Never mind, it will keep.' Magee paused to consider a new tactic. 'Paul's devoted to you,

The Fourth Cart I

isn't he? I believe he would say anything to protect you. Difficult to find the truth in such circumstances, isn't it?'

'That's your problem, Magee, not mine.'

'Are you a Mason?'

'A Mason? No,' Nick replied, his face expressing a little confusion.

'Are you a Buddhist?'

'What is this? Twenty questions? No, I'm not a Buddhist! I've never been religious in any way. Why are you asking me these stupid questions?'

'Todd Conners was on his way to a Masonic do. His throat was slashed with a knife; the handle was carved in the shape of a Buddha. I'm looking for a connection to you.'

Nick Price's eyes darted to the floor momentarily. He shook his head, grimaced and looked up at Magee. 'No, sorry, it means nothing to me.'

'What about a connection to Mansell?'

'Nah, no way. Paul's no Mason. Sorry, Magee, your trip seems to have been wasted.' Nick stood up, indicating that the interview had come to its conclusion.

'On the contrary, Mr Price, at least we've been able to eliminate one theory. Eh, Melissa?'

'Yes, sir,' Melissa put in, a blank look on her face. 'Absolutely.'

'Thanks for the coffee. It's been a pleasure talking to you,' Magee said rising to leave.

'Goodbye, Magee. A word of advice before you go, though. Don't bother hounding Paul. He's innocent. He wouldn't get involved in a murder, he's stayed clean for years. Don't waste your time on him, you'll only frustrate yourself.'

'I'll think about it,' Magee said at the door. 'It was charming to meet you, Nittaya.'

Once back in the privacy of their car, Magee turned to Melissa and smiled like the Cheshire Cat. 'Well, that was worth the visit, wasn't it?'

'Was it? You did a nice bit of verbal sparring, I'll grant you that. And you came out alive.'

'And?'

'There's more?'

'You didn't notice?'

'I noticed Nittaya. She's a beautiful young woman, isn't she? With that name, and her brother's too, I assume her mother was Thai.'

'Sorry?'

'Thailand, sir. Nick's wife must have been a Thai.'

'I've no idea. Did you notice his reaction?'

'Um, sorry no, my mind must have been on other matters. What did I miss?'

'He was rattled when I mentioned I was looking for a connection. It meant something to him, something personal. It made him feel uncomfortable, I could see that in his eyes.'

'So, you still think he's involved then?'

'I don't know. Not with the murder, no, I think not. But there's something fishy about the connection between Price, Mansell and Conners.'

'Fishy?' Melissa repeated, snorting with laughter. 'Have you been watching too many black and white detective films?'

Magee cracked a smile himself. 'I'm not that old, Melissa. There's nothing wrong with my choice of vocabulary.'

Melissa couldn't keep a straight face as she mimicked an old fashioned actor's voice, 'I say, Watson, fishy business this, what?'

'All right, all right!' Magee laughed at himself. 'Come on, let's get out of here before he sets those dogs on us.'

Chapter Eight

Magee strolled into his office rather late the next morning. An unusual event in itself which, judging from his rugged appearance, had more to do with whisky than the possibility of working late the night before. Although slightly worse for wear, he could nevertheless sense an atmosphere in the room. He caught Melissa's attention and asked, 'What's going on?'

'And a good morning to you too, sir.'

Magee sighed. The increasingly trendy concept of political correctness was not his forte. 'Sorry, Melissa, I was up late last night, bemoaning the Home Secretary's interference to Jenny.'

'I'm sure she enjoyed that, sir.'

Magee looked at his sergeant out of the corner of his eye. If his head didn't hurt quite so much, he might have had something to say about her tone. As it was, he would save it for later. He motioned for her to join him in his office. 'There's something in the air out there, Melissa, what's up?'

Melissa took a deep breath before responding. 'There's been another murder, sir. During the night. We're just getting the details through now.'

'When you say "another murder", you mean of the same mould as the Conners' case?'

'I'm afraid so, yes, sir.'

'Shit!' It was all Magee could think of to say as he collapsed into his chair. 'Tell me about it.'

'Coffee first?'

'Oh, yes please. Plenty of it. And a glass of water too.' He sat rubbing his eyes until Melissa returned. 'Thanks. Okay, spill the beans.'

'The victim is one Mike Harwood. Lives on the edge of Preston Park in Brighton.'

'Nice area, that. Who's out there, on the scene?'

'Chris Auckland is, sir. He was there by eight thirty. We tried to contact you, but . . .'

'Jenny was taking Carolyn and Jason up to the Wallands School. I was, erm, still getting ready.'

The top of Melissa's lip curled slightly. 'Right. Anyway, sir, Chris Auckland has reported in already. The victim had three young kids.' She looked down at a handful of notes in her hand. 'His wife died a year ago from ovarian cancer.'

'Damn! Did he kill the kids as well?'

'No, sir, but he did make orphans out of them.'

'And the similarities?'

'It looks like the killer crept into the house during the night. There're no signs of a forced entry. The victim was in bed when the attack occurred. His throat was slashed. He was stabbed in the chest, the dagger left in place.'

'Please don't tell me the dagger is similar. Not a Buddha effigy again?'

'Sorry, sir, but the description is the same, and I don't just mean similar.'

'Oh, hell!'

'Mike Harwood's kids found him first thing this morning. They're in a state of shock, to say the least. The oldest girl is still hysterical, I understand.'

'We'd better get over there.'

'Just one other point, sir,' Melissa added quietly. 'Guess who was discovered in the vicinity.'

Magee frowned then sighed heavily before replying. 'Not Paul Mansell? Don't say that.'

'Sorry, sir, but yes, he was there.'

'Oh for pity's sake!' Magee could just imagine the lecture he'd receive from the Home Secretary for letting a mass murderer out of a police cell to commit another crime. 'Where is Mansell now?'

The Fourth Cart I

'He's been held most of the night over in Brighton. He was picked up around two in the morning.' Melissa paused for a few seconds before continuing, 'He was soliciting, sir.'

'Soliciting? You mean he was looking for a prostitute? Oh, for god's sake, that's all I need. We've got the full trio now. Murder, religion and sex. I can see the press having a field day over this one. And I'll be lambasted for letting the bastard walk free.'

'But he seemed to have a pretty good alibi before.'

'But not quite good enough, eh? With hindsight, that is. What time was the murder last night?'

'The doctor says about one o'clock, give or take a few minutes. Mansell's arrest was logged at the station at five past two.'

'Nothing to suggest Mansell had been up to something? No blood on him by any chance?'

'Nothing, sir, sorry. It wasn't until this morning that some bright spark put two and two together. After the discovery of Harwood they figured Mansell and checked him out.'

'Come on, then. Get packed up. I'll be with you in fifteen minutes. I need another coffee first. And I suppose I'll have to let Rees Smith know. We can't have our precious Home Secretary hearing about this secondhand.'

'Good luck, sir. I'll go and get the car ready.'

Magee asked DC Collins to put a call through, an urgent call, top priority to the Home Secretary, and sat quietly, composing himself, calmly drinking his coffee, needing five minutes sanity before he went into battle. He smirked at the thought of ruining the politician's day.

His phone buzzed, shattering his peacefulness. He picked the receiver up only to hear a raging voice. 'Magee? Is that you?'

'Yes, sir.'

'What the hell is the emergency? I've just been hauled out of a meeting, an extremely important meeting, I'll have you know. You'd better have a damn good explanation.'

'I have sir.' Magee played it cool, relishing the fact that he had annoyed the Home Secretary. 'A murder was committed last night, sir. It appears to be similar to the Conners' case. I didn't want you to hear it from anyone other than me.'

'Fuck!'

'The body was found first thing this morning,' Magee continued. 'The victim was still in bed. His throat was slashed and he was stabbed through the heart. The dagger has an effigy of a Buddha carved into the handle. The victim lived in Brighton. His name was, erm, Michael Harwood,' Magee said as he looked down at Melissa's hand written notes. 'He was forty two years old, a widower, had three young children.'

'Michael Harwood did you say?'

'Yes, sir, I did. Also, similar to last time, Paul Mansell was picked up in the neighbourhood. Apparently he was looking for a prostitute.'

'A prostitute? What the fuck is the idiot playing at? Have you spoken to him yet?'

'No, sir, not yet. I'm just on my way over to Brighton now.'

'Well, crucify the bastard! Don't you dare let him go, Magee! There'll be uproar if you let him out again and I'll personally castrate you!'

'Yes, sir. Of course, sir.' He allowed himself a smirk before adding, 'What if Mansell is innocent, sir?'

'Innocent? How can the bastard be innocent? At the scene of a murder, twice in a row? He's guilty all right, Magee. Just you lock him up and prove it!'

Magee was just about to counterattack when the line went dead. He sat looking at the receiver, seething at the politician's intervention and intrusion into his authority. 'Fuck you too,' he muttered as he stood up.

Chapter Nine

'Good morning to you,' a less-than-happy Detective Chief Inspector Ryan said on shaking Magee's hand. He passed over a handful of Polaroid photos and said, 'I gather we're to give you all the cooperation and support you need for this case.'

'Thank you. Yes,' Magee replied. He knew what it was like to have an officer from another station barge into your own territory. It left a nasty taste in the mouth; it seemed to imply that you weren't capable yourself. He leant against the station's counter perusing the photographs.

DCI Ryan asked, 'Do you want to visit the victim's house?'

'No, I don't think so, thank you. The effigy on this dagger handle is identical. There's no doubt, I'm afraid; my murderer has struck again.'

'You think we've got a new Ripper on our hands?'

Magee frowned, uncomfortable with the implications of that phrase. 'He's no Ripper; he's just a common murderer.'

'But what of this Buddhist business? Doesn't it put you in mind of a religious execution? Someone seeking glorification in the name of their god, perhaps?'

'It's possible, I suppose, but I don't have enough facts to make an informed comment. And, if you don't mind, I'd prefer the religious aspect to be left out of it for the moment. I don't want the press latching on to it.'

DCI Ryan nodded. 'As you wish. But you've certainly got one sick nutter on your hands.'

'I don't disagree. Nevertheless, whoever planned these two murders is a cold, rational, calculating, very clever son of a bitch.'

DCI Ryan shrugged in response.

'Look, do you know much about the events surrounding the arrest of Paul Mansell last night?'

'I certainly do. Mansell's caused quite a stir during his visit. We picked him up at one forty-five last night.'

'On what charge?'

'Soliciting. He'd been making a nuisance of himself, cruising up and down a notorious stretch of road on the edge of Preston Park, harassing the working girls.'

'Harassing them? In what way?'

'He'd been asking lots of questions about a particular girl. Apparently, he wouldn't let it go. He kept on and on at them. Eventually, one of them got fed up, I suppose, and phoned us to complain.'

'Did he resist arrest?'

'No, but I understand that he was surprised at our intervention. He claimed that we misinterpreted the situation. We decided that a night in the cells would be a good lesson, so we threw him into one of the not so pleasant rooms. Unfortunately, first thing this morning, some idiot on the early shift handed him his breakfast tray and asked if he'd seen anything unusual since there'd been a murder close to where he'd been picked up.'

'You're kidding?'

'Nope. Sorry to say, I'm not. He's only a youngster, bit too keen for my liking. Said he was just fishing, trying to get a lead for us. The dipstick fancies himself as a detective, I reckon. Anyway, he got his just desserts.'

'How so?'

'Hah! Well, Mansell throws a fit, flings his tray at the youngster then throws him against the wall. Poor bugger's got bruised ribs now. Mansell tried to make a run for it. That's when the fun started. It was a bad decision on his part. We haven't had a runner for years, not from the cells anyway. It took six of us to contain the bastard. He's strong and unpredictable, that one, watch out for him.'

'I will. Where is he now?'

'Waiting for you in room seventeen, down the corridor, third on the left.'

'Okay, thanks,' Magee replied. 'Come on, Melissa, let's go and see what Mansell has to say for himself. It should prove entertaining.'

Magee found Paul Mansell sitting patiently in the interview room waiting to hear his fate. Melissa set up the recording machine. This time, it was going to be an official interview, no cozy informal chat.

After introductions for the benefit of the tape, Magee said, 'Perhaps you'd like to start at the beginning, Mansell. Your movements last night, please.' He turned towards Melissa and offered a smug grin.

Paul Mansell sat slumped, looking dejected. 'You won't believe my version of events.'

'Why not? Surely it won't be any less believable than last time? If you remember, I let you off then, maybe you'll have the same luck this time.'

'I'm not sure its worth bothering with. I reckon I'm being set up and the scary thing is that it's working. I might just as well wait and let you fail to prove me guilty. Anyway, if I'm inside here, the next time it happens I'll have a better alibi, won't I?'

'Okay, okay, Mansell. Point taken. Come on, though, take a chance. I promise I won't laugh. Honest.'

'Very well, if you insist. I was investigating another case. A client by the name of Ringwood. I've got his address this time, but it was all conducted on the telephone with cash delivered in advance. Ringwood's fifteen year old daughter, Jane, went missing a few weeks ago. He said he'd searched the usual places around town, and had shown her photo to several dossers in the area. He said one girl he spoke to reckoned she'd seen her hanging around near Preston Park, selling herself. I tried there last week and one woman said she'd seen the kid. I said I'd give her fifty quid if she would bring Jane along sometime. I gave her twenty pounds in advance to show goodwill. The woman promised she'd be there last night, but she didn't show. I reckon it was a set up. The whole thing must have been a scam right from the start, same as last time.'

'Why didn't this Ringwood character go there himself? He could have saved your fees.'

Paul rubbed the end of his nose before responding. 'Ringwood said he was worried he'd frighten his daughter away if she saw him. That made sense, especially if she didn't want to see her father again. If he'd turned up unexpectedly, she might have done a runner.'

'Okay, so you go along instead. What's with this harassment you were charged with?'

'I was being too persistent, I guess. Some of the women got annoyed, said I was spoiling their patch, putting their punters off. You know, those women can get mean at times, real mean.'

'Had experience of them?' Melissa put in.

'Yes. But not in the way you're suggesting,' Paul retorted. 'Purely professional experience that's all. Anyway, I'm not really interested in women here.'

Melissa blinked. 'Come again?'

'I've being popping over to Bangkok ever since I was eighteen years old. I find most British women unappealing, so many are fat with white flabby skin. It makes me shudder just thinking about it. There's just no comparison to the delicate light brown skinned girls in Thailand. I just can't be bothered with women over here, it's too much hassle.'

Melissa returned a warm smile. 'I can well understand that.'

Paul Mansell perked up. 'Been there? To Thailand, that is?'

'Five times,' Melissa replied. 'Only for short holidays though, you don't get much money or time off in this game. What about you?'

'A dozen times at least. I usually stay for a month at a time. I've had a few girlfriends there, but it's difficult to keep up any relationship because eventually I run out of money and have to return here.'

'Haven't you tried to get work out there?'

'Yep, I've tried everything over the years. I've done fashion modeling, television adverts and teaching English, but the work doesn't come easy. I've got a few links with some local businessmen, but they get involved in some pretty weird shit. I've been offered really lucrative deals, but they never come to anything. One day, I'll crack it, then I'll probably stay for good.'

'I wouldn't blame you,' Melissa responded dreamily. 'It's my idea of paradise out there.'

Magee coughed. 'Yes, well thank you, Melissa,' he interjected, 'but if you could get back to the subject of last night please, Mansell.'

'Hmm! Where was I? Oh, yes. This tart that was supposed to bring Jane along, well she didn't turn up . . .'

'So you said.'

'Oh? Well anyway, I was asking the other women whether they had ever seen Jane around. I had a photo of her; it's with the rest of my stuff outside somewhere I expect. Next thing I knew, two local boys-in-blue grab me and drag me here. They didn't listen to me; they just threw me in the cell for the night accusing me of trying to pick up an underage girl. Well, Chief Inspector, I can assure you that I am no child molester. I admit I like my Thai girls young and slim, but I doubt whether I've ever had a girl under eighteen.'

'I should hope not!' Magee was horrified at the thought. Melissa simply smirked.

'First thing this morning,' Paul continued unperturbed, 'the breakfast tray arrived with some gossip I could have done without. That's when I realized that I must have been set up. To be in the area, just like the last occasion, and only a few days ago, was just too much of a coincidence. I don't know what happened, I just lost it. Freaked out. I hate police cells as it is, and the thought of going through all this again just made me flip. I'm sorry if I hurt anyone.'

'What were you hoping to do? Escape the country? Flee to Bangkok?'

'The thought had crossed my mind, I must admit. As I just said, I've been looking for an excuse to settle down in Thailand permanently.'

'So you reckon the officers who picked you up misinterpreted the situation?'

'Yes. Mind you, I suppose it was quite understandable under the circumstances.'

'What's the address of this Ringwood character?'

Paul sighed before responding, 'Is it worth giving to you?'

Magee responded with an icy glare.

'Okay, okay! I'll write it down if you really want it.'

Magee let Mansell scrawl on a piece of paper, gave it to the officer standing by the door and asked him to check it out. After ten minutes, the constable returned and beckoned Magee out into the hallway. A minute later, Magee reentered the interview room and sat down with a broad smile on his face.

'Well, I'm sure it comes as no surprise to you that Mr Ringwood, although he does indeed live at this address, has two sons but no daughter.'

'It doesn't surprise me,' Paul muttered. 'Look, Chief Inspector, you're wasting your time. If a murder was committed last night, then your forensic team would be able to pick something up on me, yeah?'

'Oh, don't worry, Mansell,' Magee muttered. 'Forensics will be crawling all over you, very shortly.'

'Good,' Paul replied. 'I'll be out of here by lunchtime, then.'

'Hah! Don't count on it, Mansell. I've enough to keep you locked up for a while yet.'

'Yeah? Look, tell me, how was the murder committed? A knife attack, same as with Todd Conners? Is that why you're involved, the same murderer has struck twice?'

It was Magee's turn to flinch at the questions. 'You don't expect me to answer that do you?'

'Possibly not, but if I'm correct, then you must be looking for a guy with blood on his hands, literally, if not all over his clothes. Problem is, I'm clean, and you'll find no trace of blood on me.'

'You could have washed and changed nearby,' Magee ventured. 'A friend's house, for instance, and got back quickly.'

'Oh for Christ's sake! I'm telling you the truth, damn it!' He pounded the table with his fist. 'Now charge me or throw me out! I'm not cooperating anymore. I'm trying to clear my name and all I get from your side of the table is nothing but disbelief. I'm being set up and I don't know why. And your attitude really pisses me off.'

Magee sat in silence until Paul Mansell had finished his outburst. 'Okay, let's calm down shall we, there's no point in getting antagonistic. It won't help your case one bit.' The two of them glared at each other for several moments.

'Cigarette?' Melissa asked as if attempting to break the impasse.

'Please.' Paul reached across the table.

'Do you mind?' Magee said, pointing to a no smoking sign on the wall. Melissa and Paul Mansell exchanged a glance of sufferance. It seemed to make the atmosphere worse.

'What time did you get picked up?' Melissa asked.

'As I said, about one forty-five.'

'How long had you been there?' Melissa continued.

'An hour or so. As I just said.'

'Can you be more precise?'

'Yes I can, now you mention it. I was asked to be there at one o'clock exactly. The woman I'd met during the previous visit said that she and Jane would turn up at that time, and that I wasn't to turn up earlier on account of other business they had. I arrived early. I didn't see anything wrong with wandering around, so I started asking questions at twelve thirty.'

'Half an hour before scheduled time?' She sat back with a smug grin on her face.

'What's your point, Melissa?' Magee asked irritably.

Melissa scrawled on a piece of paper as Magee sat scowling at her. She winked at Paul Mansell.

Magee snatched the paper from her hand and looked at it in bewilderment. 'Shit!' He stomped out of the room.

'Seen the light has he?'

'Something like that. Let's hope your street girls remember you being there at twelve thirty.' Melissa let her eyebrows rise in a knowing signal.

'Thanks, Sergeant. Sorry, look, I can't call you by your rank, it doesn't sound right. Can I buy you a drink sometime?'

'Maybe next time I'm in Bangkok,' Melissa replied with a twinkle in her eye. 'I wouldn't mind spending more time out that way. I love the sea, scuba diving, sailing, anything to do with boats really.'

'Who doesn't? I had a week on a cruiser once. I managed it for a mate while he went off on business. The boat had a crew of six and we had to take groups of tourists out for a day's fishing, look after them, and feed them. God, I was happy that week.'

'Invite me along next time, please.'

'You know something, I reckon I will.'

'I'd better go and pacify my darling boss, he must be pretty pissed by now,' Melissa said as she rose to leave the room. 'Hope you get to Bangkok. Send me a postcard and I'll come out to meet you. The name's Melissa by the way, but only outside office hours.'

Magee was in the corridor reading the statements of some of the street girls who'd been dragged out of their beds earlier that morning, following Mansell's attempted break out.

'Didn't any of you think about checking these statements with the time of death?' Magee asked in astonishment of the uniformed officers hanging around the charge desk.

Melissa turned and headed in the opposite direction.

'Melissa! Don't sneak off. I'm not finished with you.'

'Just a second, sir,' she shouted back. 'Must go to the loo.'

Magee stared at Melissa's back as she walked away, furious at her actions.

'Listen to this,' Magee snapped, and read aloud, "I first saw him just after twelve thirty. I know that because he was new. I like to know when punters turn up for business." Magee sighed as he threw the statement down onto the counter. 'Mansell was in sight of one or more girls until he was picked up at one forty-five and charged here just after two. The doctor has placed the time of death at one, give or take a half hour. I don't believe this.'

'What's that, sir?' Melissa asked as she reappeared from her trip to the toilet.

Magee threw her a look of annoyance. 'Were you trying to help him out back there?'

'Me, sir? Course not, sir. Why would I do that, sir?'

'Because he's a handsome young man who just happens to share your passion for Thailand, that's why.'

'Handsome? Really? You think so? I hadn't noticed.'

Magee scowled. 'Don't get cute with me, Melissa. He's guilty as hell until we prove him innocent.'

It was Melissa's turn to scowl. 'I take it that what's in your hands suggests he couldn't have done it.'

Magee sighed in dismay. All eyes were focused on him as though the whole mess was his doing. Maybe if he hadn't been quite so quick to condemn Mansell, then perhaps he wouldn't be in this position, he reflected. Not that such self-recrimination helped overcome his embarrassment. 'Go and find out if he has an alibi between ten-thirty and twelve-thirty, will you, please?'

'Sure.'

Two minutes later Melissa returned, barely concealing a smile. 'He says he was out with some mates in Eastbourne. Says he left the pub just before eleven fifteen, had a cheeseburger with them before leaving then filled up with petrol at the Newmarket station about twelve fifteen. He says there should be a credit card receipt in his wallet. Says we're welcome to look, as long as we don't steal his cash.'

Magee's scowl returned. He was less than happy when he found the receipt with a date and time clearly printed on it. It certainly settled matters; He wouldn't be able to hang the murder on Paul Mansell no matter what the Home Secretary had ordered. He drew a deep breath and headed back to the interview room.

The Fourth Cart I

Magee flung the interview room door open and stared down at Paul Mansell, who was doing his best to look innocent. He bit his lip in embarrassment, detesting the thought of having to admit he was wrong.

'Mansell, you'll not be charged today, but I'm warning you, I'm getting fed up with seeing your face. I can't prove it yet, but I know you're up to your eyes in this case. If you think you're being set up, then you'd better start investigating your own clients. Don't get set up again by a nonexistent client. I won't wear that one next time, right?'

'I won't, I promise.'

'And you can hand your passport in as well. I don't want you flying off to Bangkok just yet. One way or another, you're involved. That means I want to know where you are at all times; you're not getting away from me until I know precisely what's going on.'

Paul Mansell broke into a broad grin. 'Thanks, Chief Inspector. I'll bring the passport in later today. Which station?'

'Whichever one is convenient. They'll give you a receipt. Tell them to contact me to say you've complied.'

'Can I go now?'

'I'm going, Mansell. Not you, though. You can stay until you've been dusted down. Maybe, just maybe, forensics will find the merest trace of something that will nail you. Remember this, just one fibre off your clothes that we can match to our crime scene and you'll never get to see your beloved Thailand again.'

Paul Mansell smiled as Magee left the room. Two hours later he left the station a free man. He drew in several lungs full of fresh air and stared up into the skies at an airplane passing overhead at around twenty thousand feet, chuckled and said aloud. 'Eat your heart out, Magee, you won't stop me.'

Chapter Ten

'I'm sorry for getting ratty with you. I got carried away. I was really convinced I was going to nail Mansell, but then it just sort of fell apart.'

Since leaving Brighton, Magee had sat in silence whilst Melissa had done her best to drive without glancing in his direction. They had almost reached the Kingston roundabout before Magee had spoken.

Melissa turned to catch Magee's eye. 'I think Inspector Ryan's the one you need to apologize to, sir, not me. I don't think his men appreciated being torn off a strip like that. It wasn't their fault.'

Magee cringed. 'Do I come across as a real bastard of a boss?'

'No. Grumpy, yes.'

'Carolyn says that too.' Magee reflected on the name his daughter had given him for when he was in a mood. 'Do you hate me? As a boss that is?'

'Not at all.'

Magee broke into a grin. 'You mean you like me?'

As Melissa slowed for the traffic, she turned her head to give Magee a full-on look. 'Don't push your luck, sir.'

'Would it help if I took you to lunch?'

'That depends, sir. If you mean the canteen, you can add tightfisted to grumpy.'

'I hear there's a good lunch menu at the Rainbow Inn.'

'You mean it? Your treat? Wow, yes please.' After a few seconds Melissa gave a short moan and said, 'And, of course, the pub's only a stone's throw from Nick Price's place, isn't it. Now you are being a bastard, sir. For a moment there I really did think you were trying to be nice to me.'

Magee muttered, 'Two birds, one stone.'

Melissa punched his arm in a playful way. 'Just for that, I'm having the most expensive item on the menu. And I'll tell Jenny next time I see her!'

'Ouch! You play dirty! That will cost dearly.'

At the pub, Melissa settled for a home-made ham and asparagus toad-in-the-hole accompanied by a glass of chilled Chablis. Magee stuck to a traditional ploughman's lunch and a pint of bitter. For an hour they enjoyed the atmosphere and swapped theories on how Nick Price and Paul Mansell may be involved with the two recent murders.

After lunch, they left the car in the car park having decided a short stroll up the road would aid digestion and hopefully blow away the smell of alcohol from their clothes. It also gave Melissa a chance to take a peek at the grounds of Nick Price's estate. Arriving at the front door unhindered by security guards or dogs, they found Annie, the maid, waiting for them, ready to escort them into the lounge.

Nick Price was sitting at an antique writing desk, head down, reading a document. He looked round and fixed Magee with a steely eye. 'This isn't going to become a habit, is it?'

'I can assure you, Mr Price,' Magee muttered back, 'I have better things to do with my life than come visiting you.'

Nittaya had been sitting on a sofa, making notes in the margins of a sales brouchure. She placed it down, along with a pen, and tutted. 'Honestly, what's wrong with you two? You're like squabbling children. Why can't you talk courteously to each other like adults?'

'That's just the way things are, Nit. That's life.'

Magee said nothing. Nick Price had summed up the situation well enough.

Nittaya asked in a civil tone, 'Well then, how about some coffee?'

'No. No, thank you, Nittaya. We're not planning to stay. I just want to ask your father one simple question, then we'll be gone.'

'That sounds reasonable,' Nittaya responded, and turned to her father. 'Well, Daddy? You can manage that can't you?'

'If I must.'

'Face to face, please.' Magee advanced towards Nick Price. He held his stare and said, 'There's been another murder. Over in

Preston Park. Paul Mansell was arrested near the scene of the crime. Again, you understand, that's twice in a row, now.'

'So?' Nick give an uncaring shrug of his shoulders. 'Paul's a grown man. He can look after himself.'

'The victim's name was Michael Harwood,' Magee continued. 'Do you know him?'

Magee noticed Nick Price's jaw drop fractionally. He had his answer. 'What's going on, Mr Price?'

'I don't know, Magee. Honest to god.'

'I'm sorry, but I don't believe you. You knew Conners and I assume you knew Harwood. And you know Mansell, of course. You're involved in this somehow, so don't try to deny it. Your body language confirms it. You know damn well what's going on, don't you?'

Nick flinched, his gaze shifted awkwardly in the direction of his daughter. 'No.'

The lie was obvious. Magee turned his head to see where Nick had looked. 'Do you want to talk in private?'

'No, Magee. That wouldn't help. As I said, I can't help you. I really don't know what's going on. That's the truth.'

'I'll get to the bottom of this, you know that don't you, Mr Price? It would be better for your sake if you told me all about it here and now.'

'You think so?' Nick cleared his throat. 'I don't. Anyway, I've told you already, I know nothing.'

'I doubt that, Mr Price. I really do doubt that. Lack of cooperation will harm your defence. You know that, don't you?'

Magee's choice of words startled Nittaya. 'Are you arresting my father, Chief Inspector?'

'Not yet,' Magee replied through gritted teeth.

'He's done nothing wrong since I was born, Chief Inspector. He's not the man you obviously think he is. Please stop harassing him.'

Magee backed off. 'Thank you for your time, Mr Price. I'll see myself out. Come on, Melissa.'

'Before you go, a word with Melissa please.' Melissa turned and looked expectantly. 'Were you just being nosy out there, or are you really interested in the gardens?'

Melissa looked puzzled. 'You've got security cameras out there?'

'Everywhere, of course.'

'Your gardens are beautiful, Mr Price. I live in a pokey little second floor flat. It's nice to dream.'

'Call me Nick. And I'll happily take you for a tour. Maybe a spot of horse riding?'

Melissa looked at her watch, but was distracted by a cough from Magee who stood holding open the lounge door. 'Thanks,' she replied. 'Another day perhaps.'

Chapter Eleven

Brigadier Bernard Armstrong's skills at intelligence gathering had first come to light whilst serving in the British Army as a young officer during the Malayan Emergency. Although it had been many a year since he'd been anywhere near a jungle, his skills were nevertheless honed to perfection and as sharp as ever. As the clock on the wall outside the Home Secretary's office struck the appointed hour of four o'clock, he rose from a chair on which he'd been waiting, knocked on the door and entered with the confident stride of a man half his age.

'Brigadier Armstrong,' Rees Smith said cordially. 'Thank you so much for coming over.' He gestured to the chair in front of his desk. 'Do please sit down.'

'Thank you, sir,' Brigadier Armstrong replied. He eased his slender frame into a leather chair, returned a courteous smile and waited patiently, though slightly uncomfortably, for the Home Secretary to finish the task of sizing him up.

The door behind him opened and an assistant breezed in bearing a tray of refreshments.

'Coffee, Brigadier?'

'Thank you, sir. That would be most kind.' Brigadier Armstrong helped himself to a cup off the tray and sat in a contemplative mood, stirring in a teaspoon of sugar. He eyed the Home Secretary surreptitiously, already disliking the man for the pompous way he was resting his hands against his mouth as if in prayer.

'I have a problem, Brigadier.'

'Indeed, sir?'

The Fourth Cart I

'What is your brief? In relation to me, that is.'

'I am at your service, sir.'

'Who do you report to?'

'My department is autonomous. However, you, as Home Secretary, are the head of that department. Notional head that is.'

'I see,' the Home Secretary replied. He fell silent for a couple of seconds, apparently chewing his lip. 'So you wouldn't have to report anything you did for me to anyone else?'

'No, sir. Not unless I thought it was in the national interest, that is.'

'And in that situation, who would you report to?'

'The Prime Minister, probably. Maybe MI5. It would depend on the circumstances, really.'

'And if you thought something shouldn't be reported?'

Brigadier Armstrong frowned. 'Then it wouldn't get reported, would it, sir.'

'But would it nevertheless get documented?'

Brigadier Armstrong prickled in discomfort as he observed the Home Secretary's eyebrows rising. 'Most of my department's activities result in paperwork, of one sort or another. It's unavoidable these days. But once filed, our records are kept secure. In a vault, deep underground.'

'Who could gain access to your records?'

'I am the only one with authorized access codes to the vault, sir. And in the event of my unexpected demise, I imagine it would take the Prime Minister's personal presence to get it open.'

Rees Smith's eyebrows rose again. 'Not even your secretary can gain access?'

'Certainly not, sir!'

'No documents can be leaked then, once a case is closed?'

'If a leak of a classified document occurred, then technically it could only have originated from me. And I am quite happy with the security arrangements in place for me to assume that responsibility.'

'Very well, Brigadier,' said the Home Secretary breaking into a false smile. 'Now then, there is a very serious assignment I want you to take on.'

'As you wish, sir.'

'I want you to report direct to me. No intermediaries, you understand?'

'Of course not, sir.'

'I want no one else in your department to know that I requested this assignment.'

'That goes without saying, sir.'

'And I want no written records to be kept.'

Brigadier Armstrong paused a moment to wipe away a drop of coffee from the corner of his mouth. 'That would be very difficult, sir. I do not possess a photographic memory. I would like full and proper information to hand when I report to you.'

Rees Smith returned a curt smile. 'No reports to be retained, then. Everything to be destroyed once the case is closed?'

'That would be acceptable, sir.'

'Good. Now then, I want you to keep an eye on three people. Firstly, Nick Price, a one-time petty crook from the East End of London. He's now a wealthy property developer and night club owner down in Brighton. You may well have heard of him. He's occasionally featured in the tabloids. Journalists like to have the odd bash at him, probing the origins of his wealth, asking how come he manages to secure so many council contracts, that sort of thing.'

Brigadier Armstrong's eyebrows furrowed. 'The name certainly rings a bell. A few years ago, didn't his name go through clearance for party donations?'

The Home Secretary nodded. 'I believe he has indeed made substantial donations in the past.'

'You have reason to challenge that clearance now?'

The Home Secretary stared at a document on his desk for a full ten seconds before responding. 'No. That's not why I've asked you here. I've no reason to query the source of his funds.'

'Very well. You said there are three people you want tagged?'

'I did. The second person is Paul Mansell. I don't know that much about him, except that he's an associate of Nick Price.'

'Does he have a criminal record?'

'Minor offences as a teenager, I believe. Nick Price took him under his wing as a sixteen year old wayward lad.' The Home Secretary passed a sheet of paper across his desk. 'I've written a few salient facts down, including their addresses.'

Brigadier Armstrong took the paper and cast his eyes down the sheet. 'The third person is John Mansell? A relation I assume?'

'Indeed. The older brother of Paul Mansell.'

'No address though?'

'No. Not yet.'

'And what exactly is this assignment?'

'I want you to keep Nick Price under surveillance. I'm convinced he's up to something, but I'm not sure what. And that goes for the Mansell brothers too.'

'But you don't know where John Mansell is?'

'I imagine you'll be led to him if you follow his young brother.'

The Brigadier nodded. 'You said this is one assignment. Are these three men working together?'

'That's my guess, although I have no proof. Of course, they may well be acting independently.'

Brigadier Armstrong scratched the back of his neck. 'And what in particular am I looking for?'

Rees Smith fell silent for a few seconds before replying, 'They might be perpetrators of a blackmail scam. They might also be murdering their victims.'

'I see. It sounds like a case for the police, sir.'

'It may, Brigadier. But I have no evidence. It would therefore be a waste of police resources.'

Brigadier Armstrong bristled. 'But not mine?'

'That's not what I meant, Brigadier. There have been two identical murders recently. The killer has left no trace of his presence. He is therefore smart. Far too smart for the police, I think. What I need is someone who is equally cunning, someone with an analytical mind who is not rendered incapable merely because of the absence of physical clues.'

Brigadier Armstrong was shrewd enough to see beyond the flattery. 'You want a future crime prevented, as opposed to a past crime solved?'

The Home Secretary grinned. 'That's precisely what I'm after, Brigadier.'

'And monitoring the movements of these three men may lead to the exposure of an intended crime?'

'Spot on, Brigadier. I want to know their movements. I want to know where they go, who they telephone and who they meet.'

'I understand, sir. However, if I do uncover a crime, what will be your instructions? With regard to these three men, that is?'

'Nothing. Not yet anyway. I want proof of their intention first.'

'And if I find proof?'

'I'll think about it then.'

'I see, sir. Do you have any other information to give me?'

'Such as?'

'It would help to know why you think these men are engaging in blackmail and murder.'

'Information from other sources, my dear Brigadier,' Rees Smith replied with a smirk on his face. 'Proven, reliable sources, I might add. Unfortunately, they have a right to their privacy.'

Brigadier Armstrong nodded his acceptance. 'So I just observe these men, tap their phones, read their post?'

'Yes, please,' Rees Smith replied, his smirk broadening. 'Just try to stay undetected.'

'One last point, sir. You mentioned murder just now. What if we come across one or more of these men attempting to murder someone?'

'I leave that situation to your own judgment, Brigadier.'

'I see.' Brigadier Armstrong tried to conceal his shock. 'But if we intervene and apprehend the assailant, what would you . . .'

'Brigadier,' interrupted Rees Smith, 'sometimes intervention just creates more problems. On the other hand, a lack of intervention can often bring about a most desired conclusion. You have total discretion and obviously my full support in any eventuality.'

Brigadier Armstrong was incredulous. 'Very well, sir. If those are your orders, then I shall leave you in peace.' He pocketed the piece of paper and bade farewell to the Home Secretary. Outside on the street, as he opened his car door, he gave vent to his anger. 'Bloody politicians!' he cursed in the direction of his driver. 'That man's reputation is well deserved. He truly is one smug creep!'

Chapter Twelve

'Stop moaning, Melissa,' Magee muttered as they passed through the doors of the Victoria and Albert Museum in South Kensington. 'This is worth a try, at least.'

'I'm sorry, sir,' Melissa replied with a heavy sigh. 'It's just that I detest this place. I came here when I was about eight years old on a school trip from the Wallands. I was bored senseless. I'm really not in to all this cultural and historical claptrap.'

Magee shook his head in despair. 'Well I hope to prove just how important culture is. These two daggers must mean something to someone, and any lead we can get at this stage would be welcome. We really don't have much to go on.'

'Diddley squat, to be precise, sir,' replied Melissa. She folded her arms as a moody expression descended upon her face.

'Exactly. Good choice of words,' Magee mused. He advanced towards an information counter in the centre of the grand entrance hall and caught the eye of a bespectacled middle-aged lady counting out brochures. 'Excuse me, but we have an appointment with the Curator of the Far East Department, Marcus Comyns, at eleven o'clock. Can you tell me how to get to his office, please?'

The lady peered up at Magee over the brim of her glasses. 'He'll have to come down and collect you, sir,' she said, picking up a phone. 'Who shall I say it is?'

'Detective Chief Inspector Magee and Detective Sergeant Kelly.'

Magee stood to one side of the counter and waited patiently for five minutes. Eventually, a tall, elegant but flamboyant man in his late thirties and dressed in a stylish suit, swaggered towards him. Magee took an instant dislike to the man.

'Good morning, Chief Inspector,' said Marcus Comyns, extending a limp hand. 'Do follow me, if you please. We'd better go to my office. Sorry, but it's quite a walk, this place is simply enormous.'

Magee tutted as the word enormous was accompanied by a ridiculous amount of arm waving. It was a ghastly trait he associated with theatrical, camp comedians, and one that he failed to find remotely humorous. Nevertheless, not wanting to be the root cause of any political incorrectness, he decided to keep his mouth firmly shut until they reached Comyns' office.

Magee and Melissa were beckoned to sit and then Comyns said, 'Now then, Chief Inspector, I understand you've brought something for me to see.'

Magee handed over two sealed plastic bags. Each contained a blood stained dagger. Comyns looked at the grisly items, grimaced, and placed them carefully on his desk.

'Fascinating, truly fascinating,' said Comyns, turning his attention to Magee. 'I take it these are murder weapons.'

'Yes, indeed,' Magee replied. 'Two separate murders on two separate occasions, but with similarities. I was hoping you might be able to shed some light on these knives.'

Comyns appeared to be perplexed. 'In what way, Chief Inspector?'

'Well, I'm trying to understand why a murderer would choose a weapon like this.'

Comyns' lips skewered to one side momentarily before he asked, 'As opposed to what?'

'Well, this is only speculation, but I'm assuming the murders were not random events, that they were, in fact, well planned. That would mean the murderer took this weapon with him to the crime scene. Now, I'm trying to fathom the murderer's mind. Why did he not use something convenient to hand, like a kitchen knife?'

'Ah! You mean if the murderer took a knife like this with him, then it must have some significance?'

'Exactly!' Magee gave the curator a smile for the first time. 'I'm after any background information you can give me. Are these knives culturally or historically significant? Are they associated, for instance,

The Fourth Cart I

with any particular religious rite? Can you think of any reason why they might have been used to murder someone?'

Comyns leant forward and peered into one of the bags. 'Let's start with the basics. First, we've got ivory handles. Given that there's a ban on the importation of ivory into this country, that means the knives have either been here a long time already or your murderer smuggled them in recently.'

'And how easy would it be to smuggle them in to the UK?'

'Not too hard, especially if you were determined to do it. I would imagine it would be tricky getting them through an airport, what with security the way it is these days. Easier on a ship I expect, as part of a container load, perhaps.'

'Okay, that makes sense,' Magee said. 'What else?'

'Well, the effigy itself is from Tibet. From the Geluk Order to be precise.'

'Really?' Melissa interjected. 'I thought the association would be with Thailand.'

Comyns broke into a dry smile. 'An easy mistake to make, my dear sergeant. But no, the Geluk Order is based in Tibet.'

'I don't mean to be rude, sir,' Melissa responded, 'but are you a hundred per cent sure?'

'Absolutely sure,' Comyns said, reaching for a book behind him. He flicked through the pages until he found a photograph of a similar effigy. 'Here you are. You won't find that effigy used outside the Geluk Order.'

Magee read the annotation at the foot of the page, and shook his head in bewilderment. 'I'm not sure this helps us or not.'

'Were you after a connection to Thailand?'

Magee's thoughts strayed to Melissa's comments about Nittaya being half Thai. If Nick Price's wife had been Thai, then it was probable that he had visited Thailand, or maybe even lived there at some time. 'Not necessarily,' he replied unsteadily. 'However, it might help. Why do you ask, do you know of a connection?'

'Perhaps,' Comyns said, barring his teeth. 'However, you may consider it rather tenuous.'

'At this stage in our investigation, sir, I'd consider anything.'

'Well,' Comyns began, 'there is one old story I've heard, about knives depicting Buddhist images being used in Thailand to murder people.'

'Really? That sounds promising.'

'It's only a story, Chief Inspector, I must warn you of that. There's no written record, as you'll soon appreciate. It's only what I've heard myself, whilst researching material for my books.'

'Go on then, try me.'

'Well, to set the scene, you've got to go back to the Second World War and the Japanese involvement in South East Asia. Are you familiar with that history?'

Magee nodded. 'I'm fairly au fait with it.'

'Right, well, apologies for the frankness, sergeant, but as you probably know, during the war, the Japanese soldiers were fond of sex. Unfortunately, that often meant resorting to forced sex. Estimates are that they housed two hundred thousand sex-slaves spread around Korea, China, the Philippines, Indonesia, Taiwan and Thailand.'

Melissa blinked. 'Dear god!'

'History, my dear sergeant. It's sad, but unfortunately true.'

'It wasn't my favourite subject at school,' Melissa responded with a shrug.

'At the time,' Comyns continued, 'the Japanese people had a predisposition to dominate other races. With their soldiers, that meant rape. It was something Japanese High Command was extremely worried about.'

'Why?' asked Melissa. 'I seem to recall they didn't have much respect for humanity.'

Comyns looked at Melissa in a conspiratorial way. 'Venereal Disease, that's why, my dear sergeant. It could have devastated the ranks if they weren't careful. In those days it took months to recover, and months of inactivity for soldiers meant wasted resources. Hence the sex-slaves; they were brought in specially, to encourage the soldiers to keep their hands off local girls. The Army doctors were able to monitor the sex-slaves housed in the camps, but not girls from local villages. The soldiers were told not to have sex with the locals or they would be punished. Punished for risking infection, you understand, not for committing a crime.'

Melissa snorted. 'Typical men!'

Comyns nodded. 'It's just the way of the world, sergeant, in wartime that is. Anyway, despite the risk of punishment, some soldiers nevertheless strayed. Countless millions of rapes must have occurred in South East Asia during those awful years of occupation.'

Magee gave Melissa a terse scowl. 'How does Thailand fit in then?'

'Well, Thailand was in a slightly different situation compared to other countries occupied by the Japanese,' Comyns continued. 'The Thai government signed an agreement of accord with Japan. That meant the Japanese soldiers were invited into the country, as opposed to having invaded.'

Magee raised an eyebrow and asked, 'So the Japanese soldiers were expected to be friendly towards the locals?'

'Exactly, Chief Inspector. And you don't expect your friends to commit rape.'

'But they did, I assume?'

'Of course they did. And it put both sides under a lot of strain. It was difficult for the Thais to complain, and difficult for the Japanese to admit it was happening.'

'Let me guess,' Magee said, 'the people took the matter into their own hands?'

'I can see why you're a detective.'

Magee grimaced. 'It's human nature, to want to right a wrong.'

'You're certainly right there, Chief Inspector. It wasn't long before the odd Japanese soldier or two turned up dead with a knife embedded in their chest.'

'With an effigy of a Buddha carved on the handle?'

'That's what I've heard. Sometimes, though, it was just an amulet tied around the hilt.'

'This is just hearsay, though?'

'I'm afraid so, Chief Inspector. But I did spend a long time in Thailand, during my university years, interviewing the older generation about their war experiences. They would talk openly over a bottle of whisky, but there has never been much written about their war period. Thailand has never been keen on baring its soul. Too many influential people want to protect their reputations.'

'Let me get this straight,' Magee interjected. 'You're saying that there's a historical precedence for knives bearing a Buddha effigy being used to kill for revenge in Thailand?'

'Correct. But only for a limited period, I must stress.'

'Just for rape, though? What about revenge for other crimes?'

'That, I can't help you with, Chief Inspector.'

'But the knife was left in the body?'

'Indeed. It served a purpose; it was the most efficient way of letting the Japanese know why the murder had been committed. No Japanese officer would want to pursue a murder if he knew his soldier had raped a local girl. The officer would risk punishment for not keeping his men under control.'

'Execution following a clandestine trial,' Magee muttered. 'Is that what's going on?'

'The Avenging Buddha,' Comyns murmured under his breath.

'I beg your pardon?'

'The section title, in my book on Thailand's war years history. There're about forty pages on the subject, with transcripts of several interviews. Would you care to borrow it?'

'Erm, yes, thank you,' Magee replied, pondering on the likelihood of revenge being the motive for the two recent murders. 'That's certainly an apt term of yours.'

'I suppose we're more likely to use the expression an eye for an eye,' Comyns said as he reached behind and extracted another book from a shelf.

Magee accepted the book. 'Does anything else spring to mind?'

'No. I don't think so, Chief Inspector.'

'Well, thank you for your time, sir. Your information has been very useful. It's given me direction, if nothing else.'

'You're welcome. Glad to be of help.'

'Now then, if you'll excuse us, we must be going,' Magee said getting up from his seat. 'Here's my card in case you think of anything else later on.'

'I'd better escort you downstairs.'

Magee thanked the curator as he left the building then turned his attention to Melissa. 'Come on, let's get back to Lewes. We've got something to work on now. I want you to cross reference Conners' life with Harwood's. Maybe with Nick Price's and Paul Mansell's as well. Somewhere on the way, their lives are likely to have crossed paths. Find that, and we should be able to find the killer, or at least a reason for the two murders.'

'Sounds like countless hours of fun,' Melissa replied unenthusiastically.

'You think my job is any better?' Magee muttered. 'I've yet to speak to the Home Secretary and explain why I let Paul Mansell off the hook for the second time.'

Chapter Thirteen

Lunch for Magee was a hastily grabbed sandwich and a packet of crisps from the staff canteen, eaten in his office. Even after a messy dissection, he wasn't too sure whether the sandwich contained meat or fish. At least the flavour of the crisps was clear from the label, for the taste certainly gave no clue.

He poked his head out of his office door, caught Melissa's attention at the other end of the office, nodded and made a "T" sign with two fingers. He then sat down and tapped a file with a pencil, his mind deep in thought.

'There you go,' Melissa said, putting a cup of tea down on Magee's desk. 'Do you want to talk about it?'

Magee gave Melissa a bewildered look. 'Sorry?'

'Whatever's bugging you?'

'I wouldn't say it's bugging me.'

Melissa returned a smile. 'You're like a dog with a bone at times, sir. You've got that look written all over your face.'

'Am I that easy to read?'

'Sometimes. Other times you're rather enigmatic. It's one of your sexier qualities.'

Magee felt his face burning. 'Flatterer!'

'It's how we women get on in life, sir.'

'Now that, I don't believe.'

'So, what's up?'

'Thailand.'

'Hmm. Lovely country. Fancy a holiday there?'

'That's not what I meant, Melissa. The subject's cropped up many times recently. I'm wondering why.'

Melissa shrugged her shoulders. 'The subject crops up in my life frequently. I haven't noticed anything different recently.'

'But you've been there, Melissa. You have friends who have been there. You want to go there again. The subject is bound to surface often in your social conversations.'

'So?'

'It's not the same with me, though. It's not my cup of tea. It's too hot, I imagine. Too far away.' Magee raised an eyebrow, and added, 'Too many lady-boys as well, so I'm told.'

'You don't approve of them?'

'Of the lady-boys? I saw a show last year with the family over at the Brighton Pavilion; The Lady-Boys of Bangkok. Highly entertaining, I admit, but it made me feel uncomfortable.'

'A bit like at the museum this morning, with the curator?'

'There is that side to it, I admit. But it was the medical side that really made me squirm. It put me off holidaying there.'

'Shame, you're missing out on a lot. It's like a different world out there.'

Magee tapped his pencil a couple more times. 'We have two murders in which the effigy of a Buddha features prominently. I know Comyns said it was from Tibet, but Buddhism is practiced all over South East Asia and no one else has mentioned anything about Tibet.'

'But we haven't asked, have we?'

'No. We haven't. On the other hand, neither have we asked about Thailand, yet it's surfaced. There's Comyns with his revenge story. There's Nittaya, with a Thai name and she obviously has Thai genes in her. Then there's Nick Price who presumably must have had a Thai wife.'

'Although the wife is no longer around.'

'Quite true. Price said he "lost" her. We must get to the bottom of that in due course,' Magee said, tapping his pencil harder. 'Then, of course, you got into a lengthy conversation with Paul Mansell about his travels there.'

'Like I said, sir, it's a popular place.'

'Indeed it is, Melissa, and I want to know more. From the perspective of this case, that is. Look, I'll take the Conners case, you take the Harwood case. See if we can't find a connection with Thailand. Maybe they were both out there together. Maybe they committed a crime out there that could have provoked someone into seeking revenge.'

'Fair enough, there's nothing else to do, except compile reports.'

'And I'll be able to tell our beloved Home Secretary that we are, at least, working in a positive direction.'

'I'll leave you to it, then,' Melissa said on her way out the door.

Magee picked up a file containing a host of statements taken from Todd Conners' family and associates, and spent twenty minutes browsing through them, searching for references to Thailand. Nothing came to light. He lowered the file and put a call through to Susan Conners.

'Mrs Conners? It's Detective Chief Inspector Magee. We met the other night.'

'Oh, yes. How can I help you, Chief Inspector?'

'I just wanted to ask you a question about your husband.'

'More questions?' Susan Conners uttered a sigh. 'I've given you lot everything I can already. I really don't think there's anything left to say.'

'I don't think you've been asked this question.'

'Very well, then, fire away.'

Magee thought Susan Conners sounded slightly tipsy, even though it was mid-afternoon. No doubt losing a husband, even an abusive one, could have that effect. He decided to tread softly. 'Does Thailand mean anything to you?'

'It's a country, isn't it? How many points do I score for that?'

'Ten out of ten, Mrs Conners,' Magee replied. She was certainly a little worse for wear, he could hear her gulping.

'Susan, please. Not Mrs Conners,' Susan pleaded.

'Very well, Susan. I meant in relation to your husband's affairs. Did he ever have any business connections in Thailand, or did he ever visit the country?'

'Well, yes, now you come to mention it. He was there once for a few months, although I can't see it being of any help to you.'

'Do you mind explaining the circumstances?'

'Todd flew off to Bangkok just after we finished college. He was full of bravado, said he was going to fight in the Vietnam War. He never did, of course. He never even joined an army, and I can't

The Fourth Cart I

imagine he thought he'd be recruited just because he was close by, where the Americans were resting. Anyway, by the time he'd heard a few stories of real life action, I think he chickened out.'

'What did he do in Bangkok, then?'

'Well, he settled there for a while and got caught up with various adventures. You know, real Boys Own stuff. So he said anyway, but I was always under the impression he never achieved what he set out to do. He never found himself, if you understand what I mean.'

'I do indeed understand. It's what many men hope to achieve in life. We suffer an eternal desire to climb Everest, paddle up the Amazon, to explore the world; something to test our mettle. It's a primitive thing.'

'Yep, that sounds like Todd when he was young. He didn't fulfill that ambition though. As a result, it left him empty. That's my guess on why he turned out to be such an uncaring bastard.'

'Do you have any idea why his ambition was unfulfilled?'

'No, but he came back early, rather unexpectedly to be honest. That may well have had something to do with it.'

'Do you know why he came back early?'

'No, I don't. Todd never talked about his reasons for coming home. He refused to, in fact. He used to get very upset if anyone asked him what he'd done in Thailand. He never allowed the name of the country to be mentioned in his presence again.'

'When did he return?'

'May the sixteenth, nineteen seventy three. Eighteen years ago next Thursday,' Susan responded without hesitation.

'That was quick! How come you remember so fast?'

'It was the day before my twenty-first birthday. Todd and I had been an item at college. We'd been going out for over six months before he went off to the Far East. He proposed marriage to me the day after his return, at my party. He stopped the music to make a special announcement. How could a girl forget that? He was romantic then. Or so I thought at the time. I must have been mad.'

'And the wedding?'

'Six months later. Todd promised me the wedding of the century. He said that money would be no object. He promised me he'd be a millionaire before the end of that year.'

'And was he?'

'He certainly was. Well within the year actually.'

'How did he do that? A million was a heck of a lot of money in those days.'

'No idea, Chief Inspector. Todd never really explained it properly. But I do know that he never worked hard for it. That was the curious thing about his money. He spent a whole year "studying the market" as he put it. He said he would be receiving a million pounds before Christmas that year, and he needed to do some research before he decided what to invest in. He chose property but said he would wait a while; he predicted the commercial property slump would continue that year and he was right. He picked up a lot of cheap properties in auctions around that time. That set him up to become even richer.'

'Sorry,' Magee interrupted, 'did you just say he knew he was going to receive a million pounds?'

'Correct.'

Magee's mind whirled. 'Let me get this straight, Susan. Are you saying Todd came back from Thailand in full knowledge that he would be receiving a million pounds in the very near future?'

Magee heard Susan Conners sigh deeply. 'I don't suppose it matters now. But yes, you've got it in one, Chief Inspector. Todd had it all sewn up before arriving back in England.'

'You didn't mention any of this in your statement.'

'I wasn't asked. Anyway, it's just ancient history; it can't possibly make any difference now.'

Magee closed his eyes. A million pounds! That's precisely what can make a difference, he thought. 'But you have no inkling of where that money came from?'

'None, I'm afraid. I guessed he'd done something dodgy over there and was just waiting for his payoff. I was in love with the man at the time, Chief Inspector. Todd dressed up the whole story in a way that made it seem romantic.'

'Do you know precisely how much he received?'

'I don't know precisely. He set up a company in advance, though, to use for the purchase of his properties. Those are the only records I ever managed to see. He said he would do something to impress the banks and he certainly did that. His company was set up with a share capital of one million pounds, fully paid up in cash right at the start. I had one share for legal reasons, he held the rest. No other shareholders, no loans, no outside involvement at all. He also bought this house and furnished it extravagantly. He bought his first Rolls Royce at that time too, a brand new one.'

Magee was stunned at the discovery. Maybe there was a serious Thai connection, after all. 'So,' he said, 'Thailand obviously worked well for Todd. But is there anything else about the country that triggers a memory? Do you know if he had any business associates there? What about friends from his days there?'

'As I mentioned already, Chief Inspector, he never said a word about the place from that day on. Mind you . . .'

'Yes?'

'Well, there's Nick Price, of course. He was in Thailand at the same time as Todd.'

Magee's jaw dropped. 'You're kidding!'

'Not at all, Chief Inspector. That's where they met. Todd used to hang out at the bar Nick ran in Bangkok.'

'Well, well, what a small world,' Magee muttered. He began tapping his pencil again.

'But, of course, Thailand is even more of a taboo subject with Nick.'

'It is?' Magee's pencil stopped moving. 'And why is that?'

'Because Nick lost his wife in some tragic accident there, that's why. It's affected him badly ever since, that's obvious to anyone who meets him. He's never got over her death. He blames himself, of course. At times, you can see the guilt eating away at him.'

Magee thought back to his recent encounters with the man. 'That would explain a lot,' he muttered. 'Look, is there anything else that springs to mind?'

'Well, it's just a feeling, but we occasionally went to summer garden parties over at Nick's house in Cooksbridge. There was a small group who seemed to share a past. I've only met them three or four times in all, but when they did meet up, there seemed to be a conspiracy amongst them.'

'How so?'

'Oh, you know, furtive looks, whispered comments, odd remarks. I got the impression they were talking about a past life in Bangkok.'

'Did you not ask your husband what it all meant?'

'Hah!' Susan exclaimed loudly. 'You didn't know Todd, Chief Inspector. You've got no idea of the sulks, the verbal abuse, the threats that I'd receive if I dared go against his wishes.'

'Was Michael Harwood one of that group?'

'There was certainly a Mike amongst them, but I don't recall any surname.'

'Well, thanks for your help, Susan. If you think of anything else, in connection with Thailand, I'd be grateful for a call.'

'You're welcome.'

Magee put the receiver down, sat back in quiet contemplation and let his mind absorb the extraordinary new information he'd gleaned. He certainly had direction now, he mused, but how to progress it? A firm knock on the door put an end to his thought process. There stood Melissa, a smug look on her face.

'I thought I'd make your day, sir.'

'Oh yes? How so?'

'Guess what I've found about Michael Harwood.'

'Surprise me.'

'I spoke to his sister. She said he went wandering around the world before he was due to go to university. He got as far as Bangkok and that was it. On his return, he gave up the idea of a university education and went straight into business. "Dabbling in the Stock Market", is what she called it.'

'Was he an instant millionaire? When he started out in this "dabbling", that is?'

A look of bemusement settled on Melissa's face. 'Erm, yes,'

'But not until six months or so after returning from Bangkok?'

'Are you a clairvoyant, sir?'

Magee shrugged. 'An easy guess, Melissa. When you pull off a big job, it's often best to lie low for a while. Anyway, it can often take time to find a fence, turn your ill-gotten gains into cash.'

'That's exactly what his sister said, or words to that effect anyway. She said she suspected he'd pulled something off in Bangkok all those years ago, but had kept quiet.'

'Tell me, Melissa. Did she say whether it affected her brother? Emotionally?'

'This is unnerving. Her own words were that he was haunted by his experiences in Bangkok.'

Magee sighed and rubbed his eyes. 'I take it you were saving the best bit to last?'

'Sorry?'

'Nick Price.'

Melissa placed her hands on her hips and huffed, 'You knew I was going to say that, didn't you?'

'Sorry to deflate you.'

'You can be infuriating at times, sir.'

'I'm paid to keep one step ahead.'

'You had me spend an hour working my guts out on something you knew already?'

Magee broke into a smile at seeing Melissa's frustration. 'No, sorry, Melissa, I'm just winding you up. Todd Conners' story was the same.'

'Really? So we've found our connection?'

'Looks like it. Todd Conners, Michael Harwood, Nick Price, money and Thailand. Chances are, we'll find our murderer as soon as we establish what happened in Bangkok eighteen years ago.'

'A case of revenge?'

'I should think so,' Magee said. 'I reckon they got away with several million, but something probably went wrong.'

'Eighteen years could be a long prison sentence perhaps? A life sentence, someone finally released for good behaviour?'

'Could be,' Magee agreed. 'Some other gang member doesn't get away. He gets caught and takes the rap for the others. He's just been released and has come looking for his fair share.'

Melissa frowned. 'But why murder them?'

'Maybe he tried to blackmail them first. He collects his money then murders them to maintain silence.'

'Perhaps it's not about money, sir. Maybe he has his share stashed away, but just wants revenge for being grassed up or abandoned?'

'That's quite plausible, Melissa. Yes, I like that better, actually.'

'But that begs a question, sir.'

'Which is?'

'Are there any more in the gang? Any more who are going to be murdered?'

Magee was impressed at Melissa's line of thinking. 'We need to find out who else is involved.'

'You'll have to ask Nick Price.'

Magee winced. 'That could be difficult. I can't see him admitting involvement in a crime. Especially not to me. And certainly not in front of his daughter.'

'You could bring him in.'

Magee grunted. 'And have a team of top lawyers brought down on me like a ton of bricks? No thanks, I can just see the expression on Superintendent Vaughan's face on being presented with that scenario.'

'Nick Price could be at risk himself. You'd be doing him a favour, bringing him in.'

'Somehow, I don't think he'll see it that way.'

'Then you'll just have to persuade him to talk.'

Magee groaned. Melissa was right. 'That's not going to be easy. I seem to get under his skin every time I get anywhere near him.'

'You'll just have to find a way of being more persuasive. Perhaps if you weren't quite so blunt in his presence?'

Magee narrowed his eyes. 'Okay, okay.'

'Perhaps we could go public on it. Appeal for any other gang members to come forward for protection?'

'I imagine it would be a waste of time. Coming forward would probably mean them having to admit that a crime was committed. I doubt whether any sane person would do that.'

'But if the crime was committed in Bangkok, then it wouldn't matter would it? We've no jurisdiction.'

'I don't see it helping. Just imagine if the press gets hold of the story. They'd love to steadily count the bodies off, printing large headlines like Why can't the police stop this madness? No, Melissa, while my head's on the chopping block, I'm keeping this case quiet.'

'But what about the Home Secretary, aren't you going to tell him?'

'Damn! Yes, I suppose I should. I'd better get on to him now. Let's pray he doesn't leak the story. You know what politicians are like with the press; they can't keep their mouths shut.'

'Lack of police efficiency will reflect on him just as badly, sir.'

'That's true. I'll quote you to him on that.'

'Where to next then, sir?'

'God knows, Melissa.' He slumped back in his chair, feeling his enthusiasm waning.

The Fourth Cart I

'If there's another murder in the pipeline, maybe we should just wait and pray.'

'Do you believe in God, Melissa? Or Buddha for that matter?'

'No, sir, I don't, to be honest.'

'Nor do I, Melissa. So who do we pray to?'

'Well, I don't know about prayer, sir, but I do have one small suggestion. Something we could try out with Paul Mansell.'

Magee still hadn't forgiven Melissa for her eagerness to help Mansell out during his interview. He leant back in his chair and said, 'This had better be good. Go on, then, I'm listening …'

Chapter Fourteen

Magee flinched as a piercing noise burst through the headphones he was adjusting on his head. His hand shot out to reach for the volume control. A clear voice broke through, 'Testing, testing, can anyone hear me?'

'Loud and clear,' Magee responded. 'Are you in place?'

'Yep, well at least I think I am,' Paul Mansell replied. 'I've just checked in to room 306, as per instructions.'

'Roger that. Talk to me if you spot anything. Over and out.'

Magee turned to Melissa seated in the car's passenger seat. 'Well, I suppose we just sit it out now.'

'You think this is worthwhile, sir? Not just some wild goose chase? I got the distinct impression the other day that you didn't trust him.'

'I don't. But if he's telling the truth, about being set up by these apparent non-existent clients, then we might just as well tag along behind him. It's not as though we have anything else to go on. Anyway, this is your idea.'

'But it's the middle of the night,' Melissa moaned. 'Why do we have to do this stakeout ourselves? Why couldn't we leave it to the locals to deal with it alone?'

'It's just my way, Melissa. It's the way I do things. Anyway, we are the "locals", as you put it.'

'I'm from Lewes, sir. This is Hove.'

'Close enough, Melissa. The point is, you never know, maybe we can spot something others wouldn't.'

'Like?'

'Who knows? That's why we're here.'

Melissa shut her eyes and sighed.

'Why?' Magee persisted. 'Did you have something planned for tonight?'

'A sleep perhaps?'

'I'll sleep when this maniac is behind bars, not until then.'

'This might be a legitimate client of Mansell's though, sir, in which case we're wasting our time here tonight.'

'True, but it seems to fit in with the same pattern as his last two clients. Think about it, Melissa. Mansell has never seen this client, yet a hotel room is booked and paid for in advance for him. In Hove too, even though he only lives a couple of miles away in Kemp Town. Why would anyone insist he stay here the night, wasting money, rather than expecting him to clear off back home at the end of his shift?'

'I really can't imagine,' Melissa replied. Boredom was etched all over her face.

'Mansell's been given precise instructions for his movements during this evening to supposedly coincide with the client's wife's comings and goings. It's too pat, too convenient.'

'But what if it's not this hotel? Maybe the attack is going to occur somewhere different.'

'The attack will be very close, I reckon. Certainly close enough to ensure we would check out the residents staying here at the Ranalagh, where Mansell's been booked in.'

Melissa yawned and looked at her watch. 'Nine forty-one, sir. I don't think I can stand this all night. Can I get out for a walk?'

'No!' Magee snapped. 'That's the last thing we want, you spooking the murderer. It may be someone that can recognize your face, like Nick Price. That really would wreck the evening.'

'Oh, great. Now I'm trapped here with you.'

'Go to sleep if you're bored.'

'Thanks, I will.' Melissa shut her eyes.

Magee gave a look of despair in Melissa's direction. What was wrong with the youth of today, he wondered? No staying power at all.

The evening passed slowly as Magee sat in quiet solitude next to his sleeping sergeant, his only relief the odd radio enquiry from the three patrol cars waiting in the vicinity.

At half past one in the morning a piercing alarm went off.

Melissa jerked awake and spluttered, 'What the hell is that?'

'All cars, all cars,' Magee shouted into his radio. 'Respond please, where is that alarm coming from?'

'It's coming from here,' the radio cackled in response.

'Where's here?'

'The Roxborough, sir. It's two along from the Ranalagh, going west. Hang on, there's a security guard running like the clappers.'

Magee stumbled out the car and heard a near cry of, 'Hey, you, what's going on?'

'It's the boss,' came a muffled reply. 'It's his new panic button, right by his bed.'

'Sir?' came the cackle on Magee's radio. 'Are you still there? I think an attack is in progress.'

Magee reached through the window to pick up the radio handset. 'All cars, all cars, secure the area. Move in on the Roxborough Hotel. Is anyone around the back?'

'Yes, sir,' came an unidentified response. 'There's a service path. I'm on it now. Hang on a second.'

'Come on, Melissa. Action time!'

Magee ran towards the hotel as bluish-white strobing lights from a multitude of police cars lit up the road.

'Where is everyone?' Magee shouted as he entered the hotel.

'Downstairs, sir, the owner's flat,' came a distant reply.

Magee rushed down a flight of stairs and through an open door to find a scene of utter confusion. One security guard lay collapsed on the floor; another sat on a sofa nursing a bruised jaw. Next to him lay an unconscious poodle. Behind the sofa, a pair of French doors were hanging half open, one glass panel revealing a neatly cut circular hole.

Magee moved through the flat to the bedroom. There, he found the scene he'd been dreading. An officer looked up at Magee in bewilderment. 'She's unconscious, but still alive. Gassed I reckon. He's, well, as you can see, sir. He's well and truly had it.'

Magee's eyes had been fixed on the body since he'd entered the room. Killed in the safety of your own bed, what worse scenario could you face?

'Jesus!' Melissa muttered as she walked up behind Magee.

The Fourth Cart I

'He must have woken, pressed the alarm even as he was being attacked,' the officer said to no one in particular.

Melissa leant over the bed and pulled back a bloodied sheet. 'It's the same dagger, sir.'

'No doubt about it,' Magee muttered in agreement. 'It's our man again.'

'The guard out there nearly got him,' the officer butted in.

'Really?' Magee perked up. He walked back into the sitting room to speak to the guard massaging his jaw. 'I'm DCI Magee. Did you see him? The assailant, that is?'

'Yeah, well, sort of. The bastard floored me.'

'What happened?'

'Mr Harrison, the boss, installed a panic button the day before yesterday. He drilled us for hours and hours on it. Every time he set it off we had to run, full pelt, down here into the flat without knocking.'

'You had keys?'

'Yeah. We had to race in to his bedroom. He said he was worried about being attacked at night. Reckon he knew this was coming to him.'

Magee scratched the back of his head before asking, 'Did he say why, or who it would be?'

'Nah! Sorry.'

'Can you describe the assailant?'

'A fucking Chink.'

Magee frowned. 'Do you mean he was of Chinese origin?'

'Yeah, that's what I said.'

'How do you know he was Chinese? What about Japanese? Could he have been from any other Eastern country?'

'Fuck knows, mate.'

'Man or woman?'

The security guard thought about that question a while. 'You know something? I'm not too sure. Male, I suppose. Too strong to be a woman. He nearly broke my jaw.'

'What about his height and build?'

'Smallish frame. Five foot six, maybe, maximum.'

'Any distinguishing marks, characteristics?'

'No.'

'Would you recognize him again?'

The security guard took a moment to answer, 'To be honest, no. I only really saw him for a split second. And anyway, he was wearing a gas mask.'

'A gas mask? Shit! What about an artist sketch?'

'I'll give it a go, if you like, but . . . well . . .'

'Okay, later perhaps. Which way did he go?'

'Not sure, but I expect he went straight down through the gardens. There's a path that runs along the bottom, it connects up all the properties along this road.'

Magee looked at the unconscious dog lying next to the security guard. Surely it would have been on the floor, barking at the assailant as he came in. 'What about the dog? Did you put it there?'

'No. No, I didn't.'

Magee reflected on the question of the dog's location. 'Interesting, very interesting. Our murderer has a soft spot somewhere.'

The radio crackled into life. 'He's come out on The Drive. Hello? Anyone there? Assistance required on The Drive. He's in a Renault 5, heading north.'

'This is DCI Magee. All cars give pursuit. I repeat, all cars to give pursuit.' He lowered the hand-held radio and said, 'Come on, Melissa.'

'We've got him,' came a crackled cry down the radio. 'In pursuit going up Woodlands. He can't outrun us; we're yards from his bumper. Registration number is Delta Three Four Seven Delta Tango Charlie.'

'Seal off his exit,' Magee screamed at the radio. 'Don't let him get out of the town!'

'Where's Mansell, sir?' Melissa asked.

'No idea. Let's go and check.'

By the time Magee had entered the Ranalagh, the messages coming through on the radio were not what he wanted to hear.

'. . . he's on the dual carriageway, doing over a hundred, he'll kill someone at that speed . . .'

'. . . he's going to turn on to the A23. Oh shit, that lorry's swerved too much, it's going to jack-knife. No, don't brake . . . Ahhhh!'

Magee winced as he heard the smash of glass and a resounding thud.

'Sweet Jesus! Ambulance required immediately at the junction of the A27 and A23. Oh fuck, don't lose him, let's get going!'

'... where is he? I don't believe it! The fucker's disappeared!'

Magee clenched his fists in frustration. Surely, they couldn't possibly lose sight of a car speeding that fast. 'Get a helicopter out, for Christ sake!' he shouted into the radio.

Chapter Fifteen

A waitress hovered next to the table Magee was sitting at and scowled. 'Are you going to eat that, dear? You've been toying with it for nearly half an hour. It'll be cold by now.'

'Sorry, I've lost my appetite,' Magee replied. He sat back allowing the waitress to clear away his unwanted breakfast of bacon and eggs. He stared despondently around the hotel's dining room. He felt awful, having not slept a wink, being on his feet all night. To make matters worse, he'd received a roasting from the Home Secretary, not just for the night's fiasco but also for disturbing him at six-thirty in the morning to break the news. And now he felt an overburdening sense of guilt; if only he'd done more.

Melissa waved a hand in front of Magee in an attempt to catch his attention. 'Come on, sir. Cheer up. It really wasn't your fault.'

'You think not? I'm not so sure.' Magee looked across the table at Paul Mansell. 'If only I'd been a little bit more trusting of you, Paul, then we might not be in this mess.'

'My fault is it? Thanks a bunch!'

'No. I didn't mean it like that. It's nothing personal. It's just a question of resources. I didn't have enough confidence in your story to demand more officers. That was my call. So, you see, Robert Harrison's death was my fault.'

'You're being too hard on yourself, sir,' Melissa replied. 'Our murderer might well have got away for now, but we've got his car registration number. And he left in such a hurry this time, SOCO are bound to pick something up.'

The Fourth Cart I

Magee's head sunk even lower, along with his mood. 'That doesn't cheer me up, Melissa. There are three officers in hospital. Then there's the walking wounded; Mrs Harrison, two security guards. The lorry driver is really shook up. Not forgetting the dog, of course. By the way, has it woken up yet?'

'Yes it has, actually,' Melissa responded with a warm smile.

'Shame it can't talk,' Paul threw in. 'It would have quite a story.'

'Hah!' Magee scoffed. 'Speak for yourself! You've a story to tell as well, but for some reason you're holding out. Rather like the dog.'

'Bollocks!' Paul retorted. 'I've told you everything already. I swear I'm not holding back on anything.'

Magee had a malicious look in his eye. 'I beg to differ there.'

Melissa put her hand up in an attempt to stop the bickering. 'Look, sir, maybe Paul just doesn't know what he's holding back.'

'What?' asked Paul.

'This case seems to involve the past, Paul,' Melissa responded kindly. 'Maybe it involves something from your past, but you just don't know it.'

'Why do you say that?'

Melissa continued, 'Because you would have been too young.'

'Explain, please,' Magee interjected.

'Well, sir. If these murders are being committed for revenge, as seems likely, and it concerns something that happened eighteen years ago in Thailand, then Paul would have been what, six, seven years old? It seems unlikely that he would know much about it.'

Paul Mansell's mouth fell open in astonishment. 'Eighteen years ago, in Thailand? What are you talking about?'

'That was highly confidential information,' Magee muttered in Melissa's direction. He turned to Paul Mansell and said, 'You will not repeat that to anyone.'

'But my brother John was in Thailand eighteen years ago. So were Nick and Sean.'

'Sean?'

'Sean Fitzpatrick.'

Magee rubbed his chin. 'Should that name mean something?'

'He was at school with Nick. They were friends. They worked together for years.'

'I think I remember that name from way back. Something on file about him, I'm sure. I'll look into it later.' Magee rubbed his eyes. 'Anyway, what's this about your brother?'

'I haven't seen John since he was eighteen. He left home when I was three. I never saw him again.'

'Nick knew him?'

'Yes.'

'Where is John now?'

'In Thailand, possibly, but I really don't know. Nick said he was really close to John once, but even Nick doesn't know where John is now. They just drifted apart. Lost contact I suppose, like you do.'

Magee looked at Paul thoughtfully.

A waitress approached their table. 'There's a call for you, sir. The telephone's over there by the door.'

'Thanks,' Magee replied, getting up and crossing the dining room. He picked up the phone and said, 'DCI Magee speaking.'

'Morning, sir,' a voice said. 'We've got a trace on a Renault car for you. It was hired by a Mr Somchai Polgeowit of Flat 4C Sussex Gardens in Kemp Town. The car-hire firm took the details from his driving license. I'll spell out that name for you, sir . . .'

Magee scribbled down the details. 'Great! Thank you very much. I'll take it from here.'

Magee let out a sigh of relief as he walked back to the table. 'We've got him now! Come on, Melissa, let's get back to Lewes. We need to get a search warrant issued quickly.'

Chapter Sixteen

Magee held up a walkie-talkie to his mouth and whispered, 'Are we all ready?' He looked around at the assortment of police officers spread around Sussex Gardens. He received a chorus of "Yes, sir," and the odd thumbs up sign.

Magee turned to Melissa and said, 'Action at last, eh? Just what your uncle wanted for you.'

'I'm not sure he wanted me to get quite so involved,' Melissa replied. 'I'm not sure whether I want to get this involved either.'

'Nervous?'

'Yes, sir. I am.'

'Good. The adrenaline will keep you alert.'

'I'd feel safer with a gun, sir. I'm a good shot.'

'So am I, Melissa, but I'm a family man, it's an area I'd rather not get involved in. Best left to the experts.'

The expression on Melissa's face turned from anxiety to frustration. 'Do you reckon he's inside the flat?'

'Unlikely,' Magee responded. 'If he has any sense he would have ditched the Renault by now. He must have known we were in sight of his number plate. Still, you never know your luck.'

'It's time, sir.' The remark came from behind Magee.

'Come on then lads, in we go!'

Magee's team marched along Sussex Gardens. Two officers behind Magee carried enforcers, the rest were armed with automatic rifles or hand guns. Magee halted at the front door of Number 4 and pressed the bell marked Flat C. There was no reply. He tried again, only to be met with silence. He tried Flat A instead. The intercom buzzed.

'Yes?' a slow, sexy, female voice asked in a long drawn out sigh. Magee had never heard so much suggestiveness put into one solitary word.

'Police, madam. Open up, please.'

'What have I done now?' The sexy tone had vanished.

'Nothing, madam. We just want to get inside the building. We're after another occupant.'

'Oh, well, suit yourself!'

After a long buzz had sounded, Magee pushed the front door open. Three uniformed and six plain-clothed officers bundled into the building only to be confronted by the sight of a Marilyn Monroe look-alike in a pink chiffon dressing gown provocatively standing near her doorway.

'Oh my word!' she exclaimed, 'Are you sure I can't help any of you gentlemen?'

All the men, except Magee, stood staring at the vision, their eyes out on stalks. Magee quickly appraised the woman's appearance. He was sure that police harassment featured regularly in her profession. No wonder the woman thought she was in trouble.

'Is this a bust?' she asked.

'Yes, madam.' Magee rather liked the woman's frankness.

'How wonderful! Coffee anyone? Tea, perhaps?'

All the men nodded, but Magee spoke firmly, 'If you don't mind, madam, we have work to do.'

'Shame. Later perhaps?'

Magee ignored the woman's plea and asked, 'Can you tell me anything about the occupant of Flat 4C?'

'Our oriental gentleman? No, not much. He doesn't stay here that often. When he does, though, he usually has a young man with him, if you know what I mean. He seems to like young muscular escorts. I've dropped a few hints that I can help out with any arrangements, but he doesn't seem interested. I haven't spoken to him for months.'

'Is he in?' Magee asked.

'I don't think so. I tend to notice people coming and going.'

The Fourth Cart I

With typical English restraint, Magee said, 'Well, if you'll excuse us, we'll just pop upstairs. Auckland, you stay down here just in case. Give the lady some protection.'

'Yes, sir,' DS Auckland replied. He stepped forward with a broad grin on his face whilst the others stared at him with apparent envy.

'And don't let your mind wander from your job,' Magee quipped, as DS Auckland disappeared into Flat 4A.

At the top of the stairs, Magee knocked on the front door of Flat 4C, but, as expected, there was no reply. He nodded to the two men yielding the enforcers. Four violent blows later and the door flew open.

'Check it out lads,' Magee ordered. Five officers split off in different directions.

Magee wandered around the flat, his hopes diminishing by the second. The place was empty, devoid of life. He saw just the barest minimum of furniture to make a short stay viable. There were no bills lying around, no correspondence, no milk in the fridge, no personal items. It was just somewhere to sleep and wash, somewhere for private liaisons perhaps. It was also clinical in its appearance; whoever used it didn't want to be identified.

'Damn!' Magee muttered as Melissa approached. 'I really thought we'd cracked it.'

'Maybe SOCO will be able to lift some prints.'

'I doubt it, Melissa. This place is sterile,' Magee said, running a finger along the top of the skirting board. 'He must have it professionally cleaned every time it's used.'

'Obsessive behaviour, or mere paranoia?'

'Either. Both perhaps,' Magee said absently. 'But you can't rent or buy a flat without leaving records.'

Melissa grimaced. 'More paperwork?'

'Not necessarily. Take over here, Melissa. I'm going to relieve Auckland. I've got my appetite back. Maybe our friendly lady downstairs would rustle me up a sandwich.'

Melissa stared at Magee's disappearing back with amazement. 'You wicked old bastard!' she muttered.

Chapter Seventeen

As Magee left Sussex Gardens, he gave a friendly wave back towards the woman standing in the bay window of the ground floor flat.

'You look smug, sir,' Melissa commented.

'Hmm!' Magee replied beaming like the proverbial Cheshire cat. 'A couple of bacon sandwiches and a cup of coffee, just what was needed.'

'Plus the company of a beautiful woman?'

Magee allowed an even broader smile. 'Well, that helped, I must say. She's a very intelligent woman actually, that Angela.'

Melissa's eyebrows raised a fraction. 'Angela is it? Well, well, you are a dark horse, sir.'

'She's a clever girl, Melissa, despite her choice of career. Anyway, she helped me track down the tenant via the landlord's office. I just hope it doesn't end badly for her.'

'How could it?'

'Well, with the press, I suppose. I can just picture the headlines tomorrow, The Duke, The Bimbo and The Ripper.'

Melissa looked confused. 'The Duke? What Duke? You've lost me, sir.'

'The landlord, Melissa.'

'Oh, right. Well, where do we go from here?'

'To arrest the tenant, of course. Mr Somchai Polgeowit; he's an importer of Thai products, based up near Gatwick.'

'Have you checked he's there?'

'I spoke to his secretary from Angela's flat. She says he should be back by four this afternoon. He'll be expecting us.'

The Fourth Cart I

Melissa looked even more perplexed. 'Hang on, sir. This doesn't sound right. We nearly got him last night. He must have known we were close enough to read his number plate. Yet, today, he just strolls into work as though nothing has happened?'

'Apparently so.'

Melissa scratched the back of her head. 'Odd behaviour, don't you think?'

'Maybe he's got nowhere to run. Maybe he's just waiting for us to go and get him. Who knows?'

'It doesn't sound right to me.'

'Don't look a gift horse in the mouth, Melissa. Be positive. This is it, we've got our man. We just need to bring him in.'

'If you're sure . . .'

'I am. Come on, we'll get there early, just in case he changes his mind.'

Within the hour, Magee had located the importer, Mekong Enterprises Limited, on an industrial estate on the edge of Crawley, and settled himself in a comfortable chair in the office's reception area. He waited patiently for another half hour before sighting a Thai man coming through the front door.

Magee nudged Melissa. 'This must be him now.'

The Thai man approached Magee and said, 'Good afternoon. I understand that you are police officers. How may I help?'

Magee stood up and eyed the man up and down. He was slim, around thirty years old and certainly looked capable of the physical exertion necessary to have committed the recent murders. He imagined the man with a gas mask covering his face and concluded that the hotel's security guard had been right to conclude there was nothing distinguishable about the man.

'Are you Mr Somchai Polgeowit?'

'That is quite correct.'

'I am Detective Chief Inspector Magee and this is Detective Sergeant Kelly. I am arresting you on suspicion of the murder of Mr Todd Conners, Mr Michael Harwood and Mr Robert Harrison. Read him his rights, Melissa.'

As Melissa talked, Magee watched Polgeowit's face, hoping to see a reaction. None came; the man remained expressionless, even as Melissa handcuffed his wrists.

'You are making a mistake, Chief Inspector. I hope you realize that you, how do you say, have the wrong man.'

'Yes, sir, if you say so. In the meantime perhaps you would come with us and not cause any trouble.'

'Certainly. It seems as though I have little choice in the matter. May I ask where you are taking me, though? My wife and children will be worried.'

'I'm taking you to the Sussex Police Headquarters in Lewes for questioning. You may, of course, have a lawyer present with you if you wish.'

'Thank you, Chief Inspector.' Mr. Polgeowit gave a few firm instructions to his secretary before Melissa led him away.

Magee maneuvered Polgeowit into the car, then climbed in and sat alongside him. He gave a self-indulgent smirk. He'd got his man. The Home Secretary would be happy, his Superintendent would be happy, even the press would be happy. A few hours from now, he reckoned, and he'd have his man talking. With any luck, he may even extract sufficient dirt on Nick Price to nail him as well. Life was looking up, he thought, as he lent back and relaxed the rest of the journey.

Forty minutes later, as they neared the Headquarters in Malling, Lewes, Magee's heart sunk. 'Oh, good grief,' he muttered on seeing a crowd of journalists. 'Where did they all come from?'

'Methinks someone let the cat out the bag,' Melissa mumbled.

'Probably your uncle,' Magee muttered.

'Thanks, sir. I get the blame for that I suppose?'

To Magee's surprise, Polgeowit sat calmly in the back of the car, stony faced, as the car drove through the blockade of photographers. Magee winced at the blinding flashes, yet Polgeowit made no move to avert his face. It unnerved Magee, he'd expected Polgeowit to be hiding in shame.

Magee got out the car and said, 'Process him, Melissa. I'd better go back and give that lot a statement.'

Despite his dislike for the press, Magee couldn't help feeling triumphant as he approached the reporters.

'Chief Inspector Magee,' one reporter shouted out. 'We've been told you've arrested the man that murdered the Brighton councillor, Todd Conners. Was that him in your car?'

Many other reporters shouted questions. Magee held his hands up in a request for silence. 'Thank you, gentlemen. I can confirm that an arrest has been made today in connection with those murders. I really can't say much more than that.'

'Is he the Ripper you're after?'

Magee's puffed out his chest. 'You know I can't possibly answer that.' The unsubtle gesture left the journalists in no doubt that Magee had his man, but couldn't say so publicly. Vanity got to him; he posed for the cameras and imagined the headlines running boldly alongside his photo. He smiled for the cameras, blissfully thinking that the Home Secretary would be impressed. Promotion may come his way after all.

Chapter Eighteen

Magee was on a high. He waltzed into his office, triumphantly, whistling in a carefree tone. He caught DS Collins' attention as he passed and said, 'Could you contact the Home Secretary for me, please?'

DS Collins looked at her watch before saying, 'It's five forty-five. I have a bus to catch in a few minutes.'

'Two minutes, that's all.' DS Collins gave Magee a resigned look and went back to her desk.

Magee sat in silent contemplation waiting for the call to come through. Life doesn't get better than this, he purred to himself. He picked up the receiver eager to hear the Home Secretary's congratulations.

'Magee?'

'Yes, sir,' Magee replied on recognizing Rees Smith's voice. 'I thought you'd want to be first to hear the news. We made an arrest a few minutes ago.'

'Really? Who?'

'He's a Thai man, sir, a Mr Somchai Polgeowit.'

'A Thai national, you say?'

'That is correct, sir.'

There was a momentary pause before the next question was asked. 'How old is he?'

'Um, thirty-one, I think, according to his driving license.'

'Thirty-one? Are you sure, Magee?'

'Quite sure, sir. Why, is there a problem with that?'

The Fourth Cart I

'No, not at all, Magee. I was just trying to get my head round the case. You're sure you've got the right man?'

'Quite sure, sir. There's no doubt about it following the exploits of last night. We chased a car from the scene of Robert Harrison's murder in Hove last night. The car was registered to this Somchai Polgeowit at a flat in Sussex Gardens in Kemp Town. From there, we traced the lease to his office in Crawley. There is no doubt, sir.'

'Well, congratulations then, Magee. You'll keep me informed of progress won't you?'

'Of course, sir. And I apologize again for disturbing you so early this morning.'

'Hmm,' Rees Smith murmured. 'Never mind. The important thing is you've got your man.'

'Thank you, sir.'

'Right, well, I'm sure this arrest will be seen as a fortuitous occasion, in respect of your promotion prospects, Chief Inspector. Good bye for now.'

'Thank you, sir.'

As soon as Magee put the receiver down, DS Collins called through, 'There's a Mrs Gibson on line two for you, sir.'

'Who?'

'Mrs Gibson. She sounds very distraught. And she wants to talk to you personally.'

'Oh, all right,' Magee muttered. He sighed deeply. All he wanted was for two minutes of peace before he commenced interrogation of Polgeowit.

'Hello? Yes, this is Detective Chief Inspector Magee. How can I help you, madam?'

Through a series of sobs and snuffles, Mrs Gibson said, 'I demand an explanation, Chief Inspector. I think it's outrageous.'

'I'm sorry, madam, I don't understand you.'

'You know perfectly well what I mean, Chief Inspector.'

Magee could barely make sense out of the wailing woman. 'Madam, please! I honestly don't know what you're talking about. Please, calm down, and start from the beginning.' He waited patiently for the woman to settle.

'I had a delivery an hour ago. A special delivery. It was a parcel, Chief Inspector, as if you didn't know. It contained a wreath, and in the centre of the wreath was this horrible, obscene knife. There was a most upsetting card with it as well.'

Magee sighed. There were far better qualified people than him to deal with these situations. He cursed the system for not being able to filter out such calls. 'What does it say, madam?'

'Well, the wreath was in my son's name, Chief Inspector.'

'And who is your son, madam?'

'Keith. Keith Gibson. He died five years ago, Chief Inspector, and I get a wreath today. It's most upsetting. I'm eighty-three years old next month and I could do without this sort of nonsense.'

'And what does this card say, Mrs . . . Gibson?'

'The card says, well, it has just got the number four written on it.'

Magee sighed in despair. He seemed to know instinctively where this conversation was heading. 'Mrs Gibson, this knife, is the handle carved in the shape of a Buddha?'

'Of course it is, Chief Inspector. As if you don't know!'

Magee was bemused by the comment. 'Mrs Gibson, I'm sorry, but I don't understand this. Why do you think I should know about this?'

'Because your name and telephone number are on the card, that's why, Chief Inspector.'

Magee closed his eyes in dismay. 'I'm so sorry about this, Mrs Gibson, but someone with an unbalanced mind is playing a very cruel trick on you.'

'I don't understand, Chief Inspector. Please explain.'

'I'm sorry to have to say this, Mrs Gibson, but I am the senior investigating officer in a serial murder case. I think your son was probably the next intended victim. The fourth victim, that is.'

'But why was I given your telephone number?'

'I'd rather not speculate on that, Mrs Gibson. Look, can I take some details from you. I'll come round and see you as soon as I can, if I may.'

'By all means, Chief Inspector. This is most upsetting. I would like to get the matter cleared up.'

'If I could just take your address,' Magee said, beckoning Melissa as she appeared in his doorway. 'Right, thank you, Mrs Gibson. I'll call you tomorrow. Goodbye for now.'

Melissa caught Magee's attention and asked, 'Mrs Gibson?'

'Victim number four, Keith Gibson. Well, his mother anyway. She said her son died five years ago, but received a wreath today. There was a knife enclosed in the wreath.'

'Don't tell me, our Avenging Buddha?'

'So it seems. Come on, let's go and visit our friend downstairs. He's had plenty of time alone to think. Hopefully, he'll be in the mood for talking.'

Magee walked with Melissa down to an interview room only to find an irate solicitor berating a constable in the corridor. He took in the solicitor's expensive looking suit and arrogant manner; not good signs, in his books.

'Good afternoon, sir. I'm DCI Magee. May I help you?'

'I hope so, Chief Inspector. I have been kept waiting here for half an hour, and my client has been assaulted. It's an outrage!'

'Perhaps we could go inside, sir,' Magee said walking into the interview room alongside Melissa. He sat down opposite Polgeowit and was horrified to see a large red mark on the prisoner's face.

'Chief Inspector,' the solicitor started, 'My client wishes to make it clear that he is innocent of all accusations.'

'I'm sure he does,' Magee muttered. 'They all do.'

'He is an honest businessman and has never been in trouble with the police in all his life. My client expected better from the British police force. He feels that he is being unduly harassed. His treatment so far has been far from acceptable. My client was under the impression that a man was innocent in this country until proven guilty. My client is a pacifist, a devout Buddhist and he never resorts to violence no matter how much he is provoked. Yet as you've no doubt noticed, my client now has a severely bruised face and a swollen eye.'

'I had noticed that, sir.'

'Well? How do you explain it, Chief Inspector? A self-inflicted wound perhaps?'

'I have no idea, sir. I'm sure there'll be an investigation, though.'

'I expect more than that, Chief Inspector. Someone should pay for this with their job. It really is quite disgraceful. My client is a well-respected member of the Thai community as you would know if you'd checked beforehand. No doubt the Thai Ambassador will be speaking to you shortly.'

'Is Mr Polgeowit claiming diplomatic immunity?'

'No, of course not, he is not a diplomat. But he is an extremely close friend of the Ambassador.'

'Fine. Then perhaps we can return to the proceedings. Mr Polgeowit will be treated in the same way as any non-British non-diplomatic resident.' He turned to face Polgeowit and asked politely, 'Is that acceptable to you, sir?'

Polgeowit remained silent. His solicitor responded on his behalf, 'Does every foreigner receive a black eye in a British police station, then?'

'Could we change the subject, please?' Magee pleaded. 'We'll come back to this alleged assault later.'

'We certainly will, Chief Inspector.'

Magee turned his attention away from the solicitor. 'Right. Now then, Mr Polgeowit, can you account for your movements last night. The entire night that is, say from nine in the evening?'

'Of course, Chief Inspector,' Polgeowit answered for himself. 'From eight o'clock in the evening until two in the morning I was hosting a charity fundraising party at the Savoy, in London, on behalf of the Royal Thai Embassy. There were around one hundred and fifty guests there and I believe I managed to have a few words with almost everyone during the evening. I certainly greeted each guest and bade farewell to most of them at the end.'

Magee was shocked. Surely such an alibi was not possible? He closed his eyes briefly as the image of a career in ruins flashed through his mind.

Magee was desperate to regain control. 'Do you own the flat known as 4C Sussex Gardens in Kemp Town, Brighton, sir?'

'Certainly not, Chief Inspector. My house is in East Grinstead. I am in the telephone book, did you not look?'

'You could have a second home.'

'For what purpose, Chief Inspector?'

Magee reflected on the comments Angela had made on the habits of the occupant of Flat 4C. 'I'd rather not speculate on that, sir.'

'This flat in Sussex Gardens,' the solicitor said, 'have you been there, Chief Inspector?'

'Yes, of course I have.'

'And it is relevant to this murder charge?'

'Very much so, sir.'

The Fourth Cart I

'You have taken fingerprints from this flat?'

Magee winced. 'Yes,'

'And you have compared them to those of my client?'

'I am still awaiting the results on that, sir.' It was the best, and worst, comment that Magee could come up with.

'Really? That is most interesting, Chief Inspector. Or rather most surprising, I should say. Forgive my ignorance, but I thought modern detective techniques involved things like matching fingerprints before making accusations? Or is your mind-set still stuck in the sixties?'

Magee chose to ignore the jibe and said, 'We had sufficient evidence to make an arrest, even without fingerprints.'

'Indeed? Would you care to share that information with us?'

Magee looked the solicitor in the eye. 'There was a murder last night, in Hove. The assailant got away in a hired car, but we got the number. The car hire company had a copy of the driving license which we traced to a flat in Sussex Gardens. The flat and the driving license are both in Mr Polgeowit's name.'

'Did you consider the possibility of another man with the same name?'

'That was irrelevant,' Magee shot back. 'The lease agreement for the flat gave Mr Polgeowit's business address in Crawley as well as his position in the company. Are you going to tell me there are two men called Somchai Polgeowit who are both managing directors of Mekong Enterprises Limited?'

'Of course not, Chief Inspector. But what about the possibility of someone using my client's identity as a cover, as I believe you call it?'

Magee blinked at the solicitor's comment and knew immediately he'd been duped. He turned to Polgeowit and asked politely, 'Would you mind standing in an identity parade, sir.'

'Can I go home afterwards, Chief Inspector? I think I have tolerated enough abuse for one day. My wife and children will be most concerned by my absence.'

Magee was stuck. All he had was circumstantial evidence. If the alibi proved sound, and if the identity parade failed, then he knew his case would collapse. He cleared his throat. 'Were there any photos taken at last night's party, sir?'

'Several hundred I would imagine. As host, I think I would appear in the odd one or two.'

Magee caught Melissa's eye and nodded his agreement. 'Very well, Mr Polgeowit. If this identity parade fails, then you're free to go. As long as I can also get corroboration that you were at the party last night.'

'Telephone the Embassy, Chief Inspector,' Polgeowit offered, 'I believe most of the senior staff were there last night.'

'If you'd care to wait here, sir, we'll be as quick as we can,' Magee said leaving the room.

Outside, Magee stared at the ground in horror. 'What the hell's gone wrong, Melissa? I thought this was a cast iron case?'

'It could be a bluff.'

'I wish!' Magee muttered. 'Christ, I hope you're right, it doesn't bear thinking about. How the hell could I get it so wrong?'

'I think we were led astray, sir.'

Magee nodded. 'Let's just hope we can salvage something. Look, will you telephone Angela? Ask her to pop over as quick as she can. Arrange a lift for her if she hasn't got transport. Then contact The Savoy in London, see if the party was held there last night. I'll phone the Embassy. Be careful with what you say, though, there's likely to be a heap of trouble coming this way.'

'Will do, sir.'

'And see if you can get someone to string together some Orientals from the local restaurants for an ID parade.'

'Right you are. And cheer up,' Melissa said, walking off, 'it's not the end of the world.'

'Not yet,' Magee responded, 'but it might be soon, if what Polgeowit said is true.'

Five minutes later, Magee collapsed into his office chair, rubbed his eyes and exhaled deeply. He really wasn't looking forward to the next conversation. He picked up the telephone gingerly and dialled the number of the Royal Thai Embassy. Within moments of explaining who he was, and the purpose of his call, he was transferred straight through to the Ambassador himself. He sat patiently, listening, more than talking, as the Ambassador convinced him of Polgeowit's innocence.

Magee was in a deeply depressed mood as he made his way down to the ID room. Angela, the blonde bombshell, had arrived dressed to kill. He led her up and down a line of six men, twice, but she failed to pick anyone out.

'Are you sure, Angela?'

'Absolutely sure, Jack. Sorry.'

Magee blushed at the use of his Christian name. 'Please double-check, Angela,' he begged in desperation.

'Numbers one and two are far too old; they must be sixty at least. Number three is far too young. Number four is too tall, by at least six inches. Numbers five and six are too ugly. He's not there, Jack. I'm good on faces, it's my job.' Angela gave Magee a knowing look. 'If I forgot a face it could be very embarrassing in my position.'

Magee felt a cloud of despair settle over him. Not only did Polgeowit seem to have a cast iron alibi, but now his star witness had crushed his last hope. The events of the day came sharply into focus. He'd rushed, he'd jumped the gun. He hadn't checked his facts properly. He could so easily have made a few basic, discrete enquiries beforehand. It was no consolation, but he put his negligence down to being too tired, or under too much pressure. Oh dear god, he cursed inwardly, please let this be a dream.

Melissa entered the room wearing a long face. She didn't have to speak; Magee could see by her expression that all was not well. He turned his attention to Polgeowit who was waiting impatiently nearby with his solicitor.

'Mr Polgeowit,' Magee said politely, 'you are free to go. The fingerprints and photographs we've taken here today will be destroyed. The reference to your arrest will be deleted from our records. I will start an immediate inquiry into your alleged assault. Please accept my sincerest apologies, sir, for your grief. I have no excuses to offer. I have been taken in by the deviousness of a killer who has steered me in the wrong direction, to you. For that, I am most humbly sorry.' Magee's face was beetroot red with embarrassment. He'd never felt so humiliated in his life.

'It is not good enough, Chief Inspector,' Polgeowit responded icily. 'I cannot accept your apologies. My solicitor will be corresponding with you in due course. I shall be making a very big issue about this. The whole episode has been disgraceful and I shall sue for compensation. Good day to you, Chief Inspector.' Polgeowit turned and left the room with his solicitor.

Magee slumped into a plastic chair in a dimly lit corner of the ID parade room, and everyone left him to his tortured thoughts. He wished for the earth to open and swallow him whole, to rid him of the disgrace he knew was coming his way. The case had blown up in his face. Everything that had gone wrong would be dumped on him. That fate was inevitable. It was how responsibility worked in the Force; everyone would distance themselves from him, everyone would fight their own corner citing him as the man who masterminded the disastrous case.

He sat in silence contemplating his career to date, and how it was likely to be terminated, dishonourably, in the coming weeks; he would be disciplined, made a laughing stock in the press, sued then sacked following a tribunal. His head sank into his hands and he wept openly in the solitary confines of the immediate and darkened four walls.

After thirty minutes of purgatory, he became aware of a presence in the room. He looked up to find Melissa trying to get his attention with a polite cough.

'We've just received an official complaint from the Thai Ambassador, sir,' Melissa said. 'He would like you to go to the Embassy tomorrow at eleven in the morning to give your explanation. Superintendent Vaughan has said you're to go.'

Magee nodded.

'The Super would like a word with you before you go home.'

He nodded again.

'So would the Home Secretary,' Melissa added. 'Judging by the tone of his voice, I reckon the Ambassador lodged a complaint about Polgeowit's treatment.'

'All right, Melissa. I'll see to it,' Magee responded in total defeat.

'I'll be on my way then, sir,' Melissa said quietly, turning to go.

'Sure. It's been nice knowing you, Melissa. I hope this doesn't screw up your career as well.'

'You'll be back, sir.' Melissa's response sounded unconvincing.

Magee sat for another half hour deep in thought. In other countries, he reflected, he would have been up against the wall already. Lucky for some, he thought; a bullet would be an easy way out. Eventually, he got up. It was time to face the music.

Within the hour, Superintendent Vaughan had confiscated his warrant card and ordered him to take gardening leave whilst an investigation into Polgeowit's complaint was undertaken. The Home Secretary was downright rude to him, implying that he was unlikely ever to see a penny of his pension thanks to the political embarrassment the government was likely to suffer. Finally, on his way out of the station, he was mauled by a horde of reporters who had been briefed by Polgeowit's solicitor.

By the time Magee reached home, he was an emotional wreck. By bedtime, he was drunk and near-suicidal.

Chapter Nineteen

Magee hesitated before he pressed the buzzer on the front door of the Royal Thai Embassy in Queensgate, London. A stomach churning feeling had hit him hard. He was way out of his depth. The hangover he had didn't help matters either.

The door opened. A security guard beckoned Magee inside and directed him towards a plush red leather chair. He sat fidgeting for what seemed like an hour before anyone returned. Finally, a courteous assistant put him out of his misery.

'His Excellency will see you now, Chief Inspector.'

Magee followed the assistant, feeling as though he was walking to his execution. He felt lightheaded, his mind seemingly detached from his body. Sweat broke out on his forehead as he stepped into the Ambassador's study and looked around at the magnificent opulence; oak panelling, deep pile red carpets, walls adorned with portraits of the Royal Thai Family. He gripped his briefcase nervously as he walked the full length of the room and stood like a guilty schoolboy in front of the Ambassador's enormous desk.

'Chief Inspector,' the serious looking but youthful Ambassador said, rising to greet Magee. 'Thank you for coming. Please sit down.'

'Thank you, sir,' Magee replied. The stern look of the Ambassador unnerved him. 'Forgive me, sir, but I'm not sure whether I should call you Mr Ambassador or Your Excellency.'

'My staff call me Mr Ambassador, Chief Inspector. I believe that would be an appropriate form of address.'

'Thank you, sir.'

The Fourth Cart I

'Very well. Now then, Chief Inspector. I believe you have some explaining to do concerning an assault on my dear friend Somchai Polgeowit.'

'Yes, sir, indeed. It was a most unfortunate incident. It is my understanding that an officer may have been a little over zealous in restraining Mr Polgeowit. I understand he fell awkwardly, hit his head against a wall on the way down. I take full responsibility for the matter, of course. However, I would like to inform you of the events leading up to his arrest that may explain our anxiety in handling him.'

'I would welcome such enlightenment, Chief Inspector. Please, at your own pace.'

Magee's nerves settled as he briefed the Ambassador on the murders of Todd Conners, Mike Harwood and Robert Harrison, and the sequence of events that had led to the arrest of Somchai Polgeowit. The Ambassador seemed to listen intently. Pleasing as it was, it wasn't quite the reaction he'd expected. He'd come prepared to receive a dressing down instead. When he'd finished, he sat patiently waiting for the Ambassador to respond.

'So it wasn't you, yourself, who caused my friend Somchai's wound?'

'Certainly not, sir. My Superintendent will be investigating the alleged offense. If any officer is found to have deliberately assaulted Mr Polgeowit, then that officer will be duly dealt with.'

'What punishment would he expect?'

'He would face a disciplinary charge. He may be reprimanded or thrown out of his job; it all depends on the facts and circumstances. It would certainly blight his career, if he continues in the Constabulary that is.'

'I see. Not unlike your own predicament, I expect?'

Magee sighed quietly. 'That is quite correct, sir. Last night, I was ordered to take gardening leave, whilst my Superintendent conducts an investigation. Someone else has taken over the case.'

'Someone as good as you, I hope, Chief Inspector?'

Magee fleetingly thought of Inspector Jackson. A man he detested for being pompous. A man who had sneered at him the day a younger man was promoted above Magee; a man who had last night openly laughed at Magee's woes. 'I'd rather not comment on that, sir.'

'Would you be reinstated on the case if all the charges of negligence, assault and wrongful arrest were dropped?'

Magee blinked. 'I beg your pardon, sir. I'm not sure if I understand you.'

'If my friend Somchai dropped all charges, would you get the case back?'

Magee was shocked. The question seemed to have been asked quite seriously. 'If Mr Polgeowit dropped his charges, then it would certainly help my predicament, sir. But it would not necessarily mean I would be given the case back.'

'So how could that be achieved, Chief Inspector?'

'Well, Inspector Jackson, the man who has taken over from me, would have to make a huge mistake, similar to my own. Then the position of senior investigating officer would probably be vacant again. Inspector Jackson would not be taken off the case just because I was cleared of charges, or if they were dropped. But all this talk is hypothetical, sir,' Magee replied, completely baffled. 'I'm not sure I understand your interest in the case.'

The Ambassador rubbed his chin before asking, 'Do you know much about Thai politics, Chief Inspector?'

'No, sir. I can't say I do. Thailand doesn't feature that often in our newspapers, or on television.'

'Unless there's been a natural disaster, or a murder of an British tourist?'

Magee gave a curt smile. 'Exactly, sir. We are a bit like that, aren't we? I know it's no consolation, but we're the same with most other countries as well.'

'It is normal, Chief Inspector. I imagine the majority of Thai people couldn't pinpoint this obscure little island on an atlas.'

'The media makes us ignorant, sir.'

'Indeed it does. However, if you would bear with me a minute, I hope to make you understand my position.'

'Certainly, sir.'

'Back in February, we had a military coup. It wasn't the first in our country; we tend to have coups like you have elections. Do you have any idea who caused it though?'

'No, sir. No idea at all. I had no idea it had even happened.'

'It was caused by the actions of one of your major telecommunication companies.'

'I beg your pardon, sir?'

'The company won a contract to modernize our telephone system. The job was worth billions of baht, but to win such a contract in my country, Chief Inspector, a certain amount of persuasion has to be undertaken. In this case over fifty million pounds was, erm, invested, shall we say, to secure the contract, if you catch my drift.'

'It doesn't surprise me, sir. I've found most big businesses operate like that, even in this country.'

'Indeed that's true. Regrettably though, in this case, disaster struck. The Prime Minister decided to share the money with just a few close friends. That was a mistake. A gross mistake, since normally such money would be shared by hundreds, as it trickled down from the top of government departments. As you can imagine, there were a large number of dissatisfied politicians and bureaucrats. The Prime Minister had been too greedy, you see, and it caused his downfall. In the end, there was little choice, the army stepped in and installed a temporary government. The first thing the temporary Prime Minister did was to cancel the telephone contract. The whole thing was a mess, Chief Inspector. It was a case of foreign interference damaging our national security. That's something that happens far too often.'

'I'm sorry to hear that, sir,' Magee interjected. 'However, I'm not sure that I follow your train of thought.'

'Please bear with me, Chief Inspector, all will become clear in a minute. You see, the people of my country want democracy. They do not want the army stepping in to seize control, even if it is done with good intentions. We've been promised free elections next year, on the anniversary of the temporary Prime Minister's appointment. But, Chief Inspector, there is a faction in the army that has tasted power, and have learned how easy it is to obtain. I fear that the so-called free elections may not produce the result we would hope for. If, for instance, the army manipulated themselves into a position of power, then the people's desire for a fair democracy may well lead to civil unrest. And if that happened, then my country would need all the international friends it can muster. We've been down this road before, Chief Inspector, I can see it coming quite clearly.'

'I can follow that, sir, but . . .'

'But, Chief Inspector, at the moment, there is a maniac running around this country murdering innocent people. From what you say, there appears to be a high probability that the killer is a Thai national. Also, there's the matter of last night's television broadcasts. It was particularly disingenuous of the solicitor Somchai is using to berate the British police force for racial stereotyping and racial hatred. No one likes a smart lawyer, especially one who turns on the establishment in defence of a foreign criminal.'

Magee cringed. The Ambassador had hit the nail on the head, yet he couldn't bring himself to openly agree. 'That's very perceptive of you, sir.'

'So, Chief Inspector, if these murders continue, unsolved, then I believe the British public may well turn against my country. In that situation, any Thai man is a potential murderer. It is a common reaction, as I'm sure you're aware. A whole nation can easily become xenophobic overnight. Thai residents are likely to be treated coldly by their neighbours. Thai restaurants may be boycotted, maybe bricks thrown through windows, that sort of thing. I'm sure you get the picture.'

'Yes, sir, I'm afraid I do.'

'If my worst fears materialize,' the Ambassador continued, 'then my country may well have to turn to the rest of the world for support in the near future. Britain is a wealthy and influential country and we currently enjoy a cordial diplomatic relationship. In a crisis, we would hope to count on your government's support. But if the British people have turned against us because of this murderer, then . . . well, I'm sure you understand political spin, Chief Inspector. Your government might be disinclined to help.'

'I see where you're coming from, sir, but how do I fit into this?'

'Cooperation, Chief Inspector. I'm prepared to have a quiet word with my old friend Somchai. I will explain to him that pursuing a complaint against the police could be politically embarrassing for our home country. I believe I can calm him down, although I may well have to offer other inducements. Anyway, in getting him to drop his action it would remove a thorn, a small thorn admittedly, from the Anglo-Thai diplomatic relationship.'

Magee couldn't believe his ears. 'That is extremely gracious of you, sir.'

'It will, of course, cause me a lot of grief to get Somchai to drop his lawsuit. In return, therefore, I would like to ask a favour of you. I am familiar with your expression concerning "back scratching", you understand?'

'Yes, sir. Anything I can do, I'll do happily,' Magee offered, not knowing what he could possibly do for an Ambassador.

'I believe you to be a good police officer, Chief Inspector. If this murderer is indeed a Thai, then I am extremely concerned and I am keen for the matter to be resolved quickly and efficiently. I have no wish for the good name of my country to be diminished in the eyes of the British public. But if a Thai man is involved, then he must be apprehended. Thailand has had a dream image for many years now. The Land of Smiles is a well-known description of Thailand and I want that image restored quickly. You can help me achieve that by catching this murderer and bringing him to swift justice. That will enable the British public to get over the incident and sleep soundly again. I offer any assistance you would like from my office. It will have to be kept unofficial of course, but I shall be pleased to speak to you any time you wish. I shall endeavour to obtain any information you request.'

'That is most kind, sir.'

'But in return, I would like to be kept informed on every aspect of the case as it progresses.'

'I see no problem with that, sir, provided this is kept unofficial.'

The Ambassador nodded, and smiled. 'Perhaps I can even be of help in putting forward suggestions of my own, from a Thai perspective, as it were. Whatever piece of evidence you have, I want to know about it. I wish to hear all your theories and all your suspicions. This man must be stopped. He is causing my country severe embarrassment.'

'Sir, I'm dumbfounded. I'm honoured by your offer and would gladly accept, but you've forgotten one small matter. I'm no longer on the case. You should really speak about this with Inspector Jackson, not me.'

The Ambassador grunted. 'My dear Chief Inspector, you do not look the type of man to be defeated so easily. Where is your enthusiasm? Your drive? Your devotion to duty? Are you just going to sit back and take all the abuse from those above you? Think of your career, your pension, your wife and family. Do you not want to get your position back and get rid of this incompetent Inspector Jackson?'

'Yes, of course I do. But how, sir?'

'Fight, Magee! Fight from the sidelines. Nothing is impossible if you put your mind to it. Believe me, if you want something desperately it is within your own power. Look at me, I'm one of the richest men in my country. But there was a time when I had nothing, absolutely nothing. I fought hard for my success. So should you.'

A pep talk was just what Magee been needed. 'You know something, sir, I believe you're right.'

'I am indeed. Now then,' the Ambassador said, as a devious look appeared on his face. 'That briefcase of yours is bulging, I was wondering what was in it.'

Magee returned a conspiratorial look. 'As it happens, sir, I made photocopies of a few relevant reports before I left the office last night. Perhaps you would care to have a look?'

'I am not doing anything until lunchtime. I'd be delighted.'

Magee spread his notes over the Ambassador's desk and the two men poured over the evidence and discussed theories for well over an hour. Eventually, the Ambassador concurred with Magee's own theory of revenge attacks; it was the most logical conclusion to reach.

'So,' the Ambassador said at length. 'What do you propose to do in the next few days?'

'Wait at home, sir. Until summoned that is. I have to attend a hearing next week. I'm supposed to stay at home until then.'

'And what will you do at home?'

'Well, I had intended to reread everything. Maybe I've missed something important. It often helps to start at the beginning and go along another track. It's a bit like working through a maze.'

The Ambassador sat in contemplation for a few seconds drumming his fingers on his desk. 'Let's stick with your assumption that the three victims . . . four victims, if you include this Keith Gibson, were all in Bangkok at the same time, some eighteen years ago, and were part of a team of criminals. You need to identify the rest of the men, correct?'

'Indeed I do, sir. But I don't see how I could possibly do that. As I said, I reckon Nick Price is up to his neck in this, but he doesn't seem willing to help.'

'Then you'll just have to focus on the victims.'

'I've been trying to do that, sir.'

'Assume they knew each other, those are your own words, Chief Inspector. So, how would they know each other? Work? Business? On holiday? In the same military unit, perhaps? There must be a limited number of situations for people to come together in a foreign country. After all, they have no history there, no family, no school, no village community. Where do you see them coming together?'

'I hadn't thought, sir.' Magee pondered the issue. It wasn't something he'd actually thought about yet. 'I don't know your country well at all. How do you think a group of Englishmen would get to know each other?'

'I would imagine they socialized together. Maybe they stayed at the same hotel or were simply regulars at the same bar. That would be a common occurrence.'

'That sounds logical, sir. I understand Nick Price ran a bar there. But how does it help?'

'It may help channel your efforts. We're talking about a group of young men, in their early twenties, in Bangkok. What would you have been doing in those circumstances?'

Magee shrugged his shoulders, baffled by the question.

'When you were that age, away from home, did you not write to your mother to let her know you were safe? Did you not send her photographs of exciting places you'd visited, of new friends? Did you not try to shock her with descriptions of your daring exploits?'

Magee chuckled at the memory of youthful antics away from home on scout camps. 'I certainly did that, sir.'

'Right, Chief Inspector. Now, what did your mother do with those mementos?'

Magee sighed. 'Of course! She put the photos I gave her into the family album.'

'Exactly. And you know where to look, potentially, for four such albums. Hopefully, you may find some photos or letters of interest. Something that could link them to other potential victims, or perhaps to suggestions about what heist they were involved in. That should give you something to work on during the next few days.'

'You know something, sir? You've just made such an obvious point, but we missed it. You weren't in the police before your appointment to London, we're you?'

124

The Ambassador shook his head and said, 'Not at all, Chief Inspector. But I did tell you I might be able to help, didn't I? It's always a good idea to get another perspective on an issue, especially one involving other cultures. We have a deal then? Your cooperation for mine?' The Ambassador extended his hand.

'Yes, sir. We do.'

'Strictly between the two of us, though, no one else involved. That way, we can each take the credit for the eventual outcome without anyone being the wiser.'

'Agreed, sir. My word on it.' Magee shook hands firmly with the Ambassador.

Magee left the Embassy head held high and a spring in his step. He had been given a stay of execution. He had been made to feel like a human being again. He had his pride back and he was going to put up one hell of a fight.

Chapter Twenty

Back home from London, Magee found himself aimlessly drifting around his sitting room, inches behind his wife who was vacuuming the carpet.

'For Heavens sake, Jack! Whatever's come over you?' Jenny asked, displeased at the unwanted attention she was getting. 'You've been in a very odd mood this afternoon.'

'I'm on gardening leave, love,' Magee replied. 'I feel relaxed and I just want to enjoy the rest of the day.'

'Well, get out of my way! It's worse than having the kids around my feet. What's got into you, for heaven's sake?'

Magee shrugged in response and continued shadowing his wife. Inwardly, he was still very much on a high. 'Will you be cleaning upstairs soon . . . in the bedroom?'

'Of course I will. What . . .?'

Magee looked at his wife suggestively, eyeing the lounge door.

'Stop that, Jack, it's putting me off my work.'

'The kids are out,' Magee said with a wicked gleam in his eye. 'They won't be home until six at the earliest. We've got a whole hour of uninterrupted freedom.'

Jenny stopped the vacuum cleaner and stared her husband squarely in the eye. 'Are you joking, Jack?'

'No, not at all. It's just that I've nothing to do.'

'Well I have.'

Magee pulled a face and murmured like a lecherous old man. It was part of a silly game they hadn't played for years.

Jenny broke into a laugh. 'No, don't make that noise, Jack!'

Magee grabbed his wife's buttocks and whispered into her ear. She turned and ran upstairs giggling, shouting at him to stop his antics.

By the time Magee reached the top of the stairs, he was seriously aroused, whilst his wife was almost hysterical with laughter. He gently pushed her onto their bed and slowly took his clothes off, whistling "The Stripper", leaving his socks on until last. That was always guaranteed to get a laugh, he knew. For the first time in nearly a decade, Magee made love as though he was still a teenager.

Afterwards, he lingered in bed cuddling his wife for as long as possible, knowing that the moment would soon be over.

Jenny turned to her husband, a pink tinge on her cheeks. 'What will the neighbours think, Jack? They must have been able to hear everything through the walls.'

'Sod them! They can provide their own amusement. Damn! There goes the front door.'

Carolyn, their daughter, had slammed the front door. She shouted at the top of her voice, 'Mum! I'm starving! Jane's Mum gave us macaroni cheese for lunch.'

Magee looked into Jenny's eyes and chuckled. 'How on earth did we finish up with more than one?'

'Quick, Jack, get dressed. We don't want to be caught. Carolyn will be disgusted with us!'

Magee threw himself at the pile of clothes on the floor in a panic and frantically dressed, a task made almost impossible due to a tide of hysterical giggles rising from his stomach. 'You look like a teenager caught in the act,' he said on seeing his wife fumbling with her bra strap.

Jenny tutted in her husband's direction. 'This is the last time you come near me while I'm cleaning, Jack.'

'I was only trying to give you a hand.'

'Well, keep your hands to yourself next time! Now look, you've . . . you've . . .' Jenny burst out in laughter. 'Well just look at yourself!'

Magee turned to face the mirror and guffawed at the sight of himself with his Y-fronts on the wrong way around. He turned around to catch sight of his bum as he'd never seen it before. 'Rather fetching, don't you think?'

'Oh, for heavens sake, Jack,' Jenny said in a fit of giggles. 'Never again! Do you hear me?' She gave her hair the briefest of swipes with a hairbrush and stumbled downstairs to feed Carolyn's hungry stomach.

Magee stayed upstairs for a while and sat at his wife's dressing table staring at his reflection. Well, he might have a couple of grey hairs at the edges, he reflected, but at least he wasn't past it. He hadn't performed like that in years. Perhaps he should have more holidays to perk him up, he thought. But then he felt a low coming on, as he realized from his reflection that his face was gradually turning into his father's.

Chapter Twenty-One

The warming rays of the sun fell across Magee's face as he lay in bed, blissfully content, day-dreaming sweet nothings. He could tell, instinctively, that his wife was fussing around the bedroom, but, for once in his life, rebellious thoughts kept him from stirring.

'Are you going to lie there all day?' Jenny asked. 'It's well past eight. You've never slept in so late in your life. It's a lovely day, what about going for a run, since you've got time on your hands?'

Magee knew he wouldn't be allowed to get away with such selfish behavior, especially on a Monday morning. 'I might go later. Meantime, it's wonderful just lying right here, doing nothing. It must have been all that fresh air and exercise, walking up Kingston Ridge with the kids yesterday. We really must do it more often.'

'You mean you must do it more often, Jack. You're the one that needs to get more involved with them. It won't be long now before their childhoods have gone forever.'

'I know,' Magee sighed. 'But what can I do? Get a new job?'

'Maybe, not that I'm suggesting it, mind you. Your work is what you love, I know that. But perhaps you should take it a little easier, like you are at the moment.'

'That would be nice. I'll work on that idea.'

'In the meantime, are you coming down for breakfast?'

'Yep, I've got a few important things to clear up today.'

Thirty minutes later, as Magee was finishing his second cup of tea at the kitchen table, the telephone rang. He tried to ignore the obtrusive sound, leaving Jenny to answer it.

'It's Melissa for you, Jack,' she called out.

Reluctantly, Magee rose from the table and sauntered into the hallway to take the call. 'Hello?'

A low, discreet voice said, 'How's your holiday, sir?'

'Wonderful, Melissa, absolutely bloody wonderful.'

'Really? That's good, though surprising. I thought you'd be at your wits end by now. Anyway, I just thought you'd like to know that you're missed here. No joking, honest to god, sir. The whole office will be signing a petition for your reinstatement at this rate. Jackson is being a real jerk. A real pain in the proverbial. He had us in all weekend going over the case. There was nothing to be learned, of course, it was all done just to please him and to prove he has authority over us. I suppose he doesn't want anyone accusing him of taking it easy, but honestly, sir, your good nature is sorely missed.'

'That bad is he?'

'He's that bad, sir.' Melissa paused momentarily before continuing, 'You're sounding chirpy. I feared you'd be depressed.'

'Far from it, I can tell you. To be honest, I'm glad I've had the break; it's been really enlightening. I'll be back soon, you can count on that, but don't tell anyone I said so. I haven't stopped fighting yet.'

'Good for you, sir'

'I need some support though.'

'You've got it, sir. Just name it.'

'Well, for now, I need names and addresses of the victims' relatives. I copied large sections of the reports before I left, but I didn't think relatives' addresses would be important.'

'And they are important?'

'Maybe, Melissa, maybe. I can't say at the moment.'

'You cunning old sod! You're up to something aren't you?'

'Maybe.'

'Don't tell me you're going it alone?'

'Hmm, I'd better not answer that. But I'm not taking this lying down, I'll have you know.'

'You crafty old fox! What have you got?'

'Best I don't tell you. Not if you're serious about seeing me back.'

'Sure. I understand. Give me ten minutes. I'll phone you back.'

'I'm at home until you call.'

'Right. Whoops, must go. Jackson's on the prowl,' Melissa cut off the call abruptly.

Two hours later, armed with nothing more than a hastily scribbled note, Magee found himself standing outside Cherry Tree Cottage, a quaint flint faced house halfway up The Street in Kingston, a village on the outskirts of Lewes. An elderly woman opened the door.

'Yes? Can I help you?'

'Excuse me, Mrs Gibson. I'm Detective Chief Inspector Jack Magee. You telephoned me last Friday afternoon, about the unpleasant package you received.'

'Oh yes?'

'I'm sorry about this, Mrs Gibson. I really don't wish to cause you any more distress, but there are a few points I need to clear up with you. I was wondering whether you could spare me a few minutes. If it's convenient, that is.' Magee prayed she wouldn't ask to see a warrant card.

'Yes, of course, Chief Inspector. Do please come in. Would you like a cup of tea? The kettle has only just boiled.'

Magee knew all about little old ladies whose kettle had just boiled. 'I would love a cup, thank you.'

'Follow me then, Chief Inspector. My, my, I've never met a Chief Inspector before. Isn't this exciting?'

Magee followed the old lady through to her kitchen, playing right into her hands.

'You have a lovely house, Mrs Gibson. And it's so spacious. I live on the Neville Estate. It's a bit crowded up there. I've only ever dreamt of living in a house like this. I know my wife would love to live in this village, we come over to the Juggs Arms quite often, and walk up the Ridge, but the house prices here are a little bit beyond our means.'

'Oh yes, Chief Inspector. I well understand. But then Keith bought this house a long time ago. It was large enough for Keith and ourselves to live in without getting on top of each other. My husband died twenty years ago, and Keith spent most of his time overseas, especially during winter. But he would stay here for the summer though, and help with the garden. It really is too big for just me on my own now, but I don't have the energy to move.'

'Where did Keith go overseas?'

'Well, Tibet was the country he loved most, but he hadn't been there for a very long time. India, he enjoyed. And Thailand, lots of temples to explore there. He loved studying ancient religious cultures. He was a very educated man.'

Magee waited patiently as Mrs Gibson fussed about in her kitchen.

'Now then, will you take the tray into the lounge for me, Chief Inspector? Please sit down on the sofa, make yourself comfy.'

And so Magee spent an hour listening to Mrs Gibson recount her memories. She was in a league of her own when it came to small talk about her son. She was so proud of him. Keith had accomplished such a lot in his life. He had been kind and generous and thoroughly devoted to his dear old mother. However, like so many young people, he'd gone off the rails at some stage in his life and resorted to drugs for comfort. That had been the eventual cause of his death.

As Magee had hoped, it wasn't long before the family photo albums came out. The pages turned slowly and another cup of tea was made. At one o'clock Mrs Gibson insisted on making Magee some sandwiches, arguing that he was a working man and needed his sustenance.

After lunch, Magee managed to get the old lady's attention focused on the period that Keith had been abroad. She remembered it well, Keith having sent back hundreds of photos and letters of his travels, as well as segments for his doctoral thesis whilst at university.

At length, Magee said, 'I'm particularly interested in the period that Keith was in Thailand. Would it be possible to have a look at photos from that time?'

'Of course, Chief Inspector. Oh! Just a second, where are they now? Oh, yes, Keith got very emotional one day when he discovered that I'd kept things from his past. He threw everything out, said I was silly keeping old rubbish. Most unlike him it was. Still, I rescued it all from the bin and hid it in a box. I didn't want to lose those precious memories.'

'I understand,' Magee responded in sympathy.

'Now then, where is that box? Oh, I suppose it must be up in the attic. Would you mind getting it down for me? It's a bit difficult for me to get up there these days.'

'Yes, of course. No problem. I'm sorry to inconvenience you so much.' Magee followed Mrs Gibson up the stairs. He stood staring at the attic hatch for a few moments, his stomach in knots, and offered a short silent prayer to any deity that was able to influence his fate.

He drew in a deep breath, lowered the hatch, maneuvered down a set of ladders and climbed up into the black void.

'There's a light switch to your left, Chief Inspector. Down on the floor.'

'Got it!' Magee called down as the attic lit up.

'Look for an old cardboard box,' Mrs Gibson called up. 'Over in the corner to your right, I think. Sorry about the dirt and cobwebs.'

'There's a large Co-op supermarket box here, with red ribbons around it,' Magee called down.

'That's it,' Mrs Gibson replied. 'Bring it down will you. I'll keep it downstairs now. No need for it to stay up there.'

Magee switched off the light and put the ladders back up before carrying the box downstairs to the kitchen where Mrs Gibson had laid out sheets of newspaper on a table. He laid the box down, taking the greatest of care with the historical treasure trove.

'Clean your hands over there, Chief Inspector, I'll just wipe the box down.'

At the sink, Magee turned to watch Mrs Gibson. He grinned with satisfaction, his plan so far working a treat. He bit his lip, desperately hoping that Keith's mementos included information vital to the case.

'You can use the towel on the radiator, Chief Inspector. That's right, the blue one. Now then, will you get a knife out of the drawer by the sink, please?'

Magee did as instructed.

'That's it, a nice sharp one. Thank you.'

The box was opened, the ribbon being cut with all the ceremony of a time-honoured ritual. Magee stood quite still, feigning patience, leaving Mrs Gibson to pull out various objects for which only she knew the history.

'His first Teddy bear, Chief Inspector. I can still remember him as a baby. He was so cute then. Do you have children?'

'Two. Carolyn is eight years old. Jason is five.'

Mrs Gibson sighed. 'Cherish their childhoods, Chief Inspector. It goes so fast. Soon you'll only be left with vague memories.'

Magee wasn't sure how to respond. The glaze in Mrs Gibson's eye told a sad story. He decided it was best not to intrude.

A dozen or so childhood ornaments came out of the box and then a stack of airmail letters, written by a loving son to a worried mother thousands of miles away. She pulled out a pile of papers, looked at them and said, 'No. These are about Tibet. He was there during the fifties, you know, he even got to meet the Dalai Lama. He was passionate about studying Tibetan culture.'

Magee asked, 'When did he go to Thailand?'

Mrs Gibson put the pile of papers down on the kitchen table and said, 'Let's see now. He was in India briefly in nineteen sixty nine. I remember that well because he'd disappeared for the ten years prior to that. It was a very distressing time for us. I thought he'd met an untimely death. It took me years and years of correspondence with the Foreign Office before eventually discovering he was still alive. Can you imagine ten years without as much as a postcard? It was heartbreaking.'

Magee frowned as he tried to place that piece of information in the right slot in his mind. 'But he'd been all right during that time?'

'Oh no. Not at all. Those barbaric Chinese soldiers that took control of Tibet in nineteen fifty-nine had put him in prison. He suffered terribly at their hands. They tortured him, starved him, made him do backbreaking manual work. It was awful for him. Ten years in prison nearly killed him.'

'But he got out okay?'

'Oh yes, eventually. He said it was my persistent campaign with the authorities that eventually got his case noticed.'

'So Keith left Tibet, went to India and then moved to Thailand?'

'Yes, indeed he did.'

Mrs Gibson delved back into the box, withdrew several more stacks of papers and spread them over her kitchen table. Magee picked up each one in turn and examined the contents. Most were academic works, predominantly research on Tibetan religion and culture. One pile of papers, though, caught his eye. It looked very different to the others. He thumbed through the pages, reading odd passages, noting the scribbled penciled remarks in the margins.

'This appears to be a manuscript for a book, Mrs Gibson. It's titled The Fourth Cart. Was Keith writing a novel?'

'He was indeed.'

'Is it an autobiography or fiction?'

Mrs Gibson frowned. 'I'm not sure, Chief Inspector. It was the last thing Keith worked on before his accident. I remember him spending hours every day shut in his room, the persistent clackety-clack of his old typewriter. I do remember him saying it was a story that needed to be told.'

'How so?'

'Keith had a lot to get off his chest. He was involved in something very bad out in the Far East, I'm sure of that. I can only assume he needed to explain to the world his version of events.'

'It's not fiction then?'

'I really couldn't say. I've never read it. I haven't the heart. To be honest, I don't actually want to know what it says.'

'Did Keith ever get it published, or approach a publisher?'

'No, I don't think he even finished it. I remember he got more and more emotional as the days went on, typing it. I tried to get him to stop. I tried to make him see sense, that it was doing him more harm than good. One day, he just ran out of the house, crying. It was the last time I saw him alive.'

Magee fell silent for a few moments out of respect, before asking, 'May I borrow it?'

Mrs Gibson snuffled into a handkerchief and replied, 'By all means.'

'I'm sorry if this is upsetting you, Mrs Gibson.'

'That's quite alright. I know you have to do these things. Take it with my blessing, but I'd rather not know what it contains, if you don't mind.'

'Thank you.'

'Now then,' Mrs Gibson said as she peered into the depths of the box. 'We've nearly finished. Just this left.'

The last thing to come out of the box was a photo album. Magee's heart gave a jump. His expectation leaped to such a new high he could barely resist the urge to grab it.

They sat down with the album opened on the kitchen table in front of them. Magee let Mrs Gibson turn over the pages in her own good time, each page at an agonizingly slow pace. But he knew there was no point rushing her, especially now that he had come so far. He patiently let her talk through Keith's life in picture, whilst he desperately scanned the notes that had been tenderly written alongside each photo.

Mrs Gibson halted on one page in particular, a picture of Keith with a young Thai woman on a beach. 'I had hopes for him, when he sent this photograph. He wrote saying that he'd never felt so happy in his life.'

'Did he marry her?'

'No, he didn't. It was such a shame, really. I would have loved to have had grandchildren. And I think Keith would have been a better man for it.'

'How long did Keith stay in Thailand?'

'About four years. He seemed to have settled down to a life of sorts, but then it all ended so abruptly.'

Magee was just about to ask why, when Mrs Gibson turned to the last page of the album. The photo on that page took him by surprise. Most of the others had been of Keith visiting temples or picturesque sites in the country. This one, though, was different. Very different. It showed ten men and one woman, in two rows, the back row leaning against a bar, the front row squatting on the floor. All, except one, were young. All were cheering, arms around each other's necks and holding up beer cans. All were dressed roughly, many in army khaki. And the bar, he thought, lined by mirrors, looked the seediest he'd ever come across.

Magee pointed to the photo and said, 'Do you know where this was taken?'

Mrs Gibson lifted the photo out of the album, turned it over and read aloud the slogan scrawled by Keith eighteen years ago. 'March nineteen seventy-three, the lads at Lucy's Tiger Den on Silom Road.'

'Is that in Bangkok?'

'I assume so.' She looked closely. 'A pretty rough looking bunch aren't they, Chief Inspector? They were his friends though, or so he said.'

Magee's attention was caught by what was written below the caption. 'Are those their names?'

Mrs Gibson replied, 'I suppose they must be,' and read out 'Todd, Mike, Robert, Me, Ronnie, Des, Jeff, Sean, John, Mal and Nick.'

Bells seemed to ring in Magee's head. 'May I take a closer look?'

'Of course,' Mrs Gibson said, handing over the photo.

Magee read the first three names again. Todd, Mike, Robert. Were these Todd Conners, Mike Harwood and Robert Harrison, he wondered? He flipped the photo over and took a close look at the faces. He nodded as he took in the face of the lad sitting in the bottom right hand corner. It was an all too familiar face; Nick Price. There was no mistaking his features. He'd found what he'd come for. He let out a deep sigh.

'It was the last photo Keith ever sent,' Mrs Gibson said. 'It came within a large parcel of personal mementos, and I believe he had decided to come back at that stage. He returned a few weeks later.'

'Unexpectedly?'

'Yes, that's right.'

'What happened?'

'I'm not really sure. Over the years, Keith's letters had described all sorts of adventures he and his friends had been up to. Some of them were quite outrageous, I'm sure he shouldn't have told me. Still, you know what boys are like. I expect he was deliberately trying to shock his mother. But by the end, something bad had happened, I do know that. You see, he changed inside. Something in him had died, I believe. He never did tell me what, but it was around that same time.'

Magee's eyes misted up in the emotion of the moment. He stared down into the smiling faces of mere boys. Four of them were now dead, of that he was sure. Three of them had died in the last fortnight alone. Oh, you silly, silly boys, he thought. What did you do? What went wrong? Was it so bad that you deserve to die now?

Briefly, Magee thought back to his own youth and of the capers that he had got up to with his pals. The photo could easily have been of him and his old police cadet classmates. He knew all about youthful enthusiasm and what risks lads took seeking adventure. He found himself turning aside to brush away a tear that was running down the side of his face.

Magee's reaction to the photo sent Mrs Gibson into a flood of tears. She reached into a pocket for a handkerchief and said, 'Yes, Chief Inspector. It takes me like that as well when I think about it.'

Magee coughed a couple of times to hide his embarrassment and tried to regain control of his emotions. 'Do you know the surnames of these lads by any chance, Mrs Gibson, or their addresses?'

'Not really. Keith mentioned just their Christian names in his letters, certainly no more information than that. I'm not sure whether he knew them anyway. I remember him saying that the company he kept preferred anonymity. Just part of the games boys play, I suppose.'

'Did he write after sending this photo?'

'No. It was the last I heard from him while he was away. The next thing we knew he was telephoning from Heathrow saying that he was back. It was quite a shock. He'd been away for the best part of twenty years. I didn't expect him back just like that, without any notice. His previous letters certainly gave no hint at all about coming back. I assumed something must have happened to upset him, but he dismissed the notion. He said he just got bored one day and jumped on the next airplane. He wouldn't talk about it after that. Very strange, it was, I remember. He was on edge for months. Years even.'

'Mrs Gibson, I'm going to ask you a tremendous favour. This photo is extremely important to me. Would you trust me to borrow it for an hour or so? I want to take it into a photographic shop in Lewes and get it copied.'

'It's that important is it, Chief Inspector?'

'Yes, Mrs Gibson. It's seriously important.'

'It's to do with those recent murders, isn't it? I've been following the cases in the newspaper, so I know of your involvement. That horrible note implied Keith would have been the fourth victim. You think this photo will link them together, don't you? You think someone's murdering them for revenge, isn't that what you're here to see me about?'

Magee didn't want to reply, but was caught out by Mrs Gibson's perceptiveness. He nodded in response. She may have been nearly eighty-three years old, he thought, but she was no one's fool.

'I don't want to know what happened, Chief Inspector. Keith is dead, I can't bring him back, but I can preserve his memory. I always knew something dreadful must have happened in Bangkok. Call it a mother's intuition, if you like. For months after his return, I could see fear in his eyes along with a nervous shifty look, as though he expected someone to creep up on him. He had the look of a haunted man for a long time. He got mixed up in something terrible; I've always known that. I'm not naïve; one doesn't come into a fortune overnight by honest means. Copy the photograph, Chief Inspector, find his friends and save them if you can.'

Magee pulled his chair closer to the crying woman and put his arm around her. She turned and cried hysterically into his shoulder.

'I'm sorry, Chief Inspector. I prayed the truth would never come out. Will you promise me one thing, though? Promise me you'll keep the story out of the newspapers. I don't want my son labeled a criminal by the press. Having a dead son brings sympathy, but having a criminal in the family would be too much for me to bear.'

'I just pray it won't come to that, Mrs Gibson,' Magee responded. 'But I can't promise that the details won't come out. For all I know, one of the others might speak to the press. If it's not relevant, then there's no reason for it to come out. However, I can promise you that the story won't come from my lips, and I promise I won't mention it to anyone else.'

Mrs Gibson snuffled. 'Thank you, Chief Inspector.'

Magee took hold of the photo and studied it more closely. All of the men, except one, must have been in their late teens or early twenties. The odd one out, Keith, looked much older and had a haggard face rather than a youthful one. Magee's eyes rested on one of the other men.

Magee exclaimed, 'God good, it's Paul Mansell!'

Mrs Gibson looked perplexed. 'I'm sorry, Chief Inspector?'

'This lad, down the bottom at the front. It's Paul Mansell.'

'Paul? I don't remember there being a Paul in his letters, Chief Inspector.'

'No,' Magee replied. 'You're quite right, Mrs Gibson. I'm wrong, the Paul I know would have been too young at the time this was taken. So who is he?'

'What name does it say on the back?'

'John,' Magee replied having flipped the photo over. Was this Paul's missing elder brother, Magee wondered? If it was, then Paul Mansell's involvement in the murders may not be innocent after all. He couldn't believe what he was staring at. At last, he had evidence that showed Nick Price and Paul Mansell were connected to the recent victims. He stood up and said, 'If you'll excuse me, I must move on this fast. Are you sure it's alright to borrow it?'

'Take the photo with my blessing Chief Inspector. I just hope you can use it to save someone's life.'

'I'll be back within the hour, Mrs Gibson.' On his way out of Cherry Tree Cottage, photograph in hand, Magee's mind worked furiously on the countless possibilities of where it might fit in.

Chapter Twenty-Two

Magee pressed the bell on Paul Mansell's front door, stood back and braced himself for the possibility of a fierce argument.

As the door opened, Magee politely said, 'Good afternoon, Paul. I was just passing. I wondered whether I may have a chat?'

Paul Mansell crossed his arms and said, 'You don't just happen to pass through this road, Magee. It goes nowhere. Is this visit official? I thought I heard somewhere that you'd been thrown off the case?'

'My, my, news does travel fast, doesn't it? But yes, it's true. I have been taken off the case.'

'Good! In that case, you can piss off!'

'Fair comment,' but Magee wasn't going to be put off easily. 'Look, if you're guilty of being involved in these murders then I can understand you not wanting to talk to me. But if you're innocent then I'm sure you'd be interested in helping to solve the case. After all, you told me about the hotel job, or was that simply another trick to get the police looking in the wrong direction?'

'What the hell? You still think I'm involved?' Paul sighed deeply. 'Jesus, Magee, you're a real pain.'

'Well, look at it from my point of view. You might have been trying to help, or you might have been playing games with me.'

Paul looked confused. 'Why? How? Look, I keep telling you that I'm not involved.'

'Well I beg to differ, as I've said before.'

'That's your problem, Magee, not mine.' Paul paused, frowned and added, 'Anyway, what makes you think I can help with your case? I've already told you everything I know.'

'Not yet, you haven't.'

'Magee, you're beginning to bug me. I swear to god that I have nothing more to tell you. I've been implicated in two murders and it would have been three had I not decided to cancel all my current work and cooperate with you.'

'You still haven't answered the question, why is the murderer using you?'

'I've told you already, I haven't a clue!'

'Well I have.'

Paul looked stunned. 'What? What do you mean?'

'A photograph. Something tangible that links you to three murders.'

'Bollocks, Magee! You've got no such thing.'

'Want a bet?'

'Show me then!'

'Okay, if you insist. Can we go inside though?'

'Sure. Come in.'

Magee stepped inside the flat, followed Paul into the sitting room and made himself comfortable in an armchair before withdrawing from his pocket a reprint of the photograph he'd obtained from Mrs Gibson. 'I'm sure you'll be able to identify some of the people in there.'

'Yeah, like hell.' Paul took the photograph out of Magee's hand, looked down at it and gasped in shock, 'That's John!'

'Your brother I take it?'

'Yes.'

'Where is he now?'

'I've told you before, Magee, I have no idea. He left home when I was young and never came back. Jesus, that's Nick next to him!'

'Anyone else you recognize?'

'This one's got to be Sean. Sean Fitzpatrick.'

'You know him?'

'Not that well, but I talk to him occasionally when he's around. He works for Nick sometimes. He's a strange one though. He grew up with Nick, lived in the same street, they worked together when they were young. He's always bragging how he'd been a millionaire once but spent it all on fast living. Sean reckons he had three wives in ten years and each one took him to the cleaners.'

'Where does he live?'

'Not sure. Nick told me he's being going through a bad patch these last few years. He's served time I think, for assault on one of his wives. These days he dosses around Brighton, wherever he can find a bed. Nick sets him up with a bit of work now and then. I don't think Nick really wants to, but I guess he feels sorry for him.'

'Does Nick ever talk about his time in Bangkok?'

'Bangkok?'

'That's where this photo was taken, I believe.'

'No. No, he doesn't. He doesn't like anyone to mention the subject.'

'Does he ever talk about where he got his money from? Originally, that is.'

'No way! That's not the sort of question you ask Nick. What's with this photo anyway?'

'I'm pretty sure that Todd Conners, Mike Harwood and Robert Harrison, the three victims so far, are in it. Then there's a Keith Gibson, he's in there too. He died a while ago, but I've got evidence to suggest he would have been victim number four. I've got to get positive identification of the rest because I think they did something bad out in Bangkok, and someone is now out for revenge. This might even be the murderer's death list, for all I know. If it is, then Nick and your brother are on it. Hence, there is a real connection to you. So, will you cooperate with me or not?'

'Shit!' Paul closed his eyes for a few seconds and rubbed his brow. 'Okay, Magee. You win. I'm convinced.'

'Thank you, Paul.'

'How can I help?'

'Tell me about John. I need to know about him and his relationship with Nick, and how you fit in.'

'Jesus, Magee. That's heavy stuff, a real emotional roller-coaster. I'm not sure I want to go there.'

'Please, Paul, it's important. It might help save John's life. And Nick's of course.'

'Well, I'll try, but bear with me, Magee. I may be coming on for twenty-five this month, but it hurts like hell thinking about my childhood and John in particular.'

'That's exactly what I need to know about, Paul.'

Paul Mansell settled back on his sofa and closed his eyes briefly before starting. 'I was happy as a kid, Magee, but only up to the age of about three. You see, I idolized John. He was my big brother, fourteen years older than me. One day something terrible happened, I've never been able to work out what it was. I just know my parents blamed me for it. I have these vague memories of my parents shouting at John and pointing accusingly at me. God knows what it was about. I remember John packing a rucksack. Dad took all the money out of his pocket and threw it on the floor at John's feet. John said goodbye to me from a distance, as he opened the garden gate. I was screaming and being held back by my father. I just knew John was going away, never to come back, but I've never known why.' He paused to wipe the tears flowing down his face.

'I'm so sorry, Paul,' Magee said calmly, 'I had no idea.'

'From that moment on,' Paul continued as the tears continued, 'my parents were never quite the same again. They were cold towards me, dad never cuddled me. He always looked at me in an off-hand way. My life was shattered. I'd been abandoned by John and rejected by my parents. Whatever I'd done, it must have been terrible to be punished so much.'

'Maybe it wasn't you.'

Paul wiped away at the tears. 'Oh, it was me all right. I know that for sure. My parents never let me doubt it. So, I grew up with an enormous guilt complex, feeling responsible for John's departure and my parent's neglect. I suppose that's why I started behaving badly. I had a thoroughly disturbed childhood, I regularly played truant from school and mixed with the wrong crowd. By the age of ten, I'd been lured into vandalism and petty theft. By the age of fourteen I was quite a well-known hooligan around the Arnos Grove area. It's not something I'm proud of, Magee.'

'But you broke the mould?'

'Yeah, thanks to Nick.'

'Nick Price, your saviour. Remind me, just how did that happen?'

'It was my sixteenth birthday. I'd woken up in the morning to find that my parents hadn't bothered buying me a present. They just wished me a happy birthday and said that now I was grown up I shouldn't need childish comforts like having presents to unwrap. I took that rather badly. I guess that was the one thing that I did need.

It was the final straw, positive proof that my parents didn't give a damn about me. I left the house after breakfast with no intention of going to school whatsoever. I spent the day kicking my heels with my unsavory friends, boasting that I was going to do some serious damage that evening.'

'And you did, judging from your records.'

'Too right, I did. I didn't return home that night, I was caught red-handed in the middle of a local department store smashing everything in sight. The police must have thought they had a lunatic on their hands, I was crying, screaming, hurling abuse and throwing around everything I could pick up.'

'Were you drunk?'

'No. Just angry. I didn't do drink or drugs.'

'Where does Nick fit in?'

'Apparently, Nick had come looking for me at my parents' house that day. He told them he wanted to invite me over for a chat and to offer me a job should I need one. Dad was impressed by Nick and was pleased that someone wished to give me a job, so he took Nick's telephone number. Next day, Dad phoned Nick to say that I'd spent the night in a police cell and was in really serious trouble.'

'And he came to your rescue?'

Paul choked, 'Yeah, he certainly did that. He came to see me at the station with a classy lawyer, then left to sort out the storeowner. Three hours later I was out.'

'Out? What, you mean in the clear?'

'Nick said the owner of the department store wasn't going to press charges.'

'Any idea how much damage you caused?'

'Erm, no, an awful lot, I should think.'

'And Nick paid for those damages?'

'Yeah, I guess he did.'

'Why?'

'He told me he owed John a favour.'

'It must have been an extraordinarily large favour.'

'Nick said he owed his life to John.'

'What about the charges?'

'All charges were dropped. Well, I received a strong caution.'

'Just a caution?' Magee murmured. 'How the hell did Nick swing that one?'

'He said he had friends in high places. Friends that could fix things like that.'

'That doesn't surprise me. So, you came out of the police station indebted to Nick?'

'Well, yes and no. I left the police station in tears of joy to find a Bentley waiting for me. I was driven all the way down to Brighton, shown straight into a gymnasium where Nick was working out. He made me put on a pair of boxing gloves, then he beat the shit out of me for the next half an hour.'

'Hah!' Magee said, broke into a smile. 'Now that's something I approve of.'

'It did the trick. From that moment on, we were friends. I worked for Nick, I lived in his house. I guess he became both the father and elder brother I'd been deprived of for so long.'

'You were close?'

'Yeah, real close.'

'And all this because of John?'

'Guess so. Nick tolerated my problems, tried to sort me out. He did sort me out. Well, in the main, I guess.'

'But not quite?'

'Some matters have never been satisfactorily resolved. Like where the hell is John, and why did he abandon me.'

'No clues?'

'Only that Nick and John had known each other in Bangkok for a few years, that they'd run a bar together, that they'd had a happy time. Guess this photo shows that.'

'Ever wanted to find John? To ask him what happened?'

'Yes . . . no . . . I don't know, Magee. I'm confused about that issue. I've been to Bangkok many times, as I told you. I've made a few half-hearted attempts to locate John, but something inside seems to hold me back, as though it doesn't want to face the reality of what happened.'

Magee sat in sadness. 'You know Paul, I figured you wrong. You really need to sort that problem out; you'll never settle into a normal life until you do.'

'Yeah, I know that, Magee, but where do I start? I don't want to screw up my friendship with Nick by digging too deep. He doesn't like that, you know, being questioned about what he refers to as his bad old days. On the other hand, I could really screw things up even more for myself if I did find John and he told me what really happened to make him leave.'

'I need to talk to Nick about this photo.' Magee looked at his watch. 'It's not six yet. Will you come with me, if I go now? Maybe we can clear some of this up together?'

'Sure. It's time I faced the music, I guess. Just a second, I'll get my jacket. I'll follow you in my own car.'

Chapter Twenty-Three

'Are you sure this is okay, Paul,' Magee asked as they mounted the short flight of steps to the front door of Nick Price's mansion. 'I'm quite happy to press the bell and ask for permission to come in.'

'Nah, don't worry. I've got the code,' Paul responded. 'Anyway, this place is like an open house. There must be twenty-odd staff coming and going during the day. Nick operates his entire business from the east wing. There are fifty rooms here, Magee, they all get used. One more face won't go amiss.'

'Sure? It's just that I'm not keen on the idea of arriving unannounced,' Magee mumbled. 'Things got a bit heated last time I was here.'

'Nick will be sweet as pie, trust me. He wouldn't dare cause a scene with Nittaya around.'

'No?'

'No, Nick adores Nit. God, she can twist him around her finger. He's putty in her hands.'

'I've met her already, but not Somsuk. What's he like?'

'He's the son every father would hope for. Handsome, athletic, intelligent. And a really nice person. Right then,' Paul said as the door opened, 'are you ready to do battle?'

'I've no choice. You'll give me some support I hope.'

'You bet. I'm just as interested in this as you are.'

Paul held the door to the inner hall open for Magee. 'Hi, Annie,' he said to a passing maid. 'Is Nick home?'

'Yes, Mr Paul. He's in the lounge.'

The Fourth Cart I

'This way,' Paul said to Magee, crossing the galleried hall. He opened the door to the room Magee had been in before. 'Hi, Nick!'

'Hey! Paul, good to see you.'

Magee walked in behind Paul. 'Afternoon, Mr Price.'

'Jesus Christ! What the hell are you doing here, Magee?' Nick rose from his chair as if to engage in a challenge.

Paul stepped in quick. 'I invited him here, Nick.'

'You invited him? You invited a copper, into my home? Bloody hell, Paul. I hope you've got a good reason.'

'I have, Nick. Bear with us will you?'

Nick looked over towards Nittaya who was sitting on the sofa reading a book. She glared back; be polite her eyes seemed to demand.

Nick Price appeared to relax a little. 'Well, Magee, this is a surprise, I must say. I thought you'd been thrown out of your job.'

'I'm officially off the case, if that's what you mean.'

'Meaning what? That you're working unofficially on the case?'

'Correct.'

'And you're here to pursue the case?'

'Correct.'

'I've told you I don't know anything about it.'

'You did. You lied.'

Nick's jaw dropped. 'Are you calling me a liar, Magee? In my own house?'

'Yes. You knew the three recent murder victims; Todd Conners, Mike Harwood and Robert Harrison. Then there's Keith Gibson as well, he was to have been the fourth victim.'

Nick's eyebrows screwed up tightly. 'What the hell are you talking about?'

Magee could sense Nick Price's discomfort. 'You knew all the victims in Bangkok, at the bar you ran with Paul's brother, John. Lucy's Tiger Den wasn't it?'

'You have proof of this?'

'Yep. I certainly do. Oh yes, one other thing, Mr Price, I know who the next six victims are going to be.' Magee took a moment to enjoy the shocked reaction he could see on Nick's face. 'Just as you do.'

Nick Price was well and truly speechless. Magee took advantage of the situation, caught Paul's attention and gave him a discrete nod.

'Magee has found something interesting, Nick. It needs an explanation. I need an explanation. It involves John.'

Magee brought out the photo from his jacket pocket and passed it over.

Nick hissed. 'Shit!' He stared at it for a few seconds then handed it back to Magee.

'Shit indeed, Mr Price. You're in it up to your neck, aren't you?'

'Where did you get that photo, Magee?'

'Keith Gibson's mother kept it as a memento. She let me make a copy of it.'

'Well, bully for you, Magee. But so what?'

'I want to know the story behind it. No bullshit,' Magee demanded. 'Just the plain honest truth.'

'Story, Magee? What story would that be?'

'The story about how the ten of you pulled off some big job in Bangkok. It must have been a pretty big heist. Conners, Harwood, Harrison, Gibson and yourself all seem to have become millionaires as a result.'

'I don't know where you got that information, Magee, but it's way off the mark. There was no heist in Bangkok, as you put it.'

'Really? I always did wonder where your money came from to establish your property empire. Don't tell me you just found the money?'

'As a matter of fact, Magee, we did just that.'

'Bollocks! You don't expect me to believe that do you.'

'That's up to you Magee, but it's true nonetheless. Anyway, what does it matter how we got our money?'

'Oh, it matters a lot. Believe me.'

'Go on then, explain.'

'I'm working on the theory that the ten of you were involved in some heist. It was successful, but something went wrong. Maybe not everyone got away. Maybe someone didn't get their fair share. Maybe someone got caught, thrown in jail. Whatever went wrong, eighteen years later, someone's out of jail and seeking revenge,' Magee paused to savour the look of distress registering on Nick Price's face.

'It wasn't like that, Magee.'

'How was it then? What other reason is there for someone to seek revenge?'

Nick Price hung his head as though in exasperation. 'Why do you keep saying revenge?'

'The murder weapons, the daggers, they're related to a culture of revenge.'

'Bollocks, Magee. I don't buy that. There's no one involved that could be seeking revenge.'

'Oh come on, what other motive is there? Eighteen years on, it's obvious someone is out for revenge. Did you cut someone out of a share? Did you abandon someone out there, let them take the rap?'

'No!'

'Eighteen years is a nice hefty prison sentence, is that why John Mansell never came back?'

'What? No!' Nick snapped.

'Is John Mansell free now and wreaking havoc? Is that why you took pity on Paul here when he was younger? Were you suffering from a guilty conscience over John being stitched up?'

'No!' Nick shouted.

'I've read Paul's criminal record,' Magee continued. 'It must have cost you a hell of a lot, and not only in terms of cash, to get Paul released with just a caution. Don't tell me you took pity on a poor young boy because you saw yourself in him. That's bullshit! You paid dearly for Paul's freedom. It must have hurt you, don't tell me it wasn't because you were stricken with guilt over dumping John in some shitty Thai prison!'

Paul stirred uneasily and glared menacingly at Nick.

'You're out of order, Magee!' Nick shouted, his face contorted in pain. He turned to Paul. 'I promise you that last bit is not true. John has been as free as the rest of us these last eighteen years. It was his personal decision to stay in Bangkok.'

'But he never came back, Nick,' Paul interjected. 'He never even tried to contact me! Why not? If he's been free all these years then surely he would have sent one letter at least? A prison sentence makes sense to me, Nick.'

'It's not what happened!'

Paul had tears in his eyes. 'Then talk about it, I beg you!'

'Paul, listen to me. The reason John never came back has nothing to do with this photo. There were other reasons. Personal reasons. The same reasons that caused him to flee there in the first place.

You'll have to ask John yourself. I'm sorry, but that's the way it is. I promised John I'd never talk about it.'

'But . . .'

'No "buts" Paul. I was closer to John than I am to you. Would you expect me to break a promise if I made it with you?'

Paul briefly lowered his head and stared at the carpet. He reluctantly shook his head.

'Right! Thank you. As for looking after you, Paul, I've told you this before, I owe my life to John. Seriously! I'd have been dead if John hadn't put himself in physical danger to rescue me. I was that close to death,' Nick said gesturing with his thumb and index finger the narrowness of his escape from the jaws of death. 'John saved me from a situation that still makes me wake up in the middle of the night in a cold sweat, as you well know. Every time it happens, I'm reminded of John. I owed him one. When we last spoke, just before I left Thailand, he asked me to look you up sometime, send you a birthday card, that sort of thing. He'd given me your parents address in Arnos Grove and your date of birth. It took me a long time to make contact, I know, but I eventually came searching for you on your sixteenth because of a particularly bad night with that recurring nightmare. I thought it was about time I saw how my old mate's kid brother was doing. Admittedly, I saved you from a nasty situation, but it was incomparable to the risk that John took in saving my life. It was the least I could do to fork out fifty grand for your life.'

Paul looked startled. 'Fifty grand?'

'Yes, Paul,' Nick spat out. 'Twenty five grand to pay off the storeowner and another twenty five grand as a bung to Inspector Stallard who . . . Oh, fuck, you didn't hear that Magee.'

Magee was stunned. 'You bribed a police officer?'

'Yes, Magee, I bloody well did. He was known for being bent. But don't bother trying to pursue it. Stallard got his comeuppance years ago, he got far too greedy for his own health. Anyway, he got his money's worth and some. He insisted that I found out who'd pulled off a bank raid in my old manor the previous month. You know what I think of grassing people up Paul, well I did it. It really got my goat. I exposed myself to blackmail by Stallard, but I did it for you Paul, as a payback for John. That's how much I owed him, that's how much I cared for him. So please, both of you, don't you dare insult me by suggesting I stitched up John.'

The room went silent for a while. Nittaya crossed the room to put her arms around her father.

'Shit, Magee!' Nick cursed, 'you've upset all of us now.'

'I had to ask. I'm sorry.'

'Yeah? Well, you've asked. Is that it now?'

'I need to know what happened in Bangkok.'

'I'm not prepared to discuss it. It's history. It's no longer relevant. Okay?'

'I disagree, Mr Price. I think it's very relevant. Couldn't you at least point me in the right direction? I'm convinced that someone connected to this photo is the killer. I need to understand why the killer has been using Paul. Maybe he's got something against John; hence he's taking it out on his brother. Paul's not off the hook yet, so if you have any feeling for him then help him out and that means helping me.'

'Nick, please! I'm being set up. Maybe I'm on this death list as well.'

Nick looked at Paul's pleading eyes. 'Fuck it!' he swore, sighing deeply. 'Okay, okay, Magee. But only what I deem relevant.'

'Thank you. You did pull off a job, right?'

'No, we did not. We simply found something that had been hidden years beforehand. That's the truth.'

'If the money came from abroad, then it's no concern of the British police. We have no interest in it. Okay?'

Nick Price gave a nod in response.

'Did you all come back?'

'John stayed, the rest came back.'

'Why did he stay?'

'I've answered that already. Personal reasons. The lifestyle suited him out there. He would have been frustrated back in England. His bad habits might have got him into trouble with the police here.'

'You all got equal shares?' Magee continued.

'To the penny.'

'But it took several months to clear, didn't it? Todd Conners didn't have a penny on his return. It wasn't until later that year that his fortune started mounting up. Was John the banker? Is that why he stayed?'

'One reason, yes.'

Magee stabbed a finger at the photo. 'Anyone else involved other than this lot?'

Nick paused for a moment, biting his lip and lowering his eyelids. 'No one that's relevant, Magee.'

'What about a fence? For the, well, for whatever it was you say you found.'

'Anyone else involved, as you put it, received fair commissions. There were no complaints over percentages.'

'So there were others involved, then? Are you sure they were all paid fairly? No one got fitted up?'

Nick sighed. 'The others are no longer relevant, Magee, let's leave it at that.'

'On the contrary, Mr Price,' Magee persisted, 'I think the others are exactly where the relevancy lies.'

'The dead can't walk,' Nick whispered, tears welling in his eyes.

Magee tried to work out what lay behind the slip. Did he mean the others had died since, or what, he wondered? 'Who is the woman in the photo?'

Nick lowered his head and took a firmer grip on his daughter's arms. 'Mal,' he said choking back tears. 'My wife.'

'Let me see that, Chief Inspector,' Nittaya demanded.

'Nit, please, leave it,' Nick pleaded as a fresh wave of tears cascaded down his cheeks.

'No, Daddy, I want to look. I don't have enough photos of Mum as it is.'

Magee handed the photo over reluctantly. Nittaya took it gingerly, as though a treasured object. She stared at it for a full minute, taking in the faces, the surrounding bar, as though trying desperately to remember those times.

Nick wiped his face with his hand and said, 'Nit, really, you were far too young.'

'When was this taken, Daddy?'

'It was taken at your mother's twenty-first birthday party.'

A door behind them shut with an unexpected bang. 'What's that you've got?' The question was asked by a handsome looking young man as he entered the room.

'A photograph taken at Mum's twenty-first birthday party,' Nit replied. 'I haven't seen it before.'

The Fourth Cart I

'Magee, this is my son, Somsuk,' Nick butted in. 'Som, this is Detective Chief Inspector Magee. He's trying to piece together the recent murders.'

'I've heard about you, Chief Inspector. But how does this involve us?'

'I don't know exactly, I'm trying to work that out.'

Somsuk took the photograph from his sister, stared at it for a few seconds and nodded his head. 'Where was I, Dad?'

'In bed I expect, it was past midnight when that photo was taken, and you weren't yet two years old.'

'You left us on our own?' Somsuk enquired.

'Course not! You always had someone looking after you. You were a real pain at times, Som, always determined to run off exploring at the slightest opportunity. If Mum or I weren't around you'd have Ay or Jook dancing attendance.'

'Who are they?' Magee asked.

'Ay was the maid, babysitter.'

'And the other one you mentioned?'

Nick didn't respond. He just bit his lip as more tears ran down his face.

'Jook was my mother's twin brother, Chief Inspector.'

Magee turned to Nick price and demanded, 'And where is he?'

Nick did not to respond. He turned to brush away the tears from his cheeks.

Somsuk replied, 'He is dead as well, Chief Inspector.'

'I'm sorry,' Magee said to Somsuk. 'I really didn't intend to intrude upon your family's grief.'

'That's all right, Chief Inspector,' Somsuk replied. 'Nittaya and I were only babies when the accident happened. Sadly, I can only recall the merest glimmer of a memory of my mother and uncle. It is my father who still mourns. As you can see, he has never got over the death of our mother.'

'Mr Price . . . Nick . . . look, I'm so sorry for this intrusion, but someone from your past has come back to haunt you. I think the killer is a Thai national. How would that fit in?'

'It doesn't, Magee,' Nick responded, breaking his silence. 'What makes you think it did?'

'A security guard caught sight of the killer in Hove. He said it was a "Chink", to use his precise words.' Magee caught Nittaya's eyes. 'Sorry for the offensive language.'

'A Chink?' Nick asked with a startle, as though a light had switched on somewhere in his head. 'You mean a Chinese?'

'Not necessarily,' Magee replied. 'Why, does a Chinese person fit in to the equation?'

'Maybe, Magee. Maybe.'

'How?'

'There were several Chinese soldiers involved.'

'And they could harbour a grudge?'

'One received a fair share of the proceeds, the others, well, they're no longer relevant either.'

'Dead?'

'Mostly, I expect.'

'Oh, Jesus,' Magee exclaimed. 'This is a real can of worms. How many Chinese soldiers were involved as you put it?'

'I . . . I really can't say. Far too many to count.'

Magee's eyes widened. 'Pardon?'

'We're talking half the bloody Chinese Army for god's sake,' Nick spluttered. 'And yes, some of them probably did have a grudge. In fact some definitely did have grudges.'

'Their names?'

'Haven't a bloody clue! Our paths only crossed for a few hours. We were under intense stress, introductions weren't called for.'

Magee hesitated a moment to gather his thoughts. 'Nick, look, the reaction I've had from the victims' families is that none of you lot ever wanted to be reminded of Thailand again. Someone has a grudge against you and your friends, so you must have done something to upset someone. Whoever it was, I believe that person is someone you know; someone you may even think is dead or out of the picture. Anyway, I believe that person is here, in England, right now, and intent on revenge. Whoever he is, he's extremely clever and very resourceful. And he'll soon be after you. Now, who the hell could it be?'

Nick sat down on a sofa with a dazed look on his face and ran his hands through his hair. 'Shit, Magee. You certainly know how to rattle someone. But this is all just speculation, isn't it? You have no real evidence to go on, do you?'

'No. None at all I suppose. It's mere conjecture, I admit. But your reaction proves it all for me. Now then,' Magee said as he approached Nick, with the photo held out, 'who are these others? I need to find them and warn them, if nothing else.'

Nick pointed to the men in the photo. 'That's Todd Conners, Mike Harwood, Robert Harrison and Keith Gibson. John and myself are down here.'

'And the others?'

'No way!'

'Paul said he thought one of them was Sean Fitzpatrick.'

Nick winced. 'Whose side are you on, Paul?'

'Sorry, Nick. Magee caught me unawares.'

'Oh, never mind. Yes, that's Sean Fitzpatrick down there. That's it, Magee.'

Magee was perplexed. 'Why ever not?'

'They wouldn't thank me, Magee.'

'For saving their lives? Are you kidding me?'

'No, Magee. I'm not kidding you. Sorry, but no ball. If they want to, they'll identify themselves to you. But I'm not getting involved for anything. Well, not at this stage anyway. Maybe if things get really bad, then okay. Until then, well, I'm sorry. No deal, and that's final.'

Magee didn't quite know what to say. He had met a brick wall, just as he thought he'd got his man to open up. He handed over a card and said, 'If you change your mind, here's my phone number, okay? Maybe you could do with police protection some time.'

'I can protect myself, thanks. And my family, which includes Paul.'

'If you decide to help the others, I'll keep it off the record. The others won't know you told me. Do you really want more deaths on your conscience?'

Nick shrugged his shoulders, pulled a grimace then slowly turned in the direction of the bay window, pausing for a few seconds before replying in a whisper. 'It's the risk one takes in life, Magee. The price of sin, perhaps?'

Magee didn't like that comment; it was far too close for comfort. He was just about to speak again, when he realized that Nick's eyes had misted over and were staring vacantly into the distance.

Nittaya dabbed a tissue against beads of sweat that were breaking out on her father's forehead. 'Daddy! Daddy! Are you okay?'

'Yeah, sorry, Nit,' Nick replied. 'You know what I'm like when I get reminded of the past.'

'Chief Inspector,' Nittaya said in a firm tone. 'My father is sick. Please, enough questions.'

'You're right, I'm sorry. Thank you for your time.'

'Magee, just a second, I'll see you out.'

Magee walked with Nick to the front door in silence. He stepped outside and waited for Nick to unload whatever was on his mind.

'Magee, look. Whatever's happening, it's personal, between me and the others in the photo. Leave it to us, we'll deal with it.'

'You sound as though you know who it is.'

'No, I don't. Seriously, I can't fathom it out. It doesn't make any sense to me. Look, I know we don't see eye to eye on things, and I'm still really pissed at you, but can we do a deal here?'

'Such as?'

'Information. Let me know what happens your end. Give me a chance to sort it out.'

'Why should I do that?'

'Because some of the others involved are . . . how can I say this . . . a bit too heavy.'

'You mean they've got more clout than you?'

'Yeah, I wouldn't want to piss them off. Nor would you, if you knew who they were. You'll have to trust me on that.'

'You fear them?'

Nick reflected for a few seconds before saying, 'I wouldn't want to tangle with them, Magee. They could outmaneuver me easily.'

'Really?'

'Yeah, really. There are few men I fear, Magee, but I do fear organizations. Especially those with resources.'

'You're being cryptic.'

'Yeah, I am. Sorry, but it's for your own good.'

Magee thought for a moment. 'You know something? Ever since I started in the police, I've despised you and what you stand for. I know it's irrational. Yet the strange thing is, the more I get to see of you, the less I dislike you.'

'Is that supposed to be a compliment, Magee?'

Magee smiled a little. 'I guess it is. You've got two smashing kids. You can't be all bad to have them turn out like that. You're also carrying a lot of guilt, aren't you? About your wife, I mean. You must have loved her deeply.'

Nick simply nodded his head.

'You're no longer the monster I remember from the sixties. You've turned into a human being, haven't you?'

'I always was, Magee, you just didn't see it before. Yeah, I admit I was a bit of a thug in my teens, but I like to think I've moved on. My life was hell until I met my wife, she sorted me out.'

'She was like Nittaya?'

Nick grinned. 'Yeah, just like Nittaya.'

'I'll give your request some thought. Just one thing though.'

Nick looked expectantly.

'Would you be offended if I called you by your first name? I'd prefer that, with your family around.'

Nick held his hand out. 'See you, Magee. Watch your back.'

'I will.'

Chapter Twenty-Four

Nick Price glanced at the alarm clock on his bedside cabinet. It was well past midnight, and he'd had no sleep yet. Magee's visit had been far too unsettling. He got out of bed, slipped on a dressing gown and eased open his bedroom door. A few paces along the galleried landing and he was outside his most private of rooms. He eased himself in quietly and wandered around as if searching for a long lost item. He retrieved a suitcase from a wardrobe, placed it on the bed and opened it to reveal a pile of towels and sheets. Sheets from their bed. Sheets he'd slept in, with Maliwan curled lovingly in his arms. He slipped his hand underneath the towels and withdrew a stack of photographs.

He stood for a while conjuring up fond memories. At the bottom of the stack was a copy of the same photograph Magee had shown him earlier. It had been Mal's twenty-first birthday party. And he'd only been six months older himself. They'd all been so young. Too young, perhaps, to appreciate the madness, the sheer stupidity of believing they could get away with mounting a raid on Tibet. Why, oh why, had he ever believed in Keith Gibson's tale of buried treasure? So often, he'd heard that greed kills. It was a saying that had meant nothing to him. Not until he'd lost Mal. How could he have been so insane as to risk her life?

He propped up the photograph on a table, switched on a portable record player, set the controls to re-play automatically and settled down in an armchair. As the Righteous Brothers sang their rendition of Unchained Melody, his eyes misted over. Seconds later, on the chair opposite him, Maliwan appeared, looking serene as usual.

As the arm of the record player made its way back to the beginning, Nick stood and said, 'Care to dance?'

Maliwan's answer drifted into his mind. *Of course. Don't I always?*

Nick took his wife in his arms and gently glided around the room as the song played again.

'I've missed you Mal, so much.'

I'm here for you though, my love, every night. Just you and me, just our love, forever.

Nick burst into tears. If only he could hold her all day, not just these brief interludes during the evening. He wanted to walk hand-in-hand with her in the garden, to stroll through the bluebell woods in the springtime, to kick up wet rust coloured leaves in the autumn.

'Oh, Mal,' he cried, 'please stay with me. I need you so much.'

I know, my love, I know.

Chapter Twenty-Five

Magee placed a handkerchief over the telephone's mouthpiece, cleared his throat and spoke in a low tone, 'Melissa, is that you?'

'It is,' Melissa replied. 'And that phony voice wouldn't fool anyone.'

Magee coughed, and reverted to his normal voice. 'Sorry, I'm not very good at deceit.'

'How're things going?'

'Fine, thanks, but I need your help.'

'You've got it of course, sir, but I can't risk getting caught doing anything for you. Jackson would fire me on the spot, and I don't think even my uncle would help me out of that mess either. You're not exactly flavour of the month around here.'

'I understand. You'll have to do it covertly.'

'Covertly? Ooh! That sounds fun.'

'You're in a good mood.'

'Hmm, Jackson's off kissing ass somewhere. It's giving us a break. How can I help?'

'I need to know anything that happens, immediately.'

'That won't be so easy.'

'You'll manage.'

'How are you doing, with your own digging that is?'

'It's coming on fine, Melissa. Look, don't tell anyone this, but I've got a photograph showing all the remaining victims.'

'What! How?'

'Never mind that. The important thing is that the photo contains ten men, of which four are our known victims.'

'Four? But we only have three.'

'Keith Gibson would have been number four. He died a few years ago, but his mother was sent a wreath wrapped around one of our Avenging Buddha knives the other day. The message was pretty clear.'

'How nice.'

'Quite. Anyway. I've identified three of the remaining targets.'

'How did you do that?'

'Easy, I recognized two faces in the photo, Nick Price and someone who turned out to be Paul Mansell's older brother John. The third is an old school friend of Nick's, one Sean Fitzpatrick.'

'Nick?'

'Pardon?'

'You said "Nick". It's usually just "Price". What happened to the normal derogatory tone in which you spit out his name?'

Magee's nose twitched a fraction. 'I may have misjudged him. He's actually an okay sort of bloke, albeit a bit rough around the edges.'

'Dear god, I just saw a pig flying past the window!'

'Hah, hah!' Magee muttered. 'All right, I admit I may have been wrong about him in the past. Anyway, the point is, although he's on the hit list, he doesn't know why. He says it doesn't make sense to him. So, if it doesn't make sense to him, it probably won't be any easier for us. We've obviously got some hard work ahead. And, as you're finding out, Jackson isn't up to a challenge like that. He could only solve a case if clues jumped up and slapped him in the face.'

'We're certainly finding that out the hard way. He's got some pretty stupid theories.'

'Try not to let him bother you. Focus on facts, and let me have them as soon as you can.'

'You want me to join in with the conspiracy?'

'I do indeed. I'll catch up with you later. Bye for now.'

As Magee put the telephone receiver down, he reflected on DS Kelley's choice of words. Conspiracy was a very apt term. There was certainly a conspiracy amongst the victims. But why?

Chapter Twenty-Six

Ning prided himself on his boyish looks. Like so many other Thai men, his slender frame, smooth skin and hairless body confused farang into believing he was five years younger than his real age. And given that he was twenty-one, it meant he got a lot of attention from men of a certain persuasion. Which suited his chosen profession well.

He had ten minutes spare before his next customer. Time enough to prepare the massage table, towels, oils, tissues and assorted toys of pleasure. He checked his appearance in a full length mirror, posed, and practiced standing in a way that customers could get a sensual glimpse up his shorts. He hoped he'd judged the look right, for his ten o'clock appointment had promised a very large tip.

Being anxious for customers who may not like to linger outside his apartment block, Ning was ready waiting at the intercom when the bell rang. He released the outer door lock then opened his front door for the customer's swift and discrete entry.

He welcomed his customer with his normal camp greeting. 'Sawadi, ka.'

The customer stepped into Ning's apartment and replied, 'Good evening, Ning.' He then switched to Thai and said, 'We'll talk in Thai, I believe your English is limited.'

Ning shut the door, turned and found the customer striding around the flat, poking his nose into each room. It wasn't an unusual preliminary to a massage. He well understood that some customers had privacy issues, or might get edgy about the possibility of hidden cameras or concealed accomplices engaged in theft.

The customer returned from his search and asked, 'We are alone?'

'Yes, sir, of course.'

'Good.' The customer withdrew a gun from behind him, swung it around until it almost touched Ning's nose.

Ning reeled backwards and squealed, 'Ai!'

'Don't shout, Ning. I just want to talk. Understand?'

Ning stared at the gun in horror and replied, 'Yes, sir.'

'Good. Now, here's your hundred pound fee for the massage I booked and a little extra. Five thousand pounds, Ning. For your troubles.'

'Troubles, sir?'

'For the inconvenience you're about to experience.'

A wave of panic rose in Ning's chest. 'That's not necessary, sir,'

'No. No, I suppose it isn't,' the customer agreed. He raised his left hand and caressed Ning's face. 'My, my, you are a pretty boy, aren't you? Such fresh, youthful skin. A pity if it was scarred, don't you think?'

'Please, sir,' Ning cried. 'Don't hurt me.'

'I won't hurt you if you cooperate. But I will hurt you if you don't cooperate. Do you understand?'

'Yes, sir.'

'You see, violence is necessary at times, Ning. Believe me, I won't hesitate to slash your pretty face with a knife, or burn it with acid. Be a good boy, and it won't come to that.'

'I promise, sir.'

'Good. So, treat the money as a bonus. Now, put it away. Lock it in a drawer or something.'

Ning did as he was instructed.

'Good. Now then, it's a bit chilly outside. Get dressed, please. Put some warm clothing on. You'll catch your death out there in those skimpy shorts.'

'We're going out?'

'Don't worry. You'll come to no harm. Provided you do precisely as you're told, that is.'

Ning sobbed as he slipped on a pair of jeans. 'What do you want from me?'

'Just your cooperation. I want to take you to see an old friend of mine. Ronnie Nelson, you'll like him. He's a real dear.'

'Why?'

The customer seemed to think about the question for a few seconds, grinned broadly and said, 'It's a surprise for him, it's his birthday. You're his treat!'

'Then why the gun? I would go willingly.'

'Sorry, but that's the way it's got to be. It wouldn't be so much fun otherwise. My friend and I are both into S&M. I need to do this to get aroused.'

'Do you want rough sex as well?'

'No thanks. Only the preliminaries need to be like this. Now, shoes please.'

Ning did as he was ordered.

'Good. Now, turn around.'

Ning stood obediently as his hands were bound with thin nylon rope, and a strip of sticky tape stuck across his mouth. He was led out of the apartment to a nearby car, a black Daimler Sovereign, and pushed into the passenger seat. He sat trembling, trying to loosen the ropes around his wrists as the car drove from Kemp Town towards the Palace Pier.

'Don't you enjoy this game, Ning?'

Ning grunted in response.

'Oh, well, suit yourself. It won't be long now. It's only a short drive.'

Within ten minutes, the Daimler pulled into the driveway of a large detached house on the edge of Preston Park Avenue.

'Here we are, then, Ning. Time for fun.'

Ning was dragged out of the car and across the drive. The doorbell was rung and, just as the front door opened, Ning was violently thrust forward. He collided with the owner of the house, Ronnie Nelson, and the pair of them landed heavily on the hall floor.

As Ronnie Nelson struggled to free himself of Ning's body, he shouted, 'What the bloody hell is going on?'

The response was sharp. 'Shut up, Nelson. Get up. You too, Ning. Into the sitting room, quickly.'

Ning managed to right himself despite the bonds, and followed Ronnie Nelson into a neat and tidy room in which was prominently placed a bottle of champagne in a pail of ice cubes, a decanter of brandy lying on an adjacent table.

'I see you were expecting company.'

'Yes, I am,' Ronnie Nelson replied. 'And he'll be here any minute. With a police escort, I'll have you know.'

'You mean Geoff?'

'I beg your pardon?'

'The Right Honourable Geoffrey Rees Smith sends his apologies. He sent me instead.'

'What!'

'You heard me, Nelson. Your expected guest is not coming.'

'But . . .'

'But you're on your own.'

Ronnie Nelson rubbed his eyes and looked hard at the man pointing a gun in his direction. 'What is this? What do you want? Money?'

'I don't need your money, you little shit!'

Ronnie Nelson looked taken aback. 'So why are you here then?'

'You could start with an apology.'

'Fuck you!'

'You asked.'

'You'll never get away with this.'

'I have so far.'

'You'll get caught. You'll get life. They'll throw the key away.'

'I don't think so. No one suspects me.'

Ronnie Nelson nodded his head slowly. 'No, I don't suppose they do.'

'There you go, then.'

'So,' Ronnie Nelson said, as he edged his way towards the fireplace, 'Where've you been hiding this last eighteen years?'

'In Bangkok, mainly.'

Ronnie Nelson's eyes scanned his immediate surroundings. 'Been keeping busy?'

'I have actually. Perhaps you've followed the news out there?'

Ronnie Nelson shook his head.

'Shame. You'd be impressed at what I've achieved. I've built up quite a business empire.'

'Bully for you.'

'Your ignorance disappoints me, Nelson. Still, it's of no real consequence.'

Ronnie Nelson cleared his throat. 'Look, Nick would love to see you, I'm sure. Can I phone him? Let him know you're here?'

'I don't think so, do you?'

Ronnie Nelson's eyes seemed to have become fixated on a spot near the fireplace. 'So, what happens now?'

'Up to you, Nelson. But first, tell me one thing. I've waited a long time to ask you this question. That flight out of Tibet, did you plan the route or was it all just one god-forsaken fuck-up?'

Ronnie Nelson looked angry. 'We weren't able to plan, for Christ sake! There were no charts on board. I flew by the seat of my pants. It was just an unlucky decision to go that way.' In an apparent act of desperation, he made a grab for a fire poker but was intercepted and pushed into a glass display case which shattered on impact. As he tried to stand up, he was stabbed in the thigh. He screamed as blood spurted from the gaping wound. 'Please don't do this.' He tried to stem the flowing blood with his hand. 'It wasn't my fault, you know that!'

'You could have stopped the madness. You could have stopped Geoff. You're going to pay for that mistake.'

'No, please, I beg you. Don't!' A knife slashed at Ronnie Nelson's hands. 'For the love of god, don't do this!' Despite his pleas, the merciless attacks continued relentlessly until the room resembled a war zone. 'Enough,' he murmured, as he collapsed to the floor. 'I can't take any more.'

Ning had been cowering in a corner, doing his best to evade the flying debris. As he watched a jet of blood spurt from Nelson's slit throat, he let out a muffled scream.

'Ah, Ning, there you are. Thought I'd lost you for a moment.'

'Mmm!'

'Ning, look, I'm sorry about this. But this is where you start to earn your five thousand pounds. Don't worry, it won't hurt much.'

Ning was dragged off the floor, thrown on top of Nelson's body and rolled over so that his clothes would soak up the blood. The nylon bonds were cut loose and the gag removed. To his horror, he watched a metal case being withdrawn from the customer's jacket pocket.

'Hold your arm steady, Ning.'

Ning looked on in terror as a syringe was extracted from the case and dipped into a phial. 'Please, sir. Please don't do this!'

'This won't kill you, Ning. It will just send you to sleep. But I'm afraid you'll have a bad headache when you wake up. Still, at least you'll still be alive.'

Ning screamed. 'No!'

'Look, I don't want you to be found until the morning. A cleaner arrives about eight o'clock, she has a house key, okay? I need to get away from here, and I need to leave your body for the police to find.'

'But . . .'

'No "buts", Ning. You'll be questioned by the police, but they'll release you in a day or two. Once I kill the next one, the police will realize their mistake.'

'I don't believe you. You're going to kill me!'

'Ning, listen to me. Look into my eyes. I'm going to tell you something few people know about me.' He leaned forward and whispered into the boy's ear.

Ning's face froze in utter fear.

'I want you alive for a purpose, Ning. If you fulfill that purpose, you'll live. But if you betray me, I'll be back.'

Ning looked away.

'Ning, you will not fail me, you understand. Let me make it clear to you. Number 392, Soi 4, Sukhumvit 93. I know your family live at that address.'

Ning's eyes bulged.

'Now, even if I'm locked up in prison, I can get word out. Do you really want to be responsible for the deaths of your mother, father, your two brothers and young sister? They'll all die slowly and painfully, I promise you that. You believe me, don't you?'

'Yes, sir,' Ning sobbed.

'Good, so you'll cooperate?'

'I promise. On my family's life.'

'There you go. Good boy.'

'But the police will ask questions.'

'Of course they will. And I want you to tell them everything, just don't give them a clear description of me. Tell them I was wearing a mask. Tell them you were unconscious most of the time. Tell them you were too frightened to take much in. Make it up, Ning, the health of your family depends upon it.'

'I will try, sir.'

'Good. Now then, I want you to give a message to Detective Chief Inspector Jack Magee. Give it to Magee only. He will find you, give it to him then. Then and only then. No one else, do you understand?'

'Yes, sir.'

'Tell Magee "John Mansell is the key. Magee needs to find John Mansell." Now, repeat that in English.'

'John Mansell is the key,' Ning repeated in his best English. 'Magee needs to find John Mansell.'

'Good. And you'll give it to Chief Inspector Jack Magee only.'

'Yes, sir. Chief Inspector Jack Magee only.'

'Well done, Ning. Now, hold still.'

Ning wept as the needle was inserted into a vein. 'Please don't ...'

Chapter Twenty-Seven

Melissa groaned as she saw Inspector Jackson's car pull up outside Ronnie Nelson's house. 'Morning, sir,' she mumbled in his direction.

'Ah, Sergeant Kelly. You beat me to it,' Inspector Jackson said as he closed the car door. 'Everything under control?'

'Yes, sir.'

'What's the latest?'

'Well, the housekeeper is next door having a cup of tea and being comforted. She's in a terrible state. She hasn't stopped crying since she found the body about an hour and a half ago.'

'And where is the body?'

'In the sitting room, which has been completely trashed. SOCO are sifting through the wreckage at the moment.'

'And the killer?'

'He's in the hallway. He was unconscious when I arrived, knocked out in the fight presumably. SOCO have stripped him and bagged his clothes,' Melissa paused, thinking carefully about her next comment. 'I'm not sure he is the killer, sir.'

'What? Why ever not, Sergeant?'

'Some things don't add up.'

'Really? Well, we'll see about that.'

Melissa followed behind Inspector Jackson as he strode into Ronnie Nelson's house and gave an approving glance at the two constables keeping a watchful eye over their prisoner.

'Well done, lads,' Inspector Jackson said on passing.

Melissa rolled her eyes at the inane comment and nearly crashed into Inspector Jackson who had halted at the entrance to the sitting room.

'Dear god,' muttered Inspector Jackson.

Melissa watched Inspector Jackson's face with interest, as he looked around the room. The sitting room was a mess; furniture overturned, everything breakable lying in pieces, blood over the walls. It was clear to her that the man was uncomfortable. It even dawned on her that he may never have seen such carnage, especially since most of his career had been spent behind a desk. The thought worried her. 'Do you want me to lead this case, sir?'

'No, Sergeant, I can see clearly what's happened. The victim must have put up a brave fight. Mortally wounded, he manages to knock out his assailant before his lifeblood drains away. The man was a hero. And we have our murderer sitting out there in the hall.'

Melissa was incredulous. 'Yes, sir. Very neat.'

'That's it then; case solved. We'll just wait for SOCO to tie up the loose ends.'

'Of course, sir. Perhaps I should stay on a while and make sure sufficient evidence is gathered.'

'By all means, Sergeant. By the way, what's his name? The lad over there?'

'Ning, sir. So a business card in his wallet says.'

'Just Ning, no second name?'

'He's saying nothing, sir.'

Inspector Jackson turned his attention towards the masseur sitting under guard in the hall. 'Well, Ning,' Inspector Jackson said with a disapproving look. 'Got you now, haven't we, sonny?'

Ning looked up at Inspector Jackson with tears in his eyes. 'I not do this, sir.'

'Hah!' Inspector Jackson guffawed. 'I like that! Ever hopeful, eh? Caught in the act, at the scene of the crime, knife in hand, yet you boldly proclaim your innocence. Such a wonderful case of positive thinking! Hope to get a good lawyer do you, eh?'

'I not do this, sir. Please help me.'

'Did you hear that, Sergeant? The lad wants us to help him get off.'

'I'll try my best, sir.'

'Wonderful! There you go sonny, Sergeant Kelly will get you off.'

Melissa felt more than a pang of sympathy as Ning looked at her with his pleading eyes. She nodded her head ever so slightly at him.

'What amazing optimism! Well, Sergeant, I must be off to break the news to the reporters outside. By the way, where did they come from?'

'Oh, a neighbour works for one of the major national newspapers. The story broke before we arrived.'

'Ah well, I mustn't keep them waiting. There's a local television crew out there as well I noticed. Someone has to go and talk to them, I suppose.'

'Yes, sir. I suppose one must.'

'Right, well, I'll leave you in charge, Sergeant.'

Melissa stared at Inspector Jackson's back as he marched pompously out the door, head held high. What a prize prat, she thought. 'Now then, Ning; to work. Tell me, what happened here last night?'

'I not know,' Ning replied, sobbing.

'I can't help you, if you won't help me.'

'Please, miss, I not know.'

Melissa stood over Ning, looking down at the pathetic sight of the sobbing boy. Something was wrong, very wrong, with this scenario, she realized. This boy was weak; he didn't seem to possess the strength of character to commit a cold, calculated murder. And why was he still here? Why had he not run away? Something didn't add up, she could feel it. She also knew that Magee would spot it instantly. What was it he had told her to do? That was it; stand back and take a general view, work out the most logical sequence of action and make sure the facts fitted that action. Well, something along those lines anyway, she thought. 'All right, Ning, we'll do this the hard way.'

Melissa walked into the sitting room and stood still, carefully assembling the facts in her mind in an orderly fashion. She then checked every square inch of the room. She smiled as a flash of inspiration came to her, and went out to the Daimler.

Melissa found a SOCO team member dusting the dashboard. 'Have you checked the passenger seat?'

'Not yet, no.'

'I need you to check if there were two occupants.'

'Sure thing.'

Melissa went back indoors and squatted down in front of Ning. She stared into his tear-laden eyes, and frowned as she scrutinized his face. Delicately, she touched the skin around his mouth. It was sticky.

Fresh tears ran down Ning's face.

Melissa checked his wrists. There was bruising, more like burning from a rope, but that could not possibly have come from the handcuffs. She looked up at the two constables guarding him. 'Would you give us a moment, please?'

'Sorry, we can't do that.'

'Please.'

The constables both shook their heads.

'Look, it's important. Could you at least stand over there by the doorway, give me a little privacy. You can still keep an eye on him from there, surely?'

The constables looked at each other, shrugged and moved away.

Melissa stared into Ning's moist red eyes. 'Who did it?'

Ning bit his lip, and shook his head.

'He must be caught, Ning. You know that, don't you? He will kill again. Who did it? You must tell me.'

'I can not say!' Ning bleated. 'He is evil. He will kill my family in Bangkok. He know our house in Sukhumvit.'

Melissa bowed her head, trying to think of her next question rather than thinking about pleasant times spent shopping in that road. 'Will you go to prison for him?'

'Yes. I have two brothers and young sister. He will kill them.'

'I can't help you, or your family, if you won't talk.'

'I not do this. Please do not send me to prison.'

Melissa knew what would happen to him in prison. He was too pretty for his own good. Such a nice boy as well, she thought, just like some of the friends she'd made on her trips to Thailand. Ning looked up at her with tearful, pleading eyes. She sighed and said, 'You, Ning, are going to get me into a lot of trouble.' She turned to the two constables and said, 'He's all yours. Treat him nicely, he's innocent. I've just got to convince my boss of that.'

Melissa went outside to the Daimler car. She leant over a SOCO team member who was softly brushing the door handles on the passenger side, and asked, 'Any luck?'

'There's nothing on the driver's side. It's clean. This side is interesting though. Someone was sitting here all right, although there aren't any prints on the door handle, which is odd.'

'Can you work on the theory that the driver wore gloves, that the lad indoors was a passenger and had his hands tied behind his back and mouth taped up. I need evidence to support that, so make sure he doesn't wash his face until he's tested for an adhesive residue. And would you get some blood samples from him, please? I reckon he was drugged last night.'

'Will do.'

Melissa strolled over to the camera crews a few yards down the road to listen to what Inspector Jackson was saying.

'There is no question in my mind, gentlemen, that we have apprehended the murderer. He has been caught, thanks largely to the efforts of his latest victim, who fought valiantly against the attacker. Unfortunately, Ronald Nelson lost his life in the process.'

Melissa shook her head in despair. The pompous words seemed to flow easily from the man. He was obviously on a high. Why did men have such huge egos, she wondered? She turned and walked away as Inspector Jackson puffed up his chest and almost purred at the cameras.

Chapter Twenty-Eight

Magee had been at home enjoying a late breakfast listening to the radio as the news of Ronnie Nelson's murder broke. For the first time in his life, he turned on breakfast time television, hoping for better coverage, and was delighted to see a live report from the scene. He sat tensely, eyes glued to the screen, feeling frustrated that he was not involved.

'There's Jackson!' he pointed out to his wife, as a man appeared on screen walking towards the film crew.

'He looks very pleased with himself,' Jenny replied. 'What's he done?'

'I'm not sure yet. Just a second, he's coming to the microphone.'

Magee's mood became increasingly gloomier as he listened to Inspector Jackson take the credit for the case. His heart sank when Jackson told the country that everyone could now sleep safely in their beds at night knowing that the murderer had been apprehended. It was a syrupy speech, he thought, just what the Home Secretary would love to hear.

'This crap is making me feel sick!' Magee spluttered. 'Jackson has contributed nothing to the case, yet he's acting like he caught the murderer single handed. Look, there's Melissa. Come to bask in the spotlight as well, I suppose. Traitor! Look at that, she's come over to stand right next to Jackson. Hoping some of the credit will rub off on her, I suppose.'

'She doesn't look as though she's enjoying it,' Jenny observed. 'That's her unhappy face, Jack. I've seen it before. She's not happy about something, I can tell that.'

'Well, she's smiling now! Look at that grin.' He switched the television off in disgust.

A few moments later Magee's telephone rang interrupting his sulk. He grabbed at it and snapped, 'Yes, who is it?'

'It's me, sir.'

'Melissa? What do you want? Gloating about the case are you? Well I'd rather not hear about it.'

'Have you been watching Jackson on the television by any chance?'

'Yes I have. And I suppose you've rung to rub salt in my wounds.'

'Not at all, sir. Calm down!'

'Calm down? How can I calm down when Jackson is stealing my case from under me?'

'Forget Jackson, his statement was a bit optimistic.'

Magee paused as he took in Melissa's words. 'What do you mean by that?'

'I mean, sir, that our killer is still out there. Jackson's so-called murderer is a young Thai man. We found him at the scene, almost unconscious, but he's so obviously a plant. I think it's a set-up, and not a particularly good one either, if you ask me.'

'A set-up?'

'Well, there're plenty of inconsistencies that give the game away. Jackson's fallen for it though. The killer left clues like they're going out of fashion.'

'Whoa, slow down, Melissa. I'm not with you.'

'The young Thai man, Ning is his name, is a twenty-four year old masseur from Kemp Town. I'm sure it will be easy to verify his alibis for the other murders. Jackson hasn't even taken the time to think about that.'

'He always was a bit hasty.'

'Ning has really badly bruised wrists. They're chaffed and burnt, as though his hands have been tied up tightly and he's been struggling to free himself.'

'Have you got SOCO working on that?'

'I have, don't worry. Next point is that the skin around Ning's mouth is sticky. I reckon he must have been gagged at some stage last night.'

'This is looking interesting. Any more?'

'Yes. When we found him at the scene he was really groggy, like he'd been drugged, not knocked unconscious in a fight as Jackson is suggesting.'

'So what you're saying is . . .'

'I'm pretty sure he was dumped on site. SOCO are sure there were two people in the car that brought him here, which is still in the drive, but there's no evidence of anyone sitting on the driver's side. The driver must have worn gloves, but we couldn't find any at the scene.'

'Hang on, Melissa, any cadet could piece that together in about two minutes flat.'

'Precisely, sir. The killer has made a complete fool out of Jackson. He must have meant to do it because the clues he left are so obvious.'

Magee was perplexed. 'But what did he hope to achieve? A few hours of police confusion, perhaps?'

'No, I don't think so, sir. I think he had a plan. A very clever plan.'

'Don't keep me in suspense, Melissa. What plan?'

'What's the most likely outcome? With Jackson, that is?'

'Everyone will see what a fool he is.'

'Yes, and then?'

'He'll be taken off the case.'

'And?'

'And nothing, Melissa. Someone else will take over.'

'And who might that be?'

Magee paused to gather his thoughts. 'Surely not? You think the killer wants me back?'

'Yes, sir. I think he does. For whatever reason, I think he wants you investigating the case, not Jackson. The scene was so different to the other three cases, clues literally scattered around like confetti.'

'But why, Melissa? Why on earth would the killer want me back on the case?'

'I'm not too sure on that one, sir. Maybe he likes the challenge? Maybe he's on an ego trip, battling his wits against yours?'

'It's possible, I suppose, or . . .'

'Or what, sir?'

'Maybe he can't get to someone.'

'Sorry, sir?'

'Oh, nothing, Melissa, just thinking aloud. Look, you'd better get back to Jackson before he starts to get suspicious. Thanks for this, I need to sit down and think where to go next.'

'Okay, sir. See you soon I hope.'

Chapter Twenty-Nine

Magee drummed his fingers on the hallway table as he waited for someone to answer the telephone at the other end. Finally, a voice came on.

'Nick? Yes, it's Magee. Have you been watching the news on television this morning?'

'Erm, no, why?'

'Another murder, I'm afraid.'

'Who?'

'Ronnie Nelson. Lived over in Preston Park Avenue.'

'Shit!'

'A friend, I take it?'

'Yeah, Magee, he was a good friend.'

'I'm sorry.' Magee wanted to say I told you so, but couldn't bring himself to add to Nick Price's misery. 'I assume he's in the photograph.'

'Yeah, he's the one on the far right hand side, standing up.'

'Does this news make anything clearer? We're down to five men, including yourself that is. Does it narrow your suspicions?'

'No, sorry Magee, it makes no difference. I can't believe any of the others would harm any of the others. It doesn't make sense. We were all mates, all in it together.'

'And the remaining unidentified persons? Other than yourself, John Mansell and Sean Fitzpatrick, are you going to tell me who the other two mystery men are?'

'No, Magee, sorry. No deal. Not yet anyway.'

'Well, you know where I am if you change your mind. Bye for now.'

Magee put the phone down thoughtfully and went into the kitchen to make a strong cup of tea. He sat quietly, reflecting on the inescapable fact that the killer might want him back on the case. He took the photo out from his briefcase and mentally ticked off which ones were dead. Conners, Harwood, Harrison, Gibson and now Nelson.

'Son of a bitch!' he muttered as the blindingly obvious struck him. The killer had struck them down in order, as they were pictured in the photograph. Top row first, from the left. Just a silly game, he supposed. But why was the murderer behaving like this? Was the whole thing literally a game? Was it the murderer's way of letting the remaining men know who was going to be next? If so, it seemed such a childish thing to do.

'So, who's next then?' Magee posed the question to the photo. 'Do you start the bottom line from the left or the right?'

Magee took a sip of tea, mulling the question over in his mind. Left or right? Left or right? How to decide? Assuming the killer started from the left, as he had done in the line above, then the next two victims would be the two mystery men. After that came Sean Fitzpatrick, then John Mansell. Then came the girl, Nick's wife Mal, who was dead already. Last on the list was Nick Price himself. He focused on the mystery men. Who were those two? And why would Nick Price fear them so much?

Magee needed inspiration. He rubbed a hand right over his head and looked closer at the faces. There was something about them that seemed vaguely familiar. If only he could age their looks by eighteen years or so, fatten out the faces, add the odd touch of grey hair and make their eyes a bit baggier perhaps. Yes! It was those eyes! There was something about the eyes of the larger man that caught his attention. They reflected an arrogant, condescending, almost superior, attitude. What would a man like that have done when he returned home a millionaire? What would have suited the character of such an arrogant young man? Business? The City? Power?

Magee closed his eyes in thought. Yes, power. That would be his game, wouldn't it? The public eye, devotion of his life to the public good, striving constantly for more and more power to dominate others. Politics; that would fit. This mystery man would be suited to politics.

'Oh, dear god! Jenny! Quick, come and have a look at this.'

Jenny appeared at the kitchen door and asked. 'What on earth is it, Jack?'

'This man,' Magee said pointing to the photo. 'He must have been about twenty-one when this was taken. Imagine him now, some eighteen years older, running to fat, a greyer complexion, hair thinner. Politics. A well known face on the television these days. Who do you think it is?'

'Um, well, yes, he does look familiar doesn't he? Isn't it what's-his-name, the sly one that gives me the shivers?'

Magee rushed for his Daily Telegraph and thumbed through the pages. 'Yes! Oh, yes indeed!' Magee said as he tapped a particular photo in triumph. 'There, look at that!'

'Good Lord. You know, I think you're right. Yes, it's him isn't it, Geoffrey Rees Smith, the Home Secretary?'

'And who was Geoffrey Rees Smith's best school friend? The one that fell out with him? The one who has hated him throughout his political life?'

'Oh, yes! What's his name, that bolshy militant socialist MP I can't stand. McAlister!' Jenny replied.

'Desmond McAlister. I've found my mystery men, "Des" and "Jeff". Gibson must have misspelled the name.'

'Sorry?'

'Nothing. Just thinking aloud,' Magee muttered. 'Well, well, well. That's why Rees Smith wanted to be kept informed right from the beginning. He knew what was going on even then.'

'Was that it, Jack?'

'Hmm? Yes, sorry. Thanks.' His mind was working overtime. He wanted to shout for joy. He had just made a major breakthrough. He could now understand Nick Price's reluctance to name the remaining victims. More importantly, though, he could now lay the blame for the disastrous episode with Somchai Polgeowit on the Home Secretary. He sat in quiet contemplation, mulling over the entire case and his predicament.

It was half an hour before his wife re-entered the kitchen. 'You look lost in thought, Jack. How about a cup of tea?'

'Please.' He studied the back of his hand for a moment. 'You know something, Jenny? This suspension, it stinks. I'm not going to take it lying down. It's time to get even.'

'Good for you,' Jenny replied. 'How?'

'Never mind how. Dirty is all I'll say. I'm going to show the Home bloody Secretary exactly what I'm made of.'

'That's what I like to hear. Be positive.'

'Right then, Jenny, I must work. You're sworn to secrecy by the Official Secrets Act by the way.'

'Oh dear! I didn't know I'd signed it.'

'You haven't, I'm just warning you not to gossip. There will be trouble if you mention this to anyone. You could bring the government down with that tongue of yours, so please, not a word to anyone.'

Jenny Magee's face turned bright red. 'It's not me that gossips in this house!' she snapped. 'You'll be discussing this with all and sundry within the hour, as usual, I bet!'

But Magee was deaf to the accusation. 'Now then,' he muttered, 'let's start by phoning the BBC.'

Chapter Thirty

In the depths of the night, reliving the worst moment of his life, Nick Price thrashed out wildly as he fought against clenching hands in his struggle to get to the open doorway of the airplane. He screwed his eyes up against the fierce, icy torrent of air flowing around the fuselage.

'Mal!' he screamed into the freezing cold wind. 'Mal!'

And there she was, just a few inches away, impossibly floating in mid air.

Nick grabbed hold of the side of the airplane door and reached out into the abyss. 'Please, Mal,' he sobbed, 'don't go away. I need you. I love you.'

Maliwan drifted further away.

With every ounce of strength left in his body, Nick stretched as far as was humanly possible. But it was simply not far enough. 'Mal! No!' He screamed as his wife's body drifted off into the distance. 'No! Come back!'

She was gone, her body beyond reach, drifting off into the void to disappear forever. In desolation, he jumped out of the airplane. For if he couldn't live with her, he would die with her.

His body fell gracefully through the air and a blissful sense of serenity washed over him. He would join her, alone on top of this bleak, unknown Tibetan mountain. They would end their days together, wrapped around each other, embracing death.

As his body came to hit the rocky mountainside, his legs jerked involuntary in anticipation of the blow that would crush the life out of him. The jerk snapped him to his senses.

The Fourth Cart I

'Fuck sake!' He sat up, wiped the wetness away from his face. His bed sheets were soaking wet. He tried to focus. Maliwan was dead. He would never get her back. He would never again touch her warm, loving body. Why could his mind not accept that? It had been eighteen years since he'd lost her. Was he doomed to relive this intolerable nightmare for the rest of his life? He looked at his alarm clock; five past four. He groaned wearily, he knew he might just as well get up, there was no way his troubled mind would give him any rest now.

He put on his dressing gown and slippers, shuffled out of his bedroom and quietly unlocked the door to the adjacent room. It was his place of pilgrimage; the only place in the world where he could find solace. He picked up one of Maliwan's shirts that had been left lying casually over the back of a chair, raised it to his nose and took a long deep breath. Fresh tears flowed down his face.

He looked longingly at the precious mementos of his long dead wife. Her clothes, unwashed, still retaining her fragrance that only he could smell. Her hairbrush, with a few surviving strands of long silky black hair. Her jewelry box, littered with glitzy items lovingly chosen from street vendors in Bangkok. Her photographs, a happy girl splashing around in the warm tropical seas off Dongtan Beach. Everything brought back a memory. He couldn't let go.

Nick let his hand fall on to the record player. There was only ever one record in the room; Maliwan's favourite. In the three years they'd been together, she'd never grown tired of it. He pressed a switch, closed his eyes, took his wife in his arms and glided slowly across the floor.

Nick didn't hear the door open. It was another few seconds before his daughter coughed. 'Are you all right, Daddy?'

Nick stopped dead in his tracks, his daydream shattered. 'Sorry, Nit. I couldn't sleep. I didn't mean to wake you.'

'That's okay, I couldn't sleep either. Your door was open, I came looking for you.' She walked up to her father, put her hands around him, buried her head in his shoulder and swayed to the music.

Nick allowed his arms to envelope her, just as he'd held her mother, and resumed his slow dance. 'Sometimes I can't seem to cope, Nit. I'm really sorry.'

'There's nothing to be sorry about, Daddy. I understand.'

Nick said nothing in response. He never did. He never could. When it came to his wife's death, he was burdened with too much guilt. And hatred. Hatred and contempt for the man who was responsible for her love being taken away from him.

Chapter Thirty-One

'If you don't mind, Chief Inspector, we'll record this, and air it later,' said a BBC news assistant. 'Given the subject matter, our lawyers are a little nervous you might say something slanderous. We need to be able to edit, if necessary.'

'That's fine by me,' Magee replied as a make-up artist brushed up his cheeks.

'We're ready,' a voice called through the dressing room door.

Magee was led to a small studio where he sat against a backdrop of a view over Brighton. He smiled as the well known face of Peter Johnson appeared on a video link-up screen in front of him.

'I understand you wish to make a statement about the recent spate of murders in Brighton, Chief Inspector. My assistant informs me that you know what the motive is now, that there are five more murders planned and that you actually know who the five intended victims are?'

'That is correct, Mr Johnson.'

'And you're prepared to put this on record?'

'Indeed. As I explained earlier, I was taken off the case in rather unfortunate circumstances. Nevertheless, I know that the current investigations are moving in the wrong direction. I need to get back in control to rectify that problem.'

'I see,' Peter Johnson said. 'Well, if we're ready, let's get going,'

'On three,' a woman said, holding up her hand in front of Magee.

'I am joined this morning by Detective Chief Inspector Jack Magee, of the East Sussex Constabulary, who has come here today with important news relating to four recent horrific murders,' Peter

Johnson said by way of introduction and looked expectantly in Magee's direction.

Magee smiled warmly at the camera. He was going to enjoy this. 'As you will have heard, the police apprehended a suspect at the scene of the murder of Mr Ronald Nelson in Brighton yesterday morning. Contrary to the belief of the man leading that investigation, I can tell you . . .'

'You are referring to Inspector Jackson?'

'Yes, indeed, Inspector Jackson. He believes he has the murderer in custody. I am here to tell you that is not the case. The murderer is still very much at large. However, I must emphasize that this situation need not worry the general public. The murderer is only concerned with five specific men. It is strictly a private matter between them.'

'Do these remaining five men know of the risk?'

'Certainly.'

'Do you know their identities?'

'Yes I do, but I do not think it would be appropriate for me to reveal their names. I shall be talking to them personally, soon, in an unofficial capacity, of course, since I've been suspended from duty.'

'How do you know their names?'

'They are linked to a tragic incident that occurred many years ago, in another country. I found a photograph of all the men concerned. It is that link that the killer has latched onto.'

'So they are revenge murders?'

'Yes indeed.'

'Do you know what they did to deserve to die?'

'I don't believe anyone deserves to die, Mr Johnson. It is my duty, and intention, to stop these barbaric acts from continuing.'

'But you're not currently on active duty.'

'Then think of me merely as a concerned citizen. There is no law stopping me talking to these men. No law to prevent me trying to stop their deaths.'

'Do you know who the murderer is?'

'Let's just say I have a gut feeling for who it is.'

'Do you have a feud with Inspector Jackson?'

Magee was careful in his reply. 'No. Not at all. In fact, I have nothing but praise for the man who's temporarily taken over from me. He's a good police officer. It's just that, in this particular case, he's got it wrong. The facts will bear out the truth of what I'm saying in due course. I'm just one step ahead of him, that's all.'

'Nevertheless, you're pretty much condemning Inspector Jackson.'

'He's proceeded too quickly on this latest case. He's overlooked some very obvious evidence.'

'Such as?'

'Well, let's just say he'll find that out when he reads the forensics report; there'll be no doubt that the murderer got away. The young man Inspector Jackson apprehended at yesterday's crime scene was set up, in a very crude way I must add. In fact, the crudeness was deliberate. The murderer's intention was for Inspector Jackson to fall flat on his face.'

'And why on earth would he want that?'

'So Inspector Jackson would be made to look like a . . .' Magee paused to reflect on his choice of words. 'To make him act hastily.'

'Why so?'

'Because he'd then be taken off the case.'

'Is that to the killer's advantage?'

'Yes, of course.'

'I'm not sure I follow that, Chief Inspector.'

'Because I'll be back.'

'You'll be back? Are you convinced of that?'

'Certainly.'

'But why is that to the killer's advantage?'

'I'd rather not comment on that at the moment. Let's just say it's often the way in these cases.'

'So you are putting your reputation on the line?'

'Indeed. For the sake of justice, I am prepared to make an issue of this, simply because the British public has a right to know the truth.'

'The truth in this case being that Inspector Jackson has bungled badly?'

'Those are your words, Mr Johnson, not mine.'

'Thank you for your time, Chief Inspector. We all look forward in anticipation to the next episode of this sorry saga.'

Chapter Thirty-Two

Magee's taped interview made its way on to the BBC's lunchtime news bulletin. His smart appearance, along with his well-spoken and polite manner, made him an instant celebrity. BBC Southern Radio ran with the topic of the local murder, and perceived police ineptitude, for the following hour's listeners' phone-in program.

By three-fifteen in the afternoon, Magee was being proclaimed by some as a latter day Hercule Poirot. As he drove into the car park of the East Sussex Police Headquarters in Lewes, he was confronted by a group of journalists baying for blood. He turned off the engine, wound the window down, and sat shaking his head in bewilderment as Inspector Jackson walked out of the building.

'Inspector Jackson,' shouted a reporter. 'Can we have a word from you, please?'

'Yes, of course,' Inspector Jackson muttered. 'I just wish to say that Magee is a sad, pathetic, bitter ex-policeman who's taking his frustration out on me, his successor.'

'What about his allegation that the murderer is still at large?'

'Rubbish! The murderer is locked up.'

'Are you putting your reputation at stake, same as Magee?'

'Of course I am!'

'One of you must be wrong.'

'Well it's not me!' Inspector Jackson barked back. 'Magee knows nothing of yesterday's murder. He wasn't there, I was. So what the bloody hell does he know about the murderer still being at large?'

Magee quietly exited his car and crept around to a side entrance. Hoping to avoid confrontation, he walked quickly through the corridors of power. Just as he reached Superintendent Vaughan's office, a hand grabbed his shoulder.

'What the fuck is your game, Magee?' Inspector Jackson hissed in anger.

Magee turned and smiled pleasantly, enjoying the fact that, for once, the pressure was firmly on someone else's shoulders. He could see Inspector Jackson was seething; the man looked as though he was going to explode any second.

'No game, Jackson,' Magee replied. 'You're just wrong, that's all. Perhaps you need to check your facts again. Try from the beginning. Don't forget that I was there at the start. If you work through the case, carefully, you'll find your error. You'll see I'm right. Sorry, can't stop, I have an appointment.'

'Well fuck you, asshole,'

Magee shook his head in feigned sorrow. 'Is that the worst you can do? Name calling?'

'You're finished here, Magee. I'll see to that.'

'You really are quite pathetic.' Magee turned, knocked on Superintendent Vaughan's door and entered swiftly, grateful to distance himself from Jackson's ire.

Superintendent Vaughan gave vent to a theatrical sigh. 'Oh, Jack. What on earth has got into you? Was that interview really necessary?'

'Yes, sir, I believe it was.'

'But you're off the case, damn it. You can't go around treating this case like a private vendetta.'

'But that's precisely what it is, sir. A private matter between me, the murderer and the remaining victims.'

Superintendent Vaughan shook his head in despair. 'You've become too involved, Jack. You need a break, a holiday. Stay home, take it easy. It's affecting your judgment.'

'I beg to differ there, sir. It's my judgment that's going to solve this case.'

'I do wish you hadn't taken this course of action. It's not going to look good at a disciplinary hearing.'

'It won't come to that, sir.'

'Give it up, Jack. Your pension may be at stake here.'

'It won't come to that, sir.'

'I may well be forced to take Jackson's side, you know.'

'I understand, sir. Just give me forty-eight hours, please. I need to speak to the Home Secretary to clear up a point of procedure.'

'Speak with the Home Secretary? Now just wait a moment, you can't take this matter to him. There are rules and procedures to follow.'

'Yes, sir, there are indeed rules. And that is why I must see him.'

'You're being cryptic. What's going on?'

'Sorry, sir. The Home Secretary made me promise not to tell anyone.'

'Really? This interview of yours, it's part of the Home Secretary's doing?'

'Yes, sir.'

'Good lord!'

'Quite, sir. So, please, forty-eight hours grace. That's all I ask.'

'Very well. But if what you say is true, then I expect clear direction from the Home Secretary's office. Preferably from the man at the top himself.'

'Of course, sir.'

Superintendent Vaughan puffed up his chest and straightened his lapels. 'Good luck, then, Jack.'

On his return journey downstairs, Magee found another hand abruptly grabbing his shoulder from behind.

'You're crazy, sir,' Melissa hissed. 'I'll get the sack if it ever gets out that I gave you that information yesterday.'

'Well it won't come from me. Don't worry though, you're safe. I haven't said anything so far that could incriminate you, have I?'

'No. But that's not the point. I feel vulnerable. Any second now I'm expecting Jackson to call me in for a roasting.'

'It won't happen. Calm down. Look, we don't have much time. Are you still with me or not?'

'Have I a choice?' Melissa whispered through gritted teeth.

'Not if you want me back, you don't. Do you really like the idea of working for Jackson for the next five years? Look, I can't say much, only that the Home Secretary is on my side, he will reinstate me within a couple of days. Okay?'

'What?'

'Not a word, though. Now then, the next victim is going to be Des McAlister, the politician.'

'He's next? How the hell do you know that, sir?'

Magee replied, 'Call me Poirot!'

'You sly old fox! What you said on television wasn't a bluff was it? You do know what's going on. How?'

'Never you mind. I couldn't tell you if I wanted to. Anyway, it's best I keep it quiet for now. You don't want Jackson to know, do you?'

'Christ no!'

'Good. I'll keep you posted, you keep me posted.'

'What about McAlister?'

'Leave him to me, Melissa. I'll be seeing him soon.'

'What are you going to do next?'

'It's been a stressful day, Melissa. I'm going home to relax and write up all my notes. I need to present a case to the Home Secretary that will encourage him to reinstate me.'

'What do you want me to do?'

'Sit tight and pray.'

Chapter Thirty-Three

An officious woman glared at Magee as he strolled into the Home Secretary's office late morning. Before he could introduce himself, she spat out, 'How dare you!'

Magee was taken aback. 'Excuse me?'

'How dare you invite yourself to see the Home Secretary!'

Magee squared up to the woman and retorted, 'He's expecting me. I made an appointment.'

'No you did not, you said you'd come at eleven o'clock and that he'd better be there for his own good. That is not making an appointment, Chief Inspector.'

Magee shrugged. 'Well, it worked, I assume. Anyway it's urgent.'

'Urgent? Well thank you very much. You've made him upset. Very upset. He's in a foul mood this morning, with everyone. He's already put off a meeting with the Defence Secretary because of you. I hope you don't expect a cup of coffee, I can't say I'm in the mood to make you one.'

'That's okay. I'll survive, I'm sure.'

The secretary swore under her breath, but nevertheless ushered Magee into Rees Smith's office. It came as no surprise that Rees Smith eyes were glowing with anger.

'Thank you, Dawn,' Rees Smith said. 'Leave us please. No interruptions whatsoever please, even for the PM.'

As instructed, Dawn left the room. As soon as the door was closed, Rees Smith turned his attention to Magee. With utter contempt in his voice he yelled, 'Magee, what the fuck do you think you're playing at?'

Magee remained calm. 'I'm not playing at anything, sir. It's you that's playing a game and a pretty dirty game at that.'

'What do you mean by that?'

Magee took out a photograph from his jacket pocket and threw it on the desk. Rees Smith stared at the picture for a few seconds before asking, 'Where did you get this?'

'Keith Gibson's mother kept it.'

'And why are you showing it to me?'

Magee turned aggressive. 'Don't try to bullshit me.'

'Magee! That is no way to talk to a Cabinet Minister.'

Magee spat back, 'I really don't care. You are nothing more than a little shit. I have no respect for a man who's doing what you're doing.'

'Which is?'

'Using me, allowing your old comrades to be murdered, trying to hush up this story. It's called perverting the course of justice, as if you didn't know. And that's a criminal offence, punishable by a prison sentence.'

Rees Smith put on one of his famous false smiles. 'I wouldn't call them comrades, Magee. One or two faces in this photograph are familiar, I must admit. But you know what it's like, you go on holiday, get friendly with a few people, have a few drinks. Photos are taken of a good time being had. A month later you look at them and can't remember their names. And this is some eighteen ago, Magee. I couldn't possibly be expected to remember it.'

'Bollocks! You're a liar.'

Rees Smith's false smile dropped. 'That's not very polite, Magee. May I remind you of the rank I hold.'

'I don't give a damn what rank you hold! You're still a man, you're not god. You're nothing special. May I remind you that I've organized a press conference for one o'clock this afternoon, as I told your secretary earlier this morning. After I've finished with that, some reporter will probably have a few things to say to you that might be even ruder.'

'And what exactly are you going to tell the press?'

'That you've known about the intended victims all along, that you knew who was going to be murdered.'

'Rubbish, this photo is nothing more than coincidence.'

Magee was incredulous. 'Coincidence? Four men from this photo have been murdered inside the last two weeks. The fifth, dead already, had a wreath sent to his mother last week along with a dagger. You've got a file thick with reports on the murders, from me. You got involved with this case right from the start. I thought it odd at the time, but now I know the real reason.'

'Okay, Magee, have it your way. But my story is that I met some guys while travelling the world. It just shows the sort of people you can inadvertently get acquainted with. What they did when I wasn't around, well, who knows? The fact that four died recently doesn't bother me at all. Whatever they did doesn't involve me; I'm just an innocent bystander. I do hope, Magee, that you are not going to imply that I'm mixed up with the likes of Nick Price?'

Magee snorted. 'So you remember his name then?'

'Well, yes, he owned the bar. But not the others, they were just bar flies.'

'Bollocks! You've known their names all along. That's why I could tell there was something wrong with your phone conversations with me. You were already familiar with the victims.'

Rees Smith gave a thin smile. 'So, what exactly are you going to accuse me of at this press conference of yours?'

'I'm not sure yet. Not sure that I'm going to accuse you in public, at least not at the moment. I'll call you a bare faced liar and a common thief to your face. To the press though, I'll just present the facts and let them make the accusations.'

'The accusations being?'

'That you conspired to pervert the course of justice, that you knew these men were going to be murdered and you did nothing to prevent it. In fact, I reckon you just sat back and waited. You think the murderer is one of the remaining men, and you're waiting to see who the last one left is.'

'Absolute drivel, Magee.'

'Really? I don't think so. You got involved immediately after Todd Conners' death. That means you knew what was going on at that stage. So, effectively, you condemned Harwood, Harrison and Nelson to their deaths. I'm sure the press would love to hear you answer that charge. Oh, yes, and I'm sure they'd love to hear your explanation as to how you and your comrades all became millionaires just a few months after this photo was taken. What did you do, pull off some massive drug deal?'

At the mention of drugs, Rees Smith pulled a Browning out of his jacket pocket, cocked it and pointed it at Magee. 'How dare you make such insinuations?'

Magee sat unflinching, as though a child had pulled a toy gun on him. 'You won't do that, sir.'

'Give me one good reason, Magee. One good reason why I shouldn't kill you right now? My secretary will find me rolling on the floor with your dead body. I'll naturally say that you pulled the gun on me, that you'd gone crazy after being suspended and wanted to take your anger out on me. No witnesses, I win. Who would disbelieve me? I am the Home Secretary, don't forget.'

'The entire world would know you were lying.'

'Oh? And how do you reason that?'

'Because the newspapers next week would be running front-page headlines of your conspiracy. If you'll allow me to remove a few sheets of paper from my jacket?' Magee paused, put his hand in his breast pocket, withdrew a wad of papers and threw them on the desk. 'Thank you. Now, this is a photocopy, as you can see, which means that the original must be somewhere else. In fact, it's in an envelope at a solicitor's office at this very moment. I've given instructions for the envelope to be opened in the event of my death and for the contents to be made public. I've given my solicitor no time limit. You can read it for yourself. It's all good stuff; it would make a wonderful news story.'

Magee sat in silence for several minutes whilst Rees Smith read Magee's report. By the end of it, Rees Smith had become noticeably paler. 'You bastard, Magee!'

'With respect, sir, you're the bastard around here. Now, would you mind putting the gun down, it's making me nervous.'

'I'm not so sure I shouldn't kill you anyway and take the risk that your solicitor can be silenced. Maybe I could issue a Section D notice.'

'You won't find him in time. I hired a new solicitor only yesterday. As to the Section D notice, the letter to the solicitor has specific instructions to send a copy to a European newspaper over which you will have no jurisdiction.' Magee paused to let the situation sink in. 'Now then, I have a proposition for you. Maybe we can sort something out between ourselves.'

'I'm listening,' Rees Smith said, but he didn't put the gun down.

'I understand why you want this affair kept secret. I realize that the political scandal would be enormous and may even bring the government down. I wouldn't want to be considered responsible for that. On the other hand, I can't say I give a damn whether you survive this ordeal or not. I'm indifferent to Des McAlister and Sean Fitzpatrick. I'm sure Nick Price can take care of himself and as for John Mansell, well he's disappeared off the face of the earth. The ten of you have lived this lie for eighteen years. Okay, so some big heist happened abroad, not here. But the press would still love to know about it, I'm sure. My offer is that I'll join your conspiracy. I will not tell a living soul about your involvement, or the others come to that. Your secret will die with me, okay? I'm the only one outside the group that knows your little secret. You know that the others won't say anything even after your death, if it comes to it, and neither will I.'

Rees Smith sneered. 'And just what is the price for your silence, Magee? Money?'

'No. Certainly not! I'm not that sort of police officer. What I want is only what was mine in the first place, what was taken away from me largely because of your interference and lack of cooperation. I want to be reinstated at the same rank, with the same benefits and to be put back in charge of the case. I'm a family man, damn it, that's all I care about. All these threats of losing my job and pension have worried me sick these last few days. Give me my job back and I'll sell my soul to the devil, or, in this case, to you. I do not want your money, I have principles.'

Rees Smith waved the photocopied papers at Magee. 'Your principles include blackmail, though, I take it?'

'That's not blackmail. It's equivalent to wearing a bulletproof vest. Self-defence.

'Okay, Magee, you have a deal. Shake on it?' Rees Smith held his hand out.

'I'll shake hands with the devil himself gladly, but not with you, sir. I can't say I care for your character at all.'

'Fair enough.' Rees Smith withdrew his hand. He re-holstered his gun and picked up his phone asking Magee for the number of his

Superintendent. Ten minutes later, after some firm commands and syrupy compliments about Magee's abilities and efficiency, Superintendent Vaughan could do nothing else but agree to Magee's full reinstatement and Jackson's removal from the case.

'There you go, Magee. That's my side of the bargain done.'

'Thank you, sir. I'll keep mine, I promise. Before I go, though, there're just a few things you could help me with, if you don't mind.'

Rees Smith grunted. 'You're not getting anything out of me, Magee.'

'I'm aware of that, sir. I was just hoping for your cooperation in stopping the killer, that's all. I agreed to keep your secret, but I still intend to try to capture the man and save your lives. That is my job after all.'

'No promises, Magee. What do you want to know?'

'What was the occasion about? The one in the photograph, I mean. Do you remember that much?'

'A party. A birthday party I think.'

'Whose?'

Rees Smith frowned. 'Not sure.'

'One of the group?'

'Maybe. No! No, it was Nick's wife. It was her birthday. Her twenty-first if I remember correctly.'

Magee nodded his head. At least it corroborated Nick Price's version. 'She's the girl in the photo I believe?'

Rees Smith sighed. 'Yes. She was such a pretty girl. Nick thought the world of her.'

'Can you put names to specific faces?'

'Not really.'

'From the top left, Conners, Harwood, Harrison, Gibson, Nelson. You note the order?'

'Sorry?'

'They're being killed off in sequence.'

Rees Smith stared down at the photo with incredulity. 'Fuck!'

'You hadn't realized that?'

'I haven't seen this photo for years, Magee. It hadn't occurred to me that, well . . . shit!'

'Do you know why the murderer is killing off your little group in the order that you appear in the photograph?'

'I've no idea. It's bizarre.'

Magee thought it sounded like the man was telling the truth. 'But there must be a reason this picture is important. It appears to symbolize the killer's hatred. Why would anyone hate the people in it? Hate them enough to carry out these barbaric acts of revenge?'

'I really do have no idea. Look, Magee, what is it with this photo? Why have you latched on to it?'

'I just think it's important. I can feel it in my bones. A copper's intuition I suppose. You all became millionaires around the time this photo was taken, are you sure this scene isn't a celebration? A celebration of greed perhaps?'

Rees Smith shifted uncomfortably in his chair.

Magee nodded, taking Rees Smith's uneasiness as a positive answer. 'How many people would have had copies of this photo?'

'Why on earth do you want to know that?'

'I imagine the murderer has a copy. It's his death list, he's bumping you all off in order, so it makes sense that he has his own copy. It should narrow down my list of suspects.'

'There were lots of copies made, there must have been a dozen left on top of the bar for us to help ourselves.'

'So everyone in the photo had their own copy?'

'Presumably so.'

'Anyone else?'

Rees Smith frowned. 'I can't think why anyone else would want a copy. Would you want a copy of someone else's holiday photo?'

Magee thought about it at length. 'No, I suppose not. Tell me, whatever it was you managed to pull off to make you rich, did it occur before or after this photo was taken?'

'Does it matter?'

'It certainly does.'

Rees Smith squirmed in his chair before replying, 'After.'

'So, at the time of this photo, no one had a grudge against any of you, in terms of money?'

Rees Smith grimaced. 'Your reasoning is logical, Magee. Problem is, no one had a grudge against us afterwards either.'

'Because any others involved were killed?'

Rees Smith turned a shade paler. 'I . . . erm . . . I don't know about that, Magee.'

'Nick Price told me. He said that you all got equal shares, although some people involved didn't survive. I just wanted to check with you, are you sure they all died? No possibility anyone you thought was dead could actually have cheated death?'

'No, I don't think so. The possibility of anyone surviving what happened would be too far-fetched.'

'Good. That helps. It means the killer is most likely to be someone in the photograph.'

'John Mansell,' Rees Smith replied. 'That's my guess.'

'You knew John well?'

'Reasonably well. He owned the place jointly with Nick. John worked behind the bar most of the time. He was more suited to it. Nick was a little too blunt for his own good sometimes. I chatted to John quite often. Nick wasn't keen on me, he thought I was trying to muscle in on his business interests.'

'So you reckon the murders are connected to John Mansell? Does John have a motive?'

Rees Smith nodded. 'Our friendship collapsed shortly after this photograph was taken. By the end of my time in Thailand, he hated my guts.'

'Enough to plan to kill you?'

Rees Smith closed his eyes and hung his head. 'Yes, Magee, without question.'

'And the others? Could John have killed them?'

Rees Smith reflected on the issue a few seconds. 'No. No, I don't think so. That doesn't make sense, does it? It was only me he had an issue with.'

'Is Nick Price out for revenge as well? Maybe together with John Mansell?'

'It's possible. The two of them were as thick as thieves.'

'It would explain Paul Mansell's involvement, wouldn't it?'

'Yes, maybe.'

'I was convinced the murderer was a Thai, not an Englishman.'

Rees Smith shrugged. 'Nick Price and John Mansell could be using a team, including a Thai hit man perhaps?'

'This is getting more complicated than I imagined.'

'Exactly. My very own thoughts.'

'Are you sure there was no other Thai man in your group?'

'Positive.'

'Didn't Nick's wife have a brother? A twin brother? Wasn't his name . . . erm,' Magee paused to recollect, 'Jook?'

Rees Smith averted his eyes and coughed. 'Um, yes.'

Magee noticed the body language immediately. He had touched a raw nerve. 'Nick said Jook died as well as Maliwan. In the same accident wasn't it?'

Rees Smith was visibly writhing in his chair. 'Um,' he said, followed by another nervous cough. 'Yes, he did.'

'How did Maliwan and Jook die?'

'I . . . erm . . . I don't really know, Magee. Look, this is getting out of hand. I told you I wasn't prepared to go into detail.'

'You killed them, didn't you, sir? Both of them.'

Rees Smith's eyes nearly popped out of his head. 'I beg your pardon?'

'You killed Maliwan and Jook, didn't you?'

'I, erm, how . . .'

'My god! You did, didn't you?' Magee rubbed his forehead. 'Oh Christ, that's why there's been this conspiracy. That's why Nick Price won't talk about it. You, a Home Secretary, are a cold bloodied murderer, aren't you? You killed his wife and his wife's brother, didn't you?'

Rees Smith's face turned red. 'Now look here, Magee,' he protested. Don't you dare go making accusations like that to the press or I'll fucking crucify you!'

'Well, well. At last I'm getting near the truth.'

'No you're not!'

'Oh, I am, I certainly am.' Magee slapped the side of his head. 'Oh, of course! That's why Des McAlister stopped speaking to you, isn't it? He's a pacifist. Whatever you did, you went over the top, didn't you? You did something so outrageous in killing Maliwan and Jook that McAlister stopped speaking to you on the spot. That's it, isn't it? Well, well, well.'

Rees Smith was fuming. 'Magee, you're beginning to outstay your welcome.'

'Yes, I suppose I am. Still, a double-murderer in the Cabinet, eh, who would have thought it? What happened to the security checks before you were promoted? No wonder you're concerned about the ensuing scandal if this all breaks loose.'

'This is all pure conjecture, Magee. You have no facts, and no one will bear witness against me.'

'Quite true, and each day another witness dies. You must certainly be pleased about that.'

'I am not pleased about any of this, Magee.'

'No?'

'No!'

'Does your security staff know of the danger?'

'They know of a danger, not the danger. They're on twenty-four hour red alert at the moment.'

'So there's no point in me offering you police protection then?'

'No! That would imply foreknowledge. It would be extremely difficult to explain.'

'I see. So you would prefer to die and have your reputation left intact, rather than live and face the public wrath?'

Rees Smith snorted. 'Any day, Magee, any day.'

'But your wife and children, they would suffer unbearably. Aren't you a family man?'

'If the scandal broke, Magee, I'd be hounded so much I'd probably, well, suicide is an easy way out, isn't it? If I'm going to die then I hope it won't be in vain. If my wife and daughters can escape the trauma of a scandal, then the sacrifice would have been worth it.'

Magee was astounded. 'My god, you're serious aren't you?'

'Absolutely, Magee. It's my life and my country. It's my choice. It is still a free country, isn't it?'

Magee sat staring at Rees Smith for a few moments. It gradually dawned on him that perhaps the man wasn't the monster he'd thought. He was nothing more than a desperate man trying to cover up a past indiscretion, trying to protect his country, wife and children from the consequences of the truth coming out.

'If it's okay with you, sir, I'd like to interview McAlister and offer him protection. He's the next intended victim, I believe.'

'By all means, Magee, but I don't think you'll get anywhere with him either.'

'I'd like to try nevertheless. Look, I've taken enough of your time, I'd better be going,' Magee stood to go and offered his hand, nodding his understanding. 'Good luck, sir.'

Rees Smith rose and firmly shook Magee's outstretched hand. 'Thank you, Chief Inspector.'

The handshake said it all; Magee had sold his soul.

Chapter Thirty-Four

As Magee entered McAlister's office, he was met by Ian Pendry, a solicitor. Displeased, he said, 'I'd rather hoped to talk to Mr McAlister alone. I wanted a private conversation.'

'Well, he asked for me to be here.'

Magee sat down, annoyed at the solicitor's attendance. 'Mr McAlister, have you any idea why I am here? The presence of your solicitor indicates a certain degree of expectation on your part which I feel to be unwarranted.'

'I have instructed my client to remain silent, Chief Inspector. Until we know what this is all about that is.'

Magee looked thoughtfully at McAlister who, in turn, was staring vacantly at his desk. Magee transferred his gaze to Pendry. It appeared that McAlister had no wish to speak.

Magee sat resolute, arms crossed. 'I'm not here to charge your client, Mr Pendry. I just want to talk, in private preferably and certainly off the record. I'm not sure your client would wish me to speak in front of anyone else, including yourself. I just want him to help me with my enquiries, but anything he says will not go outside this room.'

'Perhaps you would care to explain your enquiries then, Chief Inspector?'

Magee took a photograph out of his jacket pocket and placed it in front of McAlister.

McAlister gasped, looked up into Magee's eyes and said, 'You know what happened then?'

'Not everything, sir. But I do know there's a maniac intent on killing everyone in this photo. Furthermore, if you follow the order of the murders, you'll see the killer has a fixed seating plan. Bear in mind Keith Gibson was supposed to have been victim number four.'

McAlister stared at the photograph, mouthing the names of the victims. His eyes widened. 'So I'm next?'

'It looks that way, sir. Yes.'

'Do you know who the killer is?'

'Not yet. I have my suspicions, about the motive, that is. Revenge seems the most likely reason. But as to the killer's identity, no, I'm not quite there yet.'

'You know what we did then?'

'No, but I get the impression it's all to do with the deaths of Nick's wife Maliwan and her brother Jook.'

McAlister nodded. 'It was all so unnecessary.'

Pendry looked horrified. 'Please, Des! I must warn you, you're not obliged to say anything.'

'It doesn't matter, Ian, the Chief Inspector must know he can't press charges. There's no evidence and it's beyond his jurisdiction isn't that right?'

'Quite right, sir,' Magee responded. 'What happened in Bangkok all those years ago isn't my concern, though I'd love to hear the story, I have to admit. However, I'm only concerned with the present, not the past. What has been going on in the last two weeks is my only concern. I want it stopped.'

McAlister sighed, 'You can't stop ghosts, Chief Inspector.'

'This killer is no ghost. He, or she for that matter, is very much alive.'

'I didn't mean that kind, Chief Inspector. I meant ghosts from the past, skeletons in the cupboard, deeds done and regretted later. They haunt your life and catch up with you in the end.'

Pendry protested. 'Des, please, this isn't necessary.'

'Sod it, Ian. It doesn't matter now. I'm dead anyway, isn't that right, Chief Inspector?'

'You could have police protection, sir.'

'Is there any point? He'll get me in the end.'

'Don't you want to live, sir?'

'And face a political death? Politics is my life. I couldn't face the scandal. I'm sure that . . . Geoff . . . feels the same way.'

'He does, sir, if that makes you feel better.'

McAlister giggled nervously 'Perhaps we'll go out together. The press would love that, wouldn't they? Two archenemies finally joined in death, like a second-rate movie.'

'Let me help you, sir. Agree to protection. We can catch this maniac with your cooperation.'

'Chief Inspector, I die physically if he gets near me, I die in court if you catch him. Heads he wins, tails I lose. I don't think I could cope with a trial. Whoever it is, if he knows about Mal, Jook and what we did in Tibet then he'll give testimony and tell the whole world. I couldn't live with that, surely you can see that?'

Magee was temporarily at a loss for words, his mind racing. Tibet? McAlister had said Tibet, hadn't he? No one had said anything about Tibet before. What had happened in Tibet for god's sake? He blinked hard and said, 'He would be dismissed as a crank.'

'Oh, come on, don't be so naive. The press would investigate. They would do some research, the same way as you no doubt have done already. They would find enough evidence to support the killer's case. What are the chances of ten ordinary men becoming millionaires within a few months of being photographed together? That in itself is too much to be a coincidence.'

'As it's almost over, sir, would you mind telling me the story? Just out of interest that is, I'd really like to know what happened in Tibet.'

'Yes, Chief Inspector, I would mind very much. I'm sorry, but I've lived with some nasty memories these last eighteen years. I've never told anyone, not even my wife or children, especially not them in fact. We were ambushed, you see, but we hunted them down and killed them, like animals. No mercy! Then there was Mal, Jook and the Chinese soldiers; madness, murdering them out of greed. Don't you see, Chief Inspector, I should have told the world years ago about what happened. But I kept quiet. I lived a lie for all this time. How often have you heard me on the floor of the Commons spouting my pacifist beliefs? What would the press say if they knew I was a thief, that I'd killed someone?'

'Des, for Christ's sake,' Pendry interjected. 'Careful what you say, I beg you.'

'Leave it, Ian! I could have stopped this madness eighteen years ago, but I didn't. That's my sin. I've relived that part of my life a thousand times at least. Each time I try to convince Geoff that it isn't worth it; that life has to come before money. Each time I lose the argument and slowly watch Mal die, her body turning red in front of me as bullets rip her apart. If I'm to die then that's god's punishment.'

'It's not god's punishment, sir. It's man's punishment. One man, I believe, and he has no right to take anyone's life. Even with a judge and jury, I would dispute man's right to take life.'

'But that's just the point, Chief Inspector. He knows we're all guilty. He is the judge, jury and executioner, all in one.'

Magee insisted, 'He has no right to take your life, sir.'

'And we had no right to take their lives. We started it, someone else is finishing it. I'd say that's pretty fair justice. An eye for an eye, as it were.'

'So you won't tell me about it?'

'No!'

'May I ask who you think the killer is?'

'John Mansell of course. Maybe along with Nick Price, they were partners after all.'

'Why them?'

'Because they lost so much more than we did.'

'And just where can I find John Mansell?'

'Sorry, no idea. We never kept in contact.'

'I need to trace him.'

McAlister's forehead broke into a frown. 'You wouldn't ask through the press, would you?'

'No. I've promised Geoff not to go public.'

McAlister's face scrunched up. 'I'm sorry, I don't understand.'

'I promised Geoff that I would not reveal anything to anyone else. Your secret will stay with me even if you die.'

'You've spoken to Geoff about everything?'

'Yes I have.'

'The story won't come out? Ever?'

'No. Not from my lips anyway. But I can't promise anything with the killer though, once I catch him. I doubt whether a trial could be held in secret.'

'So I'm free?'

'Free to die. Yes, sir. The choice is yours. Geoff's made his choice. I was hoping you would think differently.'

McAlister grunted. 'Well, well. Good old Geoff. For once, he's been unselfish. How uncharacteristic.'

'Actually, I'd call it very selfish, sir. Geoff wants to go to the grave with his reputation intact, with an unblemished record.'

'Can't say I blame him.'

'So you'll do the same?'

'Yes! Yes, I think I will, Chief Inspector. For the first time in many a year, I'm on Geoff's side.'

'Des,' Pendry butted in. 'I don't understand who or what you're talking about, but it sounds as though you're treading on dangerous ground. It sounds to me as though you're involved in some conspiracy. I beg you to tell the truth, we'll expose this corrupt officer of the law, you'll get immunity from prosecution if you use the House to make your allegations.'

'Mr Pendry!' Magee shouted. 'I can assure you that I am not corrupt. I take great offence at that allegation!'

'Ian, please, leave it be. I doubt whether Magee is corrupt, in fact I'd say he's quite the opposite. Quite the gentleman aren't you, Magee? You could make a fortune if you sold your story to the press or blackmailed us. Yet I imagine you've sacrificed several principles for the sake of the country. Is that right?'

'Precisely. I've just had a very trying chat with Geoff. He drew a gun on me. I believe he'd actually planned to kill me. Can you believe that?'

McAlister chuckled, perhaps at the mental picture of the Home Secretary pointing a gun at Magee 'He always was a mad bastard!'

'I managed to convince him that I had honorable intentions.'

'In that case, Magee, I'll believe you as well. That must have been a really interesting chat.'

'Interesting is hardly the appropriate word. Nerve-wracking, maybe.'

'So, what do you intend to do now, Chief Inspector?'

'May I ask where you live, sir?'

'In Chelsea. Why?'

'Well, assuming you're next on the list, I'll arrange for some local officers to be posted to protect you. They won't know exactly what's going on, merely that there's the likelihood of an attack on you. Perhaps we can use the excuse of terrorists?'

'That's fine, Chief Inspector. My family is used to that.'

'I still want to stop this maniac. And I want to be close at hand if and when the strike occurs.'

'Will you kill him?'

'Execution you mean? No, I wouldn't do that for anyone.'

'But if he's shot dead resisting arrest?'

'Then that would be an accident, sir. If we had to shoot him, we would aim to maim, not to kill him, sir.'

'Perhaps you could ask your men to . . .' McAlister let the sentence trail off unfinished.

'No, sir, I could not. I do not want to be accused of murder.'

'What a shame. Sorry, Chief Inspector, it was just a thought.'

'I think I should go, sir, just in case you try to put any more ideas in my head.'

'Geoff would be indebted to you if your aim wasn't too good,' McAlister continued.

'No doubt, sir, but my aim is fine, thank you.'

Magee rose and left the condemned man in peace. He looked at his watch. Twelve forty, plenty of time for the press interview he'd never arranged. Nice bluff, he thought, as he walked away from the Parliament building. Now then, he mused, what's all this about Tibet?

Chapter Thirty Five

By late afternoon, Magee was back at the Sussex Police Headquarters in Lewes. As he returned to his section, a spontaneous round of applause awaited him. Along with a bout of whistling, cheering and back-slapping. He stood basking in the glory for a few seconds before bellowing, 'That's enough, thank you! Haven't you lot got something better to do?'

'Melissa! Come to my office please, when you've settled down, that is.'

Melissa followed Magee into his office. 'Can you let me in on what's going on now, sir?'

Magee took out the photo and gave it to Melissa. 'I got this from Keith Gibson's mother. Something big happened in Bangkok eighteen years ago. It also involved Tibet somehow. There were several deaths, including Nick Price's wife Maliwan and her twin brother Jook. There seems to have been other deaths too, Chinese soldiers, predominantly, from what I can gather. Anyway, these ten men all ended up millionaires, so they must have pulled off a big heist.'

'Is this speculation, sir?'

'No, it's fact. Someone now wants revenge, presumably for the deaths that occurred. John Mansell is the main suspect, but I can't rule out Nick Price.'

'I thought we were after a Thai person?'

'True. It is rather baffling, I appreciate that. Nick's son and daughter are on my list of suspects too. They might be exacting revenge for the murder of their mother and uncle.'

'So what now, sir?'

'All we can do is sit it out. McAlister knows he's the next target. We'll just have to join in the game. We need to relocate up to Chelsea for a few days, to keep McAlister under surveillance. Let's hope the killer doesn't realize we'll be waiting for him.'

Chapter Thirty-Six

'That really was quite extraordinary,' the deputy head of MI5 said as Brigadier Armstrong turned the video off. 'What on earth possessed the man to pull a gun?'

Brigadier Armstrong shook his head in bewilderment. 'He's desperate, Harold. And, as such, he's a loose cannon. I know we've had a few oddballs in the Cabinet over the years, but we've never really had to deal with much more than inflated egos, corruption, sexual deviancy, pilfering. But this really does take the biscuit.'

'So, what's your conclusion?'

'Well, I'm faced with a bit of a dilemma. If I run with this and it goes wrong, the government will be severely shaken by the scandal. If I go to the PM, he'll be put in a difficult position. If he doesn't take action, and the story gets into the public domain, then he's facing severe embarrassment. If he does act, then the scandal will cause shock waves. Hanged if he does, hanged if he doesn't.'

'So you haven't decided yet?'

'No, not yet.'

'I could lend you some resources if it would help.'

'Thanks, Harold. Best not to get you involved if possible. I just wanted to pass it by you, that's all. A problem shared and all that.'

'Not like you, Bernard. To be so indecisive, that is.'

'Maybe not, but then this problem is not one I've had to face before.'

'I can only make one suggestion.'

'Which is?'

'No trial.'

'Hmm,' Brigadier Armstrong murmured. 'That's about as far as I'd got myself.'

'Would you take it further though?'

'You mean no witnesses?'

'Complete erasure. It's the only way you can really guarantee no leaks.'

'I hope it doesn't go that far.'

'You think you can contain the remaining witnesses?'

'Some of them, yes. It's just the loose ends that need tidying up.'

'As I say, you have my support if needed.'

'Thanks, Harold. But I think I'll resolve this in house. Or at least I'll keep it in the family.'

'Sounds good to me. This Nick Price seems to be the resourceful type. Maybe you should encourage him to give you a hand.'

Brigadier Armstrong nodded in agreement. 'Yes, maybe so. After all, he started the whole ghastly affair. I might just leave it to him to clear up the mess. Right then, Harold, thanks for the coffee, I'd better be off.'

'Before you go, Bernard. Just one question, how on earth did you get the camera into Rees Smith's room?'

Brigadier Armstrong grinned. 'Last week he asked me to sweep his office. He's concerned someone may attempt to bug him.'

'Perish the thought,' replied the deputy head of MI5 as he too broke into a broad grin.

Chapter Thirty-Seven

'You know I hate surveillance work, sir,' Melissa said, stifling a yawn and letting her head rest against the car's window.

Magee tutted. 'Honestly, Melissa. You've no stamina have you? I sometimes wonder if you're in the right job.'

'So do I, sir. So do I. Every day, in fact.'

'So why not get out?'

'Oh, I don't know, it's sometimes easier to go with the flow rather than fight it.'

'Are you referring to parental pressure by any chance?'

'Got it in one, sir. My dad wants me to have a sound career, one with prospects and a pension. My uncle seemed to have all the answers.'

'Our beloved Superintendent Vaughan?'

'The very same. God he bores me to death. He's so . . . so . . .'

'Conservative?'

'Yes. More than that, though. Before he does anything, he thinks carefully about the correct policy, how he should react, what he should say. He isn't his own person anymore.'

'A company man.'

'Yeah, and he'd love me to be a company woman.'

'But you're rebelling against that?'

'Too right I am. Life's too short. The world's full of interesting places, full of fascinating things to do. I want to get out there, to do something with my life.'

'Sounds like an unstable character defect to me. This country's fine for me.'

'But you haven't travelled much have you, sir?'

'A bit, around Europe, before I was married, but I've learned to detest travelling. I hate living out of a suitcase.'

'I don't mean that, I mean living overseas, mixing with the local community, adapting to their culture, adopting their way of life.'

'I like the sound of that even less. Paul Mansell would agree with you though, I imagine.'

'Paul's a nice guy.'

Magee looked at Melissa quizzically. 'Seriously? You like him?'

'He's young, fit, handsome, single, seeking adventure,' Melissa said with a smile on her face. 'He's got potential.'

'He's a murder suspect, that's what he is!'

'Oh, come on, sir, does he look the type?'

'Yes, he does actually.'

'Well you're going to be proved wrong.'

'You're going to do that are you, Melissa? Prove me wrong?'

'If I can, yes, I will.'

'You'll have to stay awake if you want to get anywhere, then. The killer could strike any second.'

'How? We've got McAlister's home surrounded. How's he going to get in?'

'I really don't know, Melissa. He got in to all the other victims' houses without any trouble.'

'Well I don't think he'll bother trying. It must be obvious to him that there are police officers everywhere.'

'Not necessarily, Melissa.'

'Anyone surveying the place could tell.'

'Maybe he plans to just walk straight in.'

'More likely he's staking us out right now, waiting for an opportunity, searching for a weakness. Maybe we're looking in the wrong direction, sir.'

'Meaning what?'

'Perhaps we should be looking at all the other houses around here. Maybe we should be checking out all the neighbours' windows for subversive movements.'

'Subversive movements?' Magee grunted. 'Where on earth did you pick that expression up from?'

'I meant suspicious movements.'

'Actually, Melissa, that's not a bad idea. Come on.'

Melissa got out the car and said, 'Where are we going, sir?'

'Let's walk around the block. Alert everyone that we're probably being spied on. I want everyone to survey their immediate area, look for shadows in darkened rooms, curtains moving, that sort of thing. No discussion over the radio, the killer might be listening in.'

'At least that's better than sitting in the car,' Melissa muttered as she moved off down the road.

For the next hour, the six local officers assigned to Magee skirted McAlister's neighbourhood on the pretext of quick trips to a nearby shop or to relieve themselves.

As fate would have it, it was Melissa who spotted a car parked over two hundred yards away, with two men sitting in the front, facing down the road towards McAlister's house.

'Every few minutes they raise a pair of binoculars in this direction, sir. They've probably got night vision glasses.'

'Right. Let's go and pick them up, Melissa. Nice and casual. Okay?'

'Okay, sir. This should be fun!' Melissa chuckled following Magee down the road.

They ambled along, like a couple out for the night, on the other side of the street, disregarding the suspect car. Fifty yards past the car, they crossed the road and double-backed. At the last moment, Melissa moved into the road and they both grabbed the car's front door handles at the same time and shouted, 'Police!' at the two occupants.

Magee and Melissa each yanked a man out of the car and threw them over the bonnet. Surprisingly, the two men offered no resistance to handcuffs being strapped securely to their wrists.

'You're under arrest, you two. Do you wish to say anything?'

Both handcuffed men shouted in unison, 'Diplomatic immunity!'

'What?'

'Identity card in jacket pocket,' one of the men answered in broken English.

Magee pulled his man up and rummaged through his jacket. He found a small leather case. Inside was a card, which identified the man as working for the Royal Thai Embassy.

'Diplomat?' Magee muttered. 'Bugger! Who do you work for?'

'Cultural Attaché,' Magee's prisoner replied.

'He ordered you here tonight?'

'Yes.'

'Shit!' Magee was stumped. He stood contemplating the situation for a few moments. The professional thing to do would be to let Superintendent Vaughan know about the development and let him decide what to do. However, he reasoned his boss would be bound to phone the Home Secretary for instructions. That may complicate matters, he reasoned.

He asked his prisoner, 'Do you have a car phone?'

'Be my guest,' came the response.

Magee got into the car, flicked on the interior light, flipped open a notebook, picked up the phone and dialled the Royal Thai Embassy. His call was put through in seconds. 'Mr Ambassador? Good evening sir, it's Chief Inspector Magee. I have a new problem. I thought you may be able to help me out.'

'Of course, Chief Inspector,' the Ambassador replied. 'How may I be of assistance?'

'We're currently trying to protect Mr Desmond McAlister who I've determined to be the next intended victim. He's a Member of Parliament, so it's a very high profile case now. We've been keeping his house under surveillance this evening and we've come across two of your staff who appear to be keeping McAlister's house under surveillance as well.'

'Good lord! Are you sure they're my staff?'

'Quite sure, sir. They're claiming diplomatic immunity.'

'How extraordinary. Did they say they work for me?'

'Well, they actually said they work for the Cultural Attaché.'

'The Cultural Attaché?'

'That's what they say.'

'Oh, that's, erm, oh dear, Chief Inspector. This is a very serious matter. What are you intending to do about it?'

'I was hoping you might have a good suggestion, sir.'

'Um, no. No, I don't. Where exactly are you at the moment?'

'Just off the Fulham Road, sir, near South Kensington underground station.'

'Really? That's not far from the Embassy is it?'

'It's very close actually, sir.'

'Could you bring them to me, Chief Inspector? I'll question them here, see if I can get to the bottom of it.'

'That's fine by me, sir. I'll be with you in just a few minutes, I should think.' Magee stared at the two diplomats through the windscreen. He stroked his chin, pondering on what to do, then got out the car.

Melissa said, 'What's the plan then, sir?'

'Help them into the back seat, Melissa. We'll drive them back to the Embassy.'

'You'll let them go free, just like that?' Melissa asked, as she bundled a man into the back seat. 'Do you know what you're doing, sir?'

'No. No idea at all. However, I do know the Ambassador quite well. He's been helping me on this case. Maybe he can sort the matter out satisfactorily. I'm buggered if I can decide what to do. This is getting way above my head. First of all bloody politicians and now bloody diplomats. I think I'll ask for a transfer.'

'Back to Traffic Control, sir?'

'That sounds peaceful.' Magee buckled his seat belt. 'By the way, did you ever sign the Official Secrets Act?'

'I'm not sure, sir. Probably. Why?'

'Well I'm reminding you of it now. Whatever you see or hear from here on goes no further, right?'

'Yes, sir.' Melissa fell silent for the rest of the journey.

Magee abandoned the car right outside 29 Queensgate and, with Melissa, helped the two handcuffed men out of the car and up to the front door of the Embassy. He was met promptly and he and his entourage were ushered into the Ambassador's office without further ado.

'This is Detective Sergeant Melissa Kelly, sir. She's been working on the case the whole time with me. She is extremely discrete, sir.'

The Ambassador nodded his approval and extended his hand to Melissa. 'Do you mind if I ask these men a few questions, Chief Inspector?'

'By all means, sir,' Magee replied. He waited in embarrassment for a couple of minutes while the Ambassador snapped at the two men in his native tongue. Magee understood not one word. Not that it mattered; it was obvious by the way they hung their heads in shame that they were getting a severe roasting.

'Chief Inspector,' the Ambassador said after a while, 'who have you told about this incident?'

'Only DS Kelly here and your good self know about it so far.'

'And what do you plan to do about it?'

'I really don't know, sir. It's beyond my experience. I haven't had enough time to think it through. I made a promise the other day, sir, that I would contain the problem and not involve anyone unnecessarily.'

The Ambassador looked a little puzzled. 'Oh? May I ask to whom you made that promise?'

'I'm sorry, sir. I can't say. Forgive me, but I find myself in a very awkward situation. I need advice but I can't ask anyone for it, as that would involve me having to give explanations which I've promised not to give.'

'I see,' the Ambassador said, though plainly he didn't, judging by the confused expression on his face.

'Can you tell me what these two men were doing, sir? It would help me decide. I think.'

'Well, they do indeed work for the Cultural Attaché. Apparently he has used these two aides to stake out, I think you say, a house down the road.'

'Do they know why?'

'No. They say they just have to report all movements direct to the Attaché.'

'Why?'

'They don't know that either.'

'Don't know, or just won't say?'

The Ambassador inclined his head curtly. 'I suspect you're right. The Cultural Attaché has a very forceful personality. I imagine these men are scared of what he could do to them, or to their families for that matter.'

'Is the Cultural Attaché not under your authority, sir?'

'Of course he is, Chief Inspector. It's just that such appointments are deeply political, if you understand my meaning. The Attaché has some very powerful sponsors back in Bangkok. Regrettably, such sponsorship can result in other agendas being undertaken.'

Magee was bewildered. 'Other agendas? I'm not quite sure I understand, sir.'

'Personal agendas, Chief Inspector. Agendas that stand to benefit specific individuals, or groups, rather than the good of the country.'

Magee frowned. 'I see. Are we back to the political problems you said your country was experiencing?'

'Exactly.'

'So, now what? Can I arrest them? Take them in for questioning?'

'That would be difficult. I think their diplomatic status would prevent that. And you're now standing in Embassy property, so you're unable to make an arrest.'

'But they might be able to throw light on who the murderer is.'

'True, but, regrettably, one reason for diplomatic immunity is that diplomats can avoid undue influence by authorities such as the police.'

'So I can't touch these two men?'

'I'm afraid not. You'll have to release them.'

'What about the Cultural Attaché? Can I speak with him?'

'You may if he chooses to cooperate, Chief Inspector. I would doubt it though, given what's happened this evening.'

'Could you ask him, sir?'

'Of course I will.' The Ambassador walked to his desk, picked up the telephone and dialled a number. After a pause, he dialled another number and spoke for a few seconds. 'Sorry, Chief Inspector. His secretary says he's not contactable at the moment. Apparently, he's having a break for a few days.' The Ambassador shook his head in apparent puzzlement. 'Very odd, he usually keeps me informed of his movements.'

'Do you, or these men, have any idea where he might be, sir?'

'They think he's on holiday.'

'Can you tell me where he lives, sir?'

'At the back of the Embassy here. He's a single man.'

'Does he have a flat in Brighton?'

'I'm not sure, he's never talked about it if he does.'

'When is he due back?'

'Not until the end of next week. Maybe Thursday night, if we're lucky.'

'So until then he might still be out there murdering people?'

The Ambassador looked shocked. 'You're assuming he's the murderer?'

'What other motive would he have for this evening's activities?'

'I, erm, I really don't know. I can follow your train of thought though. Oh dear, Chief Inspector, this is all very upsetting. If the Attaché is the murderer, and he's caught and put on trial, it will cause tremendous bad feeling towards my country.'

'I'm sorry about that, sir.'

'Look, Chief Inspector, I'll get my staff to search for him.'

'Thank you, sir. But what will you do if you find him? You say you wouldn't be able to hand him over to me?'

The Ambassador contemplated the problem in silence for a few moments. His facial expressions changed from concern to worry and then from a devious look to one of enlightenment.

'Chief Inspector,' the Ambassador said at length. 'The British authorities can do very little about this matter. At best, the Attaché would no longer be made welcome in this country. He would then be requested to leave within a matter of a day or so. That's about the only action that can be taken against him. However, that process would involve you explaining tonight's activities to higher authorities. The Home Secretary would have to be informed and it would be up to him to put pressure on me to expel the Attaché.'

Magee gulped. 'I'd rather not go down that route, sir.'

'Also, of course, such process would involve the considerable dissemination of knowledge, probably involving press statements.'

Magee recoiled at the thought of Rees Smith getting involved. 'I really would rather avoid that, sir.'

'In that case, Chief Inspector, perhaps you would let me deal with the problem. One way of avoiding any publicity would be for me to send the Attaché back to Bangkok immediately. I would have him dealt with over there.'

Magee liked what he heard except for the term dealt with. The words had come out in an almost sinister tone. Still, that wasn't his concern. If the Cultural Attaché was the murderer, and was quietly disposed of in Bangkok, then that could well be the best thing for everyone involved. He glanced at Melissa to see what her reaction was.

Melissa put her hands up in front of her. 'Don't look at me, sir. This is completely above my pay grade. It's your case and I haven't heard or seen a thing. This conversation has nothing to do with me, if you don't mind.'

Magee looked back at the Ambassador. 'I think your solution might well be best, sir.' At least Rees Smith would be happy, he reflected. 'Yes, sir. I'm in full agreement with you. I'll leave the matter in your capable hands if you don't mind.'

'Good. We have a deal then, Chief Inspector?'

'Yes, sir, but I do hope you can reach the Cultural Attaché soon. In the meantime, I'm no better off. I'd better get back to my case. Thank you for your time, sir.'

'Before you leave, would you mind letting these men go?'

'Sorry. Yes, of course.' Magee nodded at Melissa who proceeded to remove the handcuffs. 'What will happen to them, sir? Back to Bangkok as well?'

'I have some questions to ask them but then, yes, I'll tell them to pack their bags. You won't see them again, Chief Inspector.'

Magee frowned at that comment. Surely the Ambassador didn't mean he would have them dealt with, as well?

Chapter Thirty-Eight

Magee made his excuses and left the Royal Thai Embassy, along with Melissa, to walk the half-mile back to McAlister's house.

Once out of earshot of the Embassy, Melissa asked, 'What on earth was all that about, sir? Why are you conspiring with the Ambassador not to pursue the Cultural Attaché? Why aren't you willing to make this new information public? I don't understand half of what's going on.'

'I'm sorry, Melissa. It's part of a very long story. And, as you can see, it's getting rather complicated. You really are best out of it.'

Melissa gave a snort. 'You can say that again! But I'm still interested.'

Magee felt a desperate need to confide in someone. 'I saw the Home Secretary the other day. I promised him I'd contain the problem and not let any more details get to the press. There could be a huge scandal if it does. It could bring the government to its knees,'

'Why? How could a murder case possibly do that?'

'Well, you see, Melissa, after McAlister, the next victim is Geoffrey Rees Smith, the Home Secretary.'

'Oh dear god! How on earth did you find that out?'

'He's in the photograph too. I confronted him, told him of my theories on the case. He pulled a gun on me, threatened to kill me. That seemed to confirm I was right.'

'Wow!'

'Exactly. That little episode is not something the press should get to hear about. You may need to know about these things, but you really do need to be discrete and keep your mouth shut. It could be dangerous to talk to anyone else.'

'I won't talk, sir.'

'Good. You see, if other people find out that you know, well, you may become expendable.' He looked at Melissa knowingly. 'Do you know what that implies?'

'Yes, sir, I do. You don't have to elaborate. Just don't tell me any more please. I talk in my sleep.'

'Well don't,' Magee said with sincerity. 'Whoever sleeps with you might become expendable as well!'

'Oh god, this just gets worse.'

'Precisely, Melissa. I'm sorry for scaring you, but you've got to realize the seriousness of the situation.'

'You've convinced me. Who else knows?'

'Just the remaining five men in the photograph, along with Paul Mansell and the Ambassador. A very tight knit little group, and the numbers are dropping daily. Sorry to involve you. Just don't involve anyone else.'

'No problem there, sir. I won't talk. I rather enjoy my life. I don't want to die yet.'

'Nor do I, so let's keep it that way. Anyway, no more talk about it, we're within earshot of the others now. Let's wander round to see what's being going on in our absence.'

The first three lookouts reported nothing new. The last had, what he thought to be anyway, precisely the information Magee was searching for.

'I've spotted him for you, sir.' The officer said as Magee drew near.

'I'm sorry. Spotted who?'

'Your spy, sir.'

'My spy?'

'Yes, sir. Melissa said you wanted us to keep an eye open for someone watching us. I've found him for you.'

Magee and Melissa stared at each other in bewilderment. 'But we just . . .' Melissa let the sentence trail off. 'Didn't we?'

'Just where is this spy of yours?'

'Over the road, sir. Second house down on the right. He's up in the attic room. The lights are off but someone's in there. The curtain is drawn back a fraction every now and then. The movement is not easy to spot. He's doing well by not drawing any attention. I reckon he's a pro. I only chanced upon him by accident. I was, erm, daydreaming and staring up that way.'

'Okay.' Magee wasn't sure whether to congratulate the man or reprimand him. 'Stay here, we'll look into it.'

As Magee walked over to the front door of the house indicated, a thought struck him. 'Melissa, this may be him. The murderer, that is.'

'The Cultural Attaché?'

'Could be.'

'The one we can't touch.'

'The same.'

'What are we going to do then?'

'Haven't the foggiest. We'll just have to improvise. Be prepared for anything,' Magee said, as he pushed a bell button. A middle aged plump woman bubbling with life opened the door promptly.

'Good evening, madam. We're police officers,' Magee said holding up his warrant card. 'I'm Detective Chief Inspector Magee, this is Detective Sergeant Kelly. May we have a word, please?'

'Oh! Yes, of course. Please come in, won't you?'

'Thank you,' Magee replied. He followed the woman into her ground floor apartment. 'Is the whole house partitioned off into flats?'

'Yes. You're quite right, Chief Inspector. Why?'

'Do you know who the tenant up the top is?'

'Right at the top? Which side?'

'On the front right as you face the house.'

'That's young Miss Virginia's flat.'

'And who is she?'

'Well, I believe she's an accountant. She works in the City, in Puddledock I think she told me once. Lovely name that, isn't it?'

'It is, though I'm more familiar with the Kent hamlet of the same name.'

'Really, I didn't know there was one. Where is it?'

'Not far from Westerham. Near Chartwell, Churchill's house.'

'Good lord. You learn something new every day.'

'You do indeed,' Magee muttered. He decided social pleasantries were over. 'Is she in? Miss Virginia, that is?'

'I'm not sure. I haven't seen her for a couple of days. Maybe she went off for the weekend. She has many friends in the country. Part of the in-crowd, you see.'

'Does she live alone?'

'Of course, Chief Inspector! She's not that sort of girl.'

'I meant does she share with a girlfriend, a flat mate?'

'Oh, I see. No. No, she doesn't.'

'Nevertheless, there is someone up there now, madam. I'd like to investigate, if you don't mind.'

'Not at all, feel free.'

'I don't suppose you have a spare key by any chance?'

'Well, yes, I do, as it happens. I'm not supposed to tell anyone, but it's for emergencies. Is she in danger?'

'Maybe, I don't know, to be honest. But it appears someone is in her flat, acting very suspiciously.'

'Very well then. But don't tell anyone about the spare key will you?'

'Of course not.'

Rather apprehensively, Magee and Melissa crept up the stairs. He whispered, 'If this Miss Virginia hasn't been seen for a few days, then she may be trapped in there now.'

'Held hostage, you mean? Shouldn't we call in then?'

'Probably, but I don't think Rees Smith would appreciate it.'

'I don't like that man,' Melissa responded, 'even though I've never met him.'

'Keep it that way. He's obnoxious.'

'What if she's bound and gagged? Maybe there's a group of them in there?'

Magee thought about the potential danger. Who else could it be, he thought, except the murderer? Perhaps he should have come armed.

They stopped outside the apartment, one either side of the door, up against the wall. Magee gave a firm knock. There was no response. He tried again. No response. He inserted the key into the door and turned the handle. The door jerked to a stop within two inches. The chain was on, the lights off, but someone must be inside. Magee looked at Melissa and grimaced.

'Police!' Magee said reasonably quietly, but firmly, from his position of safety behind the door. There was no response. 'Open up now, please. I'll kick the door down if you don't.'

'What is your name?' The words were delivered by a firm, manly voice the other side of the door.

'Detective Chief Inspector Jack Magee. I'm with Detective Sergeant Melissa Kelly.'

'What do you want?'

'I want to know where Miss Virginia is, the occupant of this flat. I also want to know why you're spying out of the window on what we're doing down below.'

'We're guests of Miss Virginia. She gave us a key, we are not trespassing. You have no right to enter these premises.'

'You're acting suspiciously with the lights off. I'm not leaving until I check the flat.'

It was several seconds before an answer came. 'Please ask DS Kelly to go away,' the voice demanded.

Magee sighed. 'I can't do that. DS Kelly stays here with me.'

'Chief Inspector, listen to me. I will talk to you, but to you alone.'

'Shit!' Magee hissed under his breath. He looked over at Melissa who merely shrugged her shoulders. 'Tell me who you are first.' Magee prayed that it wasn't the Cultural Attaché.

'Yesterday, at about eleven thirty in the morning, you made a promise to someone. Do you recall what that was about?'

'What the heck? Who's in there? No one could possibly know about that promise.'

'Well I do! And I must remind you of it. To keep that promise secure, please send DS Kelly away, out of earshot.'

Magee screwed his eyes shut. It could only be Rees Smith in there, but why? Magee nodded at Melissa, indicating her to leave. 'Okay, Sergeant Kelly's gone downstairs. Now will you open up please?'

The door creaked open slowly. Magee walked into the darkened room and the door was abruptly closed behind him. A small lamp was turned on, which lit up three men dressed casually standing alongside a variety of cameras and binoculars. None of the men was Rees Smith.

Magee cursed and asked, 'Who the hell are you lot?'

'Brigadier Bernard Armstrong. My card, Chief Inspector.' Brigadier Armstrong handed over a non-descript card. 'These men work for me, their names are not relevant.'

Magee read the card, bewildered. 'Can you explain what's going on, please? I really don't understand what you're doing here.'

'Of course, Chief Inspector. After all, you are up to your eyes in this.'

'Up to my eyes?' Magee repeated. 'I'm sorry, am I missing something here?'

'Are you saying you're not involved with our dear friend Geoffrey Rees Smith in a conspiracy to pervert the course of justice?'

'No, not at all. How dare you insinuate such a thing!'

'I must warn you, Chief Inspector, that I listened to your conversation yesterday. I have video tapes as well, so you won't be able to deny anything.'

Magee frowned in puzzlement. 'Just a second, Brigadier, you seem to be accusing me of some criminal activity.'

'You said it, Chief Inspector.'

'I think we have our wires crossed here. I'm involved in nothing illegal.'

'It didn't sound like it during your meeting with Rees Smith yesterday.'

Magee scratched the back of his neck and gave a moment's thought to how the conversation might appear to an outsider. 'Can we discuss this? I think there are aspects of the case you may not be aware of.'

'By all means, Chief Inspector. Take a seat, I do like a good chat.'

Magee sat down and rubbed his chin, wondering where to start. He decided to begin with the photograph. He extracted a copy from his jacket pocket. 'Have you seen this photo before, Brigadier?'

Brigadier Armstrong studied it for a few seconds. 'No, I haven't.'

'Do you recognize anyone in it?'

'McAlister and Rees Smith, in their early days by the look of it. What's this about?'

'This photograph was taken in Bangkok eighteen years ago. Shortly afterwards, these men got involved in some sort of heist. I'm not sure what, no one will tell me, but I believe it involves Tibet and I believe several people were killed, murdered by Rees Smith himself is my guess. Anyway, the point is they were obviously successful because they returned home multi-millionaires.'

'The source of McAlister's and Rees Smith's fortunes?'

'And the reason they fell out with each other.'

'Hmm,' Brigadier Armstrong murmured. 'Interesting. Do you know what happened?'

'No. Not yet. But I will find out, eventually. I always get there in the end.'

'That's important to you?'

'Indeed it is, sir. You see, this photo is closely connected to the recent series of murders I'm investigating in Brighton. Todd Conners, Mike Harwood, Robert Harrison and Ronald Nelson are in this photograph and were all victims. Another would have been a victim had he not been dead already. We know that because his mother got a message recently making that very clear. Whoever is killing these men off is doing it in accordance with the seating plan in this photo. I therefore know that Des McAlister is next. Then it's Rees Smith's turn.'

One of Brigadier Armstrong's eyebrows raised. 'Good Lord!' he responded.

'I was suspended from duty last week for being too keen, and an idiot called Inspector Jackson took over the case. However, it seems the murderer wanted me back on the case so he deliberately set up a red herring at the last murder scene to make Jackson look a fool. I was able to use that as a weapon against Rees Smith to get my job back. All I want to do is solve this murder case and keep my status in the Force. Unfortunately, I've upset a few people along the way. Like Rees Smith, for instance, since I've accused him of being involved in something pretty ugly.'

'Why does the murderer want you on the case?'

'I don't know, sir, although I have a suspicion.'

'Which is?'

'Well, it's just a hunch, based on what I know about the remaining men in the photo. To start with, the main character in all this is Nick Price. That's him down on the bottom right hand side of the photo. It was his bar in Bangkok where this photo was taken, but he's now a wealthy property developer living down near Brighton.'

Brigadier Armstrong nodded sagely. 'I thought so. Rees Smith suspects him, I believe. He instructed me to put Nick Price under surveillance last week.'

'I'm glad to hear it. He is involved, although his involvement may just be peripheral since he seems to be an okay sort of person, a family man. But I can't rule him out. He's a sick man, he suffers terribly from guilt over the death of his wife. I know him from the past, in our teenage years. He's quite capable of murder and I get the odd glimpse of him as a man who may be mentally unbalanced.'

'Rees Smith is right then? Nick Price is the main suspect?'

'It's not that clear cut, sir. There are several others on my list. Equally probable, I should think.'

Brigadier Armstrong reached for a pen and notepad that were sitting on an adjacent coffee table. 'I'm listening.'

'Well, there's Sean Fitzpatrick, an old acquaintance of Nick Price. He's in the photograph. He seems to have blown all the money from the heist. I'm told he's nothing more than a dosser these days, getting drunk frequently, ranting in bitterness about his ex-wives. I haven't spoken to him yet, but such a character could well be trying to blackmail the others.'

Brigadier Armstrong took a pause from writing and said, 'Do you know who John Mansell is?'

'Yes I do, sort of. He's in that photo as well. He was an intimate friend of Nick Price and jointly owned the bar with Nick. But he seems to have disappeared years ago, so I've not been able to make contact. I'm more familiar with his younger brother, Paul. Nick took Paul under his wing after he became a mixed-up sixteen year old hell-raiser. It seems that the murderer has been using Paul; he's tried to frame him in three of the murders so far.'

'For what purpose?'

'I don't know. Possibly out of hatred for John, but that's just conjecture.'

'So your hunch with the murderer is what, precisely?'

'Well, no one seems to know where John Mansell is, so I reckon the murderer can't find him either. I believe he wants me to do his dirty work for him. I reckon he's hoping I'll track down John Mansell.'

'Interesting idea. Rees Smith asked me to trace him too. I've certainly had no luck.'

'Also, I think the murderer's using me to flush the others out into the open so he can pick them off more easily. That's why I'm here now. We've been scanning the surroundings, looking out rather than looking in.'

'Very interesting, Chief Inspector. And just who do you suspect of being the murderer?'

'I have an even longer list of possibilities.'

'I'd like to know them.'

'First, there's Rees Smith. Now he's in a prominent position in the government, he's vulnerable. His history could catch up with him. Maybe someone is blackmailing him. Best thing is if he kills them all off.'

'Including you, I take it?'

'Yes indeed, sir. I got rather carried away yesterday. I was under threat of losing my job, my pension, everything I've ever worked for, and all because of something Rees Smith did in his youth. I threatened him with exposure. If you know about our meeting, you probably know what happened next.'

'He pulled a gun on you.'

'Precisely, sir. And I think he was fully prepared to use it. He'll do something very silly, very soon, I fear. Even if he isn't the murderer, he might become a murderer to stay on top of the situation.'

'You've thought this through well, Chief Inspector. Who are your other suspects?'

'Well, first of all, we have to determine motive. Revenge is most likely. Several people got killed eighteen years ago, so the murderer is probably taking his revenge for someone who died.'

'And those possibilities are?'

'Nick Price, since he lost his wife, Maliwan. I'm pretty sure she was killed in the heist itself, and I have the impression it was Rees Smith that killed her. Anyway, Nick Price is still extraordinarily distraught about her death, even now.'

'I see. Grief is certainly a powerful emotion. Next?'

'Nick Price has two children. Somsuk and Nittaya. They must be suspects as well, since they lost their mother along with her twin brother, their uncle, at the same time. Family revenge there, of course.'

'Any others?'

'Paul Mansell. I'm not convinced of his innocence despite the fact that I believe he really had been set up. His brother, John, walked out on him when he was just three years old. He's still very cut up about that. There's been no indication that John's alive, maybe he died in the heist, or was caught and imprisoned in some Bangkok hellhole. Paul might know the truth and be avenging his brother.'

'No others, I hope?'

'I'm afraid there are, sir. There's something running alongside this murder business, something I can't quite yet put together.'

'Please elucidate.'

'All the victims have been killed with daggers that have an ivory handle carved in the shape of a Buddha. There is an historical connection here; Thai people used them against Japanese soldiers during the war to take revenge for rape.'

'How on earth does that fit in?'

'I think the murderer is a Thai national. I think he's trying to murder everyone in the photograph.'

'So that means the murderer is a different party entirely.'

'Sort of, sir. Obviously not someone in the photo, but he's certainly still very much connected with the photo.'

'Could it be a she instead of a he? What about the girl in the photo?'

'The girl is Nick Price's wife, Maliwan. As I said, she's dead.'

'Ah!'

'Nevertheless, sir. I believe she's a very large part of the jigsaw.'

'How?'

'It's a gut feeling. This photo is relevant to the heist, and she, I believe, was killed over greed. Someone wants to settle old scores.'

'How does she fit in with your mystery man then?'

'Ah, that's the problem, sir. Nick Price won't talk about other people involved in the heist. All he says is that they're dead.'

'So we're either dealing with a ghost, someone they've all forgotten existed, or someone that was presumed to be dead?'

'Exactly, sir. That's why I need to know the story behind the photo. I need to examine the evidence, rather than get bogged down with the emotion of it all.'

'McAlister and Rees Smith? Won't they help?'

'Hah! They've both said they'd prefer to die rather than let the truth be known.'

'You're caught up in a real hornet's nest, aren't you, Magee?'

'I certainly am, sir. And my boss, Superintendent Vaughan, doesn't know about it.'

'You're going to have to proceed very carefully, Magee. And alone, unsupported, I expect.'

'Indeed, sir, but I have to say it's rather nice unburdening this lot onto you. I don't feel so alone now.'

'Hmm.' Brigadier Armstrong drummed his fingers on his knee. 'You know something, Magee, I think we could help each other out. You see, I'm involved in the case from the National Security point of view.'

'Guarding the Home Secretary?'

'Yes and no. My brief certainly requires me to protect the Office of the Home Secretary, but as to the man, well, he does seem to have a rather chequered past, or so it's emerging. The man could easily overstep the mark, in terms of carrying out the duties of his office.'

Magee was astonished. 'You're implying he's expendable?'

Brigadier Armstrong rubbed his chin thoughtfully. 'I'm afraid so, yes. He's dug his own grave, politically and maybe even physically as well. Whatever he did in Bangkok has come back to haunt him with a vengeance. It would be extremely difficult to stop the truth coming out now. When it does surface, he'll be lucky to get away with a simple resignation. If he committed a serious crime, even one committed abroad eighteen years ago, the press will crucify him.'

'So you've been tagging along, watching from a distance, hoping maybe that things will sort themselves out nicely?'

'You never know, Magee. You just never know. However, I won't leave things to chance, I'll be there waiting to make a move if things don't go the right way.'

'You mean you want the murderer to succeed?'

'No. Not necessarily, Magee. I'd be quite happy for the murderer to be killed, and for the Home Secretary to live. Provided the story stops there, of course. No leaks, no Sunday newspaper interviews, no memoirs published.'

Magee sighed deep. 'Rees Smith just got too greedy, I suppose. Wasn't content with wealth alone, he wanted the power that could be bought with it, didn't he?'

'Power corrupts absolutely. Rees Smith could have had a life of luxury, somewhere quiet and low key. Instead, he craved a life centre stage. He's paying for that decision now.'

'If you don't mind, sir, I'd like to try to stop this madness. It is my duty, after all.'

'Of course, Magee. I don't mean to belittle your position. You come across as a good police officer. I apologize unreservedly, I assessed you incorrectly. You'd better be getting back to your troops. Good luck.'

'Thank you sir.' Magee got up from the sofa. 'Well, I've no doubt we'll be seeing each other again.'

Magee left Brigadier Armstrong to his task and meandered slowly back to the street wishing he'd simply stayed in bed for the day. A completely new perspective had been added to the case. Who could make decisions concerning the fate of a Home Secretary? The Prime Minister? Brigadier Armstrong himself? Did the man have that much power? Who the hell was the Brigadier anyway?

Magee felt that he was losing his grip on reality. It felt like the world was going mad. All this business with politicians, ambassadors and intelligence service officers was just too much to get his head around.

'You certainly took your time, sir,' Melissa said when Magee came up alongside her. 'What was that all about upstairs?'

Magee shook his head. 'You don't want to know, Melissa. Forget it happened. I feel as though a large hammer has just pummelled my brain. I wouldn't want you feeling the same way. Someone has to keep a level head. This case is getting far too complicated for my liking.'

'A problem shared?'

'Is a problem doubled in this case. Whatever happened to simple straightforward murders? That's what I want to know.'

'Fancy a drink? There's a pub down the bottom.'

'We shouldn't really,' Magee protested half-heartedly as Melissa slipped an arm under his and gently steered him down the road.

'Come on, one drink won't hurt.'

Magee felt a headache coming on. 'Will you visit me in hospital, Melissa? I think I'm losing my sanity. This case is really getting to me.'

Chapter Thirty-Nine

Des McAlister zapped the TV off with the remote and sat staring at a blank screen. As bedtime approached, the seriousness of his predicament intensified. Two of his old comrades had been killed in bed. Just how safe would he be, with Magee and his men patrolling outside? It was the thought of his wife and kids being attacked, as well, that made the burden of keeping quiet his dreadful secret almost unbearable.

'You know something, dear?' Amy McAlister ventured. 'I'm almost glad of this security alert. We haven't seen so much of you during the evening for years.'

Des McAlister smiled falsely at his wife. Inside, he was a bag of nerves. 'This time, Amy, it really is very serious. More so than ever before.'

'We overcame the problems before, dear. I daresay we'll do so now.'

'I'm not so sure,' McAlister muttered. 'Look, Amy, if anything happens to me, let the kids know I love them won't you?'

'Oh, Des!' his wife cried. 'Don't speak like that!'

McAlister fidgeted with the TV remote. 'I'm sorry, Amy. I just have a bad feeling in my bones, that's all.'

'Well I don't, but you've upset me now.' Amy McAlister rose from her chair. 'Look, I'm going to bed. I'll read for half an hour or so. Join me when you're in a more positive mood.'

Des McAlister nodded and leant back in his chair to contemplate matters. Theft and murder. Of those, he was guilty. How was he to explain them to Amy and the kids after all these years? Should he even bother? Why not let the inevitable happen? At least death would bring salvation. No awkward questions, no recriminations, no looks of astonishment. There again, it would leave the kids with no father. Could he do that to them? Which scenario was worse? He closed his eyes. Please God, give me one last chance to redeem myself.

As if in response to his prayer, the telephone rang. He grabbed at it.

'Good evening,' the caller spoke in a muffled tone. 'Is that Des McAlister?'

'Speaking. Who is this?'

'Sorry, the line's bad,' the muffled voice continued. 'I'm in a public phone booth, I can hardly hear you. Hang on, I'll just give it a whack. There! Can you hear me better?'

'Yes, a little better, but it's rather crackly. Look, who is this?'

'It's Nick. Nick Price. Do you remember me? It's been a long time since your days in Lucy's Tiger Den, hasn't it?'

'Nick Price? Yes, of course I remember you. Dear God, I haven't heard Lucy's Tiger Den mentioned in years.'

'Great days, weren't they? Look, sorry, but there's no time for social pleasantries. You're aware of the recent murders, aren't you?'

'Yes, I am. Chief Inspector Magee has warned me about the problem.'

'What are you planning to do about it?'

'Well, nothing, really. Magee has my house under surveillance. What more can I do?'

'You can fight back, for one thing.'

'No. No more fighting, Nick. Enough is enough.'

'We can stop him. We must silence him ourselves.'

'Kill him you mean?'

'No, not necessarily.'

'What then?'

'Did Magee tell you about his suspicions, that the killer is a Thai person?'

'He mentioned the possibility. Why?'

'Well, did Magee also tell you that the Thai Ambassador is keen to catch the killer, if he is Thai, and send him back to Bangkok? That way, there'll be no trial in this country. If anything, there'll just be a secret trial in Thailand. No one will ever know what's happened.'

'But how could that be achieved? How can the Ambassador catch him?'

'Well, we need to set a trap, and we need your help to pull it off. You're his next victim and we need you to draw him out into the open. You won't have to fight, Des, I promise you that. I'll do any fighting that's necessary along with the help of the Ambassador's staff. You see, the killer's an embarrassment to the Ambassador. I've been talking to him myself tonight and he explained everything. All we have to do is bring the killer into the open. There will be no court case, no media exposure, life will go on as normal. Do you understand that, Des? You won't have to fight in any way whatsoever.'

'What about the police?'

'There's no danger that the police will be involved either, we're doing this without Magee's knowledge.'

'Really?'

'Yes really, Des. Do you like the sound of it so far?'

'Of course I do, Nick. My god, if only it were possible. Please, let's do it.'

'Good man, Des. Right. There's a small element of risk though, but I'm sure you'll agree it's worth taking. We have to set you up as bait. A bit like tying up a goat to a tree to catch a tiger, I'm afraid, but there's no other way. There's a small park at the bottom of your road with a war memorial in the centre. Do you know it?'

'Yes indeed. I often jog past there on the way over to Hyde Park.'

'Good. We reckon the killer is watching your house. He's just waiting for the right time to strike. We want you to lead him to the war memorial where we'll be hiding in the bushes. Do you understand?'

'Yes, I understand.' McAlister was aware that he'd begun to shake.

'I'm phoning from near the park right now and four of the Ambassador's staff are getting into place at this very moment. I want you to slip out of the back door, make your way along the alleyway and down to the park. We've seen a couple of policemen down that way, but they're in hiding and won't have time to react if you run past fast enough.'

'I'm fit, I can do it!'

'Course you can, Des. There's just one small problem though. There's a police officer stationed near your back gate. You'll have to think of a way to distract his attention. He'll be expecting someone to break in, not out, so you should have an advantage over him.'

'And the killer?'

'He should be nearby, probably hiding in a neighbouring road waiting for his spies to tell him what's going on. They'll spot you and tell him. You should have a couple of minutes spare at least.'

'When do we go?'

'No time like the present, Des. Don't think about it, just do it okay? Go now!'

'Right. I will. Right now.'

'Good. We're all here waiting for you, Des.'

McAlister replaced the receiver and breathed deep. This was it. The opportunity he'd prayed for, the one last chance he'd desperately sought. Good old Nick Price; a man of action, a man to depend on. Everything would be all right now, he said to himself as he grabbed a coat out of the under-stairs cupboard and walked into the kitchen.

'What are you doing, dear?' Amy asked as she poured herself a mug of hot chocolate.

'I'm not tired, dear. I thought I'd go out and chat with the police. They must be terribly bored. I might even make them a cup of tea. Anyway, I could do with a breath of fresh air.'

'What about the terrorist threat, dear?'

McAlister laughed at his wife's suggestion. 'As you said earlier, it's just a threat. We'll get through it.'

'Well don't be too long, will you? You know I can't sleep if you're not in the house.'

'Half an hour at the outside, I promise. Okay?'

'Okay then. See you later. Turn the lights out, will you?'

'Sure,' McAlister said as he slipped out the back door.

Des McAlister's house was a Georgian terraced town house with a long walled garden and a service pathway at the back. He sneaked down the flagstone path he had laid himself many years ago, knowing precisely where to tread so as not to make the slightest noise. He soon reached the back gate and stood staring at it and the seven foot high wall running the length of his garden. He bit his lip, stifling a curse; he hadn't oiled the gate recently. He knew the rusty hinges would make enough noise to wake the entire neighbourhood.

There was no alternative. He had to go over the top in order to avoid catching the attention of the officer on the other side. Shaking his head in dismay, he removed an old chimney pot from the rhubarb patch and placed it near the wall. With one hand grabbing the top of the wall, he eased himself up onto the pot. Gingerly, he peered over the top, withdrawing immediately when he saw a police officer squatting on his haunches just a few feet away.

McAlister stepped back down on to the lawn trying to think of a solution. The only idea that occurred to him was a bit too violent for his liking, but time was running out. He had no other option. He crept over to the garden shed and picked up one of the two dozen sandbags he'd bought in a panic after the great storm three years earlier. He went back to the wall carrying the sandbag, shifted the chimney pot two feet to the right, took a deep breath and climbed back on top of the pot. The officer was still there, seemingly oblivious to his antics.

McAlister gripped the sandbag in his right hand, held the top of the wall with his left, leant slightly over and swung the sandbag down from the side. The bag arced and slammed into the side of the unsuspecting officer's head. The hunched man keeled over. Stunned, McAlister hoped, rather than dead. Unfortunately, there wasn't time for him to stop and find out. He jumped down from his chimney pot, opened the gate and turned towards the park and his salvation.

McAlister came across no one during his mad dash, and within three minutes found himself in the centre of the park, his back to the war memorial statue, trying to make out shadows in the dark.

'Nick?' McAlister hissed. 'Nick, where are you?'

A bush rustled less than thirty feet away and a figure crept out in a crouching position.

'Over here!' The kneeling man hissed back.

'Jesus, Nick, I'm scared shitless.'

'That's okay,' the crouching man whispered back. 'I understand. We're all around you.'

'Are you armed?'

'Yes, we are. Why?'

'I could do with a gun. I feel so vulnerable.'

'Are you sure? I didn't think you liked guns.'

'I'll make an exception in this case.'

'Well, okay, just a second, I'll come over.' The crouching man withdrew into the bush and re-emerged clutching a bag. He jogged over to McAlister in a bent position, keeping his head down. Then he stood up quickly and, with a violent swing of his arm, hit McAlister on the side of his head with a cosh. McAlister flopped to the ground unconscious.

Chapter Forty

Brigadier Armstrong frowned as McAlister's back door opened letting light flood in to the garden. He cursed loudly on realizing what the man was probably going to do, 'Damn, he's going along with it!'

'He's doing a runner, sir?'

'I believe he is, Ian. Bloody idiot! Haven't you traced that call yet?'

'Any second now, sir. Here we go. Yep, it was made from a public phone box down near the park.'

'And exactly where is our friend Nick Price?'

'He gave Phil and Jamie the slip earlier this afternoon.'

'Brilliant,' Brigadier Armstrong muttered. 'Voice match?'

'Could be Nick Price, not too sure. It's got some vague similarities, but it's being distorted, possibly electronically.'

'What about anyone else we know?'

'No, no matches found.'

'A fine evening for cock-ups, if I may say so, gentlemen. I think we may have a situation developing. Who says leave it, who wants to get involved?'

The two surveillance officers in the room along with Brigadier Armstrong shrugged their shoulders in indifference.

Brigadier Armstrong was unimpressed by the response of his men. 'I'm glad that's not me out there. All right, stick to your headphones and binoculars you wimps, I think it's time for me to take a walk around the block.'

Chapter Forty One

Magee stared at his radio in despair. 'Damn it!' he spat out. 'Why the hell isn't Nixon responding?'

Melissa yawned. 'He's probably fallen asleep, sir.'

'Where the hell is he? He should have reported in at least five minutes ago.'

'Do you want me to go and look for him?'

'Yes please, Melissa. He should be round the back.'

As Melissa jogged off in search of the officer who was not responding to his radio, Magee checked his watch. Eleven twenty-five. The other murders had occurred well past midnight. An hour or so to go, he pondered, if tonight was going to be the night it happened, that is. Unexpectedly, his radio crackled into life.

'Sir,' Melissa screamed, 'He's out cold. He's been sandbagged!'

'Who has?'

'Nixon, sir. He's sprawled on the ground, unconscious. The back gate is open. The attack must be in progress.'

'Shit!' Magee gave swift instructions into his radio and rushed across the road to McAlister's front door. He banged on the door, pressed the bell and shouted, 'Open up! Open up!' Despite being prepared for this eventuality, now that it had happened he was quite shocked. There seemed such little likelihood of the murderer getting away with it.

The front door opened and Magee found himself looking at Melissa. 'Has he gone out past you?'

'No, sir.'

'Then he must still be in the house. Okay lads,' Magee said, letting five other officers in to the house ahead of him, 'Spread out! Search each room. Melissa, you stay here by the front door.'

'What on earth is going on?' Amy McAlister called down from the top of the stairs. 'Who are you people?'

'Police, madam,' Magee responded. 'Where is Mr McAlister?'

'Des, you mean? Well, I think he's still downstairs somewhere. I haven't heard him come up yet.'

Magee pointed to two of the officers and said, 'Get up there, you two. Give her some protection and search every nook and cranny. You others, come with me.'

Amy McAlister screamed hysterically at the sight of two burly police officers advancing towards her. Two minutes later, one returned downstairs and broke the news to Magee that the upstairs rooms were empty. In dismay, he went out into the garden but was greeted by the sight of an officer walking towards him gesturing his frustration with his hands. He reached the obvious conclusion; the murderer was not on the property, nor was McAlister. 'Damn!' he muttered and went back inside in search of Amy McAlister.

Standing guard in the front hall, Melissa jolted at the sound of a soft knock on the front door. She opened the door in trepidation and asked of the gentleman standing there, 'Can I help you?'

Brigadier Armstrong smiled warmly as he gave Melissa a brief once over with his eyes. 'Are you Detective Sergeant Kelly?'

'Yes I am, why?'

'I'm taking charge. Tell Chief Inspector Magee I'm here will you please?'

'And you are?'

'Brigadier Armstrong.'

'And that makes you ...?'

'You wouldn't want to know that, my good sergeant.'

'Oh, right. I see,' Melissa replied. 'Well, er, I'll go and find him for you, sir.'

Magee was upstairs, in a bedroom trying to calm Amy McAlister.

'He said he was just popping out to chat with the officers on duty,' Amy McAlister stuttered through her tears.

'Why would he do that?' Magee asked.

'He said they must be bored. He was going to make them a cup of tea.'

'Did anything unusual happen tonight? Did he speak to anyone? Was there a phone call earlier, for instance?'

'Yes. Yes there was, actually. Just before he put a coat on to go outside. Oh, dear god,' Amy McAlister sobbed. 'Where is he? What's he done?'

'I don't know yet, I'm sorry.'

Melissa interrupted. 'Excuse me, sir. There's a Brigadier Armstrong downstairs. He says he's taking charge.'

'Tell him I'll be down in a minute. Give him whatever he wants. Anything at all.'

'Right. Say no more.' Melissa said as she touched the bottom of her nose.

Magee stayed with McAlister's wife for a few minutes. He just couldn't understand the mentality of Des McAlister. He had obviously walked into a trap. But why on earth had he gone out in the first place? What had the phone call been about? Another of the murderer's games perhaps? Was there no end to this stupidity? Magee left Amy McAlister to console herself as best she could.

Downstairs, Magee found Brigadier Armstrong giving out commands thick and fast. Within minutes, several police cars arrived carrying more men and a selection of powerful torches. Police dogs were offered a variety of McAlister's dirty clothes and shoes, and their handlers raced off into the night with their animals straining at the leashes.

The trail left by McAlister was less than twenty minutes old, fresh enough for the dogs to follow. The alleyway McAlister had run down only went in one direction. Soon, the dogs came out onto a narrow suburban road opposite a small public park. By the time they reached the park's entrance they were barking furiously, knowing they had found their mark.

As Magee raced into the park, he shone his torch in the direction that the dogs were straining. In the distance, he could make out a vague shadowy outline up against the war memorial. As he drew nearer, he slowed down, and then stopped, horrified. The outline was that of a body; a hideously distorted body.

Desmond McAlister had been gutted like a pig at an abattoir. Strips of intestines lay on the ground or hung down from his waist. His head hung at an impossible angle, almost severed at the neck. The knife sticking out from his chest looked bizarrely redundant.

Two of the police officers, young novices, gagged and vomited. Magee turned his torch away out of respect.

'Is he dead?' Someone at the back of the search party asked.

Brigadier Armstrong grunted. 'Don't be bloody stupid! Take the dogs around the area. See if they can pick up any exit trails.'

Magee walked as close to the remains of McAlister as his stomach permitted, reached for his radio and barked orders for arc lights, canvas sheeting to veil the victim and several bags to put McAlister's remains in.

The dogs failed to locate anything. The only trail picked up led to the main road then disappeared. The murderer had got away from right under Magee's nose. He was sickened by the events of the evening and bitterly regretted his promises to Rees Smith and the Ambassador. He wanted to tell the world about this monstrosity and to see the murderer caught, sentenced and put away for ever.

Chapter Forty-Two

The murder of a parliamentarian during the early hours of Sunday morning featured predominantly amongst news items for the remainder of the weekend. First thing Monday morning, as Parliament sat in session, the Home Secretary was given the floor to offer a personal tribute to his old friend.

Magee caught the speech on a radio in his office. After a couple of minutes he spat out, 'What absolute rot!'

'Shush,' rebuked Melissa. 'I think this is really moving.' She leant over Magee's desk and turned the radio up louder.

On the radio, Rees Smith was saying, 'So I would ask the House to join me in observing a moment's silence in memory of a man who devoted his life to serving the nation to the best of his abilities.'

Magee had had more than enough of Rees Smith. The silence was welcome. 'At least he's shut up.'

'It's very touching, sir. Didn't you hear the emotion in his voice when he talked about McAlister once being his best friend? You've no heart.'

'I've no heart for this bollocks, I know that.' Magee hit the radio off button with a resolute thud.

'Well I think it was a beautiful tribute. That must have been the best speech of his life; it really seemed to come from somewhere deep inside.'

'Well I say it was the sickest, most hypocritical garbage I've ever heard. What really galls me is that he probably prepared it in advance, days ago. It was too slick to have been written yesterday, especially if he'd been grieving as much as he says he has.'

'Perhaps he's written one for himself as well.'

'Hah!' Magee grunted. 'You know something, that wouldn't surprise me in the least.'

'Do you ever show sympathy, sir?'

'Yes I do actually, but only for deserving cases. Rees Smith is not on any such list.'

'Talking of lists, he's next. What do you intend to do?'

'Nothing, absolutely nothing. Brigadier Armstrong is keeping an eye on him, but then he's got security clearance, whereas we haven't. How the hell are we supposed to keep him under surveillance without letting Special Branch know what's happening?'

'So we just sit and wait?'

'Until he asks for our help, yes, I think so.'

'In the meantime, what's the plan?'

'I want to visit Nick Price again. Officially, this time. He gave Brigadier Armstrong's surveillance team the slip on Saturday, so it could well have been him who made the mystery telephone call to McAlister's house. We need to conduct a search.'

'He'll love you for that.'

'Unfortunately, it can't be helped. My list of suspects is being whittled down rapidly. Most of the remainder either live in Nick Price's house or are close to him. Come on, let's go.'

Magee picked up the paperwork, gathered his team together and left Lewes at the head of a convoy four cars and a van headed out to Cooksbridge. As he drove through the gateway to Price's Folly, and up the long tree lined drive, he couldn't help feeling he was finally nearing the end of his quest.

The arrival of the police vehicles in the front driveway elicited prompt action from within the manor house. Before Magee had rung the doorbell, Nick Price was standing on the doorsteps looking ready for a fight. Magee handed over a search warrant.

'You're kidding me!' Nick protested as he read through the warrant. 'You've got a nerve, Magee.'

'I'm sorry, really. But it's got to be done.'

'Why, though. Why on earth do you still think I have anything to do with these murders? I'm not violent, Magee, I'm a family man. Everyone's told you that.'

'There are other people who live here, Nick.'

Nick Price looked shocked. 'You mean you suspect Nittaya and Somsuk? Are you nuts?'

'Not at all. Now, if you'll please stand aside. Okay lads, let's start upstairs and work our way down.'

'Magee, please. This is really inconvenient.'

'I'm sorry, Nick, truly.'

'Please be careful in the house. Please don't touch any of her things.'

Magee was puzzled at the odd remark. He nodded to his team and replied, 'Don't worry, we'll be careful.'

'Daddy! What's going on?' Nittaya called out from somewhere inside the house. 'No! Don't you dare touch that!'

'Magee!' Nick shouted. 'Stop this now!'

'Tell me what's happening, Nick,' Magee said wandering up a magnificent wooden staircase, 'and I'll stop.'

'I can't do that, Magee,' Nick shouted up at him. 'I really don't know! I keep telling you that.'

Most of the first floor doors surrounding the open galleried landing were propped open, an officer in each room delicately sifting drawers. Magee stopped outside the one door that was shut. He tried the handle. It was locked. He turned to find Nick Price standing behind him, eyes glaring red. 'Key, please.'

'That is a very private room, Magee. What's inside is very personal. I really would prefer you not to go in there.'

Magee looked expectantly. He held his hand out. 'Key, please,' he repeated.

The look on Nick's face was enough to kill, but the man did as he was asked. He opened the door, motioned Magee to enter and followed behind shutting the door.

Magee thought he'd entered a time warp. The furniture, curtains, wallpaper, everything screamed nineteen seventies fashion. And it was all plain, cheap, unglamorous, understated, not at all what he'd expected to find in this palatial house. His eyes adjusted to the dim light, took in the nature of the photographs and clothes scattered around and recognized the morbid nature of the room. A foot high statue of a Buddha, centrepiece of a shrine, caught his attention. He wandered over to it, his eyebrows furrowing at the strange collection of offerings adorning the statue and its surroundings. 'Are you a Buddhist?'

'Me?' Nick asked quietly. 'No, I have no faith in any religion. How could I, after Mal was taken from me?'

'What's with this statue then?'

'It was Mal's. She kept it in our room. She would worship in front of it first thing every morning and last thing at night.'

'Why do you keep it?'

'Why keep it? Why do you think? Same as everything else in here, Magee. Everything's hers, just as she left it in Bangkok. I come in here to remember.'

'Nick, these memories, they're destroying you. You need to let go.'

'She was the love of my life, Magee.' Nick spoke softly, his eyes misty. 'I'd never known the power of love until I met Mal. She gave meaning to my life. She changed me, deep down inside. She gave me warmth. She gave me Nittaya and Somsuk. She gave me happiness.'

Magee sighed. The room was an unhealthy reminder of the past; a past in which Nick Price was trapped. Magee had seen rooms like it before, a shrine to an obsession. And obsessions often led to abnormal behaviour. 'Tell me what's happening, Nick.'

Nick Price sat down, ran his hand over the record player and stared trancelike towards a chair on the other side of the room. The music started and he hummed along quietly to the classic words.

Magee was taken aback. 'Are you okay?'

'She comes to me, Magee, whenever I'm in here. We dance sometimes, or just sit and talk about the kids. She was so special to me. She didn't deserve to die.'

'I'm so sorry.'

'After the accident, I just wanted to hold her close, just one last time. It's not right, to be denied a funeral. I could never forgive Geoff for that, nor could John, I suppose.'

'Did you kill them, Nick?'

'I'd like to kill Geoff. I told him then that I would.'

'And the others?'

'Why? That's what I can't understand,' Nick continued appearing to be lost in his own thoughts. 'Why kill the others? John wouldn't do that, he had no reason. They were his friends.'

'You think John Mansell is the killer?'

'It has to be John, or me. It can't be anyone else. No one had any reason, any motive, other than John and myself.'

'So you admit it was you?'
'It must have been me.'
'Are you making a confession?'
Nick Price's head rolled from side to side in time to the music.
'Nick? Talk to me about the murders.'
Nick rocked backwards and forwards in his chair. Tears were running down his face. 'Mal says she did it.'
Magee was stunned. 'Excuse me?'
'She's here now. She says she killed them.'
Magee looked around the room. There was no one else present. 'Why did she kill them, Nick?'
'For revenge.'
'Revenge for killing her?'
'Yeah. It was so unnecessary. Geoff lost it, you see, he flipped. If only he'd stayed calm, it wouldn't have happened.'
'Geoff was responsible for the death of your wife?'
Nick Price nodded his head.
'What about the others, Nick? Why did Mal kill them?'
'They just stood back, they let Geoff do it. No one challenged him. They could have stopped him, if they'd really wanted to.'
Magee sighed. It was obvious Nick was deeply disturbed, maybe even in danger of losing his mind. This wasn't the first time he'd seen the man act so strangely. In such a case, would a charge stick? Would a jury convict? Was it fair to even try? 'Nick,' he finally said, 'These murders have to stop. You can't murder a Home Secretary.'
'I know. But Mal will get him. She's told me that. She's got a strong will, that one, you won't be able to stop her.'
Magee's ears pricked up on the comment. Did he mean Nittaya instead of Maliwan? Were they in it together?
The record had stopped. Seconds later it restarted automatically. Nick hummed along with the words, lost in his own world, his eyes moist and out of focus.
Magee sank forward in his chair, cradling his head, thinking how true was the old adage life goes on after death, but paralyzes those left behind. How in the name of hell was he ever going to sort this mess out, he wondered?
'Come on Nick.' Magee got up and laid a hand on Nick Price's shoulder. 'You're going to have to come with me.'

Chapter Forty-Three

Magee thought the change in Geoffrey Rees Smith's demeanour was remarkably since the last visit to his office in Westminster. The man appeared to be on a high, a genuine smile in place for once.

'You've arrested Nick Price I hear. About time too! Has he confessed yet?'

Magee sat down without been asked. 'Not as such,' he replied.

'Not as such? What the hell is that supposed to mean, Magee?'

'He said that Mal did it?'

'Mal did it? But that's preposterous! She's been dead for eighteen years.'

'So I gather. Nick's being assessed at the moment.'

Rees Smith guffawed. 'Assessed? It sounds as though you should just throw him in the loony bin and chuck the key away.'

'I'm doing this by the book, sir. He'll be examined over the course of the next few days by a variety of doctors. If he's clinically insane, then it may prove impossible for him to stand trial.'

Rees Smith grimaced. 'Well, as long as you've got him under lock and key, then I'm safe.'

Magee took a few seconds to respond. 'I wouldn't be too sure about that, sir.'

Rees Smith appeared perturbed. 'Why do you say that?'

'I haven't proved that the murders were committed by Nick Price. Some issues have yet to be cleared up.'

'Issues?' Rees Smith responded, a frown appearing on his face. 'Such as what?'

'Well, there's the issue of the unknown man, possibly of South East Asian origins. The one seen by the hotel security guard in Hove.'

'We've discussed this already, Magee. It was a hit man. Or possibly Nick Price's son, Somsuk. I assume you've arrested him as well?'

'Of course, sir. We're holding Nittaya, Somsuk and Paul Mansell for questioning as well.'

'Good.' Rees Smith broke into a smile. 'I've nothing to fear then.'

'Only your past, sir.'

'Excuse me?'

'You've only your past to fear.'

Rees Smith snapped, 'And what precisely do you mean by that?'

'Something McAlister said. He said that your past would catch up with you, eventually. He thought his own punishment was inevitable.'

'Hah!' Rees Smith chuckled. 'Des was a fool.'

'I'm not so sure, sir. I still need some answers before I throw the book at Nick Price.'

'Answers to what?'

'Questions like, where are the remaining knives? Is there just one more knife, presumably for you, or are there four more left, making ten knives in total?'

Rees Smith retorted, 'Buggered if I care!'

'I think you should care, sir. It would be dangerous to let your defences slip at this stage.'

'The game is over, Magee. Well and truly over. There is nothing more to fear.'

'I wouldn't be so sure.'

'Explain yourself, Magee!'

'There's an anomaly in this case. You all say that Nick's wife Maliwan is dead.'

'That is correct.'

'My problem is that Nick mentioned to me that he was denied a funeral and that he could never forgive you for that. What did he mean by that?'

Rees Smith frowned again. 'I don't see this as being relevant, Magee.'

The Fourth Cart I

'Please bear with me, sir. Is it true that there was never a funeral for Maliwan?'

Rees Smith bit his lip before answering, 'No, there wasn't.'

'Why was that, sir?'

'Because we had no body to bury!'

'Again, sir, why was that?'

Rees Smith squirmed uncomfortably.

Magee nodded thoughtfully. 'Am I right in thinking that her body was left somewhere? Dumped, maybe? Is that why Nick Price has never been able to forgive you? Because not only did you kill his wife, but you deprived him of the ability to bury her with dignity, denied him a grave to visit?'

An ice-cold expression appeared on Rees Smith's face. 'You may leave now, Magee. The case is closed. You will not trouble me anymore. Understand?'

'Yes, sir. I quite understand.' Magee rose from his chair. 'Just before I go though, please think about the logic of what I've just being saying.'

'Which is?'

'If you never buried her body, if she was indeed dumped somewhere, then how can you be so positive she really is dead? Can you be absolutely one hundred per cent sure Maliwan is not behind these murders? After all, of everyone in that photograph, she's the one with the biggest grudge against you. You all survived, you all became millionaires. She didn't, did she?'

'Bollocks!' Rees Smith shouted at Magee's back as he walked out of the room, 'You know nothing!'

Chapter Forty-Four

Nick Price's confinement lasted a full week. On the last day, Magee travelled to the hospital in Haywards Heath hoping to receive the doctor's assessment first-hand. He had been waiting patiently in a reception room for an hour before a white-coated doctor entered and caught his eye.

Magee rose from his seat out of politeness and asked, 'How is Nick Price, sir?'

'He's reasonably fit for his age, Chief Inspector. And he's quite sane. In fact I'd go as far as to say there's really nothing wrong with him at all.'

'Will you discharge him then?'

'Absolutely. You can take him away now if you like.'

'Thank you. I'm sorry to have wasted your time; I really thought he'd gone over the edge.'

'Far from it. He's as sane as you or I. Well, me, anyway.'

Magee ignored the doctor's attempt at humour. 'What about the flashbacks he suffers from? Aren't they serious enough to cloud his judgment? Isn't it possible for him to do things he can't remember later?'

'You're clutching at straws, I'm afraid. Yes, he's suffering anguish, guilt, depression and anxiety. That's because he's never recovered from the loss of his wife, even though it's been, what, nearly two decades. Some people never get over the death of a loved one, especially when there's no chance of getting closure.'

'No funeral you mean? No body to grieve over, no one to say goodbye to, no grave to visit?'

'Precisely. He may stay the same for the rest of his life. Sad, really. There are many people in the world suffering the same condition. Usually, it's a parent whose child has been abducted and not found.'

Magee nodded his understanding. He'd met a few grieving mothers in his time. 'What about his mental state with regard to murder?'

'We're all capable of murder, Chief Inspector. Whether we're sane or otherwise. I suggest you stick to hard evidence.'

Magee shook his head. 'That's my problem, sir. I don't have any, but I need to keep him locked up.'

'Well, I'm sorry, but I can't do that for you.'

'I know,' Magee replied in a resigned tone. 'Thank you anyway for all your help.'

'You're welcome.'

'I'll take you up on your offer if I may, of discharging him now. I'll take him home.'

'Sure, if you'll just wait in reception, I'll get one of the nurses to bring him out to you.'

Magee thanked the doctor and approached the reception desk. He signed out, sat back down and picked up a Country Life magazine. It was half an hour before Nick Price emerged, ashen-faced. He looked ill.

'Nick, I'll give you a lift home if you like.'

Nick nodded his head and followed Magee out to the car park. As he got inside the car he said, 'You know something, Magee, I've been in hospital too many times in my life. I nearly didn't get out on at least two occasions. I've learned to despise them.'

'I'm not keen on them myself. They're far too depressing for my liking.'

'There was a young nurse in Saigon once, she was the only good thing I've ever come across in a hospital,' he paused and stared out the window for a few moments. 'I've done a lot in my life, Magee. I've done many things I wish I hadn't. I've suffered a lot too, but I've never really been bad, not in the evil sense. I couldn't commit murder, not the cold blooded, calculated type we're up against at the moment. Whoever's been doing this is sick. Really sick. A right mental case.'

'You know I was hoping it was you.'

'Yeah, I know, Magee. You're still trying to nail me for what I did as a kid.'

Magee smiled. 'Old habits die hard.'

'I'm sorry to disappoint you.'

'Actually, though it pains me to admit it to your face, I'm glad it isn't you. I've spent a long time talking to Nittaya and Somsuk these last few days. I wouldn't like to see them suffer with you locked up for life.'

'I'll take that as a compliment.' Nick returned a smile in Magee's direction. 'Look out!' he screamed, as a lorry pulled out from the T-junction they were approaching.

Magee realized it was too late to steer clear of an accident, but he quickly turned the wheel to avoid the worst. They braced themselves for the impact as the car spun to the left, up on to the pavement and into a low wall.

'Bloody hell!' Magee cursed. 'Are you all right?'

'Yeah, I'm okay, but we've got company.' Nick pointed to six armed men rushing towards them.

The last thing Magee recalled, before passing out from the effects of a spray gas, was watching Nick Price being forcibly removed from the car.

Chapter Forty-Five

'I have your girls.'

The words made Rees Smith freeze in fear. He closed his eyes in despair. This was one of those telephone calls that every father dreaded. How was it possible? What had happened to the Special Branch team that was supposed to be guarding them along with his wife? 'What do you want?'

'To talk. We have unfinished business.'

'About what may I ask?'

'Mal, of course.'

'Of course,' Rees Smith repeated, as though it would make sense. It didn't to him. 'Where, when?'

'Right now. Let's get it over with.'

Rees Smith sighed deeply. 'We need to talk about this.'

'We do indeed. Save it for six o'clock this afternoon, Shoreham Airport.'

'How do I know my girls are safe?'

'You don't. Come alone or they'll die, same way as Mal did.'

The telephone line went dead. Rees Smith stared at the receiver in his hand for a few moments before replacing it. 'Now, who the hell was that?' he murmured. He leant back in his chair to contemplate matters.

An hour later, Rees Smith stood in front of his dressing room mirror looking pleased at the image. Dressed up in army camouflage outfit, it reminded him of his time in Bangkok in his younger days. He struck a pose with a revolver.

He laughed loud. 'Oh, yes! I like it!' He placed the revolver and a handful of cartridge cases into his jacket pocket and casually made his way downstairs as if there was nothing untoward. He opened his front door and smiled at the two guards posted there by Brigadier Armstrong.

'Fancy dress party! Good costume, don't you think? I should just be able to make it on time if I rush. The wife's there already, I expect. Must dash, see you later.' And with that, he left the two guards standing, totally confounded.

He covered the distance from his house to Shoreham Airport within twenty minutes, pulled into the Airport's car park, turned off the engine and sat pondering what to do next.

As if in answer to his question, a young Thai man walked over to his Range Rover, inclined his head and motioned for Rees Smith to follow. His body shaking badly, pumped full of adrenalin, a nervous cramp knotting his stomach, he nevertheless did as instructed. It had been years since he had felt such a buzz.

Three minutes later, Rees Smith was beckoned to climb into a small, old airplane that looked horribly familiar. He shook his head, declining the offer. His escort jumped on board and Rees Smith's jaw dropped as his two young daughters, bound and gagged, were dragged into view. He climbed the short flight of steps without further ado. The escort slammed the door shut and the airplane rolled forward for take off.

A man, sitting crouched in front of another armed escort, looked up and smiled in Rees Smith's direction. 'Glad you could make it, Geoff.'

Rees Smith looked over at Nick Price. Seated beside him were Nittaya, Somsuk and Paul Mansell. 'I can't say I'm surprised to see you lot here. I knew you'd be behind this charade somewhere.'

Chapter Forty-Six

Nick Price shook his head as Rees Smith stumbled slightly before sitting down. 'Actually, Geoff, you've got it wrong. We were forced here at gunpoint. This is not our doing.'

'Really?' Rees Smith muttered as though he didn't believe it. 'So just who is in charge around here?'

'We haven't worked that out yet,' Nick responded. 'I honestly thought it was you.'

'Sorry to disappoint you, I'm sure. What about John, though? He's not here, I notice.'

'Paul took a pounding on receiving his invitation to this party,' Nick replied. 'I can't see John being responsible for that. Not to his own brother.'

To everyone's shock, one of the escorts brought the butt of a gun crashing down on Nick's skull. As he collapsed, spread-eagled on the floor, the escort shouted in broken English, 'You be quiet!'

'Daddy!' Nittaya shrieked. She sank to the floor next to her father and cradled his head. She looked up at the escort and demanded, 'Why are you doing this?'

The escort gave no answer. He stood expressionless, gun pointing at Nick as he lay moaning in agony. Slowly, the airplane rose above the sea and leveled off at ten thousand feet. Five minutes later a curtain shielding the cockpit was drawn back and another Thai man, dressed in army camouflage kit and sporting a backpack, came into view. He leveled a revolver at Rees Smith and said, 'To business, then. Stand up, Geoff.'

Rees Smith stared at the gunman quizzically. 'Who the fuck are you?' For his trouble, he received a smack in the face with the side of a gun.

'Don't be insolent, Geoff. Just do as you're told.'

Rees Smith frowned. He looked across at his two daughters cowering in fright. He wiped blood away from his lip and stood up.

'Right, Geoff. Stand toward the middle.'

As Rees Smith complied with instructions, he glanced down at Nick, and remarked, 'Still acting innocent?'

Nick looked up at the gunman. It was not a face or figure he recognized.

'Nick, get over there,' the gunman ordered, gesticulating with his gun. 'In your position.'

Nick rolled his eyes but didn't move.

The gunman waved his gun in a threatening manner. 'Nick! I said over there, now!'

'Daddy, please do as he says!' Nittaya put her arm around her father and helped him crawl in the direction indicated.

The gunman turned to Somsuk and said, 'Somsuk, go and lie down at the back. You take the position of the General.'

Somsuk looked bewildered, but did as he was told.

'John, stand over here, next to me.'

Paul Mansell frowned, as though trying to decide whether the order was meant for him. After a moment, he edged forward a few feet to the indicated spot.

'Mal, come and stand here, my love.' The gunman looked at Nittaya expectantly, but she did not move. 'Mal, I said come and stand here.'

Nittaya stared at the gunman in puzzlement. 'Me? You want me to stand over there?'

'Yes, my love.'

Nittaya moved into place. She looked down at her father, seemingly for guidance. None came.

'Right. We're all in place,' the gunman said. 'This time, we do it right. Open the door, Geoff.'

Rees Smith roared, 'What? Are you crazy?'

'No, Geoff. I'm not crazy. Nick said to open the door, don't you remember? We've got to throw as much out as we can.'

Rees Smith screwed his face up. 'Who the hell are you?'

The Fourth Cart I

The gunman ignored the request and barked an order in his native tongue. One of the escorts moved towards the door and opened it.

The gunman had to shout to make himself heard over the ensuing noise. 'You remember the shock we felt when this door was opened? The freezing air that gushed in, sucking the air out of our lungs? You remember the panic as we ripped away everything we could and hurled it out?'

Rees Smith shouted, 'This is not happening!'

The gunman turned his attention to Nittaya. 'Mal, lie down on the floor. Now!'

Nittaya lowered herself to the floor. She looked at her father in desperation.

'Lie down, Nit,' Nick said. 'Feet towards the back end. Stay still, try not to move.'

'What's happening, Daddy?' Nittaya cried. 'What's this all about?'

For the briefest of moments, Nick exchanged eye contact with Rees Smith. There was no other explanation for it; they were being forced to relive a moment of madness from their past. He felt his head swirl with a mixture of painful memories and unanswerable questions.

The gunman turned towards Paul Mansell and barked, 'John, kneel down beside Mal.'

'Paul,' Nick shouted, as he snapped out of his reverie, 'get down here. Lean over Nit.'

Paul did as he was told.

'General, pull your gun on Geoff!'

Somsuk remained in a motionless confusion.

Nick shouted at his son, 'Do it, Som. Do exactly as he says.'

'But I don't have a gun, Dad.'

'Role-play for god's sake! Use your imagination.'

Somsuk nodded and held his right hand up in the shape of a gun.

The gunman crouched down next to Paul Mansell, then looked up towards the middle of the airplane. 'Now then Geoff, it's your move.'

Rees Smith had a look of fear on his face. 'This is absurd. It can't be happening. Who the fuck are you?'

'Look around you, Geoff,' the gunman replied. 'Look at this airplane, doesn't it look familiar.'

Rees Smith screamed, 'You're barking mad!'

'It's a Prince 3A, Geoff. The Prince 3A, to be precise. You wouldn't believe how long it took me to find and restore it.'

Rees Smith caught Nick's eye and shouted, 'What the fuck is going on here?'

Nick looked at the positions of the people around him. History was repeating itself. And in the same airplane? That really was surreal. So surreal, in fact, he wondered if he was hallucinating. Maybe it had been the blow to the head that was affecting his sight. 'I think you'll find this is called a re-enactment, Geoff. Have you never re-enacted this scenario in your dreams? In your worst nightmares?'

'No, I have not!'

'Well I have, Geoff. A thousand times, at least. It never goes right for me, either. It always finishes badly, the same way as before.'

'Then why re-enact it for god's sake?'

'Why, Geoff? I'll tell you why,' Nick continued. 'To get it right, of course. To re-write history. To change what happened. To be able to live with myself.'

Rees Smith snorted. 'What the fuck are you talking about, Nick?'

'Enough!' the gunman screamed. 'Do it Geoff, make your move. Go on, grab Mal's legs!'

Rees Smith screamed, 'Shit! Who are you?'

'Do it!' the gunman screamed. 'Now!'

Rees Smith bent down and took hold of Nittaya's legs. 'This is insane!'

'Daddy?' Nittaya sobbed. 'What's he doing, Daddy?'

'It's okay, Nit. There's nothing to worry about. This is going to work out fine. Just hang on in there.'

A gun fired. Rees Smith grunted as his left arm recoiled from the impact of the bullet. He looked down at the reddening mark on his sleeve and snarled at the gunman crouching alongside Nittaya, 'You bastard, you'll pay for that!'

'You're the bastard, Geoff,' the gunman screamed back. 'You always were. And it's you who are going to pay for it!' He fired again and again, pumping more bullets into Rees Smith's torso. He threw the gun aside, withdrew a knife from his waist belt and lunged at the Home Secretary, screaming, 'You murderer! You fucking murderer! You took her from me!'

Rees Smith courageously fought against the frenzied attack. But as his body weakened, he turned his attention to Nick Price and shouted, 'Nick! Are you with me or against me?'

'I'm with you, Geoff,' Nick shouted back. He caught Paul's attention and flicked his gaze towards the escorts.

Above the din of the airplane's engines, Rees Smith shouted, 'Save my girls, Nick.'

'Let's do it!' Nick screamed back. 'Now!'

Rees Smith lunged at his attacker, his hands clawing at the man's face. Chunks came off in his fingers, yet they were of latex rubber not flesh. A brief look of puzzlement on Rees Smith's face changed to one of shock. 'No!' he screamed, as he found himself looking at a familiar face. 'It's not possible. I killed you!'

The gunman laughed insanely. 'Welcome to hell, Geoff. You threw Mal out like trash, so guess what I'm going to do with your daughters?'

With a surge of strength borne out of desperation, Rees Smith wrapped his arms around the gunman's body, sidled over to the door, wrenched him off his feet and threw him out into the abyss with a parting shot of, 'And as I said last time, don't fuck with me!'

As Paul and Somsuk wrestled with the escorts for control of their guns, Rees Smith sank to his knees, his left hand vainly trying to pull the obscene knife out of his side. With his right hand he pulled the revolver out of his jacket pocket, held it out and cried, 'Nick, use this!'

Nick dived for the revolver and shouted back, 'Stand away, Som!'

Somsuk just managed to jump out the way as his escort caught a bullet in the middle of his chest.

'Paul!' Nick screamed. 'Get out the way!'

Paul Mansell turned his escort to face Nick and then dived for cover.

Rees Smith had a contented smile on his face as he crashed to the floor. He looked in the direction of his two daughters and silently mouthed the words, 'I love you.'

Nick rushed to the girls as Paul wrenched the door closed. 'Okay, you're okay,' he said to them as he untied their bonds.

The two girls crawled over to their father, crying, 'Daddy!'

Rees Smith whispered, 'I'm so sorry, my darlings. I love you so much.'

'Daddy! Don't die!'

Nick knelt alongside the girls. There was blood everywhere. Far too much for the man to survive. 'Geoff, hang on there, old mate.'

'Nick, please don't tell anyone what really happened. Let it go to the grave with me.'

'Don't talk, Geoff, save your strength.' But it was too late. Geoffrey Rees Smith's eyes closed, he exhaled one last time and his body lay still.

Rees Smith's girls screamed in unison, 'Daddy! Please! No!'

Epilogue

'That's about it, I suppose,' Paul Mansell said, as he finished dictating his statement.

Melissa had been interviewing Paul Mansell for thirty minutes in one of the five rooms Brigadier Armstrong had commandeered that evening in the small airport's main building. She stopped writing and looked him squarely in the eye. 'And you've never seen this gunman before?'

'No.'

'Even though he's probably your mystery client?'

'As I've said already, I never met my last few clients. Cash only, in advance, through the post.'

'So you've no idea why this man wanted to kill Rees Smith?'

'None at all, he certainly didn't explain it.'

Melissa shook her head. 'Honestly, Paul, you're no good at lying. Your body language is all wrong.'

'I'm not lying, Melissa,' Paul responded with a slight grin on his face.

'DS Kelly to you. This is still official business.'

'So when can I call you "Melissa" then?'

'Not here, that's for sure. Take me on holiday to Thailand and then you can call me anything you like.'

Paul gave a wicked smile in return. 'Really? I might just do that. I'm going as soon as I can. What about you, are you free to go?'

Melissa sighed. 'Don't tempt me. The paperwork from tonight alone is going to take a month to complete.'

'Leave it to Magee, come fly away with me to paradise!'

'I can't! I've got work to do. You stay here a few minutes, we're not through with you tonight yet. Your stories aren't entirely consistent with each other.'

Magee hadn't yet finished interviewing Nick Price when Melissa came opened the door and stepped into the room. He caught her eye, only to be disappointed when she shook her head. He hung his head despondently. Was he never going to get the truth from anyone?

He sighed deeply and said, 'Nick, for god's sake, for the hundredth time, what the hell really happened up there tonight?'

'And as I keep telling you,' Nick replied as he massaged the back of his head. 'I'm buggered if I know. Whoever that gunman was, he was insane, pure and simple. I really don't know what he was playing at.'

Brigadier Armstrong leaned forward on his chair, looked into Nick Price's eyes and asked, 'And you'll keep to that story?'

'Story?' Nick grunted. 'It's no story, it's the truth. Some nutter kidnapped us all. God knows what his game was, but if it hadn't been for Geoff we'd all be dead. He's a hero, that man.'

'But the knife we recovered,' Magee interjected. 'It's got a carved handle, same as with the other killings. Geoff was the intended victim, so someone known to you must be responsible for the attack. You swear you didn't recognize any of the Thai men involved?'

'We're going round in circles here, Magee. Watch my lips, I swear I did not recognize any of those bastards!'

'Not even the one that was thrown out?' asked the Brigadier for the tenth time in an hour. 'The one we're assuming is the killer that Magee's after?'

'Never seen his face in my life.'

'But he's dead now, right?' persisted Brigadier Armstrong. 'You're sure of that?'

'I don't know. I assume so. Geoff threw him out. We were about ten thousand feet up over the sea, so I guess he must be dead. Hard to see how he could survive.'

'Bugger,' Magee swore. 'We're still no nearer establishing who the killer is.'

'Bugger indeed,' added Brigadier Armstrong. 'And I suppose there's no chance of finding the body out at sea?'

'Unlikely. If it ever washes up on a beach it will be unrecognizable.' Magee took a deep breath. 'Damn! This is no way to close a case. I need to identify the killer to determine motive and eliminate other suspects. Without a body, I've got nothing but conjecture.'

'Sorry, gents,' Nick replied with a shrug of his shoulders. 'I don't really care who he was, just so long as he's no longer a threat to my family. Can I see my kids now, please.'

Magee turned to Melissa. 'Have you finished getting their statements?'

'Yes, sir.'

Brigadier Armstrong took a deep breath and said, 'Right then, Mr Price. You are free to go. Sorry the debriefing took so long.'

'No problem, Brigadier, sorry I couldn't be of more help.'

Magee caught a glint in Nick Price's eyes. There was more; that was painfully clear from his body language.

Brigadier Armstrong got up from his chair to leave and said, 'Well, there's nothing more for me to do here, Magee. It's getting late and it's been an eventful day. I'm dead tired. I'll be off now.'

'Thank you for all your help, Brigadier.'

'You're welcome. Oh, by the way, Magee. I'll need to have a debriefing session with you. I'm far too tired tonight. Can you come to my office up in London, say Wednesday afternoon? Just after lunch?'

'Of course, sir.'

The Brigadier looked at Nick Price. 'Nice work by the way, Mr Price. In bringing the airplane down that is. A really cool landing for a novice in a crises, so the tower said. In fact, they found it hard to believe it was your first time. For an old machine like that, they said you seemed to possess a remarkable familiarity with the controls. Especially since you managed to disengage it from auto-pilot and head back towards Shoreham before calling the tower.'

Nick shrugged. 'I had some practice, years ago. A friend had a similar model, I flew with him on occasion. Not that it helped much today. I was close to panicking. I reckon I'd have ditched it over water and jumped the last few feet if I'd been alone.'

'Far riskier,' replied Brigadier Armstrong. 'It would have been like hitting concrete. Anyway, it was nice work. So I'll say goodbye to you, Mr Price. I trust we won't have the need to meet again.'

'And why would we?'

'Secrets and lies, my dear man. They have a habit of being exposed. Eventually.'

Nick Price feigned a look of innocence. 'What's that supposed to mean?'

But Brigadier Armstrong merely gave Nick Price an odd look, his eyebrow arching, and turned his attention to Magee. 'Now then, Magee, I assume you'll leave the press announcement to me?'

'Of course, sir.'

Brigadier Armstrong looked at each of them in turn before saying in a serious tone, 'Geoffrey Rees Smith died valiantly tonight rescuing his kidnapped daughters. Let's not give the press any other version.'

'He saved me and my family, as well, Brigadier,' Nick responded. 'I owe him that.'

'You do indeed, Mr Price. Well, then, Magee, I'll leave you to it.'

Magee looked menacingly at Nick Price.

Nick feigned a hurt look. 'What?' he demanded.

###

Other books by the same author
The woes of Nick Price continue in The Fourth Cart II, a sequel to this book.

The Fourth Cart II:
One sunny afternoon, Nick Price took a stroll through Lumpini Park in Bangkok with his family and friends. At some stage, a joke was cracked, he laughed and placed a hand, intimately, on a young man's shoulder. The event was unremarkable, except that twenty years later a witness testifies that the young man had been Khun Sa, the legendary drug lord from the Golden Triangle.

Set against the backdrop of civil unrest in Bangkok in May 1992, DCI Jack Magee visits Thailand to explore Nick Price's murky past in the hope of identifying Khun Sa, unaware that he has been set up by the intelligence services like a goat to catch a tiger.

Printed in Poland
by Amazon Fulfillment
Poland Sp. z o.o., Wrocław